OF NIGHT AND BLOOD

THE COVETED: VOL. 1

BREA LAMB

Of Night and Blood

Copyright © 2023 by Brea Lamb

Cover art by Madison Lee, @matzia_mouse
Map by Lindsey Staton, @honeyy.fae
Edited by Laura Allan, @lauraroseallan
Edited by Annalee Poureetezadi, @annptoz

For every dreamer who finds joy in getting lost between the pages of a book. May you never forget that you are worthy beyond measure and that you are no one's but your own.

WELCOME TO THE WORLD OF

THE COVETED

Demon Realm

Haven

Forest of Tragedies

Sophistes

Elpis

Kratos

Dunamis

Andreia

The Royal City

Eros

The Sea of Akiva

The Mist

Mortal Realm

PRONUNCIATION GUIDE

Adbeel: Add-buh-hail

Andreia: On-drey-uh

Asher: Ash-er

Asta: Ah-s-tuh

Augustu: Uh-gus-too

Ayad: Eye-ed

Bellamy: Bell-uh-me

Betovere: Bet-O-veer

Bhatt: Buh-ah-t

Bhesaj: Beh-saw-j

Braviarte: Brah-vee-ar-tey

Calista: Cuh-lee-stuh

Cyprus: Sigh-prus

Daniox: Dawn-wuah

Davina: Duh-vee-nuh

Dunamis: Doo-nuh-miss

Elpis: El-pus

Eoforhild: U-for-hill-d

Eros: Air-O-s

Farai: Fair-eye

Genevieve: Jen-eh-vee-v

Graham: Gr-am

Harligold: Har-leh-gold

Henry: Hen-ree

Herberto: Air-bear-tow

Ignazio: Eye-na-see-O

Ishani: E-shaw-nee

Isolda: is-ole-duh

Jasper: Jas-pur

Kafele: Kah-fey-lay

Kratos: Cray-tow-z

Lawrence: Lor-ence

Lian: Lee-en

Luca: Loo-cuh

Maybel: May-bell

Mia: Me-uh

Mounbetton: Mon-bet-tun

Nayab: Nay-eb

Nicola: Nee-co-lah

Noe: No-ee

Odilia: Oh-dill-E-uh

O'Malley: O-mal-lee

Papatonis: pah-puh-tone-is

Pino: Pee-n-yo

Ranbir: Run-beer

Raymonds: Ray-mun-d-s

Salvatore: Sal-vuh-tor

Selassie: Seh-lah-see

Sipho: S-eye-f-oh

Sophistes: So-fee-st-es

Stella: S-tell-uh

Sterling: Stir-ling

Tish: T-ish

Tristana: Tris-tah-nuh

Ulu: Oo-loo

Windsor: Wind-soar

Winona: Why-no-nuh

Xavier: Ex-ay-vee-er

Yarrow: Yahr-r-oh

Youxia: Yo-shaw

Zohar: Z-oh-hawr

GLOSSARY

Afriktor: Omniscient creature that lives in the Forest of Tragedies.

Air: Element sub-faction with the ability to wield Air power (i.e. create wind).

Betovere: Also known as Fae Realm, made up of five islands that are inhabited by the fae species.

Earth: Element sub-faction with the ability to wield Earth power (i.e. grow flowers).

Element: Faction of fae with the ability to wield elements.

Ending: Term used by fae that means death. It is believed that the fae will sense when Eternity calls them home, and that is when they will choose to pass on.

Eoforhild: Also known as the Demon Realm, this is the continent that the demon species reside on.

Eternity: The sentient place that fae power comes from, as well as the higher power they pray to and believe their souls return to after death.

Faction: Term used to group together fae with similar powers (i.e. Readers or Shifters).

Fae Council: Group of fae who aid the King of the Fae Realm with decision making.

Fire: Element sub-faction with the ability to wield Fire power (i.e. create a flame).

Healer: Faction of fae with the ability to heal.

Honey Tongue: Ability to influence beings with the sound of one's voice.

Lady/Lord: The title bestowed on demons who reside over one of the five territories in Eoforhild.

Magic: General term for abilities that are thought to be bestowed by gods, wielded most notably by demons.

Moon: Ability to wield the raw magic from the moon (i.e. wield shadows).

Mortal: General term for the humans who do not live indefinitely.

Multiple: Shifter sub-faction with the ability to alter their appearance in indefinite ways, though they can only maintain that form for a short period of time.

Navalom: Creature that lives in the Forest of Tragedies and feasts on memories.

Oracle: Term for a being who can see both the past and the future without touching a being. This ability is rare and believed to only be possessed by fae.

Power: The general term for abilities gifted by Eternity, wielded by fae.

Prime: Member of the fae council who is in charge of particular specialties that are needed to maintain the Fae Realm (i.e. trade or coin). They live in The Capital.

Reader: Faction of fae with the ability to read the past or future.

Royal Court: Members of the fae council who are the strongest in their respective sub-faction. They are chosen to represent said sub-faction and live in The Capital (ie. Royal Healer or Royal Fire).

Shifter: Faction of fae with the ability to alter their physical appearance.

Single: Shifter sub-faction that can alter their appearance into one chosen form for an unlimited amount of time (i.e. wolf or panther).

Siren: Water folk with the ability to have legs on land and a large fin underwater. Can lure their prey with their singing.

Sub-faction: Term used to represent fae who wield the same power.

Sun: Ability to wield the raw magic from the sun (i.e. wield light).

Tomorrow: Reader sub-faction with the ability to read the future of anyone they touch.

Warden: Title bestowed on the second strongest member of each sub-faction. They rule over their respective lands.

Water: Element sub-faction with the ability to wield Water power (i.e. create waves).

Whisp: Creature that can turn their body into various forms, such as black mist, bubbles, etc.

Wraith: Creature with the ability to blend into their surroundings, their form fading and turning them nearly invisible. Often called ghosts by the fae, though they are living beings.

Yesterday: Reader sub-faction with the ability to read the past of anyone they touch.

Youngling: The fae and demon equivalent to a child.

ACT I
~ DENIAL ~

PROLOGUE

Asher Daniox had always been told she was special.

As Mia Mounbetton, the queen of the Fae Realm, wove the five-year old's hair into intricate braids and hummed a lovely tune, Asher felt abundantly special. The pair sat facing a golden wall bare of decorations except for the sole painting depicting the great Fae Realm. Like she often did, Asher found herself staring at the islands, attempting to decipher where she fit in.

"Mia, why do I not have a mama and dada like everyone else?" she asked, her small voice showing no signs of hurt, just simple curiosity. The queen's fingers halted, causing Asher to wonder if she was not allowed to ask such a question.

"Well Asher, I was hoping to save this conversation for when you were older, perhaps not until you started Academy. However, I will tell you now. Your mother and father were dear friends of mine, and they had been spending a day in the gardens with you and my son, Baron—"

"You have a son?" Asher asked, cutting off Mia's story. The queen flicked Asher in the back of the head, scolding her impolite behavior.

"Mind your manners now, we do not interrupt others. But yes, I had a son. That day, demons came. Their goal was likely to kill Baron, but your mother and father fought bravely against them. They both died, along with my sweet son. You barely survived. Guards found you with your little ears mangled, left in the cold to perish."

Mia began braiding again, effectively ending the conversation, but Asher thought the story did not seem finished. No, to the youngling, the story seemed wrong somehow. When the queen finished, Asher reached up to her ears, which were always deliberately hidden underneath her long brown waves. Tears pricked her stormy-gray eyes upon feeling the jagged tops. She looked at the beautiful points of the queen's ears, her heart breaking at her own inadequacy.

For the first time in her life, Asher felt true sorrow. She opened her mouth to object, but Mia shushed her, motioning for her to practice the piano forte. As she stood, indescribable pain overcame her, and she sensed something in her chest swell. She was unsure what had happened until Mia cried out. Asher turned around to see that the queen was grabbing her head, pulling on her hair and clawing at her skin as if she were on fire.

"Please, Asher, stop!" she screeched. Asher blinked and suddenly Mia's face relaxed, her body going slack. The queen opened her eyes and looked at the youngling. Asher feared retribution for what she somehow did, staring at her shaking hands in horror. Mia merely smiled though, a joyous and triumphant lift of her lips. "It seems we have work to do, little love."

CHAPTER ONE

The stark difference between the heat in my cheeks and the cool kiss of the wind was a welcome relief. I could still feel the anger rising from the pit of my stomach, threatening to boil over. Was I seeing red, or was that just the shade of the roses seeping into my vision?

I tried to take deep breaths, but the scarlet petals brought back the sound of his dingy, lust-filled voice.

"Your beauty rivals that of the most luscious flower."

The thought of it made me want to eviscerate the rose bushes entirely. I looked down to see that my knuckles were gaining a white hue from gripping the balcony railing so tightly. I could not fathom how anyone could be so incredibly vapid, with nothing to offer but his own arrogance.

"That dress becomes you, Your Highness."

Foul. Absolutely foul. After attempting to court me for over three months, Sterling Windsor had yet to mention anything other than my physical appearance. If Kafele was to be believed, then I also knew the prince had much more vulgar things to say about my body when I was not present. Nicola's betrothed had never given me reason to doubt him before, so there was no cause to do so in regard to the annoying man.

If one could call him that. Being nearly two hundred years older than him made me reluctant to do so. Which was another rather revolting aspect of this soon-to-be union. He was practically a child in comparison to me. In fact, I was well into my eighteenth decade when he came to be.

I suddenly felt sick thinking about what I must have been doing when the boy prince learned to walk.

Perhaps if Sterling was not trying so desperately to fit into a place where he, quite honestly, did not belong, then I could see past the superficial; although, the age might still haunt me. How many more times could I sit through breakfast while he said obnoxious things like "Your eyes are especially dazzling today, Asher"? Or walk with him while he showcased one of the most jaded personalities I had ever come across? Or politely tell him once again to keep his hands to himself without smacking him across the face? Worse yet, how could I do this for a lifetime?

My spiraling was interrupted by the click of the double doors opening behind me, and then the steady tap of heels on concrete. Each step towards me echoed, the sound of pure confidence sending birds scattering. I knew who it was before her lilac perfume wafted my way, but the scent was further confirmation that the queen stood to my left.

"I was unaware that the view of the gardens was worth missing out on your own introductory ball," she said, the edge of her lips tilting towards the stars above. Her tangerine hair was cut to her shoulders, hanging lower in the front than it did in the back. A small shake of her head sent locks waving back and forth.

Despite being well over six hundred years old, there was not a wrinkle on her face other than at the corners of her light blue eyes. She stood a few inches taller than me, towering over most females. From head to toe she was a compilation of straight, harsh lines. Gold petals made up her gown, sewn together to form a tight-fitting masterpiece that showed off her figure perfectly. The outfit was both regal and youthful, complimenting her skin, which was as pale as the moonlight.

Mia was every bit the glorious figurehead a queen should be. Her mere presence was a reminder that I was not. Many across the realm had not hesitated to share the same concern, but it was still never fun hearing it in my own head.

"I thought introductory balls were to allow a member of the royal family to meet their potential suitors, not be obsessively followed by a mortal boy." The queen chuckled, quickly trying to muffle the sound with a gloved hand.

After a year of planning this ball, we were unable to cancel, but it was still clearly for show. Just to follow the traditions and pretend as if the eligible bachelors of the realm had a chance to win me. I was no more than a means to the crown to those dancing in the golden palace at our backs—a prized and feared creature that might offer them endless wealth and favor. Even with whispers of my engagement spreading across every isle, many fae still hoped they might be able to convince the king and queen to pick their son instead. Not that any of those sons would even speak to me.

"This was much easier back when it was I having balls thrown for me to meet my future king consort." The vague response did nothing to settle the unrest simmering inside me. Of course it had been easier for her. She had a ballroom full of Elements, and the strongest won her favor. Just as it had always been. Far simpler than my circumstances.

"I cannot do this anymore Mia. If not for the fact that he does not see past what I can give him, then because he is so mundane, I find myself wondering if he will bore me to death one day," I whispered, having at least enough self-control to not mention his inappropriate behavior. Not only would it make no difference, but it would also only serve to upset her. "I do not like him in the slightest, and I dare say he would not like me very much if I did not come with a title and immortality."

My voice was harsher than I meant it to be, and I could see concern flash across Mia's face before she quickly schooled it back into neutrality.

"Asher my dear, you are simply new to this. Relationships take time to build and grow. This one will flourish if you give Prince Sterling the chance to become comfortable. Can you imagine being removed not only from your home, but from your entire realm, and living with beings you have never met?" she asked, her features softening. "Would you be an exciting and vibrant suitor in that situation? Are you even trying to be one now?"

Her words cut deep, but the truth of them was evident. I had not thought about how isolating it would feel to be around creatures so vastly different than yourself. Although it did not excuse his less than savory actions and words, I could see how alone he might feel.

I sighed, looking up, hoping to find some sort of answer in the stars. My hand instinctively went to the small amethyst at my neck, twirling it between my forefinger and thumb. "I know you are right, but I guess I always thought that I would marry for love."

That I would choose something for myself, was what I wanted to say. I rarely had the chance to make my own decisions. If I had complete autonomy in every other aspect of my life, I might be more agreeable to the situation.

"You can marry for something far greater, Asher. You can marry the man who will bring great prosperity to your kingdom. And along the way you can learn to like him, to be happy with the life you will build together." The respect I felt for Mia prevented me from speaking the truth that was on the tip of my tongue: an alliance is not love. Despite the way she cared for her husband, I knew there was no love there. King Xavier once told me that marriage should be a partnership rather than a relationship, and Mia felt the same.

"You are right. I promise to make more of an effort to get to know Prince Sterling," I vowed.

A simple thing, saying one will try, but it was enough for her, it seemed. Her wide smile was contagious, and it relieved my face of the angry flush.

"I will be inside shortly, I just want a bit more fresh air," I said, smiling up at her. Mia nodded and kissed my forehead before walking back into the grand ballroom. The second the doors closed my shoulders slumped. The conversation drained me, and I felt like more of a husk than a princess.

I stood there for a moment, taking deep breaths and attempting to convince myself that I could one day enjoy the company of a boring pervert. I loudly snorted at that and turned to face the doors. My body met resistance suddenly, causing me to stumble back. Hands grabbed my arms, steadying me. I looked up to see a pair of icy blue eyes.

"Hello," the fae said. His husky voice did not quite match his youthful grin that formed, dimples popping up on either freckled cheek.

I took a step back, straightening the skirts of my gold gown out of nervous habit. His gaze followed my hands and I felt surprisingly bare for how covered I was. Then his eyes met mine, and embarrassment flooded me as I apologized, "I am so sorry."

"No, it is I who should apologize; I was not paying enough attention," he said, his smile so wide it made me feel warm despite the chill in the air.

"There is no need to apologize, but I thank you for doing so," I responded, looking at him a bit more openly now. The burgundy jacket and trousers were a surprising choice, as were the many gold rings that adorned his fingers. The outfit hugged his body and showed off what had to have been fairly intense training. His dark hair was cropped and messily styled, with short pieces falling down his forehead.

I realized I had not heard him exit the ballroom and wondered how he could be so quiet with the stone beneath his feet.

Briefly I considered ending the conversation there, but I could not keep the curiosity at bay. "I do not believe we have met, you are?"

My attempt at nonchalance must not have been believable, because the handsome stranger's eyes crinkled in amusement, that smile still lifting his cheeks. I could see the weather was already causing him discomfort as his ears and nose quickly pinked. Why would he care to be outside?

He bowed deeply, peeking up at me through thick lashes. "My name is Bellamy, Princess. It is a pleasure to make your acquaintance." The raspy words sent tingles up my spine. What an interesting name, one I had never heard before, in fact. Bellamy grabbed my hand and placed a quick kiss to the top, the ivory tone of his skin a striking contrast to the bronze of my own. My breath hitched and entirely inappropriate thoughts filled my mind.

I was no better than Sterling.

"Well, Bellamy, it was very nice to meet you. I hope you enjoy the beautiful night and the rest of the ball," I hastily responded.

Walking around him towards the doors, I attempted to hide my face, with cheeks heated for very different reasons than when I came outside. My foot snagged on something, causing me to tip forward. A hand grabbed my waist, catching me before I fell. Bellamy pulled me up, my back becoming flush with his chest. I felt his breath tickle my ear, and there was now no denying what I felt low in my stomach.

"Are you okay?" he asked, sliding his hand across my stomach and making no noticeable effort to separate our bodies. I turned over my right shoulder and looked up at him. Concern coated his features, but amusement sparkled in his eyes.

I began to pull away and felt his arm tighten around me before letting go. His reluctance to release me brought a devilish smile to my face.

"Twice you saved me tonight, Bellamy. It seems I am in your debt," I said, my voice coated with honey and desire.

I knew exactly what I was doing, and despite how wrong it was, I could not stop myself. I turned to face him, keeping us close. The smirk he gave brought a dimple to one cheek, and suddenly I could see where the husky voice came from.

"I would never dream of accepting debt from you, Princess," he said, placing his hands behind his back.

Uncertainty filled my mind. Did he not feel that same electric shock that I did where our bodies met? Was I making a fool of myself? I took a large step back, furrowing my brows. Clearly, I misread the situation. What was wrong with me?

"Of course not. Have a splendid night Bellamy."

I made haste in hopes of avoiding further embarrassment, or worse, intrigue. With a gloved hand on the brass knob, I stopped. As if against my will, my head turned towards the invisible pull at my back. My eyes met Bellamy's, who was staring back at me with a level of intensity that made me shudder. I did not look back again as I entered the ballroom, the music dragging me into reality once more.

CHAPTER TWO

I spotted Kafele Selassie and Nicola Salvatore dancing in the center of the room, grace and beauty incarnate. Nicola's curly brown locks bounced and swayed with their every move, keeping in time with the music. Her full lips were tilted up in a shy smile, but the gleam in her hazel eyes was mischievous. The red gown she wore mirrored wine with its color and fluidity, making it seem as if she were floating.

Kafele wore the classic black that every other male wore, except for Bellamy apparently, and his single gold earring shined brightly under the lights. Through his well-kept beard I saw his broad smile, the black hair and his ebony skin making his teeth appear even whiter. He looked down at her with so much adoration and love that their dance felt too intimate to be watched. Or perhaps that was the slight red hue to his lips that matched hers, suggesting they were far closer than that at some point in the evening.

Giving myself a break from the agonizing torture that was true love, I headed to the table full of food, my stomach growling violently at the sight of the delicious spread. Glancing at the two thrones on the far end of the room, I checked to make sure Mia was not looking my way when I popped a sugary pastry in my mouth. I was not supposed to be indulging in sweets for the foreseeable future due to my "rather full figure," as the castle seamstress called it.

I had always been aware of the fact my size was not that of most young females around me, but it never seemed to be a problem until the agreement with King Lawrence was made. He was the only one of the mortal kings who was willing to spark an alliance, even with the offer of my hand on the table. Mia knew I needed to impress Prince Sterling in order to make the truce work. After all, he had the right to reject the marriage.

Regardless of my desire to make peace with the Mortal Realm, I did not feel as though I should have to marry a crown prince to do so. I remembered protesting that it would leave the mortals of his lands without an heir, but Xavier said that Sterling's older sister, Genevieve, was in line for the throne. So that meant I needed to fit into a smaller dress, apparently.

My hand instinctively reached down to my soft stomach. Where most were flat, I was round. This included other parts of my body as well. I recalled the other night when Nicola and I challenged each other to swim nude in the lake behind the castle.

Where her breasts were small and perky, mine were full and slightly hung. Where her hips flowed smoothly down to her thighs, mine curved out. A small part of me understood the reason for restricting my diet, but I mostly loathed it, especially now that I was being watched.

Snatching another sweet just to defy everyone, I ate it and once again watched the dancing pairs in front of me. Two males sweeping across the room caught my eye, and I instantly knew that the couple was Jasper Cromwell and Farai Sibanda.

Many of the fae my age were married or betrothed, with this couple being the former. Farai willed his nose into that of a pig, causing Jasper to let out a laugh. The two Shifters seemed to have a running joke, always attempting to make the other laugh at inopportune times. Seeing them made my chest ache. More often than not, I felt left out and lonely despite my own engagement.

Lost in thought, I did not hear someone approach me until I felt hot breath on my cheek.

"Would you like to dance, Asher?" Sterling asked, placing his hands on my waist from behind.

Even through my many layers, his touch made my skin crawl, every glorious tingle that lingered from Bellamy's hands fading immediately.

Rage threatened to take over when his hands slid down to my hips. Sucking in a deep breath, I moved out of his grasp and turned to face him.

In truth the prince was rather handsome. His golden curls were thick and shone in the light. His brown eyes were large, and his blonde eyelashes framed them in a beautiful way. He was average height for mortal standards, though that was shorter than most males in our realm, standing at eye level with me. His skin had begun to tan from the weather in the Fae Realm, but the autumn chill was slowly returning it to that pink hue it had been when we first met.

The black tunic he wore had gold stitching to match not only his hair, but also my gown. I had picked out a silky black fabric, but instead was put into one so gold it reflected the light. Not that I was surprised, I never wore anything other than gold.

The bodice was pulled as tight as it would go, and the skirts flared out, weighing me down. My crown sat atop my head, golden branches reaching towards the sky, diamonds accented throughout. It was a smaller, less grand version of Mia's, made to represent her Earth power. Xavier's was golden flames instead, bigger than necessary, but Fires were proud like that.

The crown atop Sterling's head was also gold, but adorned with startlingly large emeralds and rubies, highlighting his title and his wealth.

As if we all were unaware somehow.

My problem was not with his appearance, but rather his arrogance.

"Prince Sterling, as I have asked many times, please do not touch me without my permission," I said with the most respect I could conjure, which was not a lot.

He smiled as if I did not just remind him of his own indecency. Placing his hands behind his back, Sterling took a slow step towards me, his eyes falling to my breasts. I let out a small cough, catching his attention and bringing it back to my eyes.

"Yes, you have. I am sorry for being inappropriate," he responded. I thought I heard a hint of amusement in his voice, but his tone was mostly sincere. I should move on; Mia would want me to. "You are just so beautiful it is hard to keep my hands to myself," he whispered, getting close to my ear again.

He was simply nervous about what the night signified, I told myself. Or excited. Maybe both. Our impending marriage was terrifying and… well, terrifying. I knew I was struggling to find words that would fit the arrangement, which would leave us bound together for the rest of our days. Xavier and Mia had not gone into detail about how the magic would work, but they confirmed that for as long as I lived, so would Sterling.

My lips formed a thin line.

"Thank you, but be that as it may, I still do not wish to be touched without being asked first," I stated bluntly, taking another large step back.

His smile turned predatory as he quickly closed the space, barely leaving room between our bodies. My hands began to shake with fury at his blatant lack of respect. Before I could do something foolish, Sterling spoke again.

"Would you dance with me, Asher? I promise to be well mannered. I just want to dance with my bride-to-be." Sterling held out his hand, waiting for me to agree. To submit.

My eyes veered to the left where I felt the stares of King Xavier and Queen Mia watching us intently. They both had smiles on their mouths, but their stiff body language told me they were nervous I would mess this up.

Was Sterling aware we had an audience? Had he waited to ask me until he knew I would be in a position where I could not deny him? I felt in my gut that the answer was yes.

Relenting, I grabbed his hand and allowed him to lead me to the dance floor. Surprising no one at all, Sterling chose the center of the ballroom. His eyes were ignited with lust, bright and blazing. I knew that this was not only for me, but for the attention and power that being with me brought him.

Mia had explicitly told me not to ever use my power on him, but I could sense the ambition pouring from him, projecting my way.

Months ago, when I was hopeful something beautiful could come of the arrangement, I resented her for taking that option from me. Normally I was against invading someone's privacy and stealing their choice from them, but I wanted to know whether or not he was a good man, if he deserved my love. However, I found ways around it by involving my friends. Each time Sterling said something less than savory about me to them, they faithfully filled me in. Still, I often considered what I could learn about him if I had not been forbidden from his mind.

Sterling guided my hand around his neck, wrapping his left with my right. I felt his warm fingers trace from my upper back down to my hip, squeezing before he started to move us. Only the fact that we were surrounded by other dancing couples stopped me from smacking that smug smile off of his face. Or better yet, kicking him right between his legs.

The thought of him weeping on the floor, clutching his groin, had me smiling wide. This seemed to convince him I enjoyed his touch, because he pulled me all the way into him and rested his forehead on my own. I attempted to push him back gently, but he held firm.

"We are being watched, Asher, please do not make a scene," he whispered, his hot breath fanning my face.

I backed my head away to see his eyes on my lips. I knew what he was planning before his head moved towards mine, but I had absolutely no way to stop him. As he leaned forward, I closed my eyes tight, cringing at the memory of his mouth on mine. Right when I felt his lips graze my own, someone cleared their throat, and he pulled back. I opened my eyes to see Bellamy standing beside Sterling, rage clouding his eyes and a tight smile on his lips.

"Sorry to interrupt, but may I cut in?" he asked. It did not go unnoticed by Sterling that Bellamy was directing the question at me, not him.

I felt Sterling's other hand wrap around my back, his hold tightening. The boy prince opened his mouth to decline, or possibly argue, but I firmly gripped his hands and freed myself.

"Of course, this is my introductory ball after all. It would not be fair to only dance with Prince Sterling," I responded, stepping towards Bellamy. Sterling looked from him to me, then back. He was seething, and I knew that this would cost me later, but did not regret it.

Anything to avoid kissing him.

Sterling stomped off to the side of the floor, and when he turned, his eyes immediately went to us as I put my hand in Bellamy's. Smirking and radiating satisfaction, Bellamy lifted our hands, his other going to my mid back. I placed my free hand on his shoulder, and we began to dance. "Thank you."

"You do not have to thank me Princess, no one should be touched against their will." Again, I felt silly for thinking that his intentions were anything beyond basic decency. My skin flushed, heat rising to my cheeks. We spun in silence for only a few seconds before he spoke again. "Who is that male to you if I may ask?"

His question took me by surprise. How did he not know? Everyone seemed to be aware of the bargain the mortal king made with ours. It was why no one had asked me to dance tonight, despite this being my introductory ball. Why they allowed a mortal to hoard all of my attention. Why their parents flocked to the king and queen to sway them to pick their son instead. That, and they were all terrified of me.

"He is to be my husband," I whispered, the words tasting like poison in my mouth. Acknowledging it in front of a stranger was more painful than only thinking it. More than that, it was reality that stung me. I was not going to get out of this marriage. There would be a day where kissing Sterling, and more, would be expected of me. Required of me.

"You do not seem to be very happy about that," he responded, his head tilting to one side. No one but my friends had ever said that out loud, not daring to point out the fact that my union was already tense and less than ideal. It took me off guard to hear that he was paying so much attention. Which is probably why I spoke without thinking.

"I am a gift of good faith between the fae and the mortals. I had no choice in my future husband. It is hard to be excited." My eyes grew wide and the hand I had placed on his shoulder flew to my mouth. I considered taking the memory from him then and there to avoid whatever repercussions would come from my blatant disregard towards Sterling, but before I could, Bellamy let out a quiet chuckle.

"Honesty is a brave trait to have, you do not have to fear what I will think of you." His hand grabbed mine from my face and he said, quieter this time, "And I will not tell a soul any of the words you share with me." He kissed my palm this time, sending sparks up my arm and to my heart, setting a ferocious beat.

My eyes slid over to the royals, who were conversing with the Prime of Trade and the Royal Air. If either of them saw this, the strange fae might not leave The Capital alive. I worried my bottom lip at the thought of being the reason yet another died. Bellamy returned my hand to his shoulder, as if he could sense the stress building up inside of me.

I looked up at him apprehensively, not fully believing in his promised discretion, though *his* life was the one that depended on it. Our eyes stay glued together for a moment before he continued.

"Honestly, he seems like a bit of a twat to me, but that goes without saying. You can trust me with your words, Princess." I nodded my head with wide eyes, a chuckle escaping my mouth.

CHAPTER THREE

"Asher," I said after a few moments of dancing in silence. He lifted one eyebrow in question, cocking his head to the side. "My friends call me Asher. I would like for you to as well."

His smile illuminated his face, infectious and charming. I could not help but smile back.

"Well, Asher, tell me more about..." My name sounded sweet coming from his mouth, and my eyes wandered to his lips. I quickly reminded myself that it was disrespectful to continuously be thinking inappropriate thoughts about this male. What was he saying?

"What?" I asked, knowing there was no way I would be able to recall what he said.

He chuckled, and the butterflies dipped lower. Something felt different about the way I was reacting to Bellamy. Maybe it was due to the way Sterling had just treated me, and how his words had the opposite effect.

As if thinking his name summoned him to me, Sterling placed his arm between Bellamy and I, halting our dance. It was then that I realized we had drifted so close we were sharing the same breath. I felt Sterling's arm yank me back, separating me from Bellamy and also hurting a bit. I knew better than to react, but it was an off night.

"Sterling, I told you to keep your hands off of me!" For the second time during the ball, my hand went straight to my mouth. I felt the fear and knew what I would see if I turned around. Looking over my shoulder, I saw that Xavier and Mia were both standing, their eyes piercing me, anger filling the room.

I looked away, surprised to see that Sterling was not glaring at me, but at Bellamy.

"Sterling, I apologize. Please, dance with me." I moved to grab his arm, but he shook me off with enough force to send me back a step. Before I could even acknowledge what happened, Bellamy grabbed the same arm of Sterling's that I had attempted to.

"You should reconsider laying hands on the princess," he said, his voice promising violence. Sterling did not back down, instead getting closer to Bellamy. Their faces were only inches apart, and I could see that both of them were breathing heavily in anger.

"She is mine, and I will do what I want with her. You will do well to mind your own business and not touch what does not belong to you, peasant!" The power in the room started to swell and suffocate as all in attendance tuned in to our conversation.

I felt my stomach drop when Mia put her hand on my shoulder and squeezed. She would not be happy about this. Xavier came over, his crown making him seem even taller, more daunting. His face was red with fury, or perhaps it was the fire within him that began to simmer.

It took every ounce of my being not to snap at Sterling. I was no one's but my own. I was not a prize to be won or a gift to be given, regardless of the agreement made between our realm—or what I said to Bellamy before. Arguing would be unwise now though. In fact, it would only get me in more trouble.

Xavier seemed ready to end the fight before it started, and I knew that would only mean destruction. So instead, I closed my eyes and honed into everyone in the room. I could sense them—Elements, Readers, Shifters, Healers—calling to that well of power deep within them. At once I grabbed hold of their minds.

Everything is fine. Enjoy the ball. Ignore the childish antics of the two in the corner. Dance.

Just like that, everyone was dancing and laughing once again. Everyone except for Sterling, Bellamy, and the royals. We all stayed in our tight circle, and to avoid further issue, I grabbed onto the minds of the angry males on either side of me.

Take this outside. Now.

They both straightened and began walking towards the hall. I did not bother to check that the king and queen were following; I knew they would. My heels tapped on the marble floor as I struggled to keep up with Bellamy and Sterling stomping ahead of me.

The second they pushed open the double doors that led to the long hall, they faced off. Both were radiating fury, and I wondered what could possibly have made them this mad when neither really knew me. What would they do next? Pee on me like an animal to claim me as their territory?

"You dare to speak to me like that again and you will find yourself in a much scarier place than a hallway," Sterling said, voice dripping with acid and fists clenched at his side. Bellamy looked him up and down, then laughed. Actually *laughed.*

That only enraged Sterling further, causing him to step forward once again. I tapped into Bellamy, trying to assess his power, to adjust for the potential danger. The second I did, I felt the burning heat. He was an Element, a Fire to be specific. And he was strong; I could feel the hum of his power, the way it fought to break out. His mind was hectic, full of darkness and heat, painful to be in.

I thought about grabbing onto his mind again, but decided that taking away his free will once tonight was plenty.

"Both of you stop!" I whisper-yelled. "Sterling, I think it is time for me to go back to my chambers. Thank you for the dance. I hope you have a good rest of your evening." He hesitated, fists still clenched, chest practically against Bellamy's stomach. There was too much tension in the air to stifle it on their own without coming to blows.

Go find a willing girl to dance with and do not think of me again tonight.

Sterling knew what my powers were, but he would be unaware I was using them until later. By then it would not matter, excuses would be ready and lies spun. Fae were notorious for manipulation, but my abilities went beyond that. As Sterling whirled towards the double doors and exited the hallway, I faced the king and queen. Both visibly angry.

Xavier spoke first, face red and finger pointed at Bellamy. "I do not know who you are, but you will surely pay for—"

"I will escort him out. Thank you for the ball." Before they could argue, I pushed Bellamy's back and said, "Go."

Once he began walking, I sped up to get in front and lead the way. Looking back, I noted the fire rolling around Xavier's fingers, his whole body shaking. If he ever saw Bellamy again, I had no doubt in my mind that he would end the young fae's life.

Strangely enough, it was Mia who seemed more angry. The stiffness in her features and the clenching of her jaw told me so. I turned away from her, but her voice stopped me in my tracks. "Remember what is at stake, Asher."

How could I forget? I started walking again, not turning back this time.

The moment that we were out of ear shot and sight of the royals, I felt Bellamy's presence move to my side. I looked over to see his hands in his trouser pockets and a smile on his face, both dimples on display.

"What could you possibly think is so funny?" I asked, baffled at his amusement. My head began to pound, a sign I was using too much power.

"Your mortal prince is easily angered, especially seeing as he was the one who touched you against your will. Again." Despite the smile on his face, I could see the flames blazing in his eyes.

Elements had personalities that mirrored their power—Fires were easy to anger and full of passion; Earths were strong willed and brave; Waters were calm and collected; Airs were wild and free. Knowing that Bellamy was a Fire made sense of his short temper.

All fae carried traits unique to their powers, like Elements. That was likely because of the separation of the factions, but could also be genetic.

The Shifter Faction was unpredictable all around, with both Singles—Shifters who have only one form that they can hold indefinitely—and Multiples—Shifters who have many forms that they can only hold for a short period of time—favoring spontaneity over structure. They are wild, strong, and easily the bravest of fae.

The Reader Faction was comprised of Yesterdays—those who saw the past—and Tomorrows—those who saw the future. Tomorrows were usually fairly antisocial, which might have been because they were constantly asked questions about what they saw in the future of those around them. Yesterdays were much more energetic and outgoing.

Last was the Healer Faction, the largest of the four. They were lively and adventurous, with respect considered important among them as well.

My parents had both been Readers. My mother was the Royal Tomorrow, as she was the strongest of her time. My father was also a Tomorrow, and together they read not only the future of the royals, but also any put on trial for crimes against the crown. They, along with the Royal Yesterday, assessed someone's past and future, determining whether or not they had committed the crime and how they would affect the future of the realm.

It hurt to recall the loss of them, but the knowledge that I survived what they did not was even more painful. Mia and Xavier lost their son in the same attack, so we rarely discussed the topic. It made me afraid to ask about what my mother and father were like. Had they held the same temperament as most of their faction? Was I like them at all? I knew bringing them up reminded the king and queen of what they lost: their heir, their only child, their pride and joy. I was thankful they took me in, but we would never be to each other what was lost.

I often wished that I could have lived on Isle Reader, just to feel closer to my parents and see where they grew up. But even if the royals allowed me to go, I would never be accepted. I was no Reader, and outsiders were not treated well. Each fae lived on the island that represented their faction, required to marry within to keep bloodlines pure.

The faction islands surrounded The Capital, which was where all younglings went to harness their power and learn to control themselves. It was the only time that fae would live with factions outside of their own. Although, they were still separated, each having their own building where they learned, ate, and slept. Being left to live on Isle Reader would have likely gotten me killed.

Bellamy was similarly out of his depth here at The Capital. I was unsure of his reasons for attending my ball—unless he thought he might be able to secure a marriage with one of the other attendees—but recklessness was not tolerated, insolence even less so. He was a flame walking on thin ice, tempting Eternity.

"He is not my prince, and you had no place interfering. You embarrassed me."

You forced me to use my powers on you. On everyone. To be the monster they all think I am.

His head snapped in my direction as if he heard the thoughts running through my mind. He opened his mouth to speak, but I held my hand out to silence him.

"Regardless, Sterling is my betrothed whether I like it or not, and our issues are simply that, our own. I thank you for standing up for me, but I do not need the help." Each word that left my mouth was sharper than the last.

"Asher," Bellamy said, putting himself in front of me to halt my steps. "You do not know me, and I do not know you. I understand why it was not my responsibility to stand up for you. I apologize for upsetting you in any way. I did not seek to do so, and I deeply regret it."

I knew he was being honest, could feel the genuine tone of his words and understand a vague tenor of his thoughts. Still, something was off.

I noted the way he wiped his hand on his pants, seemingly removing the sweat. Was it simply nerves? I could find out if I wanted. The mind was easy to take control of, but doing so felt invasive and manipulative. In fact, I was called "The Manipulator" by many of the fae in our realm, their fear of the unknown leading them to hate me.

"I accept your apology," I said, trying to get my mind to focus on the conversation. We had stopped at another pair of double doors, both of us facing the other. His dazzling eyes and full lips were too distracting, and I found I could not stay annoyed for long.

I knew the best thing I could do for both of us was walk away before I made a poor decision.

"These doors here will lead you out to the gardens, if you follow the path to the right, you will find yourself at the front of the castle where you entered. I am afraid that if you do not leave soon, then you may be subject to far worse horrors than Sterling's foul attitude. I hope you have a good evening, Bellamy."

Right as I took a step away from him, Bellamy spoke.

"Wait," he said, voice low and husky again. "Would you care to take a walk, Asher?"

CHAPTER FOUR

I knew it was dangerous, and so very stupid. Yet, I found myself nodding. My body moved towards him as if he was the center of gravity. The corners of his lips lifted, but he did not dare smile fully, likely knowing by the look on my face it would be unwise to gloat.

We began our walk in silence. The night was still chilly, and neither of us were necessarily dressed for it, but it was nice to enjoy the gardens with someone other than Sterling for once. Bellamy reached out and plucked a rose, twirling it between his fingers.

"A peace offering," he said, holding the flower out to me. I grabbed it, only to be stuck through my glove by a thorn. "Oh gosh, I am so sorry."

Reaching out to my bleeding finger he gently touched it with his own, making heat pool in my stomach.

"It is nothing, just a bit of blood," I said with a wave of my other hand. The small dot had already stopped bleeding and was threading back together.

After we passed the last of the roses and entered the section with lavender, I felt his arm graze mine, electricity racing from the point of contact down to my toes. Then his fingers brushed my skin too, and my stomach spun. A simple touch, far too innocent to be getting so worked up over. I needed to stay calm before I scared the poor male.

On our left we came up to a concrete bench hidden within the lavender. Bellamy gestured to it with his hand.

"Would you care to sit for a moment?" It was an invitation that was different than what I was used to. He had chosen to ask if I cared to, rather than ask if I had time or if I was allowed. I smiled, moving to sit.

The second I did the cold bit into my thighs through my gown. I let out a sharp hiss, drawing Bellamy's attention. He pressed his body into mine, his skin growing warmer by the second. His hand moved towards my chest, and for a moment my thoughts were hazy with anticipation. He stopped just shy of my breasts and cupped his hand, calling on his fire.

A small flame sat in his palm, heating the air and casting a red hue over his bright blue eyes and black hair. I felt silly for what seemed like the thousandth time this evening. I did not recall having such promiscuous thoughts before tonight.

"Fires never cease to amaze me," I said quietly, watching the flame whip in the wind but never burn out.

King Xavier was also a Fire, and when I was a youngling he would do tricks for me with his flames, juggling them or throwing them in an arch and letting them land in a bucket of water. Queen Mia was an Element as well, but an Earth. She very rarely used her power in public. In my experience, when a fae let their power lay dormant for too long, they would begin to feel pain as the gift ate away at their body. Which was why Mia found ways to use it inconspicuously, like throughout this garden of hers. She often did small displays in front of me as well.

"I do not believe anyone's powers could be considered as impressive as your own," he said with nonchalance. "It is quite the gift to be able to bend the mind to your own will."

The words held no malice in them that I could detect, but that did not mean he was okay with my choice to strip him of his autonomy.

"I apologize. I cannot say I enjoy using my power, but it would have caused many issues for the crown if the fight had continued, or escalated for that matter. I wish I did not have to use it," I admitted. Shame was the price of a power like mine, and I paid it often.

He seemed to consider that response for a moment, then looked into my eyes. When we locked gazes, it felt as if he could see into my soul, like he had a hold of my mind rather than the other way around.

"You should not hate your power, none of us should, it makes us who we are. Our powers give us strength and provide us with the opportunity to be better than those before us. Yours in particular has the potential to change the world as we know it," he said it with such conviction that I found myself nodding, though most of the fae would disagree.

"My power is greatly feared throughout the realm. I am sure even on Isle Element they share stories of the wicked princess who will steal your mind in the night." I rolled my eyes, and Bellamy let out a breathy laugh. "Or would you tell me they believe I am some kind of miracle?"

Some did. They thought I was the symbol of a new age, a blessing to the realm. Either way, I was more of a figurehead than an individual, which I struggled to accept.

"Rumor has it that when you take the mind of your enemy and crush it, their sins flash before their eyes. Some Airs say that they will hear you call to them on the breeze when the reckoning day comes. I have also been told that you will kill us in our sleep if we do not eat our greens." At that he chuckled again, and I could not help but crack a smile as well. "We mostly talk of the dark-haired beauty that will save our realm though."

I let out a loud laugh.

"I highly doubt that. Fae tend to run at the mere sight of me," I responded. It was common for not only castle staff, but residents of The Capital as well, to cringe when they ran into me. Even those who worshipped at my feet as if I was a god often chose to not speak to me directly. Though it was standard practice of the fae to live at the mercy of Eternity rather than the gods, anyways.

"I am not running," he said, smiling down at me. I looked up at the stars to hide the blush that crept onto my face. Knowing that Bellamy was not scared of me, that he actually enjoyed my presence in some way, sent a rush through my body. It almost seemed as though I was not the Manipulator or the princess to him, but rather I was simply Asher. "So, tell me more about you. What do you enjoy doing?" he asked.

From the corner of my eye, I saw him look up as well, but he left his hand and flames in front of my body to keep me warm. A kind gesture that I had already begun reading into, as per usual.

"No one has asked me that in a long time," I murmured. His eyes found mine, his brows scrunching together.

I could not tell if it was disbelief or sorrow that flashed on his face, but whatever it was, he recovered quickly. His smile was radiant, full and dimpled. I could not help but smile back at him, though my answer was uninteresting at best.

"Reading mostly, and I often enjoy playing the piano." Beyond that there was not much to me. I liked the way books whisked me away to a new place, another life. Music, that was a different kind of escape. It gave me power that did not take over minds, but enchanted them. "I also enjoy being with my friends. They are incredibly mischievous, and they treat me as if I am just like them. I find that their presence grounds me, reassures me. Though with us all recently reaching our second century, most of us are marrying and starting anew."

He continued to look at me, his eyes squinted slightly. Like he was trying to make sense of a complicated puzzle, one with missing pieces. I probably sounded like a bore, but how could I explain without sounding like a fool? I wanted to have excitement and adventure in my life, to do more than merely exist, but it just was not realistic.

"Does the beginning of marriage usually mark the end of friendship?" he asked, surprising me again.

I chose not to look over at him to avoid seeing the pity I knew he was feeling. His question sounded genuine, but there was a tinge of disdain in there that made me wonder if the idea of marriage was appalling to him.

"No, but they will visit The Capital less often. We met at Academy, and after all graduates were sent back to their factions—apart from Nicola, who lives here—we remained in touch secretly, though I am truly only close with a couple from Isle Shifter now. I am given slight leeway with them since they are wed. Once we are all married, it will be difficult to see one another, as we will have responsibilities that keep us on our respective islands. Especially with my own union meaning I will begin preparation for ascending the throne," I said with a shrug.

I tried not to dwell on the fact that so much was being taken from me to make peace with the Mortal Realm. Our future was contingent on this marriage, this alliance. The Demon Realm was active, slaughtering fae. We had known that their king, Adbeel, was biding his time since the Great War, so when the mass murders began last year, it was little surprise. How they got to the fae lands undetected was puzzling though. Especially with the impenetrable mist that surrounds their lands.

Then again, we were not privy to details of demon magic. No one was alive that had fought in the Great War those many millennia ago, and by some wicked blight of the demons' making, no Yesterday has the ability to see that far back. We believed the demons corrupted our minds with whatever evil shadow magic they rendered from the Underworld where they derived. It was no secret that they came to our world to conquer.

Even worse, talk of King Adbeel's son, The Elemental, had surfaced eighty years ago. He was a dangerous addition to an already highly feared enemy. No one knew what he looked like, or even his age, but we all knew that he was capable of harnessing all four elements. Local gossip suggested that the demon king had abducted a fae and used her to breed the male, but no one knew for sure how a demon came to have the ability to call upon the elements when they were normally black magic wielders.

Our council meetings were filled with horrific tales of The Elemental tearing holes into the ground to suck fae into awaiting molten rock and ripping heads off with nothing but his hands. We once received word during a ball that there had been an attack staged by the demon prince which resulted in seven fae being flayed alive. Worse was the time that an entire village in the Single Lands was nearly burned to the ground, which The Elemental seemed to take credit for as the mark of all four elements had been burned into a tree just outside of the wreckage.

The entire realm relied on not only my powers, but my future husband's army as well to keep us safe from the demons and their monarchs.

"If I refuse to marry Sterling, I risk the safety of my subjects. I risk the wrath of the demon king. I risk allowing more fae to be senselessly murdered," I whispered. I was unsure if I was even talking to Bellamy, or if my words were a reminder to myself.

"That is a burden that should never have been forced on you. There are strength in numbers, and in will. The mortals should know that. No one is safe when those in power seek more of it. Requesting a marriage alliance seems, to me, more presumptuous of what they can truly offer than anything else," he said, rolling his eyes. I chuckled, nodding. It felt like he took the words out of my mouth.

"Tell me something about you. What do you do in your spare time?" I asked, eager to move on. He smiled at my obvious attempt to steer the conversation away from myself, his gaze remaining tilted up to the stars. When he answered, it was in a soft and faraway voice.

"I like to adventure. Staying still is uncomfortable to me. I want to do more, be more, than a husband or a father or a soldier. I want to be someone, not just anyone." I thought that statement made sense. He did not seem to enjoy the idea of marriage, and being held down would not suit someone always on the move.

"That is not to say that I would want to be alone. I would like to find a partner that loved the idea of seeing the world like I do, and perhaps loved me even more." He turned away from the sky above and set his icy stare on me. "Has anyone ever told you that you are stunning, Asher?"

Hearing my name on his lips sent a wave of ecstasy through me.

I looked away, easing some of the growing tension. Bellamy's stare continued to set my skin ablaze, as if he enjoyed the tension, wanted to bring it to a breaking point. My cheeks heated, a blush forming. I murmured an awkward thank you, twiddling my fingers and trying to recall a time when I had been this flustered.

Though there were also very few who thought to talk with me this deeply, to understand me beyond my body or my power. I felt Bellamy's finger slide under my chin, guiding my face back in his direction. When I peered up at him once more, I could have sworn black mist swirled in his eyes. A blink and it was gone, a figment of my imagination perhaps.

"I mean it," he whispered.

We held eye contact. Whatever the connection was that sparked between us seemed to peak, because without a second thought, I crashed my lips to his. There was no hesitation as he moved his hand into my loose hair, gripping the thick, brown locks and pulling me impossibly close. His other hand released the flame and went to my back, warming me. I reached up, dropping the rose, and put both of my hands on either side of his face, grazing my tongue across his lips. He let out a raspy moan and opened his mouth for me.

The kiss was electric and fiery and all consuming. My breath quickly sped up when he tugged me onto his lap. My legs moved to either side of his thighs, and I felt him harden beneath me. Everywhere our skin touched left a trail of goosebumps. When the tips of his fingers slid under my gown and up my calf, I nearly melted, shivering against him. He broke our kiss and looked at me, moving to hold my face with both hands. "Are you cold?" he asked, his voice somehow deeper than it was earlier.

"No. Well, yes. But I am not shivering due to the cold," I said sheepishly.

He smiled, running his fingers down the side of my face until he reached my chin, gripping it. He was the most attractive male I had ever seen, somehow both innocently handsome and dauntingly sexy. His striking jaw and freckled cheeks were a beautiful contrast, and I realized I could do this for days without growing tired.

"Shall we continue our walk?" he asked, voice a mere whisper against my lips. I returned the smile before offering a quick peck to his mouth. Then I slid off him slowly, giggling at his sharp intake of breath. As I offered him a hand up, I watched intently when he adjusted his trousers, horribly dirty thoughts flooding my mind.

We walked through the extensive gardens, our hands grazing every so often, and Bellamy told me of his grand adventures. Swimming to the bottom of an ice-cold lake, sword fights in the desert with his best friend, sailing across miles of the sea, working on a farm and finding chickens to be rather violent creatures. Memories of riding horseback through the snow, his disastrous attempt at making fire rain when he was a youngling, the first time he ever kissed a female—who apparently had been at least a head taller than him. "I had to stand on a bucket." He chuckled.

In turn I told him of my own, far less interesting, life. We discussed how Nicola, Jasper, Farai, and I would secretly meet in Academy, breaking the rules of fraternization. I told him of Nicola and I's tradition of swimming nude in the lake, named my favorite books, attempted to explain how I felt when I played piano. I too shared the story of my first kiss, which ended disastrously with me accidentally grabbing hold of his mind.

"I mistakenly spoke to him within his head. Poor male ran away crying in fear," I said, the two of us laughing.

And when we realized we had strayed well past the exit he intended to use, we faced one another. Our noses were red from the cold, lips swollen from stolen kisses along the way, and I decided that I had been right. This—being with Bellamy—was something I could do for a lifetime. He leaned in again, his hands moving to my cheeks, and I thought of how much easier it was with this stranger than it had been with Sterling.

At that I froze.

I could not be doing this. I was engaged, spoken for, even if unwillingly so. Panic swallowed the lightheaded feeling of lust, intrigue, and genuine interest.

"I should go," I croaked, stumbling backwards. He stood there, his hands still in the air, confusion and what seemed to be hurt on his face.

Impossible, that was what we were. One night could ruin everything, could sentence so many innocents to death. If even a single soul saw the two of us out here, Sterling could find out. I could lose my chance at uniting the fae and mortals, at fighting against the demons who terrorized us all.

And Bellamy, he could lose far more—his life. If Xavier caught him with me...well I already knew what would happen then. Had experienced it. I took one last look at the Fire, memorizing a face I would likely never see again, before bolting back down the path.

The second I reached the doors I thrust them open and slammed them behind me. Breathing fast not only because of exerting myself during the short run, but also because I could still feel the tingle of Bellamy's hands on me. Every fiber of my being urged me to go back to him, to finish what I started. Instead, I continued the walk to my chambers, praying to Eternity that I did not see Sterling or Mia on my way.

Luckily, the hallway was empty, sounds from the ballroom filling it. I imagined the party would go on for several more hours, as they usually did. I kicked off my shoes, hoping silence would aid me. My bare feet quickly went numb from the cold, but it was easy to ignore, because the unchecked and dissatisfied part of me was still uncomfortably aroused.

My dress swished against my hips and felt heavier than at the start of the night, the bodice horrifyingly tight. I was eager to get the ugly outfit off, and to be on my own. The gold gown and shoes matched the palace, which was not a particularly welcome thought. Every surface of this place was the same color, with minimal design and decoration. It was always eerie how empty the large structure was, how far it felt from a home. When I was a youngling, I could not walk the palace alone without having a breakdown. I did not have that problem any longer, but was still in a hurry to get out of the now silent hall.

Halfway to my destination, I felt something. Someone.

Terror shot through me at the sudden and distinct inkling of being watched. The hair on my arms prickled and rose. I willed my legs to go faster, reaching my power out as a precaution. Nothing—no one— nearby. Still, I maintained a quick pace.

By the time I made it to my chambers I was convinced that I had gone mad. First, I yelled at Sterling. Next, I kissed a stranger who was most definitely not my fiancé. Then, I convinced myself I was being stalked by...I did not even know what. Was the full moon playing tricks on me? I slammed my doors shut and locked them with the hopes of a night spent alone, not needing any further chances to make a fool of myself. Hands pressed firmly against the cool wood, I took a deep breath. Or I tried to take a deep breath. The bodice truly was ridiculously tight.

I slowly turned towards the bed, untying the form-fitting top. My room was just as bare as the rest of the palace. It housed only the necessities such as a bed, small tables on either side to hold lanterns, a wardrobe, a small desk with a chair, and then a door leading to my adjoining bath chamber. The large four-poster bed took up most of the room, and every surface was gold.

It had looked the same for nearly two centuries. Decorating never seemed a priority when I preferred to be in the library, or the market, or the music hall, or really anywhere else. Anywhere that I did not have to stare at the uneven paint on the floor in the center of the room. Anywhere that I did not have to force back the memory of screams.

With that dark thought I finished undressing, letting the layers of fabric hit the floor with a small thud. I walked to my bath, noting that it was filled to the brim. Mia must have sent someone up recently, because the water inside was blissfully hot as I slipped in. I submerged myself, enjoying the way I felt weightless for once, as if the world did not sit atop my shoulders. The heat flooded my system and brought my mind back to the feeling of Bellamy's flame in front of me.

Awareness of my surroundings was not at the top of my priority list just then, so it was quite the surprise when I heard the low bass of Xavier's voice. I shot up, water sloshing in the tub and over the edge, drenching the tile. Rubbing at my eyes with the heels of my palms, I finally blinked away enough of the water and soap to see the king's angry expression.

He offered me a towel, scratchy and golden, without a word. I nodded, taking it to wrap around myself as I stepped out of the tub. Hot fury radiated from him, blazing through my head and making me wince. I had known what I did tonight would come back to bite me, but was not expecting it immediately. When I had grabbed a robe and tied it around my waist, Xavier finally spoke.

"You disappointed me tonight, Ash. Your recklessness and disobedience put the future of this realm at risk, and you know it," he said, voice smooth but face a deep red.

I nodded, walking up to him and bowing my head. He sighed, placing a thumb under my chin to raise my face. I looked up at him, at the only father I had ever known, and watched as his face relaxed. His skin faded to pink, then back to his pale tone.

"I need you to behave, Ash. We must please the mortal prince, we must present a strong team to our subjects, and we must stick together as a family," he whispered.

My smile was not strong, but it was genuine. I knew he loved me, Xavier. Both of the royals did. More than I deserved, really. But I also knew they loved their realm more, far more, and that meant I would always come second to the ambition that maintained it. His smile faltered slightly, his hands gripped onto my biceps, squeezing enough to wrench a gasp from my lips.

"Do not *ever* undermine me that way again."

CHAPTER FIVE

"Good morning," I said over breakfast the next day as I took my seat opposite the queen and to the left of the king. As always, Sterling sat beside me, prepared to occasionally brush his fingers against my hand when I set down my spoon or press his knee into my thigh between courses. It annoyed me to no end.

"Good morning, my flower, how did you sleep?" Mia asked, a smile on her face. Her golden gown clung tightly to her torso, the intricate ties and buttons in the front holding her stomach and breasts in. She had cosmetics on already, her lips and cheeks a youthful pink. Her hair was loose, the orange such a startling shade that it took precedence over even her golden crown, which was littered with diamonds.

Xavier matched, his own tunic a shiny gold that appeared almost metallic. He too wore his crown of gold and diamonds, his black hair pulled back behind his head in order to draw attention to the menacing symbol of his reign.

Sterling, who stood out in his forest green top, spoke before I could.

"I do apologize for not walking you to your chambers, it seems I had the sudden urge to dance the night away." His face was lit up with a handsome smile, but his tone was accusing.

After falling asleep, I had not thought again about the excuses I would need to make for Sterling. However, it seemed they would be unnecessary, as Mia was prepared. She cut back in, tone still light and welcoming.

"Unfortunately, Princess Asher had to maintain your safety before disposing of the disrespectful male from last night. I daresay he might have been a danger if given the chance," she uttered, clearly feigning concern. Mia was not known to be afraid of anyone, no matter their power. Even I, with all my unknown and unheard of abilities, did not scare her in the slightest.

A small thud could be heard under the table, and Xavier's face briefly contorted in pain before he added, "Yes, we did promise your father that we would keep you safe after all. Asher merely did her part, and she begs your forgiveness for the intrusion of your mind."

Normally, I would have maintained my look of impassive agreeance, but last night had jarred me, and it showed through the disbelief on my face. My previous unfaltering façade with Sterling had been slowly cracking, but it shattered at my introductory ball, and I was struggling to maintain a semblance of it.

Sterling caught my slip, narrowing his eyes at me. Before he could comment, I set down my spoon and faced him fully, my knees pressed to his thigh this time. It was something I knew he would enjoy, perhaps enough to quench his doubts.

"King Xavier is right, I am horribly sorry for what I did to you. There are no excuses, at least, none that are good enough to justify such an action. However, I beg for your forgiveness, and I do hope you will see the remorse in me that I so deeply feel." Lies, all of it. Yet, my smooth tone, sultry and submissive, was enough to halt him. To ensure my success, I even reached out and took his hand from the table, wrapping both my own around it and pressing them to my heart.

Sterling startled at the contact, so used to my reluctance with physical intimacy that even this small action was a surprise. I nearly smirked in triumph when a smile formed on his face, one that reached his eyes and brought small crinkles to their corners. Unfortunately, that meant I had no reason to pull away as he leaned forward and placed a kiss to my lips.

It was not a ravenous kiss like Bellamy's had been, rather a soft and slow joining that seemed to say, *this is only the start*. I considered that, a life full of being touched and complimented by Sterling. No sparks or warmth filled me, no emotions other than impatience at the length. For the rest of my existence, I would endure this loveless coupling, and never would I feel how I did last night.

An old and welcoming sense of panic came to me, which had been my companion for months. A dear friend that reminded me no escape was coming, no help. I would marry the boy whose lips felt like concrete, whose touch sent unease through me, whose personality left me exhausted. I would marry Sterling.

When we broke apart, I was forced to smile, to feign enjoyment. A flush filled my face, though I knew it was not from embarrassment or lust, but grief at the life I would never have.

"I forgive you, Asher. You are my future, and I would not dare risk a life with you over such a pesky creature. That man—I mean *male*—shall get what he deserves in the end. And I will have you, a prize grander than any other," the prince declared. It might have been a pretty speech if it were not for the gleam in his brown eyes that told me his motivations were far more selfish, more ambitious, than merely being at my side.

Still, I plastered on a small smile, placated and devoted as ever. When I moved to free his hand, he maneuvered to quickly clasp onto one of mine, entwining our fingers. Apparently, I had been far too convincing. Yet, I knew that if I let on my reservations, doubt might once again creep into the prince's mind. With my orders not to use my power on him, I was forced to allow the affectionate hold.

Adjusting to face my breakfast once more, I was met with a joyous look on Mia's face. She was proud. I could feel it radiating from her, projecting. Xavier looked just as pleased, even eager. They knew what an alliance between the fae and mortals would mean, and I had finally shown my first sign of submission.

"Back to my question, how did you sleep last night, Asher love?" Mia inquired once more, a newfound spring to her voice. I fixed that same look of reserved giddiness onto my face, allowing my voice to lift as well. We remained that way, chatting and smiling during all three courses of breakfast, which I dutifully pushed around rather than eating.

Throughout that time, I allowed my mind to stray to Bellamy, who had adventured to every inch of the fae lands. This was a rarity, even among fae of high standing, but he had managed it, had seen the realm in its entirety.

Why could I, the crown princess and future queen, not do so as well? The idea that I was limited in such a way suddenly felt ludicrous. Mia and Xavier had always insinuated my place was at The Capital, where I could rule on a throne of gold. But how could I rule a realm I had never seen?

Xavier was discussing my natural leadership, his tone that of respect and delight. He too was proud of who I was and would be. Confidence poured over me. I was going to be an incredible queen, one which had never before been seen. Once again I rallied, prepared to ask to see more of the realm that I would preside over.

"Xavier, Mia, I wonder if I might ask a favor of you both?" Their eyes snapped to me at once, the happiness draining from their faces instantly. I had asked before, though they never outright denied my request, the pair always managed to steer the conversation away from talk of travel.

Xavier recovered slower than Mia, who at once brought forth a smile again and said, "Of course, love. What is it that you ask?" I braced myself for the possible denial, which Xavier appeared ready to provide. There was no sense in being upset if I was told no, though I hoped for a different answer.

"I want to travel, to see the realm," I said softly. The royals both cringed at my words, as if I had insulted them somehow. Could that be why they remained hesitant? Did they think me not thankful for the roof over my head and the food in my stomach—for my place in their family?

Reassuring words formed in my mind, ready to be offered as penance for my foolishness, but Xavier had finally found his voice.

"Ash, why are you so eager to leave? This is your home, no place is more important than The Capital. We need you here, where you can learn, rule, and remain safe. The demons would do anything possible to end your life, as they have to so many of your subjects." The low timbre of his voice was absolute, though it was edged with a feel of somberness, as if it pained him to say it.

I nodded, no longer attempting to hide my displeasure. The royals offered tight lipped smiles, both of them reaching out their hands for me to place my own in. Sterling kissed the back of my left hand before letting go, his face full of understanding in this one thing, for he was also confined to the island.

I gripped Xavier and Mia's hands, feeling comforted by the fact that I had them. My parents might be gone, but I was not alone. I would never be alone.

"We love you, Asher," Mia said.

"Forever," Xavier added.

"And always," I finished.

***

After breakfast, Sterling offered to walk me to my chambers. I wanted to say no, so badly that I nearly did without thinking. But I felt the way the royals eyed me, and heard Xavier's warning echoing in my mind.

"Your recklessness and disobedience put the future of this realm at risk."

With the weight of a world I feared I could not carry, I agreed, taking Sterling's hand. We walked mostly in silence, fingers entwined. He rubbed gentle circles on the back of my hand with his thumb, humming an unrecognizable tune.

"You know, Asher, for what it is worth, I believe that you should be able to see where your kind live. They are your subjects, and this is your realm, you should know it like the back of your hand," Sterling said in a hushed voice.

I turned to him, bewildered by the statement. He merely looked straight ahead, a small smile on his face. What could I say to that? He was right, I needed to know my realm, but I could not agree. Not without verbally disagreeing with the royals, which would be the very disobedience that Xavier had reprimanded me for last night.

Sterling peeked at me from the corner of his eye, gauging my reaction to his words, to his lifeline. I maintained a stoic expression, my hand twitching in his slightly.

"In fact," he continued. "I was thinking that perhaps once we are wed, we might work on seeing it together. And after, I would very much enjoy it if you allowed me the honor of showing you the Mortal Realm."

A trick, that was what this likely was. He wanted leverage, submission, *something*. Because there was no reality in which he would fight on my side in that way. No future in which we would be a happy couple that traveled and ruled with grace.

So I stayed silent, listening as he described his home, his kingdom, the lands beyond. I smiled and laughed when warranted, all the while his hand held mine, grip tighter than it needed to be. As if he were holding me to him with every ounce of his strength, unwilling to let me go.

When we arrived at the double doors to my chambers, he turned to face me. Big, brown eyes glanced quickly down at my breasts, then settled on my lips. This time, I could say no. We were alone, it was not necessarily appropriate, and I could claim I was tired. Yet, all I could think of was the disappointed look in Xavier's eyes last night.

With the battle of mind and heart ending before it began, I rallied myself, planting my feet. Sterling cupped either side of my face, licking his pink lips, then leaned in. I scrunched my eyes, wishing I could embody any other place than this one.

Our lips met, and I felt nothing. He settled for a soft joining at first, sighing into the way our mouths molded together. Then he grew hungrier, took more. I kissed him back, meeting his tongue with slightly less force and energy.

Sterling did not seem to mind. One of his hands slipped to the back of my neck, the other slid down to my lower back. All the while I wondered when he would be satisfied enough to leave me alone.

This might have been exactly why he offered the freedom of traveling once we were wed. He wanted me to make the marriage easy, to give and give until I was nothing but a shell of what I once was. Everything I had would gladly be offered on a silver platter, and when I withered away I would know that despite all of the unhappiness, I had saved my kind.

CHAPTER SIX

A knock at the door startled me, causing me to play a note off key. It was a nasty sounding lapse that made my teeth clench. Embarrassing.

I looked up to see Xavier walking in, his face grim. I froze, instantly filling with dread. It was always the same expression, a look of remorse, of regret. Without a shadow of a doubt, I knew exactly what the fae king was here for. These days never got easier.

I stood, walking away from my piano forte. I followed Xavier through the halls of the golden palace, so bright and shiny, vastly different than my corroded and corrupt soul.

When we reached the courtyard, which held at least one hundred fae gathered in a crowded circle, I felt my throat close. It was a larger crowd than normal. Whoever stood on the wooden stage in the center must be important.

Even worse.

We made our way through the bodies of fae. Some were sobbing, others grinning. Many had blank faces, though fury radiated from them. No matter who stood there, most viewers felt this way. Looked at me with hatred in their eyes—with terror.

Being powerful means you are coveted, but it also means you are feared. I was both a prize and a punishment.

Xavier and I finally reached the wooden stairs, our every step echoing out into the gloomy sky. It would rain today, it always did on sentencing days. They were not held often, but when they were, the rain faithfully came.

At the center of the platform kneeled one male and one female, not touching or even looking at one another. Smart. Though it would not save them, not if they were here. Public reapings occurred only when there was not a shadow of a doubt on the guilt of the accused.

And only when they committed one crime in particular.

Xavier and I stepped to the side of the two fae, every set of eyes in the crowd locking on mine. It would be I who was blamed by the angry, the vengeful.

"On this day, I stand before you with a heavy heart. For today, we must deal a sentence to the two accused on their knees in front of you. Today, we seek justice," Xavier said, his voice booming.

Many in the crowd shuffled at his words, unrest building. Their thoughts hit me as if they were saying them aloud.

Liar! Stop! Evil! Wrong! Kill them! Corrupt! Please! Die! Die! Die!

I fortified my mental shields, forming gates with a golden lock, stacking hedges, pouring concrete, building walls. Anything to block out their voices as they merged into one long, hateful string.

"Marybeth Wells and Jameson Telladair stand accused of a crime greater than any other. Together, they have broken our most sacred law, risking the only defense we have against a wicked enemy. Both have endangered not only themselves, but you and your families as well," he said.

I shivered at his words, thinking of a time when it was I who had made those mistakes. I who had risked the lives of those I loved.

Someone in the crowd hissed, a sharp sound that had everyone flinching. Xavier ignored it, continuing as if he had not noticed the discontent.

"Marybeth, a Multiple of Isle Shifter, and Jameson, a Water of Isle Element have fraternized for more than two years. Here they kneel, guilty of selfishness and treason. Guilty of mixing power, therefore weakening it." He knelt down next to Marybeth, who began sobbing at his nearness. With his hand, he gestured towards her stomach. "Here they kneel, with a youngling they so carelessly created, knowing it would poison our realm."

Shocked gasps, then complete silence. My eyes bulged as I took in the small swell of her belly. A youngling. They had conceived a youngling.

My disbelief created weak spots in my shields, and suddenly I felt not only the horror in Marybeth and Jameson's minds, but also their love. For each other and for their unborn youngling. A single tear ran down my cheek, and I quickly wiped it before Xavier noticed.

"The punishment for this crime has long since been written. We must uphold our laws, for if we do not, we allow weakness to fester in our kind. With weakness comes death at the hands of the cursed demons, who desire our demise above all else. When two of us decide to put ourselves above the realm, the realm shall fall. Therefore, it is with great sorrow that I sentence them both to death. For if not them, then all of us shall surely perish," Xavier said, his voice taking on a tone of finality.

Screams and shouts, the two fae grabbing each other in a desperate embrace, guards pushing back the crowd. A crowd of Marybeth and Jameson's family and friends. A crowd to witness what happens when you break the law of fraternization.

Xavier looked to me, waiting. I dipped into a shallow bow, ignoring the way the fae cursed and threatened me. Though I knew better,

I bent down to the accused, getting on my knees before them. Xavier would hate this, my show of remorse. It undermined our laws, made it look as though even royals did not agree with them. Still, I did it.

"I will make it quick," I whispered to them out loud rather than in their minds. They did not need more fear than they already had.

The two nodded, their arms around each other. Just before I closed my eyes, I watched as they shared one final kiss, one last goodbye.

And then their bodies slumped to the ground as I shattered their minds.

Above, the rain began to fall.

***

I spent the next two days in my chambers, forcing myself to stare at that discolored spot on my floor. I did not eat, did not drink, did not sleep. I stared and stared and stared at the repercussions of my own crimes.

For two days I punished myself for the lives I took, including the love I lost.

CHAPTER SEVEN

"What about these, Ash?"

I looked over to Nicola, who was holding up blue delphinium and violet hydrangea. She was sitting cross-legged in the grass, her curls pulled up into a high bun and her tanned face bare. Her apricot dress was a loose and whimsical cotton piece that blew in the soft wind. Her cloak was the opposite, a heavy black wool that looked far more comfortable than my own.

We had spent the majority of the morning planning for her wedding next month. Mia had invited her and Kafele to be married at the palace, which was an honor even most court members would never receive. I knew the queen did it for me, although I was not sure if it was so I could be with my friend during this time, or because she wanted me to bear witness to how exciting a marriage could be. The difference between Nicola and I though, was that she loved her betrothed. I rarely managed to tolerate mine.

"I like them. I think the colors go well together, and they will look beautiful with your dress. They are unique, like you," I responded.

"Good. I want our wedding to be different than others. I want to be original," she said, lifting her chin a bit. I smiled, knowing that originality would never be a problem for Nicola. We sat there in silence for a few minutes, organizing all of the supplies we had put together.

Nicola was nothing short of perfectly organized, with charts and drawings and truly anything she could think to depict or plan. I wondered if knowing who she was made these things easier for her, like second nature.

I loved that about her. How strong-willed and confident in herself she was. Nicola took everything thrown at her and threw it back with double the force, never stumbling.

I heard her let out a deep sigh, and when I looked up, she was peeking at me from the corner of her eye.

"Okay Nicola, what is it you are dying to say?" I asked, rolling my eyes. Her smile grew at my question. Since we were young, she had always done this, hoped I would catch onto her hints of interest and speak up first. She was clever and cunning, which made her all the more fun.

"Who was that you were dancing with the other night? The one who nearly ripped Sterling's arm off?" she asked, facing towards me. She leaned in a bit and said, "He was quite possibly one of the most attractive males I have ever seen. Apart from Kafele, of course."

I never used my powers on Nicola, so she would be the only one who continued to watch what happened that night other than the five of us who went out into the hallway.

"I only got his first name. Bellamy. He was very…interesting," I said, unable to find better words to describe him. I doubt I could do him justice.

"Oh my gods, Asher, did you have sex with Mr. Interesting?" she asked, squealing a bit at the end. I quickly shushed her and gave a bit of a shove, making her lean over laughing. I had done the same to her the first time she told me about Kafele, and when they had sex I made jokes for weeks about him being quick off the mark. Poor male only lasted a minute or so. I guess I deserved this.

"No, do not be daft. And keep your voice down before Sterling hears and sends an army after him!" I hissed, trying to stay serious. I failed when she wiggled her eyebrows at me, falling into a fit of laughter. I was always planning on telling her about what happened, but I was nervous to do so outside where we could be overheard.

I looked around us and saw no one. Reaching out with my power, I sensed a groundskeeper on the other side of the castle trimming a hedge, but no one else.

"If you must know, we might have kissed," I answered, trying to sound casual. Nicola's mouth dropped open and her eyes grew wide.

"Ash, I was kidding. I cannot believe you actually kissed him. How exciting!" she said, clapping her hands together. "Tell me all about it. Did you like it? Was he any good? What did he taste like?"

I lowered my voice to a whisper, "It was amazing. I have never felt a spark like that before, like lightning in my skin. And yes, he was good at it. So so wonderful at it. He tasted like fire and cinnamon and sunshine—"

"How does someone taste like sunshine?" Nicola asked, giggling.

"I do not know how to explain it, but he was warm and clean and...like the first ray of sun after a long and stormy winter." At that, she smiled, and I knew she understood. I would never dare say that this feeling Bellamy gave me was anything like what she and Kafele had, but I did feel a pull to him. Like he was a magnet guiding me to his side.

"Will you see him again?" she asked, her voice impossibly softer.

She knew this would be the most damning part of the conversation. One which should not be occurring at all. Nicola I could trust, it was the listening ears that I could not. Truthfully, it did not matter. There was no future in which the Fire and I would be together.

"I do not know Nicola, will I?" I asked jokingly.

Nicola was a Tomorrow. The first time we met, she said that in her dream, which was what she used to call the visions she saw upon touching another fae, we became best friends. She had been the only one brave enough to read me and, to this day, remained the sole Tomorrow to have read The Manipulator.

She rolled her eyes. "Stop avoiding the question."

I would have loved to see him even once more, but not only would every suiter have left The Capital immediately after the ball ended, I also did not know how even a single minute with him would lead to anything other than trouble. Mia and Xavier would likely die of fright if they found out what I did, let alone that I had the desire to see him again, and Sterling might call for Bellamy's head. Of course, Xavier would deliver it whether requested or not.

"It was exciting and sexy, but it was also incredibly stupid. Risking myself is one thing, but if my marriage to Sterling does not happen, then our entire realm could be in danger." I sighed. Futile as it was, a part of me had always dreamed of finding a handsome stranger that would fall madly in love with me. Apparently, Eternity liked to play jokes on the hopeful.

"You cannot carry the world on your shoulders Asher. If you marry Sterling, you will be giving up your happiness for a realm that does not even respect you." Her words stung, and I was positive they would stick with me for some time. The truth was not always easy to hear, and it was usually hard to forget.

"I know that, I witness their hatred everyday Nicola," I snapped. I knew that she was not being mean intentionally, she never was when she said those things that felt like a stab to the chest. Yet, her good intentions never seemed to take away the hurt of such a horrible truth.

Nothing in the world would make me happier than having the fae accept me. Each day I woke up and attempted to fight back against my nature, to mold myself into the princess—and eventual queen—the fae deserved. Each day I seemingly failed.

"I am sorry, I just meant that you give up more than you should to the ungrateful. You deserve happiness. Sterling is dull at best and deranged at worst. Look how he treats you when he is still vying for your heart. What do you think a marriage to him will be like?"

Again, she was right, yet I still felt anger rising within me. I never enjoyed talking about Sterling with her, because there was no changing the situation. All it did was serve to upset us both. Nicola would not share with me what future she saw for my impending husband and I, but I knew that she did not enjoy whatever ensuing life would come of the nuptials.

"Marriage is about gain, Mia tells me as much daily. I am only doing what nearly everyone else does. You are the exception Nicola, not the rule." Determination lit her eyes, and she looked as if she might further argue. I spoke before she could. "Because of that, it would be careless to see Bellamy again. I would never be able to get away without being seen anyways. Besides, I would have no way of finding him."

Just then, soft footsteps sounded behind me. I turned to see Jasper and Farai walking towards us, hand-in-hand. They were a beautiful couple, so much so that it was hard not to stare at them. Jasper had let his hair glide down his back freely today, the straight black wave blowing in the wind. He was growing paler as the cold months came crashing down upon us, but his cheeks always held a pink hue. His strong jaw and broad shoulders paired with his wide brown eyes and thin lips had always made him appear more ethereal than most. The kind of beautiful that made you question reality.

Farai was a unique sort of handsome. His ivory hair was cropped short recently, a change from his normally shoulder-length style. His irises matched, an equally colorless hue. He was larger than Jasper, in height and bulk. Years of training as a soldier for the Isle Shifter military forces had chiseled him into a living sculpture. However, it was the male's skin that

OF NIGHT AND BLOOD

brought others flocking to him, piquing their interest. Rather than a single tone like most fae, Farai's skin was both a creamy pearl and a rich brown. Patches of the two colors warred on him like an abstract painting, an alluring and captivating anomaly.

"Ash baby, when are you finally going to say no to the gaudy gold?" Farai asked as he sank into the grass beside me.

I looked down, eyeing the thick gold trousers and scratchy short sleeve tunic. I had originally planned to wear a long sleeve to hide the bruises on my arms, which were taking uncharacteristically long to fade, but my hideous gold cloak covered them well enough.

I too hated my clothes, but Xavier and Mia preferred we represent the color of the royal seal. To them, the color signified our love for our realm and separated us as royals. I understood the sentiment.

"I am pretty sure I will be buried beneath gilded dirt, Fair. But I do so appreciate the hatred for my wardrobe," I teased, rolling my eyes at him. Farai was in all black, as he often was. Though his obsession with the color did not seem excessive, rather it was flattering, making the shade of his hair and eyes stand out in bold contrast.

Jasper huffed beside me. Nothing displeased him more than my attitude towards the rules that had been set in place for me. His belief was that I let them walk all over me, whereas I argued that there was no need for me to fuss over small things such as clothes. If it made the royals happy, then it was the least I could do after they had given me so much.

All three of them loathed my choice to submit. Of all those decisions I had agreed upon, it was Sterling that they most adamantly argued against. Concern from them had not been a surprise in the slightest, because they were all desperately in love. Their understanding of my situation, my life, only went so far.

"You look beautiful, as you always do. I think what Farai meant was that you deserve the chance to blossom on your own, to become who you want to be," Jasper said, rubbing my back softly.

The three of them shared the same solemn and troubled expression, surrounding me with their pity. I knew why they worried. In fact, I appreciated their love for me. Nothing other than my absolute trust in that love would have helped me at the start of my relationship with Sterling, when I had been desperately attempting to form a connection.

He had seemed kind and intelligent, not to mention he was incredibly handsome. I had been willing to see past his young age and his shameless touching because of that. But behind my back he was cold and calculated, lustful and conceited, hateful and conniving. It did not warm him to my friends, and they were quick to inform me of their opinions.

After I confronted him, he was more direct about who he truly was. The mortal prince was all too glad to strip the façade, because he knew I would do whatever the royals said either way. And they were insisting upon our marriage.

I shook my head, fighting off the tears welling behind my eyes. I would not cry about that ridiculous child. He could be my king consort; I would not allow for that to mean anything other than someone at my side for show. Someone to supply armies and help us win the war that we all knew was coming. Someone to please Mia and Xavier. If forced, perhaps a youngling.

"Anyways, who was that dashing male you were dancing with at your ball? He was positively delicious," Farai said, licking his lips. Jasper chuckled, slinging his arm around his husband and flicking his cheek. All three of them looked at me with wide smiles, Nicola not offering the slightest bit of assistance. One of them prodding me was enough, I did not need all three.

"No one I will ever see again," I grumbled, my tone dripping annoyance. Such a pointlessly dangerous conversation. Jasper rolled his eyes, straightening his amber vest and matching trousers, the cream long-sleeved tunic smooth beneath. He possessed the kind of casual grace that sparked jealousy among males and females alike.

Farai on the other hand was a beautiful disaster, with his perfectly messed tunic and trousers, buttons askew and hair wild. He shook his head, as if my choice of words was incredibly irritating. Maybe to them it was. Because how could they understand what it is like to owe everything to someone the way I did to the royals?

"I need to go grab something from my chambers, I will be right back," I said, jumping up and practically running from them. They all watched me, not remotely convinced. But I did not care, I needed to be alone.

With impressive speed, I rushed inside, prepared to hide away until the three of them came to retrieve me by force. My eyes frantically searched the hallways as I ran, my power tasting the air as well, praying to Eternity that I did not run into Sterling or the royals.

When I finally, thankfully, grabbed the handles to my doors, I yanked them open and closed them behind me with a sigh. I had still been searching the area, subconsciously looking for unwanted guests. So the other mind, all black shadows and fiery sunshine, alerted me to my visitor before his husky voice.

"Hello, Princess," Bellamy said.

CHAPTER EIGHT

Bellamy laid sprawled out on my bed, hands behind his head and smile wide, as if he belonged there. Standing against my door, hand to my chest and breathing heavily, I was too startled to pretend he did not look as though he did.

"What are you doing here?" I hissed, thoughts racing at the many possibilities of awful ways this could end. Bellamy's burnt head on a spike being one of the more horrid scenarios. Though not nearly as awful as watching him slump at my feet on a wooden stage.

His smile did not falter in the slightest as he sat up, his tight black tunic stretching over his arms and sending uncomfortably erotic images through my mind. As if he could hear my thoughts, Bellamy smirked, eyes alight with a wicked gleam that I needed no part of.

"I am here to bring you on an adventure," he said with a casual shrug.

I wanted to grab him by the shoulders and shake him, to ask him how he could not see the danger, to push him out the window because it would be a cleaner and safer death. Instead, I remained standing, the same baffled look still on my face.

I needed to tell him to leave, to panic or run or yell, *something.*

"How did you get in here?" I asked instead. He quirked a brow, clearly amused by my reaction. His scent floated in the air, and I realized that I would be doomed if anyone came in here today, because the smell alone would be telling.

The Fire was uninterested in the growing danger, far more intrigued by me if the way his eyes stayed trained on my own was any indication. His mind was strange, like a canvas that had been painted a solid color. There was no dimension to it, not like there had been the other night.

"Desperation can get you anywhere," he said as he stood, then began walking my way.

His steps towards me were not quick, but rather slow and calculated, as if behind that relaxed and confident exterior was a male who feared my rejection. I could taste it slightly, the chilly nerves that radiated from him despite that solid canvas.

"I do not know what that means, but you need to leave, *now.* It is not safe for you to be here," I said just as he made the final step and closed the distance between us, our bodies nearly touching. Foolish, that was what being next to him like this was. Foolish and dangerous and so, so intoxicating.

"Careful, Princess, I am beginning to think you do not want me here," he said, gesturing behind him to my room. A part of me ignited at his words, his insinuation. I could not fight off the many ways I did want him here from flashing through my head. Hypocritical of me to say the least.

"Careful, Fire, I am beginning to think you cannot take a hint," I said, back still against my doors. He smirked, placing one hand in the pocket of his trousers and the other above my head. As he leaned in, my breath caught, eyes flicking to his lips before I regained my wits and stared back into his icy gaze.

His eyes did not meet mine though, instead they honed in on my arm, where my cloak had slipped off my shoulder. My bruises, which had faded to a greenish hue, now sat on full display.

"Who did that to you?" he asked, his voice a deep growl. I winced at my careless mistake, covering my arm once more with my cloak.

"It is none of your business. Now, what do you actually want? Hurry up and tell me, then leave before someone sees you and cuts off your head," I said, my words a rush of nerves and stress. I had not planned to ever see Bellamy again, let alone be sharing the same air as him once more. It was unnerving. Hypnotizing.

He shot a glare at my now covered arm, then sighed.

"Spend the day with me. One day, and then I will leave you alone if you wish," he said. His eyes were wide, pleading.

A tempting offer to say the least. In fact, it was too tempting. Had I not just been discussing my desire to travel and live? Had Sterling not insinuated yesterday that he would take me to see the world if I were willing to marry him? The timing of it all was suspicious, and I was in no place to be running off with strange fae males.

Still, there I stood, considering saying yes as if it were not the absolute worst way to spend my day. As if I would not be marking him for dead just by being this close to him.

His own eyes slid down to my lips, not attempting to hide it as I had, and I felt all of my sense leave me. My head nodded, the slightest dip of my chin to signal that I agreed to the idiocy. That gorgeous smile returned in full force, taking over his face and making his dimples widen as if someone had placed their thumb to both his cheeks.

Making this stranger happy was unnaturally exciting, my own eagerness to experience something new bleeding into the joy that seeped from him. Sadly, I would need to crush his hopes, because there was no way we were getting out of this castle, let alone off the island, without being noticed.

I meant to say as much to him, but Bellamy was quick to hold out some sort of ball, a mischievous smile on his face. It was a deep green and only half the size of his palm.

"Do you trust me, Princess?" he asked, offering his hand.

I swallowed hard as our eyes connected, the same tug from the night of my ball telling me to say yes.

"I do not even know you," I answered instead, my words coming out with much more conviction than I felt.

"Let's change that," he whispered, pulling my arm around his neck and wrapping his around my waist. Before I could question his forwardness, he took the ball and slammed it onto the ground.

The color seemed to be ripped from the world around us as the cinnamon scented smoke surrounded our bodies. Suddenly I felt as though my skin was being stretched and ripped, a slight cry releasing from my mouth. Just as soon as the pain started, it stopped.

"You can open your eyes Asher," Bellamy said into my ear.

Realization that the world was not a black void hit, and I opened my tightly scrunched eyes. The sea was in front of us, the sun reflecting off the calm expanse of blue. Below our feet there was bleach-white sand where my golden floor had just been. Fear and curiosity were at war in my mind, which formed an overwhelming tornado of questions. The most obvious ones left my lips.

"What just happened? Where are we?"

"You are safe, you just portaled," he said, voice deep. I felt his heart racing against my right hand and realized how close we still were. When I dropped both hands to my side, I felt his grip on me tighten a bit. "I assume they have yet to show you based on your reaction, but it is not a new creation."

I remained silent, too confused to speak just yet.

"And you are in the place I call home," he added. When I finally lifted my gaze from the ground to his eyes, I saw that he was staring at me rather intently.

"I find it hard to believe that I would have not heard of such a miraculous tool," I responded, the accusation in my tone obvious. Impossible as it was that I just went from one spot to another in an instant, it was even more improbable that there was nothing suspicious about the magic.

"Check with the king and queen, I am sure that they will admit to their knowledge of portaling. Tell me, is it so hard to believe that they would refrain from giving you knowledge of a way to leave without detection?" he asked, eyebrows raised. He had a point there. That did not mean I had to like it though. In fact, my rage seemed to rise within me at his knowing response.

I squirmed out of his grip and took a handful of steps back. Spinning in a full circle, I slowly took in my surroundings. We were on a crowded beach; the air was cool and the wind was fierce. At least I knew he was not planning to murder me. Yet.

In the distance there was a strange red hue to the sky, as if somewhere far out at sea a fire raged. It stunned me momentarily, the sight of something so odd and out of place. Especially in comparison to the beauty of the beach and its occupants.

Everywhere around me fae of all colors and sizes and ages walked about. There were younglings splashing around in the chilly water, their parents not far, laughing at their antics. Young fae in their prime also mingled, the styles of clothing varying as much as physical appearances.

Off in the distance, many white buildings I assumed were homes could be seen, beyond that, a dark structure loomed. It appeared to be a castle of sorts, black and ominous, leaching the light from the day.

It sent chills down my spine.

Facing him once more, I latched onto that anger and brought it to the surface, letting it spill from me. "If you ever take me anywhere against my will or knowledge again, I will not hesitate to take everything that makes you unique and warp it into something you do not recognize. In fact, I will gladly shatter your mind with barely a thought," I said, my finger pointed at his face.

The male remained still, listening to my threats without a word.

"I am not a pawn, a toy, or a pet. I am not just some princess waiting to be carried off or a female begging to be rescued," my voice went down an octave, sounding utterly lethal. I closed the space between us until we were breathing the same air, and I did my best to look down on him despite the height difference. "I am an immensely powerful being that offers kindness to those who are smart enough to treat me with respect, and promises wrath to those stupid enough to wish harm on me. So, before we continue our little adventure, tell me, Bellamy, are you smart or are you stupid?"

Bellamy did not react the way I had hoped. Instead of cowering or submitting or even looking stunned, he smiled. His eyes wrinkled at the corners and his dimples deepened. For a moment I caught a sense of his mind, and I realized he had found my speech…endearing. Was I losing my touch?

"I would like to think I am smart, but I find myself growing increasingly stupid in your presence," he answered, cupping either side of my face with his warm hands and leaning in. Just before our lips met, he paused. It felt like a question, as if he were waiting for permission.

As mad as I was, there was still no part of me that wanted him to stop. He seemed to feel that, because he brought his lips to mine. The kiss was timid and slow. His tongue was in my mouth, wrapping around mine. One of his hands slid to the back of my head, pulling me closer somehow. My hands moved of their own accord, grabbing onto his short, dark waves. I heard him let loose a little moan before pulling away.

To my surprise, he leaned his forehead against mine and smiled down at me. His cheeks were flushed, making his freckles less noticeable.

Despite how frustrated I was with him, I also had to admire how utterly free Bellamy was. Something I had never associated myself with by any means, but that I longed for.

I pulled away again, knowing that I needed to keep my wits about me. This male had just taken me across islands without my permission, kissing him was idiotic at best. Even though I knew that, my stomach still flipped at the sight of him licking his lips.

"If you would still like to spend the day with me, I would greatly enjoy showing you where I live," Bellamy said, holding his hand out to me just as he did in my chambers.

"What if I say no?" I questioned, my eyes forming into slits.

"Then we go back to the palace," he answered with a shrug. I knew he was being sincere, but I felt as though I should show at least some sort of self-preservation instinct.

"Swear it to me," I demanded.

"You want me to swear what exactly?" he asked with a raised brow. A fair question, I supposed.

"Swear to me that you mean me no harm and that you will never take me somewhere against my will again," I said.

Without hesitation, Bellamy got down on both knees in the sand.

"I, Bellamy, swear to you, Asher, that I mean you no harm. I swear to never take you anywhere you do not desire to go. And I will do you one better Princess, I swear to protect you for as long as you are at my side."

He stood up and once again reached out his hand. This time, I grabbed it. A smirk formed on his lips as he interlaced our fingers. The way his hand felt in mine, our fingers tangled, was strange. It was as if they had always belonged this way, joined. I looked up to see his eyes down as well. Could he too feel that strange pull? The sense of rightness? Without warning, Bellamy began stalking forward, tugging me with him. Together, we walked off the beach.

When the sand turned to stone, we came upon a small market. There were vendors selling a variety of goods ranging from shimmering silks to lush spices to intricate pottery. The stalls themselves were simple, plain even. They appeared to be made of driftwood, the sun and salt-bleached wood shining and providing little distraction from the creations of those running the stands.

My eyes lit up at the sight of it all. I felt Bellamy looking at me but could not manage to pull my eyes away from the wonders of what was in front of us. "Is it normal to feel the urge to touch and taste and see everything?" I asked, mesmerized.

"Females often ask me that, but we are in public Asher." I swatted his arm, rolling my eyes. He merely let out a deep chuckle. "Yes, the first time I came to the market I spent hours here. There was not a single booth I had yet to see by the time I left," he said, smiling down at me.

"Then let's go see it all," I whispered.

CHAPTER NINE

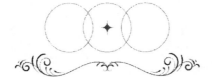

Our first stop was to a baker that was selling sweet pastries with sugary powder on top. Bellamy introduced her as Leela, and said she had the best sweets in the market, which made her blush a deep scarlet. I had no coins with me, but Bellamy did, and he seemed more than happy to oblige as he handed her the payment. I ate the first bite and moaned loudly, earning a smile from the female. A minute later I had already devoured the entire thing. She gave me a second one, this time coated in chocolate, for free and kissed my cheek goodbye.

I continued eating the pastry as we were walking to the next booth, reveling in the way I could enjoy a sweet in public, as if it were normal. Out of nowhere, Bellamy lightly gripped my arm, halting me. I looked up at him, eyes squinting from the sun peeking through the gray clouds overhead. I felt the warmth of his hand touch my cheek just before he wiped the side of my mouth with his thumb. He held my stare as he put it in his mouth and sucked off the white powder, pulling it out with a pop.

Heat flowed to my cheeks, and I had to clench my thighs together in an attempt to calm myself down. Clearly, I was deprived. Or depraved. Bellamy winked at me and then began walking towards the next vendor we had been on our way to. My knees were shaky, but I willed my legs to move towards the teasing fae ahead.

We made our way around, each fae flashing Bellamy a wide and genuine smile. Many even came up to him, bowing their head slightly and welcoming him home. Their somewhat formal tones confirmed what I had already guessed based on the well of power I had sensed within Bellamy, he was likely the Fire Warden's son. I did not recall much about Isolda, but I knew her to be a strong and fierce Fire. The respect Bellamy was being shown would make sense of the heir to a leader such as herself.

Throughout our time of browsing, Bellamy and I went back and forth asking the other questions. His favorite color was red, which I could have guessed. Mine was green, like sage leaves, though gold made up almost the entirety of my wardrobe. When I asked what his favorite scent was, he surprised me and said it was vanilla.

"Like the smell of you," he had said, making my cheeks burn.

Our conversation continued like that, a give and take that I had never had with anyone other than Nicola. Even Jasper and Farai had never asked me some of these questions. And I was glowing under his attention, bathing in the heat of it. Until he asked what my greatest fear was, and I froze.

I could not share with him those concerns, those horribly intrusive thoughts. There was a fine line between discussing my least favorite food and sharing those deeper feelings that had led me to unspeakable acts. I shook my head, to both rid myself of those memories and to tell him I could not—would not—answer that question.

His eyebrows pinched together and his mouth opened slightly, as if he was poised to argue my refusal. I rushed ahead, aiming for the closest booth. It was the largest in the market, the wooden walls chipped and sun-bleached. Clothing of endless styles and colors littered every surface. The booth was beautiful and chaotic, exotic in comparison to what was sold at The Capital. The male at the counter smiled at us as we approached, and as luck would have it, Bellamy let his previous question go.

"What do you have for me today, Pino?" Bellamy asked the male. This seamster was visibly aged, which meant something for fae. He had to be at least five millennia with his graying beard and wrinkling tan skin. He was likely nearing his Ending, but still he was at his booth, faithfully creating masterpieces.

Fae might be immortal, but we aged and lived and died nonetheless. We called it the Ending, because we believed that we would sense when Eternity had decided our story was at a close, hear when it called us back home. It seemed Pino had not felt that tug just yet.

I reached out to touch a silk slip that hung from a beam above. It was a beautiful sky blue, similar to Bellamy's eyes. The way the light reflected off of it made it seem almost iridescent. I could not imagine wearing such a stunning garment. Something that was not gold.

"It seems your *friend* already has an item in mind," Pino said. I turned back towards the two males and saw that they were having some sort of silent conversation. Bellamy glared daggers at the seller, taking his handsome face and warping it into something menacing. Pino did not back down, instead he raised his brows—a challenge. I felt the need to step in as the tension grew.

"I do not believe I have a need for it, but it is lovely, as are all of your pieces. Your talent is extraordinary," I said, bowing slightly. Talent was something fae prided themselves on. The arts were a big part of our realm, and it would be rude to not recognize his abilities. He beamed at that, pushing Bellamy out of his way and coming over to me.

"Well, you are a delight! Thank you my dear, one can never hear too often that their passion is fruitful. I am Pino Augustu. If you care to try anything on, I have a room in the back to do so," he said.

I walked away from the slip and further into the small, enclosed space. The wooden walls were covered in finished pieces ranging from trousers like my own to gorgeous gowns. The deeper into the room I went, the more beautiful the clothing got.

I found a simple red dress along the back wall. It was made of a thicker material than silk and had a plunging neckline. The back was barely there as well, making me wonder if it was possible to wear undergarments at all with it. The sleeves were short, sheer ruffles, and the garment itself reached the ground.

Mia would faint at the sight of it, and the castle seamstress would likely suggest I was too big to wear it. I meant to walk away, but Pino was there watching me intently.

"You find yourself called to the piece, yes? So why not just see how it makes you feel before walking away from it?" A question like that would normally be uttered from a Tomorrow, but I also knew very little about fashion, so it could be more common knowledge regarding clothing than a premonition of sorts. I grabbed the dress and followed him to the back.

Pino showed me to the small dressing room, which appeared to have been a closet before being repurposed. It had nothing but a small hook on one wall and a long mirror on the opposite. He closed the curtain behind him and left me to the daunting task of trying on such a promiscuous piece.

Taking my time to undress, I let my mind wander back to Bellamy. For the first time in my life, I was struggling to understand a male's intentions. Dating had not been hard before. In fact, it was quite easy. My desires were communicated and fulfilled. Hesitation had never been in my vocabulary.

Until now.

I sighed. It was a waste of my time and energy to attempt any form of companionship with Bellamy. I was marrying Sterling whether I wanted to or not. With my boots discarded and my trousers on the floor next to my cloak, I grabbed the hem of my top and lifted it over my head.

I again considered if I was supposed to wear undergarments with the dress.

I quickly shimmied out of them before I lost my nerve. As I pulled up the dress, I made a silent vow to have Bellamy loan me the coins regardless of whether I liked it or not, because this was horribly unsanitary.

The dress was tight, which nearly brought tears to my eyes. Why was I subjecting myself to this? As I cursed myself, the dress finally slid up, catching under my bare breasts. I tucked them both into the remaining fabric, then slid my arms into the small sleeves.

Instantly I regretted not facing the mirror to begin with, as I now had to somehow convince myself to turn and look. After counting to five a total of seven times, I finally spun to face my reflection.

Every part of my body was on display, even what the red material covered. My nipples were taught, and bumps raised on my upper stomach at the chill from the plunging neckline. My stomach was more obvious in the skintight dress, but the small draping was flattering in a way I had yet to experience. I made a half circle so I could look at my back and gasped at the sight. The back was so low that my undergarments would have shown. I was genuinely fearful that my rear might make an appearance, but in a way that gave me a thrill.

Overall, the dress was confidence made tangible. I could not recall a time I had ever felt as strong, sexy, and sophisticated as this; especially not with so little on. Just below my collar bones, the small amethyst lay against my tan skin. The silver that held it coiled around the jagged and imperfect stone, wrapping it like vines. My heart gave a jolt, but I fought back the memory.

The suede curtain was moving in the breeze, catching my eye. I chose to act on a whim, pulling it back.

Both males were gone, so I went in search of them, willing my bare feet to stay silent. With how little the booth was, I knew it would not take long to spot them. My guess proved right when I found them around the corner, huddled closely and whispering. Neither seemed to notice my arrival, continuing the tension-soaked conversation. Both were stiff and seemed to radiate anger.

Fires, I thought with a roll of my eyes.

"You are taking more of a risk than you should be. What will she mean to you in the end? What will happen if you go on this way?" Pino hissed, his questions laced with venom. Did he mean me?

"Watch your mouth, I am not the only one who might take offence to that," Bellamy snapped back. The way his voice deepened sent shivers down my spine. I had never pictured being afraid of the dimpled male, but a part of me was now.

"She is a liability at best! You need to get this over with. Do not make me regret allowing your secrets to stay hidden. What do you think he would say if he knew the real reason you left? Or the reason you asked to stay?" So much was being said that I could not make sense of. Who were they talking about, and what secrets did Bellamy have?

What had I done to become a liability? Was it because I was engaged? Did Pino feel I was too much of a risk to allow on their land? It would make sense. Being with me could lead to a horrible ending for Bellamy, one I would not wish on anyone, but I had witnessed firsthand. Perhaps Pino was right to wish me gone.

I wanted to keep listening, but I knew that if I did, I would likely get caught. I cleared my throat and took a step out into the open. Both of their heads snapped in my direction, the fire within Bellamy scorching in his eyes at the sight of me. He seemed to hold his breath.

Pino's features were the first to soften, turning into a joyful surprise. His mouth popped into an O shape, and he rushed over to me to adjust the dress.

"I do not think that I could have made a better fitting dress if I tried," he said to me, all signs of the previous anger gone.

Smiling at the old male, I allowed myself a quick look at Bellamy. He was standing a few feet away, drinking in every inch of me. I could see the red tinging the tips of his nose and pointed ears from here, likely from the argument. For a moment his gaze locked onto my bruised arms, his fists tensing. Then he took a deep breath, his body relaxing.

"You look stunning," Bellamy commented. I felt my own cheeks go red, my hand reaching up to twirl my necklace.

Pino let out a cough that sounded like a repressed laugh and rushed out of the cluttered room.

CHAPTER TEN

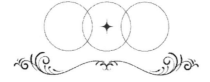

Bellamy and I sat there in silence, both of us staring at the other. My power begged to burst free, sensing my desire to know what he was thinking. I watched his eyes move slowly down my body, the tension growing. My own eyes caught the flushed points of his ears again.

"I wish I had your ears," I blurted.

The second the words left my mouth I felt foolish. I often chose to ignore my deformed ears, but with Bellamy it seemed I was prone to speaking without thought.

"I mean, I just wish mine were normal," I clarified.

His smile quickly faded, turning into a tight line.

"Your ears are beautiful Asher, being different is not a bad thing," he said. "Besides, are they not a sign of your resilience?"

"Being the sole survivor of a demon attack is not necessarily something I enjoy recalling, and my ears remind me of it every day," I shared, surprised at my own vulnerability. "I often wonder if it bothers the king and queen as well. Seeing where the demons cut off the tips of my ears surely reminds them of the friends and child that were taken from them."

Their son had the same thing done to his ears before they killed him, which was probably why Mia preferred my hair to be long and down, hiding the reminder. On special occasions, she would place golden cuffs atop them. They came to a point, replicating what mine surely would have looked like in a better world.

"What about your own feelings, do they not matter?" he asked, tilting his head to the side. In truth, I spoke of my feelings and thoughts so rarely that I doubted anyone knew to ask. Mia and Xavier both cared for me more dearly than I could have asked for. Everything I had and was came from their kindness, generosity, and love. If I made my feelings known, they would care. Right?

"I find it difficult to talk about how I feel, but I know if I expressed myself more, everyone around me would move mountains to help." Even as I said the words, I was unsure if I believed them. Just a few nights ago I was telling Mia I did not want to marry Sterling, and she was willfully ignoring my reasoning. Did what I wanted and thought truly matter to her? It was not rare for someone to love you but not respect your independence.

Yet, I could not help but think of how selfish those desires I held were. Would I really risk the safety of my realm simply because I did not particularly enjoy my betrothed? I saw the way Xavier and Mia moved, their beautiful reliance in one another. No, they did not love, but they did find a way to make their marriage seamless, comforting. I could likely do that if I tried.

The problem was that I did not want to try.

"You seem to do just fine discussing your feelings with me," Bellamy noted.

He was not wrong, though I wished he was less aware. Refreshing and easy, that was what Bellamy had been. He was a male I knew I could also find that comfort in that Mia had with Xavier. Without a doubt I knew I could also find love there, if I gave myself the time and freedom to do so. But I did not have that luxury.

"Tell me something," he said.

"What?" I asked curiously.

"Why are you marrying that mortal?" he asked. His body leaned towards me in anticipation of my answer.

I thought over it, gauging if I should admit that I would do anything for Xavier and Mia. They raised me as their own, loved me despite my flaws, saved me from myself. And the realm, my kind, those were things worth sacrificing for.

There were times long ago when I thought the opposite, when I blamed the royals for losses that I did not want to accept fault for. Pain I put on them when really it was my own to bear. Never again would I do that to them. Even being here was a risk to it all.

"Why does that question take so much consideration?" he asked quietly, still standing across from me. I looked down, avoiding his eye contact which would surely cause me to say something ridiculous.

"I find it hard to believe that you would like what I share," I answered honestly. No one ever did. It was my life to do with as I pleased, so no one's approval but Xavier's and Mia's truly mattered. Yet, I found myself wanting Bellamy to accept my choices as well.

"Try me," he countered. His thumb idly twisted one of the many rings adorning his fingers. This one was a gold band that had a symbol for each of the elements on it.

Twist. Fire. Twist. Air. Twist. Earth. Twist. Water. Around and around it spun. His eyes never left me, his interest radiating from him.

"I often feel as though I am no one," I began instead, answering a question I had previously avoided. "Do you want to know why I liked this dress? It was because I would never get the chance to choose it any other time. Every part of me is a perfectly thought-out design made by everyone but myself. I eat, sleep, and dress according to what I am told. I do so out of guilt, but also for the betterment of the realm. I am the story of nightmares amongst our kind, and I wonder who I would become if I was left to my own devices. What I might morph into. Who I might hurt. My greatest fear, it is myself," I finished, sucking in a deep breath.

Bellamy responded almost immediately, as if he needed no time to form the opinion.

"What if the being you are meant to be is far superior to the one others have crafted you into? A rendering will never be as beautiful as the original, as the life and flesh and breath of that which inspired it. I believe we all are afraid sometimes. Of others and ourselves. No one is completely sure of themselves, but your doubt will prevent you from becoming what you were destined to be." He spoke as if he somehow knew what my future held. A tangle of words that threatened to tear down everything I had ever been told. Everything I had ever believed.

"And what was I meant to be?" I asked, lifting my chin, challenging him.

Bellamy walked towards me, stopping just an arm's length away. He looked at me intently for what felt like years, seemingly fighting an internal battle. It was clear whenever the war within him ended, because he answered, "A queen."

Then he took the last step and crushed his lips to mine. His right hand tugged my hair, making my head tilt back. When I felt his tongue slide across my lips, begging for entry, I opened my mouth. Soft fingertips grazed my mutilated right ear, sending a shiver down my spine. I had never allowed anyone to touch my ears except for Mia. Even I avoided them at all costs. The way Bellamy caressed them though, it was electric.

Heat pooled low in my stomach, and I gripped his top to tug him closer. His body was solid under my fingers, so strange when paired with his soft facial features. The dimples and freckles living in constant contrast to the strong jaw, high cheekbones, and toned body. My grip tightened, eliciting a low growl from deep in his chest, and then he broke our kiss.

Before I could wonder what I did wrong, I saw him squat down and grip my thighs, lifting me off the ground. He maintained eye contact with me as he quickly took us back into the changing room, where I shut the curtain behind us. My back hit the wall with a thud, and Bellamy's lips met my own again. There was nothing sweet about the way our mouths connected. It was pure savagery and need.

He ground his erection into me, causing me to let out a small cry. The male took that chance to drag his plump lips up my throat, giving a soft nibble to my chin. Then his mouth was at the crease between my shoulder and neck, sucking and biting. My vision was clouded with ecstasy at the feel of him all over me.

I wanted more. I wanted everything. Anything he would give me. There was an animalistic need to the way my body arched into his, a hunger that could only be satiated with more of him.

More. More. More.

"Do you want me, Princess?" Bellamy asked against my skin. What a stupid question, a ridiculous one. Of course I did. How could I not? With untamed fervor, I nodded. "I need to hear you say it, Asher."

The way he said my name, like a prayer, should have been outlawed.

"I want you, Bellamy," I said with a gasp. He moaned, one thumb hooking around the fabric above my breast.

"Ahem." I heard from behind the curtain. I froze, embarrassment and shock flooding my mind, washing away the arousal Bellamy had brought forth within me. My attempt to push the male only resulted in him gripping me tighter. His face was stern, and I could see that he was not finished with me, and not at all happy with whoever was outside.

"What?" Bellamy snapped, his eyes still on mine.

"As much as I hate to ruin your fun, I am pretty sure Pino will kill you if he finds out you are attempting to have sex in his changing room. On top of that, I have been waiting for you for half an hour. Let's go, chop chop," the voice said, clapping in time with the last sentence.

Bellamy rolled his eyes, then leaned in and kissed me softly. The act itself was no more intimate than what had just occurred, but somehow it felt like a different kind. A kiss that said, *we have all the time in the world.* Though that was the opposite of what we truly had.

Just as I was beginning to come down from the high that was the taste and feel of him, he slowly lowered my body to the ground, making sure to let that bulge in his trousers rub between my legs. I moaned at the contact, my need returning in full force.

He rotated us, his back leaning against the wall now, arms snaked around my waist to keep me against him. We shared a look of mutual want. I could not deny the physical attraction, but there was something else there in his icy eyes. A different kind of want.

I pushed away then, not wanting to see whatever look he offered. Not wanting the vulnerability of his desires when I knew I could never fulfill them. This would be all we had. If we were truly stupid, we might even be able to sneak around together for years to come, and even that small choice could lead to his body hanging from the gallows. Or worse.

A brief image of a charred body and my piercing screams filled my mind, but just as quickly as the scene came, I had pushed it away. Once more numb to it all.

Bending over to pick up my clothes, I felt him. In that strange silent way he moved, Bellamy had come to me. He was there at my back when I jolted upright, mouth against my ear as he whispered, "You are magnificent, Asher. And you will be mine."

I froze, not sure what to say to such a bold statement. There was no denying the butterflies that swarmed my chest and the fire that ignited in my core, but my mind knew what my body refused to acknowledge, we could never be.

Bellamy was living in a fantasy with a female that has been perfectly curated to be everything the realm desired. I would never live up to it, even if Sterling was not in the way. No part of me was safe or stable, and I knew that.

I moved my head, looking over my shoulder to find our lips only inches apart once more. He stared with a level of intensity that was nearly unsettling.

"I am no one's but my own," I said, finality and resolve seeping into the words.

With one last wistful look, I turned to head towards the curtain. Just as my fingertips grazed the cloth, Bellamy spoke.

"We shall see, Princess."

CHAPTER ELEVEN

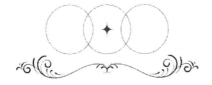

Outside the curtain was a strikingly beautiful female. She had short straight hair the color of a bright summer sky, and her slightly slanted eyes were brown with golden flecks, almond in shape. Her white teeth were larger than average, but so were her lips, making them rather symmetrical. She radiated strength and grace, and when I reached out to her with my mind, I could sense a spring breeze: an Air.

"Wow, has anyone ever told you that you are hot?" she said, whistling. Her eyes roamed over me from head to toe, and the intensity of her stare made me blush.

"Li, you are scaring her. We will meet you there," Bellamy said. I turned back just in time to see him roll his eyes at her. I let out a small giggle, enjoying seeing him annoyed. She flashed a toothy grin and stepped closer to me, clearly enjoying Bellamy's reaction.

"I do not know Bell, I like it here. Especially when your *friend* finds me so amusing. I am Lian by the way. Lian Youxia."

OF NIGHT AND BLOOD

"Seriously Lian, go. Now," Bellamy's voice rang from behind me. She groaned loudly, heading to what I assumed was her shop. "I am sorry, she speaks before thinking," he said, rubbing his hand up my arm. The touch was comforting and seductive, so I took a step away, needing to leash my emotions.

"It is fine, so do I." I shrugged, pulling my trousers on and quickly shoving my undergarments into a pocket. Then I took my arms out of the small sleeves and put on my tunic, shimmying the red fabric down my now covered legs with an embarrassing amount of effort. Once that was done, I threw the dress over my shoulder and quickly tied my shoes, adding my cloak last. When I looked up, Bellamy's eyes were on me. "What are you staring at?"

"You, Asher. I could watch you do that all day and never grow tired of it. Although, I think I would much prefer you take them off," he said, pulling me back into him. I smacked his arm and went up to where Pino was standing at the front of his shop. Bellamy followed, quickly catching up to me, that dimpled smile on his face. "Pino, we are going to take the dress."

"Delightful, let me get a bag." He placed the dress in a satchel and handed it to me. Then he gripped my hands tightly, looking me in the eye with a glazed expression on his face. "I know who you are, Princess Asher. I know what you can do," he said, sending chills down my spine.

Pino's eyes rolled to the back of his head, and his voice dropped, lowering to the all-encompassing tenor of a Tomorrow as they prophesized.

"Your magic is a force, a strength previously unheard of and ever reaching. As you find the light and dark, you shall see they will guide you if you dare heed their call. When you do, a prince you will lose, a prince you will gain, and a king you will hold. And when the moon paints the sky red, retribution will light fire to the realms. As promised by the true queen who defied her false destiny, when two worlds collide and history repeats, from it will come the salvation. From it, love will defeat vengeance. But if you fear what you do not know or do not understand, you might find yourself dead before you have even lived. And so the world will fall not far behind. No matter the choice you make, your reign will be the end."

Instinct took over and I snatched my hands away, taking a few unsteady steps back.

"You are not an Element at all, you are a Reader. A Tomorrow," I said, backing into the wall. Bellamy's face was full of dread, setting me further on edge. "And that female, she was an Air. I thought we were in the Fire Lands. Your home," I said to Bellamy.

I looked back and forth from him and Pino, confused and horrified. Why was there not only an Air, but also a Tomorrow here? It was forbidden to travel beyond your assigned Isle. And what did he mean by the princes? And the part about dying before I have lived? Why would the realms burn? I tried to calm my gasping breaths as the information sank in.

"Please Asher, let me explain," Bellamy said, reaching for me. His plea set off another warning alarm in my head. Something was off about this place, this moment. My eyes continued to dash between Pino and Bellamy, both with faces frozen in regret and guilt.

"Are we actually on Isle Element?" I asked, panicking slightly and focusing my gaze on Bellamy. Where would a place that had multiple fae factions exist? It was forbidden for us to intermingle like this, and it seemed that both males in front of me were hiding a rather important detail. I had assumed we were on Isle Element, but apparently, I was wrong.

He hesitated, glaring daggers at Pino. The Tomorrow was frozen, his eyes scanning my face as if trying to decipher me. Or perhaps the prophecy. "Thanks a lot," Bellamy hissed, finally bringing Pino back to reality. "No Asher, we are not, but I never technically said we were—"

"Take. Me. Home. Now," I said, forming fists with my hands so tightly that my nails bit into my sweaty palms. He did not move, so this time I yelled. "Now!"

"No, Asher, Princess—"

"Do not call me that!" I screamed, my hand flying to my chest. My racing heart thumped violently against my palm.

I was quickly losing my cool, and the shallow breaths were making me dizzy. Bellamy stepped towards me, and I flinched back, recoiling at the idea of being touched by him. The hurt in his eyes at my evasion meant nothing as his lies made themselves known.

The Fire jumped for me, grabbing me tightly as smoke leached the color from the world once more. The force that felt as if it was tearing me apart taking my breath away. Just like that, we were in the gardens outside the palace. Once I gained my bearings, I pushed away from him, not wanting his hands on me.

"Why did you lie?" I asked, tears welling in my eyes. "What did you stand to gain from today? Were you hoping for a crown?"

"No, Asher, of course not!" he said, stepping towards me. I knew that if he got ahold of me, if I felt his skin on mine, that I might falter.

"Do not come near me!" I said, putting more space between us. I wrapped my arms around myself, trying to hold in all of the emotions that threatened to break free from my chest. My mind raced, needing to think, to understand. He had ulterior motives, but I could not see them through the hurt. "I was honest with you, I was open with you, and you lied to me. Do not stand here and lie again."

"I mean it, Asher, I have no intentions of ruling over the Fae Realm. Please, you have to believe me." Bellamy's voice went up an octave, sounding strained and broken.

"Oh really? 'You will be mine,' that is what you said earlier." My accusation hit home, because he flinched at hearing his own words back. "Do not ever come near me again," I warned, before once again running from him.

When I got into the castle, I was slightly sweaty despite the cold. Tears streamed down my face, and all I could think about was how I risked everything to spend the day with a stranger who clearly manipulated me. My heart felt as though it might burst.

Reality slammed into me, reminding me that this day would always end in sorrow. Regardless of Bellamy's actions, we would never be together. My future was with Sterling, and it was time for me to accept that fate.

"Are you okay?"

Of course he would be here.

Sterling stood outside my doors, looking at me with confusion and concern. I was surprised to see both, as I never thought he truly cared. Wiping away my tears, I nodded, hoping he would be uncomfortable enough to leave me alone. "You are clearly in distress Asher, what can I do to help?"

I decided since I was throwing all caution to the wind, I might as well allow myself this one thing. I reached for Sterling's mind, seeing that he was in fact worried for me. His head swirled with thoughts of what could have gone wrong, each more vague than the last. Until he suddenly thought of Bellamy.

"I am okay Sterling, I just need rest," I said, trying to step around him. He moved quickly, faster than I was aware a mortal was capable of, stepping in front of me.

"Why will you not let me help you? I am here, Asher, I want this engagement to work, but you make it so hard. Every day you become more unbearably difficult, even though I do everything I can to make you happy. You give me nothing." His words stung, and my grief turned into red hot anger.

"I make it hard? I am unbearably difficult? You touch me without consent daily, you have no personality beyond self-obsession, and your only desire is to wear a crown and bind your life to mine so you do not die an old man in a few decades!" I screeched, pushing his chest with all of my strength.

I forgot that mortals were far weaker than fae, but was reminded when he slammed into the wall with a loud thud. I ran to him, spewing apologies from my lips, but when he looked up, I saw that he too was now wrath incarnate.

"You stupid bitch!" He slapped my face so hard that my head whipped to the left, and in my surprise at the sting, he kicked my legs out from under me.

My head hit the floor first, sending a shockwave of pain throughout my body. I cried out, opening my eyes and seeing nothing but black spots for a moment.

"You are lucky to have me, lucky to be mine when you are so unwanted by your own kind," he spit, his words venomous. I felt his hands grab my own and pin them above my head. I tried to fight back, but the pain was searing.

"Please, Sterling, stop," I begged, tears once again flowing from my eyes. He chuckled, getting on top of me. I felt his breath on my lips and knew that he would be able to do whatever he wanted to me right now. I tried to struggle under his grip, tried to call to my power, but each time I moved the pain in my head peaked.

"I do not think I will." Then his lips crushed into mine, forcing them open and shoving his tongue down my throat. I sobbed into his mouth, pleading with him to stop. One hand remained on my wrists, the other roaming my body over my clothes, unwanted and vile caresses seeming endless.

Finally, he halted. I did not dare open my eyes, not wanting to see his joyous face. Not wanting to see his eyes roam over me.

"I am saving you for after we are married my love, but I thank you for the kiss. Perhaps now you will be more accommodating to my advances. Maybe we will even see what your mouth can do when it is not talking back." My sobs grew louder at his words and what they insinuated.

Still, I remained unspeaking. I tried to stop the tears, but the pain and the violation were too much to bear.

"You should be glad to know that thanks to the peasant from the ball, your parents seem to think it is in our best interest to show a united front," Sterling continued. "We are to be wed in a fortnight. I look forward to consummating our union, beautiful."

He kissed me one more time, gripping my neck so tightly that I could not breathe. When he let go, I gasped, coughing uncontrollably.

"I will let the Healer know that I saw you come in hurt, I might even mention I suspect a certain dark-haired creep from the ball." With that he got off me.

Some of the tension left my body, thinking he would leave me alone. He must have noticed my relief at his absence, because his foot slammed into my stomach, causing me to scream out in agony. He quickly reached down and put his hand over my mouth, shushing me. Then he was up, and his foot hit me again. And again. And again.

When his energy and anger died out, he leaned down to place another kiss on my lips. With a final smirk of victory, he stood and left, the sound of his shoes tapping on the gold marble growing distant.

CHAPTER TWELVE

When I could no longer hear him, I curled into a ball. I stayed that way until my sobs stopped and my pain eased. As my vision came back, I looked up. An arm's length away from my chambers, that was how close I was. I could make that.

I forced myself to stand, wobbling as I walked the two steps to my doors, crying out at the sharp pain in my head and below my chest. I opened one and quickly locked it behind me.

Every part of my body hurt, but if I let myself think about it, I would break. I turned around to find a cloud of gold satin and gossamer hanging from the beams of my bed. At the sight of the hideous wedding dress, I found myself shattering at last.

In that moment, one that would seem so inconsequential to anyone else, I was swallowed whole by the grief of a life I never had the chance to live. To me the gown was a mark of an impending future I had no say in, one that would rip every ounce of joy that I once had. I fell to my knees, landing so hard that I heard a crack as I made contact with the golden floor. Sobbing, with no fight left in me, I laid down and closed my eyes.

I was unsure how long I had been lying there when the Royal Healer, Tish, and her assistant found me. She awoke me with a light shake and soft words. At the sight of her concern, I remembered I was supposed to lie, but the pain—both physical and emotional—drained me. I felt hollow and sluggish, like a raging sea emptied, forever just a husk of what it once was.

When I did not answer her questions, she gently pulled off my clothing. At the sight of my body, she gasped. Was it that bad? I wondered how I would possibly make up a good enough lie when I could not bring myself to even care what happened anymore.

Giving up never seemed like an option before. I thought I could push and struggle and manage. I would not give in; I would not submit. Even if I had to marry Sterling, I thought it possible to still govern my life. He would not dare test me or harm me when he knew of my power. I was infinitely stronger than him. Yet, I was the one in pain while he walked off smirking.

Maybe I could blame my emotional state, or the fact that he caught me off guard. But really it all came down to my own incompetence. I was untrained, unsure, and unconfident. In the grand scheme of our future together, I knew he would always be in control.

Tish got to work healing me, sending her assistant to grab Mia. The pain I felt when she began touching my stomach was red hot, causing bile to rise in my throat. A second later I vomited all over myself, choking on it. Tish lifted my head, and her touch sent another shockwave of agony through me. At my scream she set me back down and inspected her gory hand. Her eyes went wide, and she immediately got to work on the wound.

Every minute of the healing brought on pain and then relief, until I felt nothing but a light throb throughout my entire body. That was when Mia walked in. Her face was no longer perfectly blank and complacent.

No, she was the embodiment of fury, from the shake of her fists to the set of her jaw. I had never seen the queen look so flustered, so angry.

Mia rushed over to me, kneeling in the pool of blood at my head. Her soft golden gown soaked up the color, and I wanted to tell her that she needed to move or it would be ruined. But the lump in my throat and the ache in my heart stopped me.

"What happened to her, Tish?" Mia asked. The venom in her voice promised retribution, but Tish would provide little help with the vengeance Mia sought after. I meant to speak, but my voice was missing, or perhaps I was lost inside myself. A child alone in the woods, searching desperately for a way out but never finding it.

"I do not know, Your Grace. She has yet to speak," the Healer responded, her voice solemn. I thought I felt something from her, a sort of unspoken truth. "The extent of her injuries makes me believe she was attacked. She had five broken ribs, bruising around her throat, a fractured skull, and a black eye. It seems she also fell rather hard on her knees, as the bones there were bruised heavily. From experience I must say, it is rare for such a powerful being to be taken down so easily. With Asher's powers, I find it hard to believe that she was harmed by someone she did not know."

She looked at me then, communicating to me what she would not say to Mia. She knew.

The list of my injuries shocked Mia, as well as Tish's statement. She seemed eager to continue the conversation, but apparently did not want me to be a part of it. "Put her to sleep for me, Tish. She needs to rest if she is to enjoy the first day of her ceremony preparations tomorrow," Mia whispered. Of course she would still be thinking of the wedding, even after hearing the news of my attack. If I told her Sterling did it, what would happen? Would she call off the wedding? Would she stand up for me? I had thought the fight left me, but maybe not.

"Mia," I said, my voice hoarse. She looked over at me with wide eyes, as if she were surprised to hear me speak. Her hands went to my head, softly stroking my hair, a tear beading down her cheek. The love that radiated from her gave me courage. I could trust her to save me.

"Yes, my love?" she whispered. Tish looked back and forth between the two of us, her power pulsing in her palms as she awaited further confirmation that I should be put to sleep. I took a few deep breaths, hoping that if I focused on the way my chest inflated rather than the quick beating of my heart, I would maintain the composure I needed to speak this truth.

"Sterling," I tried to say. My voice broke, and I let out a strained cough. Mia shushed me, still weaving her hand through my blood-soaked locks. Her expression softened, and I knew she was misunderstanding before she even spoke.

"He knows. He is the one who found you. That poor boy is terrified for you," she said, a delicate smile on her face that did not quite reach her eyes. I shook my head fiercely, needing her to see that she was wrong. The movement sent a piercing pain into my temples. I spoke before I could convince myself not to.

"No, he attacked me. He hit me," I said, tears threatening to spill again. "He kissed me and touched me—he—please Mia, please," I begged. For a moment, anger lit her face again, her power swelling. This is it, I thought. She would end the engagement and banish the boy prince. She was going to save me.

Bellamy's words came to mind. *What about your own feelings, do they not matter?*

Despite my incertitude about that statement before, I realized in this moment that Mia did care. She would not let me suffer in this way. The queen would move mountains to save me from pain. I breathed a sigh of relief, because the last few months of fear were over. I would be free.

But then she schooled her face back into that neutral composure she always wore. "Put her to sleep, Tish. Now." Her hand left my hair, her heat disappeared from my side. As Tish touched my cheek, the

Healer's eyes filled with sorrow. I sagged as Mia disappeared from my line of sight. I would marry Sterling, and my entire life would be a series of pains and tragedies every day after.

My eyes closed before the tears came, but I knew in my heart that in my sleep I wept.

CHAPTER THIRTEEN

I woke up in a daze, my brain fogged and my eyes crusted. Light shone in through the many windows that lined the southern wall of my chambers. At some point in the night, I must have been moved to my bed, because I was tightly wrapped in my blankets with pillows under my head. I stared up at the golden mesh above, letting all of yesterday's events come back to me.

Bellamy's touches, Pino's premonition, my discovery of the deception that took me away from the palace, Sterling's attack, Mia's failure to help me. My wedding. All of it swarmed me and threatened to wreak havoc on my psyche.

I pushed every memory and every pain to the back of my mind. I needed to get through these next two weeks, I could break later. My limbs felt sore and tired, but my head ached the worst. I grabbed the cup of water off of my bedside table and drank it in one long gulp. Though it left me out of breath, it also quenched my scorching thirst.

I sat up, feeling the leftover ache of the previous night. Today would begin the planning for the elaborate celebration that royal weddings entailed. Fae would come from all over to witness the marriage, and the festivities would go from sunup to well past sundown. Sterling and I would leave after for the consummation ritual, which would have guests flicking water at us and praying to Eternity for a fruitful marriage, toasting us with sweet wine and kissing our palms. Many would openly discuss things they did to ensure pregnancy, and it would be expected of me to immediately begin attempting to bear children. With fae it was difficult to conceive, which was why our life spans were seemingly never-ending. If we died as early as mortals then we would never reproduce, and the fae would go extinct.

To my knowledge, no mortal had ever married a fae, and for good reason. I myself was surprised when Xavier first told me about the betrothal. Mating outside of one's faction was outlawed in the Fae Realm due to a mass dilution of powers. In fact, there was a time many millennia ago when fae were attacked by demons and had no way of protecting themselves due to the reduction of power within our realm.

So many died during that dark age. Now, it was a part of our history that reminded us of what—and who—we stood to lose. This was why I was baffled when Xavier told me I was to marry a mortal. Power, especially mine, was coveted in our realm. If Sterling and I had younglings, would they be able to manipulate minds? Or would they be without fae power at all? To this day we were unsure how I came upon my gifts, and I dared say it seemed unlikely to be wielded by half mortals.

Then of course there was the fact that I was the only of my kind. On a deeper, more intrinsic level, I would never be matched properly. Before Sterling, I had been worried I might not marry, because who would pair with me? If an occasion occurred when someone expressed interest, Xavier and Mia were quick to remind me that it was forbidden, that they would find my match, and what the consequences would be if I chose to disregard their rules. Which I did of course do, but in secret and only for a night of pleasure. Never more. Not after I suffered the consequences the first time, that is.

Swinging my legs over my bed, I slowly lowered my still sore body. When I was steady on my feet, I turned around and yanked down the golden wedding gown. With more energy than I thought I could conjure, I marched to my bathing room and hung the offensive piece. When it was up and glowing like the sun of a new day, I covered it with a blanket, refusing to look at it again until I needed to.

The dress was a reminder that this marriage with Sterling was my only chance, my only choice. Bellamy, he took a great risk even being alone with me in public. It was no secret that being caught with me could lead to an untimely end.

I reveled in his lack of fear, but I now suspected that it was more due to how he might use me rather than enjoying my company. Acknowledging that forced me to also see that I would always be used, at least by those who I did not call family or friend. No suitor would be with me for anything other than gain. So Sterling, who was foul and evil, was simply one version of the many.

I think that Mia knew that. She was aware that I would have little in the way of options, so last night she did all that she could, she gave me rest in hopes that I might face this upcoming marriage with a clear head. Intelligence and cunning would keep me from getting hurt like that again, so I would sharpen my mind and harden my heart these next two weeks.

With that fact in mind, I rung the pully system that would alert the handmaidens of my need for bath water, ready to wash away the memory of last night and push forward. Within minutes three of them were carrying two large buckets each of steaming bliss. When they finished filling the tub, I thanked them. They all curtsied before leaving me to my washing.

The second my body sunk into the warmth I moaned, finally relaxing as the smell of vanilla—my favorite scent—wafted my way. But when my eyes closed, visions of curly hair, brown eyes, and pain flashed through my head. A sense of urgency came over me, making my eyes open wide.

Move, my mind seemed to tell me, *keep going.*

So I did.

For the remainder of the day, I refrained from being still, even to sit and eat. Especially to sit and eat, as I knew who would be at the table, wearing false pity and providing empty threats. Sterling would want to convince everyone that he did not lay a hand on me, and that he would kill anyone who did.

He was a skilled fighter, as were most mortals. He once told me that in the Mortal Realm, children were taught from an early age how to fight against fae and demons, to go head-to-head with a power wielder and live to tell the tale. None of us truly knew what the demons were capable of, but still the mortals prepared.

His heroic defense of my honor would seem very in line with his capabilities, though many understood that I needed no protection when I could grab onto any mind. That was not true though, was it? The mortal prince had me incapacitated so easily, as if I was nothing.

Perhaps I was.

By the time I went to look for Nicola, she had already finished with her wedding planning for the day. Her hair was left down, her curls wild. Her blush dress had long, loose sleeves and a flowing skirt, which she had paired with a white cloak. My gold gown hugged me closely, threatening to prevent me from breathing.

Together we walked the long path from the palace grounds, stopping at the golden gate. The guards, wearing black armor with the fae sigil etched across their chest plates, looked at us and immediately opened the gates. Two more guards came from inside their small station, following us as we walked down the tree lined path.

When we came upon the market, a surprising pang of sadness hit me. I was well aware that Bellamy had misled me yesterday, though where I had been taken, I was unsure. Still, I enjoyed my time with him, as well as seeing the market there and meeting the vendors.

Those who held booths rented them, traveling by day to get here, and leaving at night, causing it to be a cold and calculated place. Sellers did not talk to, laugh with, or befriend one another, but rather sold their product and left. Their booths were luxurious and large, painted gold like the rest of The Capital. Each vendor also dressed in elegant finery, adding to the emptiness of it all. Talent was rampant among them though, making for a fantastic shopping trip every time.

When the market closed in the evening and the booth holders left, the silence became a living entity. Sorrow and hopelessness often found their way to me in the night, especially as of late with Nicola constantly away with Kafele. Only certain fae were permitted to remain on the center island, including my family, the members of the fae council, The Capital guards, and the students at Academy. Which meant Farai and Jasper were often not allowed to visit.

The council consisted of the Primes and the Royal Court, an exceptionally large group of fae that loved to argue and give me headaches.

There was a Prime for every need of the realm—coin, trade, military, agriculture, and diplomacy. Since no living fae was powerless, we chose those most qualified, regardless of their faction. They would be offered residence within the palace.

Our Royal Court contained a representative from each sub-faction, which was what we called the groups who possessed each power type. This meant that one Healer, Multiple, Single, Yesterday, Tomorrow, Air, Earth, Fire, and Water would live within the palace as well. Only the strongest candidate from each sub-faction would be offered the position. Though, offered seemed to imply choice, and there really was not one.

Whoever was chosen to sit on the fae council had to be married, therefore unlikely to fraternize. This also meant their families would live in the palace, too.

I recalled saying how confusing it all was when Xavier first tried to explain the inner workings of the council to me.

"We must be diligent in maintaining the safety of our realm, Ash. That means allocating jobs to others. I sit at the head of the

council because I rule the realm, I cannot also worry about how much coin we have or speak on behalf of the needs of those in the Fire Lands. I must know my own limitations, which means a *very* large fae council."

It made some sense, and anything that allowed Nicola to remain with me was brilliant in my eyes.

Nicola's father took over for my mother as the Royal Tomorrow after her death, which was why we had been joined at the hip for so long. In fact, we only separated when she would travel to Isle Reader to visit her fiancé.

She became betrothed to the Warden of the Yesterday Lands after visiting Reader River and seeing him across the way. From what Nicola has shown me, it was love at first sight.

Kafele was named Warden due to his ranking within his sub-faction. His strength as a Yesterday was second only to Ulu Kekoa, who held the position of Royal Yesterday—the title granted to the representatives of each sub-faction on the fae council— and lived in The Capital with his family.

I cannot recall how many times I had asked Nicola to think the memory for me when she came home with the happy news, the beauty of it a thing of rarity. Despite him technically taking her away from me, I did adore Kafele. It would be difficult not to like the male that loved and cherished my best friend.

When we got to the open cobblestone square, the small buildings bordering it like a fence, my chaotic mind had at last slowed. Nicola must have noticed, because I heard her let loose a breath, as if she had been holding it in for some time. "Are you going to tell me what it is that happened?" she asked.

I had gone back and forth all morning on whether or not I would tell her. On the one hand, I knew Mia would be against anyone knowing. Actually, she would be furious if I risked the marriage by spreading the tale, even if just to Nicola. On the other hand, I was breaking. If my mind rested for even a moment, I would feel rough hands gripping me and hear a harsh voice in my ear. Thinking of having her to shoulder some of this pain with me, to hold me, it would make all the difference this next month leading up to her wedding and then her permanent move to Isle Reader.

Instead of speaking, I grabbed onto her hand and pulled her to the edge of the market where a booth remained empty for the day. When we stopped, I turned to face her, making eye contact as I projected the memory into her mind. She was used to me doing this, speaking to her without talking, but at the violent memory, her entire body stilled. Tears ran down her face as the scene played out from my view. I was unable to stop my own sobbing while I relived the violent attack. By the time Sterling walked away in my memory, I was shaking uncontrollably, my arms wrapping around my torso as if to hold in the wretched pain. To hide it.

Nicola replaced my arms with her own when the memory faded as Tish put me to sleep. I latched onto her, knowing that I would receive no such comfort from the female who was, for all intents and purposes, a mother to me. In my ear, Nicola whispered, "I will find a way to save you, Asher."

I nodded, but we both understood she would not be able to. Nothing and no one could save me now.

ACT II

~ ANGER ~

CHAPTER FOURTEEN

Eight days after…everything, Sterling finally caught me. It followed an especially long council meeting.

Each member of the fae council, along with myself and Xavier, attended the weekly meetings. We all sat at a long wooden table that had a map of the entire world carved into it, with Xavier at one head and myself at the other. As the future queen, I had been a part of the council since leaving Academy. Xavier led the group, as each king before him had done. I would lead it one day, no matter what my husband-to-be believed.

Traditions could be broken.

The rest of the room was covered in smaller maps, thorough as they could be, as well as any and all information regarding the Fae Realm. Each member of the council had dedicated desk space lining the four walls to prepare, store, and organize their information. On the double doors was the sigil of the Fae Realm, a shield with the infinite symbol of Eternity on it. Everything was painted gold, just like the rest of the palace.

Many arguments came from the discussions. The Prime of Coin, a Fire named Graham Raymonds, was often at the center of these disagreements, and it was no different this time.

Graham had made a sly comment regarding the newly appointed Prime of Agriculture, Davina Yarrow, who was an Earth. Normally the position went to a Healer, as Isle Healer was where most farmlands were in our realm.

As expected, Davina did not take it well. She was young for a Prime, barely three hundred and fifty years. Graham on the other hand, was well over a millennium, and thought himself superior to all but Xavier, even me. When Davina shot branches as thick as full tree trunks at Graham, who then set them aflame, Xavier looked to me. Unlike Mia, my father figure thought of me as a diplomat, a leader, a strength. Our bond was strong because of it, as he made me feel purpose, though he was still quick to dismantle that confidence with the strike of a hand if I stepped out of line. That was the way of the Fires. They were strong-willed and enjoyed control, a perfect example being Graham.

So, when the fight broke out and the power of everyone at the table began to simmer, giving a heaviness to the air, I stood. "Enough!" I shouted, raising my arms, palms facing the two Elements.

Sit. Silence. Breathe.

The two sat, mouths shut and eyes wide. Ishani Bhatt started visibly shaking on my left, and a silence filled with terror engulfed the space.

"You are not younglings, you are members of the fae council. Everything you do, every word you say, holds weight and merit. You do not have the benefit of making mistakes," I said, allowing my audible voice to drop to the tenor of my mental one. "Heed this warning, your strength and cunning put you in this seat, but I have no qualms with removing you from it. Each of you possess power and knowledge unlike any other in your respective land, now act like it."

Slowly, I sat back down, letting my glare rest on each of them, moving over Tish faster than the others. When my eyes met Xavier's, he was grinning ear to ear.

Still, it was exhausting. On the best day I merely tolerated the idea of becoming queen. Though it gave my life meaning, a reason as to why Eternity put me here, it was also a burden. I would rule a realm of fae who feared, despised, or worshiped me, none of which were preferable. The rest of my life would consist of this same thing, manipulating minds to get what I wanted, and being either loved or hated for it.

Which was why these meetings wore through my joy, and I was on a very low supply of it already.

Ignazio Salvatore, the Royal Tomorrow who was also Nicola's father, spoke of the prophecy Nicola had dreamt of the night prior. I was not fully listening anymore, a wave of pain sweeping across my eyes and temples. He mentioned something about a *great power* and said that Nicola was rather disturbed by it.

Many Tomorrows had been upset upon discovering that Nicola was planning to marry Kafele, as she would then cross Reader River and live within the Yesterday Lands, forfeiting her ability to hold any other position of power. Xavier once told me that Nicola was the most powerful Tomorrow he had ever met or heard of, far surpassing her father and my mother. Ignazio was enraged when Kafele proposed, going as far as to beg Xavier to forbid the union.

The king had refused to do so.

Eventually Ignazio accepted Nicola's choice, and instead had her aiding the fae council by sharing her readings and prophesies. It was a compromise she had been more than happy to make, and Ignazio never failed to bring more information from her to each of these discussions, always giving credit to his daughter.

When we finally left the meeting room, the council quickly dispersing, I saw Sterling leaning against a wall. He stood casually with one leg bent at an angle, his foot pressed flat against the golden wall. I cringed at the sight of him, which made his smile grow. To him, he had the advantage between us. What he did to me made him stronger in his eyes, a dominant figure.

He was wrong.

I would not let him see how broken he made me. The pleasure of knowing I lie awake at night, plagued by memories of his touch, would not be his. Let him think he had the upper hand, let him believe he was above me. I would show him just how wrong he was.

"Hello, beautiful," Sterling said with a joy that told me he was remorseless.

Holding in any further displays of emotion, I nodded to him and walked on. I knew he would follow, but still I was taken aback as I felt his hand grip my shoulder and turn me around. He reached up and tucked a piece of hair behind my ear.

"So sad that such a gorgeous canvas was forever ripped," he whispered, his pointer finger running across the flat top of my ear.

My eyes darted around the hallways, making sure everyone had scurried off to get to work and avoid angering me again. Then, with a wicked smile, I reached out and traced my thumb across Sterling's bottom lip. His eyes went wide as I touched his full pink mouth. Then, I slowly slid the tips of my fingers down his jaw, his neck, his torso, until finally I reached his growing erection.

With no hesitation I grabbed it, squeezing not for pleasure, but for pain. Then, I latched onto his mind, scratching and clawing to make him all the more aware I was there. He shrieked in pain, and I felt a wave of nausea wash through him. There was a strange taste to his mind, earthy and distinctly animal.

"Listen here you little wretch," I seethed, my hot breath puffing into his rounded ear. "I know you think yourself invincible after that little stunt you pulled, but I would like to remind you who I am. I am the heir to the fae throne. I am The Manipulator. I am the holder of minds and the breaker of souls. Feared by even the strongest of fae. I can end you with a mere thought. I am your superior in every way, and one day I will be the queen which you cower before."

Just to prove my point, or perhaps to simply be cruel, I released my grip on his penis but tightened my hold on his mind.

Bow.

Sterling leaned forward, making a truly pathetic attempt.

I said BOW.

Lower he leaned, practically folding in half. Tears streamed down his face. Five days ago, I would have felt guilty, but as he wept there— that smug smile finally gone—I felt nothing but pure triumph.

Bend the knee, mortal.

Sterling crashed to his knees, so similar to the way I fell that night, the resounding crack giving me déjà vu that was both painful and exhilarating.

"Touch me again, dear fiancé, and I will show you why they tell horror stories of me to children and younglings who misbehave," I said, my voice still full of that deeper tenor that forced others to do my bidding.

As if this moment could not get any better, a small puddle formed around the golden-haired mortal. I laughed then, an evil, throaty sound that confirmed I was every bit the monster my subjects thought I was.

Today I was okay with that, proud of it.

"Asher!" I heard a furious voice call from behind me. I turned slowly, knowing who it was and dreading the consequences I would face. Mia stood a few paces away, her expression livid. She did a quick jog to close the space, shoving me out of the way and leaning down to Sterling. "Release him," she ordered me, the threat in her voice deadly.

Immediately, I obeyed. The moment I dropped my hold on Sterling, his upper half hit the golden marble, crumpling as consciousness left him. Mia slowly turned her head towards me, and when our eyes met,

I saw something I never had before—hatred. With a snap of her fingers, thorned vines wrapped around my arms and torso, shredding both my golden dress and my flesh. A yelp of pain escaped my lips before I silenced myself.

"How dare you lay your hands on him, Asher, he is to be your husband!" She raged, her hands flying in the air as she spoke. I wanted to hold my ground, to ask her why he went unpunished after he attacked me. Instead, my head tilted towards the floor, eyes averting her gaze.

In my heart I knew that I did not want to disappoint Mia, the female who raised me, guided me, loved me. But how many times had I thrown up into the toilet when my shirt grazed my skin and brought memories of his touch? How many times a night did I wake up screaming for help to find that waking up was the true nightmare? He deserved pain. More than that, Sterling was owed death. My power urged me on, built up from that well in my chest, and simmered.

I held tight to every ounce of control I possessed, trying to leash the fury before I murdered the boy prince and found myself dead too. Mia shouted orders at her handmaidens, who ran to fetch Tish. Guards who heard the commotion finally deemed the issue in need of their presence, looks of disbelief on their face when they saw the blood-soaked vines around me and Sterling on the floor unconscious.

"Take her to her room in the low level," she ordered one of the guards, who immediately grabbed my entwined hands to guide me away. "I think that Asher needs to be reminded of her place."

***

The walk to my second room was excruciating. Not only because of the thorns slashing through my skin, but also because I knew that Mia would have Xavier come for me. My low level room was where I was sentenced when I misbehaved enough to warrant this extent of punishment. It was rare, but not unheard of.

We got to the room with the wooden door, and I sighed in relief. The magic used on this space, an ancient kind even I was not privy to the knowledge of, created a sort of barrier. Once I passed the threshold my powers were siphoned from me. Each minute in here was painful, but the thorns were worse. I gladly walked in, every vine falling to the floor and instantly withering. My old, black bed still sat in the corner, familiar in the worst way. Nothing else, save for an assortment of my toys from my youth, resided in the room.

This part of the castle was the sole space left untouched by the gold, still the original gray of the rock in which the palace was built. The only paint that graced these walls was used to sketch ancient runes, most likely that which fueled the magic. They were different than the language of The Old Ones, far more ominous in appearance.

I turned back towards the guards, who stood watching me from the doorway, their fear prominent on their faces. "I apologize, but I cannot recall if either of you are a Fire?"

My teeth clenched, that hollowing feeling of my powers draining sending a steady flow of pain throughout my body. I would not last long in here without succumbing to the fatigue and agony. A small fire from outside of the door could make the situation a little less horrid.

"No, My Princess, we are not," the taller of the two said, his shaggy brown hair swaying with his head. I let out a long-suffering sigh, my shoulders slumping with the weight of the day, and the week.

"Well that is rather unfortunate seeing as it is colder down here than the soul of the lovely Prince Sterling," I murmured. One of the guards, the taller fae who had spoken before, attempted to disguise his laugh with a cough. That made me smile, but barely. Then the smaller, younger fae stepped forward. His baby blue eyes and blonde hair gave him a sort of innocence that was different than most of the guards. In fact both of them seemed unfamiliar and out of place.

"Servants talk, Your Highness, and I think it imperative you are made aware that those in the castle know the truth of your attack," he spoke with conviction. Behind him, the other guard stood straighter.

"You are our future Queen, the one whose power will guide us into a new age. You are our protector, and we are yours. The prince will never lay another finger on you so long as we are here," he declared, one hand falling to the hilt of his sword, the other forming a fist over his heart.

"Your kindness and devotion are both duly noted," I responded. My smile was worn, exhausted, but it was the best I could call forth. Just then, steps sounded from above, and I knew my time of simple happiness was over. "However, it seems safety is fleeting. I thank you, but I beg of you to never speak those words to me or anyone again." Quickly, I pushed the guards out of the room, popping my own body out enough to shove into their minds.

The king comes, no matter what you hear from this room, stay still and stay silent.

Both guards' eyes widened at the sound of my voice in their minds, the taller one shivering. I made a mental note to ask their names when this was over. Right on cue, the tune of Xavier's boots rang down the long, stone hall. I pulled the heavy wooden door shut on myself and heard the click of the bolt as the two locked it. I peered through the bars on the door and gave a small smile followed by a quick nod.

"Good afternoon, Luca, Cyprus," Xavier said, his voice stoic and kind. My teeth ground together as I prepared for a vastly different tone when he entered this room. At least I knew their names now. Rushing to the bed, nearly tripping as I attempted to navigate in the dark, I sat in the corner with my eyes facing down. I pulled my knees to my chest and waited.

Chills ran down my spine as the menacing tune of the door creaking open hit my ears. Xavier slammed it shut, shaking the small cot of a bed. Still, I looked down. My breath hitched as he approached, it had been so long since I was brought here that the fear almost felt foreign. When he stopped in front of me, his golden boots glowing in the light of the fae fire he left floating behind the bars, I at last looked up into his eyes, seeing the storm-raged waters.

"What were you thinking, Ash?" he asked. His disappointment was that of a father to his daughter, but I knew that my punishment would go far beyond familial. This would be a king punishing his subject. More than anything, I wanted to explain to Xavier what Sterling did to me, how I was abused at his hand. When I tried with Mia, I thought perhaps she would help me, but I was wrong. Without a shadow of a doubt, I knew that Xavier would not either. Which was why defending myself, attempting to make him the pleased father he seemed in that meeting, would be futile.

"I apologize, My King," I replied. The tears registered before the pain as Xavier's hand made contact with my cheek. My head snapped to the side, and I wondered how far this would go. Begging and pleading were pointless, that much I knew from experience.

"Apologies will not fix what you have done, you insolent female. Have I not loved you? Have I not given you everything, including my kingdom? Have I not treated you as an equal to that of my most trusted council members? Just today, I watched proudly as you handled strife amongst some of the strongest fae to ever exist. Yet here you sit, apologizing for attacking your betrothed as if the issue is not far greater than a simple accident or misguided decision." Every word hurled my way stung just as deeply as the slap.

"Sterling is traumatized, he sits in the infirmary shaking as if he were in the middle of a blizzard in the Tomorrow Lands. He has confided that he is prepared to end the engagement. One, need I remind you, that our subjects are relying on to ensure their safety," he fumed. A small part of me was eager to know that I might yet relieve myself of the abusive boy, but the far greater part of me cowered in dread and despair. If I failed to marry Sterling, then I likely doomed the fae.

Xavier leaned down, his hot breath hitting my face. "Sterling is willing to allow this transgression to go unpunished, but he requests a lofty price." A price? What could he possibly want? "You will wed tomorrow, no delays or arguments. You will resign your position on the council and forfeit it to him. Moreover, you will wear a blocker."

As Xavier spoke, he pulled out a thin, brown band. I knew that on the underside would be the same markings that littered the room, because this band held the same magic, but on a condensed and far more potent scale.

I gasped, horrified at the sight of the bracelet. I had the same one as a youngling due to how unpredictable and dangerous I was with my newfound powers.

Occasionally, Xavier would have me tear into the mind of a traitor or a criminal, my job being to recover the truth and prove the scoundrel guilty. More often though, I was ordered to publicly shatter the minds of fae who fraternized, like I had the day after my ball. I was a murderer that claimed to have a conscience, a moral code of sorts. But at least I had the strength to manage only taking life when I was told. As a youngling, I had killed more than I cared to remember before they finally deemed it necessary for me to wear the thick leather band around my wrist. It was meant to be a fail-safe, a last case scenario.

"For how long?" I dared ask, shaking with the memories of how painful it was to wear a blocker day in and day out. The way my body would convulse, the eternal fatigue, the extreme weight loss, the unbreakable fevers. We thought I might die if I did not stop wearing it. Which was why I spent the majority of my first years with powers training relentlessly, obsessively.

"For as long as he wishes you to," Xavier proclaimed, his casual shrug conveying the words he would not say—his pleasure is worth your pain, Asher. "Now stand, we have to make quick work of this."

I stood, and as I took the beating, the one I knew in my heart I deserved, I wept for the life I once dreamt of but would never have.

CHAPTER FIFTEEN

Morning sunrays shone through the wall of windows in my chambers, alerting me to the start of the day. I had yet to sleep, afraid of the nightmares that I might conjure in that state of limbo. Throughout the night I violently vomited into a bucket laid at my bedside, the blocker on my wrist pulled so tight it itched and left welts. The first day would be the worst, but it would not get much better.

I had yet to move since Tish visited me after Xavier brought me to my chambers. I decided now was as good a time as any to get up, so I edged off the bed and into my adjoining bath chamber. Inside I was bombarded with the puffy gold dress hanging on the far wall. On a table sat piles of cosmetics, pins, jewelry, lotions, soaps, and a plethora of other items. The chamber smelled sickly sweet, with lavender, rose, and jasmine hitting me so powerfully that I nearly gagged. A written note lay on top of the counter.

Please get ready as quickly as possible. I cannot wait to see how beautiful you look. -M

As if they were waiting behind my door for any sound of movement, an assortment of handmaidens rushed into my chambers. They gave no hesitation as they began directing me to the bath. The water they brought in was as hot as freshly lit coals, but I had no energy to do anything other than wince when I sat. My limbs and hair were pulled in opposite directions, warring with one another. A brush was taken through my blood-crusted hair, and then water was dumped over my head. Gold was painted onto my nails after one handmaiden dug red flakes of my blood out from under them, ever the theme of royalty. My body was scrubbed raw, the scent of soap mixing with the already heavy air, creating a putrid smell.

When I was lifted out of the bath and sat on the chair in front of the table full of irritating vials and bottles, the first tear fell down my cheek. One look into the mirror had me cringing. My eyes were bloodshot and puffy, with purple splotches underneath. My hair was still fairly knotted even after being brushed through and washed, but Maybel, my personal handmaiden, was giving her best effort to separate the matted section.

One handmaiden started rubbing my naked body down with a lotion, making me slip a bit on the seat below. I felt accosted and violated, but they did not seem to care. Orders from the queen no doubt. As Maybel began weaving my hair into braids that she coiled around my head like a halo, another started with my face. She painted my eyes and lips a gaudy gold, adding pink to my cheeks. Maybel finished with my hair and placed a gold diadem adorned with diamonds into a small space she had left for it atop my head. A pair of gold slippers were slid onto my feet, then I was pulled up.

When I saw Maybel reach for the dress, I inwardly cried out. I wanted to beg her, anyone, to stop this. To save me. But it was too late for that. Perhaps it was always too late.

I was guided into the fabric, then it was secured to me as tightly as it would go. The corset pinched at my skin suffocatingly, but I ignored it. Every fiber of my being told me to run, but instead I went numb, allowing myself to be pushed, prodded, and prepared. I was a sacrificial lamb being sent to the slaughter, a peace offering to a mortal king that needed us more than the reverse. The demons would not stop with taking over the Fae Realm, they would terrorize the mortals to the South as well. A river of blood would be all that was left of the once proud and boisterous humans.

Yet here I was. Giving myself over to an evil and malicious child. A boy with no regard for others. A mortal with violence and pride running through his veins. I was doomed no matter the angle I chose to view the situation from.

When I was fully dressed, the handmaidens dusted my body with glittering gold powder before dispersing, most likely to tell Mia I was finally ready. Maybel was the only one to stay behind, offering me a small smile. I did not smile back.

Her hands went to unclasp my necklace, and I found myself swatting them away, protecting that one last piece of myself. For a moment, I thought she might wrestle it off of me, the look on her face suggesting she was likely ordered to remove it. In the end though, she relented, instead fastening gold clasps onto my ears, the points mimicking the ears I had stolen from me.

It was rare that Mia allowed my hair to be up, so the jewelry was of little surprise. My ears were a grim reminder that no one wanted.

She eyed me for a moment, her joy fading with the realization that I was miserable. Still, my handmaiden offered no comfort, no aid. She simply nodded her head and said, "It is time, Your Highness."

I attempted to take in a deep breath, but the dress did not budge. I would need to manage with the little air that was making it into my lungs. Maybel started walking, exiting my chambers. I kept pace with her, having no idea where this would be held. Luca and Cyprus were waiting outside my doors, both noticeably angry, but as silent as the grave.

Together, the four of us wove through the palace. I realized we were to be wed in the ballroom when I heard music from behind the golden doors. "You will enter once the doors open, Princess Asher," Maybel said, curtseying and then walking the opposite direction.

Once she left, I began to waver. My palms were sweating, and my mind was racing. Should I hide? Should I run? I looked between the two guards, and I had the distinct feeling they would let me do either.

Before I could make a choice, the doors lurched open. Xavier was there, his long black hair pulled back, his thick and muscled frame covered in gold satin. Silver lined his coal-colored eyes, the tears not quite spilling, and he was waiting for me with his hand out. Bellamy came to my mind then. The way he held his hand out to me, asking me to trust him. Had he heard about the wedding? Did he think it revenge for his lies?

Regardless of his feelings and thoughts, I was still here, taking Xavier's hand. Bellamy did not matter, because I was walking down an aisle, fae surrounding me on both sides. I was a gilded toy being passed onto a child, wrapped like a present. These fae would bear witness to it, they would tell the story again and again, spreading the good news of the princess's marriage to the mortal prince. Of our salvation.

There were gold painted roses on every surface, covering seats and tables and a huge arch at the end of the aisle. Golden petals were spread on the walkway, and I heard them crunch under my slippers as we walked. How Mia put this wedding together in one day was beyond me, although the tackiness of it made me think it was not too hard.

Sterling stood under the arch, dressed head to toe in gold as well. The smile that lit his face made him look so beautiful, which made me all the more angry. His curls were messy in a way that added to his charm, and the crown atop his head was different, still gold, but larger with diamonds. It was a symbol of his new status, of his future title.

Mia stood off to the left, also dressed in gold. We were a group of statues, created for viewing pleasure. I had always known it. My entire life was molded to fit standards the public set forth for the royal family. This marriage was the culmination of two centuries of designing and perfecting Princess Asher of the Fae Realm.

We continued our too quick walk towards Sterling. Every step felt heavy, like I had stones strapped to my feet. I searched the room for Nicola, but she was nowhere to be seen. Abruptly, we stopped in front of Sterling. My eyes shot forward just as Xavier took my clenched fist in his. He brought my hand towards Sterling, who was practically diving for me. This would be the death of me.

As our fingers met, red splattered across my face.

For a moment, everything was silent. Then the screams started. Sterling stood in front of me, looking down at the dagger that had pierced his chest. I shot back, ready to defend everyone in the room, when I locked onto a pair of icy blue eyes.

CHAPTER SIXTEEN

Bellamy stood there in the center of the room, a smirk on his lips and violence in his eyes. I was frozen in place, unsure of what to do. Xavier was running at Bellamy, fire blazing in each of his palms, but just as he was about to hit the handsome fae, Bellamy ducked, shoving up with his shoulder into the king's exposed stomach. Xavier went flying over him as if carried on a phantom wind, his crown falling off of his head and his body slamming to the floor. I heard Mia behind me, and turned to see her and Tish leaning over Sterling. They were trying to save him.

Why did that infuriate me?

"Did you miss me, Princess?" I heard in my ear. I turned just in time to see Bellamy as he wrapped an arm around me. I whipped my head towards Mia, who watched in horror and outrage as thick smoke swirled around me. I was prepared this time when we ripped through time and space, the pain nothing in comparison to last night.

When we landed, I stumbled back. The lack of food, the blood loss, little to no sleep, and the anxiety took hold of me. I felt myself tip before I realized I was fainting. Bellamy must have thought I was fighting his grip, because his arms let go of me. The last thing I saw was his concerned face as I fell backwards, and everything went black.

***

I awoke sometime later to find Bellamy sitting in a chair, watching me. I moved to sit up, realizing that I did not recognize the chair he was in. My eyes roamed the room. The walls were the same burgundy as his outfit from the ball, with black furniture placed accordingly throughout the space. I saw a pair of glass double doors shaped like an arch on the far wall that revealed a dark, star-filled night. On the table to my left was a plate of eggs, some sort of meat, and toast with jam, a steaming mug of what I assumed was tea beside it.

The sheets covering me were the same reddish hue, and I noted that the side to my right was not slept in. It was then that I realized I was in different clothing. I silently wondered who had seen me naked, cringing at the violation. I tapped my ears, finding them without the golden tips. I blanched as my hand shot to my neck, but the amethyst still lay there. Whoever had changed me had removed the ear cuffs and the dress, but somehow knew to leave my necklace.

"Where am I? What is happening?" I demanded, scooting back into the headboard of the bed in an attempt to put more distance between us. He seemed to scowl at my action.

"You are in my home. I had to get you out of the palace after I killed your fiancé," he said nonchalantly, as if murder was a daily activity. Even his body seemed relaxed, comfortable. His voice was different. Still that deep and raspy tone, but now with a heavy and slow drawl.

"Why?" I asked, the panic settling in my stomach like a boulder. Fear rose through me as the memories of my wedding came flooding back. My wrist stung, but when I looked down, the blocker was gone. I gasped, tracing the large welt wrapping the circumference of my wrist.

It was off. How did he get it off? Why did he take it off?

"Why did I kill him? I was made aware of the state a Healer found you in, and was told you suggested your soon-to-be husband had done it. I would much rather have tortured a confession out of him, but we had very little time." His casual shrug and even tone were unsettling, made worse by the fire blazing in his eyes. Did he feel no remorse for ending a life? I could not recall a time that I was not left useless by the pain and guilt of doing so.

"If you mean to ask why I took that disgraceful band off of your wrist, that is because it is an abhorrent practice, one made to weaken and even kill the wearer," Bellamy hissed. On his face was a look of pure hatred, for the blocker or for those who put it on me I was unsure.

"Will you kill me next? Is that why you took me?" I asked, trying to make sense of why he brought me here.

His head tilted to the side like he was thinking through his answer, which further terrified me. Would he torture me? Did he save me only to take care of me himself? Subconsciously, I trapped my bottom lip between by teeth, tasting blood. A habit that used to anger Mia, but something I struggled to quit.

"No, I will not kill you. I have no reason to," he said matter-of-factly. I did not believe him, but my powers seemed uneager to find out. Before I could even consider reading him, he said, "Nor do I want to."

"Why am I here?" I asked again, stalling.

Killing him would be easy, but I had a feeling I would be unable to get out of wherever this place was. Sheer will could only get me so far. I tried to tap into my powers, but I sensed nothing from him. Did the severity of my injuries obstruct them? Was it due to aftereffects of the blocker?

"I told you, because I—"

"No, I am not asking why you are here. I understand that somewhere in your psychotic mind you thought murdering someone was the best option, so you had to run. I am a lot of things, but stupid is not one of them. I am asking you why you brought me here." His eyes narrowed, body going rigid.

"You were not safe there," he said, anger adding a clipped bite to his voice.

"Oh, and I am safe here? With a murderer who will probably slit my throat the second he finds I am not useful for whatever it is he needs from me?" I was growing angry too, the fear mixing with it to create a dangerous combination.

A rough gust of wind blew the doors open, but I ignored it. The power in my chest swelled, pulsing. Bellamy stood, as if he could sense what was happening and wanted to calm me.

"Do not come near me. You are a monster!" I shouted, fighting back my power before I killed the male.

Thick flurries of snow flew through the doorway, sticking to my skin. My head whipped to the side, staring at the clear night sky in confusion. Then I felt the earth shake below the bed, and I lost my balance, hitting the mattress with enough force to knock the breath out of a mortal.

I looked up to find Bellamy shaking, his rage having at long last won the battle. His arms were slowly catching fire, causing his tunic to burn and ash to flutter in the wind. The flame that was now past his elbow was not the red and orange hues I so often saw from Xavier. No, this was black fire. The angrier he grew, the more violently the elements around us reacted.

It was then that I recalled something Farai told me years ago, about a powerful half-fae.

"I am telling you Ash, he is hot!" Farai said. I rolled my eyes, finding the entire conversation absurd.

"Demons are some of the most notoriously hideous creatures alive. Being half fae does not fix that. There is no way he could be even remotely attractive," I countered.

"Well Raven told me that she heard he looked fae. Not like just any fae either. Apparently, he is insanely gorgeous," Farai gushed, twirling a piece of his pale hair, his equally white eyes alight with mischief. Raven was a notorious gossip, there was no way that anything she said held merit.

"Are you going to let your boyfriend fawn over a demon prince like this, Jasper?" I asked, hoping he would end the conversation. There were too many listening ears and vengeful hearts around to have such a reckless discussion.

"As long as he still plans to marry me someday, then I do not mind. Plus, I also heard the mysterious prince was able to use every element, even hotter." Jasper laughed, pieces of his long black locks falling from the bun atop his head and framing his face, skin pink from being in the sun for far too long.

"Well Raven told me that he eats the hearts of his victims and makes sacrifices to the Underworld, which is how he got those powers," I said, choosing to ignore my previous point of Raven's unreliability.

"The forbidden love part goes a long way too, then," Nicola swooned. I found the statement sent chills up my spine. Everyone loved a tragic tale, until they lived it.

I snapped back to reality, my heart racing at the sight of Bellamy as he wielded all four elements.

"You are The Elemental," I whispered.

Then I took the knife next to the plate of food, and proceeded to hurl it at him.

CHAPTER SEVENTEEN

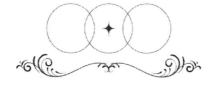

Bellamy's entire body lit up in those black flames as the knife sliced into his chest. His clothes burned away, leaving him naked and revealing dark ink snaking across his skin. The wind blew fiercely through my hair, making it hard to see. I felt the chill of the snow hitting my cheeks and stinging my eyes. Below, the ground still shook as he ripped the blade free, tossing it to the floor.

Without allowing myself to consider the consequences of my powers failing, I latched onto Bellamy's mind. I knew it worked when the rage I anticipated was invading my senses. Unmanageable sorrow fell upon me next, taking me by surprise. The pain he felt was so excruciating that I cried out at the weight of it, but I did not let go of his mind.

Flashes of what I assumed were his memories flooded my vision. A castle atop a hill. An aged male with kind eyes. Lian laughing with another fae female. A gray cat licking its paw.

Then I saw myself, alone, reading a book in the grass outside the palace. Quickly it switched to Sterling and I sitting on the shore of a lake, he was talking about something as I stared off in the distance. The image morphed into me making my way through The Capital market, nearby fae giving me a wide berth.

All of a sudden, my back came into view. My head was tilted up towards the star filled night as my hands gripped the balcony of the palace, the music from my introductory ball coming to a crescendo in the background. In the same setting, I saw Bellamy reach his foot out and…trip me, catching me before I fell.

After, I saw as I walked through the palace hallways, my golden gown swaying. I sped up in the memory, and I knew this was when I had sensed someone watching me walk to my chambers. Then it was me, standing in the red dress, my hands behind my back. My face appeared again, here in this room, on his bed, asleep.

Memories that he could not possibly have, but somehow did. He had been watching me, spying on me for who knew how long. I panicked at the images, gripping his mind and pressing on it. Every element winking out at my attack, and he nearly collapsed to the floor, the glass doors slamming shut with a loud bang.

Just when I stood, bracing my feet to end him, to shatter his mind and make a run for it, a wave of black fire pushed me towards the edges of his mental walls. I could nearly feel the burn of it, scorching my powers out of his mind and leaving me gasping.

"You are blocking me," I said, trying to remain calm. To act as if I was not slipping into a violent hysteria. Without a word, his eyes bore into me, and I knew he saw through the façade. "How do you do it?" I asked.

He gave me no response.

"Are there so many secrets in there that you must keep me out?" My words came out harsh, clipped. I tried to relax to avoid him spiraling again, but I was not sure if I could.

"My secrets are not public information for a reason, Asher." I rolled my eyes, shaking my head at him. He could abduct me from my wedding but I could not ask a question? Figures.

"You will not try anything like that again. Ever," he growled. I assumed he meant attempt to kill him, though I would neither ask nor agree. I would try again, we both knew it. "There is a bath waiting for you through that door if you need it."

Without another word he got up, unfazed by his own nudity, covering only his wound as he left the room, slamming the door on his way out.

I stood there for a few minutes, unsure of what he meant or how I should react. When I finally snapped out of the daze, I moved to the door. Locked. I figured as much, but it still enraged me.

I walked over to the glass doors that went outside. I saw the soft sand of the beach and assumed we were likely wherever he had brought me earlier today. Wait, was it today? How long was I asleep?

Pushing back those thoughts to avoid more panic, I reached for the doorknobs. Also locked. As if I could somehow escape over the sea. My anger seemed to bubble inside of me. I tried to calm down by pacing the room, hoping it would right my mind.

When that did not work I took Bellamy up on the offer of the bath. I smelled wretched, like I was left out in the hot sun for days on end to rot. My heart felt corroded and decayed, so there was definitely some truth to that.

To no surprise, the bathing chamber was entirely black and red, mirroring the bed chamber. The only difference was that candles lit the room rather than fae fire, or whatever that was floating near the ceiling.

I could smell Bellamy in the air. I cringed at the way my heart leapt when the scent of cinnamon and smoke enveloped me, as if my emotions were not totally in line with my common sense.

I reached down to pull off my clothes, only to find that the thin silk hid very little, which made my cheeks blaze in embarrassment. More than that, I was furious at the fact that someone changed me without my knowledge.

Ripping the flimsy material off, I lowered my body down into the deliciously warm water, a moan escaping my lips. Even the relaxing and soothing bath with hints of vanilla could not hold back the dark and brooding thoughts for long.

How was I ever fooled? How did I think him to be a regular fae? I recalled only sensing fire within him, but he also somehow blocked me on multiple occasions. I had never met anyone capable of that, not even Mia could stop me from breaking into her mind—not that I had since the day my powers manifested. Even without the blocking, I was still drawn to him in a way that would have convinced me to ignore all caution.

He was a wicked temptation, and he knew it. Every smile, touch, and word were calculated from that moment we bumped into one another on the balcony of the palace. Fooling me a second time would not be so easy. I began washing my hair and body with the products laid out on the small table near the bath, once again being hit with the scent of the demon fae.

My memories of that first night when we danced, laughed, walked, and kissed were triggered by the strength of the smell. Every moment had felt so right, like a piece of me had been reunited with the whole. I risked not only my future, but also the lives of every fae in the realm just to spend one more day with him. Like he was a sweet wine and I was a long-time addict. Even so, it had seemed as if he was inherently good, like the wine was healing a sickness. Looking back, I knew that I was being manipulated, used.

My anger forced me out of the bath, needing me to move, to act. I grabbed onto a nearby towel, which was, of course, black. The soft fabric felt better than the ones at the palace, which were stiff and left balls of lint on my body. Another tactic to reel me in most likely. I would not submit,

I would not give in. No matter what I had to do, I would find my way back home. That was a promise.

"Stupid, murderous demon!" I shouted.

"He is definitely something," I heard from behind me. I whipped my head around to see Lian standing by the door, her hands on her hips. She was dressed in all black, her blue hair pulled back. She had a large sword strapped to her waist that shone even in the dull fae light. Black lined her eyes, looking much more lethal than the last time I saw her.

"Why are you here?" I asked, not attempting to be kind when I knew it would get me nowhere. Lian did not seem to care, plopping down on the large bed. She pointed at the chair Bellamy had been sitting in, where a small pile of black fabric sat.

"Figured you would want some clothes. Pino made them for you, he based the measurements off the dress you got. There are more items in the wardrobe, but Bellamy picked those ones out. I helped Pino make this set." I looked from the clothes, to her, then back at the clothes again. Suspicion rose within me, and I glared over at her as I walked to the chair.

Lian turned away to give me some privacy, a small mercy. The undergarments were a perfect fit, sliding up my thighs with little effort but holding snugly enough not to slip. The trousers were a bit loose, but in a way that felt intentional. The tunic had enough space for my breasts, allowing room to breathe. The comfort the soft, clean fabric brought was a bright side to an otherwise horrifying situation. "He made all of these? In a day?" I asked, suspicious once again. How long had they been planning to take me?

"You have been in and out for three and a half days. You peed the bed twice. It was funny." She snorted. My cheeks heated in embarrassment. For reasons I was unsure of, I hoped that it was not Bellamy watching over me when I relieved myself in his bed. That explained the smell though.

"How long will I remain a prisoner of The Elemental?" I questioned when I finished pulling on the socks, hoping to gain any information I could from the Air.

She sat up straight and folded her arms across her chest.

"Why would you assume yourself a prisoner? Perhaps he saved you from a prison disguised as a sanctuary." Her vague response only served to annoy me, causing me to tighten the thick boots too much. I unthreaded them and began again, letting out an exasperated sigh.

"The doors are locked and I have yet to be told where I am. I was also brought here against my will and knowledge. Again. I imagine being a prisoner is fairly similar to that," I said.

Lian scoffed.

I stood up, walking towards her. She backed into the bed frame, brows furrowed.

"Are you afraid of me?" I asked, not at all surprised.

"Last I checked, you were able to control minds. I would prefer you did not make me jump off a cliff or forget who I am. Fear can be healthy," she responded, her nonchalant tone a stark contrast to her shaking body.

"Well, I prefer not to do any of those things, so perhaps you should speak to your demon master about what he tells his subjects," I retorted. "Now move over."

To Lian's credit, she did not hesitate to drag her small frame to the right side of the bed. Making rather slow movements to ease her discomfort, I sat next to her. When I first woke up, I was unable to focus too much on the details of my surroundings, but now I had an unknown amount of time on my hands to lay idle.

Near the glass double doors sat a large wardrobe, black as night with red detailing that looked like bloody vines. The dark chair Bellamy had sat in was paired with a sleek black desk that had nothing on it, as if it were rarely used. No lanterns sat on any of the tables, instead the light somehow danced midair. The light itself was different than the fae fire that lit the palace, it had a sun-like glow to it and seemed to radiate energy.

Above the large black bed hung red silk curtains that draped down to conceal the mattress, allowing for privacy if needed. The ground was also black, feeling similar to marble. Both colors dominated the room, ominous and heavy. The black floors made the four walls seem as if they expanded forever, an endless vortex of darkness and blood.

Similar to being at the mercy of The Elemental. I had no idea what his plan was for me, why he so desperately needed me here. As I sat there with Lian, I thought of ways that I might try to find out.

CHAPTER EIGHTEEN

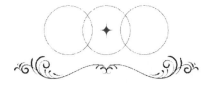

"So, where are we?" I asked, trying to sound casual.

It occurred to me that we might be in the Demon Realm, seeing as I was their prince's captive, but there were so many fae that I was unsure.

Plus, our histories always referred to the Demon Realm as nearly unlivable, full of volcanoes and black sludge in place of rolling hills and soil. I saw her roll her eyes, and I figured that meant she had no plans of telling me anything. My suspicions were confirmed when the minutes dragged by in silence. I felt awkward at best and considered asking her to leave, but then I realized she was more than likely guarding me. As if I needed a babysitter to hold my leash and keep me in line.

"Fine, do not tell me," I grumbled, crossing my arms.

In the quiet, my thoughts strayed to the pain Sterling inflicted on me, then the blood gushing from his chest. I could still hear the screams of the fae around me, see Tish panicking with her hands around the wound, feel Sterling's hand ripping from my own. Was I sad that he had died? Truthfully, I was not. I myself had wished him dead days ago. But what did that make me? Ghastly, among other things.

Weak, that was another. Frailty was what allowed me to be attacked, and I wondered if today would be different if I had been trained in physical combat rather than focusing solely on honing my powers.

Xavier and Mia always said that it would be a waste of time and potential to teach me combat, but now not knowing seemed rather foolish. Was it ignorance that convinced them I would never need to use my fists, or something else?

"Is there anyone here who can teach me combat?" I asked, turning my head towards her. The question took her by surprise, her eyebrows lifting and mouth falling open. I maintained my stare, deciding I would not back down on this.

"You truly think we would teach you to fight when you are already a danger enough as it is?" she asked, astonished by my inquiry. When she put it that way, I did seem dense. "And how is it that you grew up with the royal family but did not learn combat?"

"The king and queen told me it would be a waste of my abilities. I spent all of my time at Academy sharpening my power." I shrugged. As heavy as the day felt, it was nice to talk to someone casually.

"Of course they did." She scoffed. I could feel her rage, and silently wondered what could be causing it. That simple curiosity was all it took for me to unwittingly slip past the flimsy barriers of her mind.

Horror shot through me as I saw a female lying bloody in the grass, a pair of hands trying to halt the red liquid from seeping through the neck wound. Lian's hands. Nearly screaming from the pain and wrath the memory brought forth, I pulled out of Lian's mind. I was not used to others projecting as she did, and perhaps my own exhaustion left me vulnerable to such a thing.

"I need out, now," I said, pushing myself to stand before I vomited on the bed that I apparently soiled twice already. My pulse quickened and a cold sweat broke out on the back of my neck. I had used my powers too much, allowed too many outside emotions, thoughts, and memories to flood me. I wrung my hands and began pacing once again, needing to move and exert the energy filling me.

So much, too much, had occurred over the course of the last few days. I tried and failed to reel in the ferocious beast inside of me, the one that always wanted to break through, that craved retribution and death— The Manipulator. Keeping her at bay was normally easy, as I was often secluded and around less tension. Right now I was overwhelmed and surrounded by fae. I could feel them, all around me, their powers and minds on edge.

I grabbed Lian's mind again, holding on tightly and adding a bit of rage into my mental voice.

Escort me outside, now.

She stood up, back stiff and eyes blank. I hated this, controlling beings, forcing them to do my bidding. But I needed out, immediately.

We walked to the door and Lian knocked quickly five times, then slowly twice more. I made note of the beat, but was not sure I would be able to match it later on. The door opened, and the tallest male I had ever seen poked his head through. His hair was the color of the tip of a flame, like an orange beacon. His face was covered in freckles, different than Bellamy's that graced only his nose and cheeks, but similar in the way they added that charm. The male's full pink lips were set in a frown, and his green eyes looked down to us with suspicion. Lian pushed past him, guiding us out into a long hallway.

The walls on either side were full of beautiful paintings. I tried to resist, but I could not help slowing to look at them. There was no rhythm to the madness, no cohesive pattern, but that made them all the more beautiful. Some of them seemed abstract, with random colors and shapes merging and flowing in a way that looked alive.

There were more realistic ones as well. Some of those were of fae, some of mortals. I was surprised to see art of the Mortal Realm here, it was rare to collect anything they created.

A million questions rushed into my mind, but a deep voice sounding at my back startled me.

"You should not be out here." I whirled around, my hand flying to my racing heart. The orange-haired male stood in front of me, which made me aware of how much larger he was than me. His menacing stance was all the more terrifying with the violence that shone in his green eyes. Where did Lian go?

"You scared me, you creep," I said, searching for any way out of his reach.

Despite his intimidating stature, his pale cheeks reddened at my insult. Fear took control and my power grabbed onto his mind, filling my senses with blinding light. I had never felt a power like this, but it reminded me of the strange fae fire floating in Bellamy's chambers. Before I could make a command, the male grabbed onto my wrist, yanking my body forward. I tried to rip out of his grip, but he tightened his hold and shoved me. I flew back into the wall, hitting with a loud thud that sent a painting crashing to the ground.

I gasped when he grabbed me by my hips, lifting me up and over his shoulder. Beating my fists as hard as I could against his back, I let out screams for help, knowing it was pointless but doing it anyways. I latched onto the male's mind, not bothering to search or open myself up any more than I needed to.

Put me down you orange oaf!

The male stopped in place, slowly setting me down. The second my feet hit the ground I smacked him across the face, the loud slap ringing down the empty hall.

Of course, with my attention diverted for even a moment, the male regained his consciousness. With a snarl he shoved me against the wall again, this time using his body to press against mine. I let my mind open to his, thoughts of violence and fear pounding into me. He looked down at me, a sneer on his face.

Get your hands off of me you foul prick!

My mental voice was not usually so distraught, so untamed, but it had been a rough week. I shoved at him the second he took a step back, but I was not letting go of his mind.

Take me outside immediately.

His body whirled in the opposite direction, his gait steady and robotic. I followed closely, fuming with pent up rage. Our turns became confusing as we walked through the large residence, which I thought could be considered more of a manor than a home based on the size of the interior. Everything was black and red except for the rows of paintings. The smooth, glass-like black floors met our feet with loud clicks, and the vaulted black ceilings reverberated the sound back at us.

Finally, we arrived at a pair of large doors made out of a red wood.

"This male could use an interior designer," I muttered. "I mean honestly, what goes through someone's head when they create a disaster such as this?"

"Well beautiful, you could always ask me if you are that curious." I froze, shoulders reaching up towards my ears and jaw clenching.

CHAPTER NINETEEN

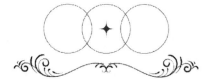

"Can none of you announce yourselves?" I asked, rolling my eyes and crossing my arms over my chest.

Bellamy wore a red tunic that was left partially unbuttoned, revealing his ink-covered torso. Now that I was not focused on calming him down, I could see that the thin black lines almost looked like veins. His trousers were black and perfectly pressed, his hair combed to the side with those same few strands hanging forward over his forehead. He had on black shoes and a luxurious red cloak that seemed to be fur lined inside.

"Can you resist taking control of another soul's mind for more than a day?" he countered, raising an eyebrow. When I stayed silent, my fists clenching and my blood boiling, he gave a smirk. "How about we both promise to stop, then kiss and make up?"

I did not miss the step he took towards me as he spoke, his eyes on my mouth.

"I would rather take my chances with pumpkin back there." I scoffed, pointing my thumb at the gigantic fae behind me.

Looking over my shoulder, I saw that same fae seething. I realized then that he would no longer be under my compulsion, and he was likely not excited about what I did. I shrugged, knowing that apologies would change nothing, especially when I did not mean it.

Bellamy chuckled, but his eyes narrowed in on the male at my back.

"I have her from here, Henry," he said, waving off the male. Henry mockingly saluted Bellamy and glared down at me before walking the opposite direction of the double doors that he had nearly led me through.

So close. So painstakingly close.

With my eyes focused intently on the fae, desperately wishing I could have had him walk me through the doors and back into my chambers at the palace, I did not notice Bellamy approach.

"If you are so interested, then why not follow him?" he asked, his breath hitting my ear.

His question took me by surprise. Did he think I was lusting after the male who clearly loathed me? I maintained my gaze as I spoke, not wanting our lips any closer than they already were.

"Seeing as he looked like he might rip my head off the second you turned around, I would wager he is uninterested." Bellamy's chest met my back then, sending chills down my spine.

"Anyone that would dare think harm upon you would die at my own hand, Princess. And let me tell you, I have yet to see a male in your presence seem even the slightest bit disinterested." Hidden meanings beneath his words started to swirl in my mind.

Why would he care if someone hurt me? Did that mean his feelings were real? Was he referring to someone in particular? Did I even care?

"Lucky for you I am perfectly capable of taking down anyone who comes at me," I said, twisting my body to face his. Bellamy's gaze slid down to my mouth, and he pressed his body into mine once again. He licked his lips, then let his eyes wander up slowly. When his bright blue irises locked with my own, our lips just a breath away, I whispered to him. "And I am far out of their league, seeing as they associate with demons."

As I spit out the words, I used all of my strength to shove his chest. Though my body responded to Bellamy, my mind thought of another way I had been pressed down, forced.

He laughed at my aggression, but that did not surprise me—he was clearly deranged.

"Ah Asher, how you wound me. So, do divulge your reason for holding poor Henry captive," he asked, his smile not quite bringing out his dimples. I crossed my arms over my chest again, feeling defensive.

"You tell me nothing and you expect me not to keep secrets as well?" I retort. This time his smile lifted fully, both dimples appearing along with the crinkles at the edges of his eyes. Damn him for being so handsome.

"Interesting that you did not openly refuse to answer. Are you suggesting we each divulge a secret?" he asked, head tilting to the side. I was not suggesting that at all, in fact my only goal was to be annoying, but any information would be invaluable right now.

"Can I ask you anything?" I questioned. I refused to be tricked into learning something derisory and inconsequential.

"You can, but I do not promise to answer it." At his response I began stomping down the hallway I came from, not at all sure of where I was headed. "How about you ask first?" he added, his tone making me halt my childish march.

Why did he sound as if he were desperately yearning for my question?

"Fine," I said, not turning around to face him for fear of what I might see. I could not afford to be deceived by him again. Instead, I stood there, thinking hard about what I could ask that he might answer. What would hold weight but might seem innocent. "That fae, Henry, what were his powers?"

I heard his intake of breath, but by the time I turned around he had schooled his face back into a cocky smile.

"Well, someone has found a way to surprise me it seems," the demon said with a chuckle.

I glared at him, wishing I could take his mind and force answers out of him. Just to see, I reached out and was met with quiet, emptiness, as if no one was there. If I pushed harder, I could sense a wall of flame—hot and impenetrable—but doing so made me dizzy.

"Stop doing that, it is impolite," he chided.

I gasped. "How did you know I was trying?"

"Oh no you do not, one question. And the answer to your first one, is light," Bellamy said, as if that was all the explaining one would need.

I blinked, too confused to respond.

"I like the way you look when I puzzle you," he said, smiling widely. I quickly relaxed my face, not needing him to feel any way towards me other than afraid if I wanted to maintain control over the conversation. Though honestly, I did not feel as though I had it at the moment. "His ability is light. He can call to it, weaponize it, create it."

"That is impossible," I said, my brows knitting together.

Why was he lying to me about something so small?

Unless I was wrong, and the male was not fae. Looking at Bellamy was an obvious hint that I ignored—there were some demons who did not look much different than fae. I thought back to the way Henry looked. He had that bright hair that distracted from everything but his height, and that face full of freckles. His jaw was not as defined, body not as bulky, but still handsome.

"You are figuring it out, I can tell." I looked up at him again, noting the way he leaned towards me, as if excited to see my mind working through the puzzle.

"Henry is not fae is he?" I asked. He smiled then, his head shaking slowly back and forth. I was right, they had demons who looked like us, so much so that I did not even hesitate to assume we were the same. "Do all demons look fae?" I inquired, desperate to know more, to have a fighting chance against these creatures.

"Nope, we were only each allowed one question and I answered two. Your turn now, where were you trying to go?" he pushed. What was I supposed to say? I was mindlessly wandering? I wanted to somehow find someone to teach me to fight? I needed to get out of this fancy prison? They all gave off an innately naive feel, but there were no better answers coming to mind.

"I felt trapped. So much has happened, and I am overwhelmed. I have no one, I cannot defend myself against a mortal boy let alone fae or demons, I am unaware of whether I will live or die, and no one has bothered to tell me where I am. I have been assaulted, kidnapped, beaten—" Cutting myself off before I shared too much, I averted my gaze to my feet to avoid the pity that was steadily filling his eyes. I would not be looked down on. "Do not give me that look; if you want to show remorse, then take me home."

"Home? Asher, that was not a home. You call this a prison, but what is the difference? Why can you not see that the life you were living was not worthy of you?" he asked, stepping towards me.

I backed away just as quickly as he crept forward, but my back hit the wall. When Bellamy was about three steps in front of me, he stopped his pursuit. Apparently, that was not a rhetorical question.

"I was loved and cared for and given everything there. I had a family, a community. Here I have nothing, I am nothing. Why bring me here Bellamy? To torture me? To brainwash me? To use me? What is your motive?" My voice was full of acid, like poison coming from my mouth. Regret was something I felt very rarely, but a small part of me wished I treated him better.

Tragic as it was, that part of me needed to be squashed. She was weak and easily exploited. I would beat that part of myself down until she was nothing, because I could not afford to be at the mercy of a sycophant.

"You know nothing of love, I can promise you that. You know only the tactics of a corrupt monarchy that used and abused you for years without you even realizing!" he said, voice rising without fully yelling. I pressed my head back in the wall, looking up at him with a scowl.

"What do you know about my life? How long were you sitting in the shadows stalking me like a lunatic?" I shot back. He was not without fault, and he knew nothing of who I was or what I lived. I was lucky to have the life I did, lucky to be afforded such opportunities.

"You would be surprised Princess, I know much more than you think I do." He closed the distance between us, once again bringing our faces inches apart. Cinnamon and smoke wrapped around me, like his scent was a tangible thing.

"Take me home," I demanded.

He would not take me back, but I had to try this way before I attempted to flee, because that was not going to start or end well, and everything in between would be horrid too. He placed a hand on my cheek then, cradling my face. His features softened but his eyes blazed on like an uncontrollable fire of rage wanting nothing but to consume.

I was in the lion's den. Even worse, I was enjoying it. To my discontent, that part of me was not rooted out fully yet.

"Why can this not be home?" he whispered. I thought he would kiss me, but instead he took a deep breath and started walking towards the double doors. Anger and sadness warred over my heart, because I had yet again been fooled by his act.

"You speak of home as if you did not steal me away. As if you did not kidnap me against my will. I would rather call a mud puddle my home than this place, here with you. Because at least the mud puddle does not act like a hot spring. You are no sheep offering sanctuary and love, Bellamy, you are a lion waiting to attack, and I refuse to be the lamb that falls prey to you." My voice faltered, shaking with uncertainty and outright ignorance. I knew that what I said was truthful, so why did I struggle to believe it?

"Then follow me," he said without looking back at me.

"To where?" I asked, a bit of terror shooting through my veins. At that, he turned around, his face the picture of serenity.

"To train you into a lion."

CHAPTER TWENTY

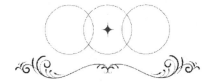

I stood rooted in place, mouth agape, for a few moments. Bellamy patiently waited with one hand on the handle of the door, watching my reaction. I thought about what he said and wondered if he might be lying. Would he really teach me to fight? Lian was right, I was a hazard enough with just my powers, let alone with the ability to physically attack.

If he was not lying, then it would be idiotic of me not to take him up on his offer. I needed this advantage if I were ever going to make it home. Mia and Xavier would be furious with me for learning, but after everything that had transpired over the last week and a half, I imagined they would find it in themselves to see that the guaranteed benefits far outweighed the possible consequences.

I nodded my head and walked towards the doors where Bellamy waited. I did not miss the small upwards tilt of his lips before he pulled the door open. It was still dark outside, the stars and moon lighting up the green lawn and the sea beyond. The dewy grass smelled heavenly, allowing me to take my first full breath since I had felt Sterling's hot blood spray across my face.

Bellamy continued forward, but I stopped, tilting my face towards the sky and closing my eyes. I missed the gardens of the palace, the way the scent of the flowers comforted and grounded me.

My still damp locks made the already chilly air feel even colder. I missed the way Mia braided my hair as well. How she would surprise me by weaving flowers through the brown strands, growing them from thin air. My hands moved to my hair, pulling it all into a single plait, eyes still closed and face still up. If I was not taking in such deep breaths, I might not have noticed the change to the air, the smell of smoky cinnamon wafting towards me.

My eyes flew open, locking on Bellamy's with little effort, as if my body was hyper aware of his. He slowly unlatched his cloak, the muscles in his arms and shoulders straining against his tunic as he slid it off in the most outlandishly obvious show of his assets.

I was ashamed to admit heat pooled low in my stomach. When he smirked as if he knew the way he affected me, that shame turned into anger.

Bellamy brought the cloak around my shoulders, his fingers never making contact with my skin.

"Your eyes are so beautiful—gray, like a storm cloud," he whispered, his breath visible in the frigid night. Our bodies were nearly touching. He stared at my irises as if he were seeing them for the first time.

I never enjoyed talk of my eyes, because the memory of someone else's love for them hurt a piece of my soul that I had long since buried. Even worse, any compliment geared towards my eyes was a reminder of another prince.

"Sterling used to say it was his favorite feature of mine. He enjoyed pointing out the color, as if he could think of nothing better to note," I said, my voice flat.

I did not know how to feel about the late prince. Bellamy killing my fiancé and then taking me provided little time to process. Was I mad at Bellamy? Thankful? Scared?

The demon prince's jaw clenched, his neck tightening at the comparison I made. Abruptly, he turned and walked further into the grassy area. I followed, not knowing what else to do. The tension in the air was thick when he whirled around to face me. We squared off, my mind on high alert for what he might do. But Bellamy did what I had quickly come to associate with him, he relaxed his body and smiled slyly. He was many things, but dejected was not one of them. I admired the way he could shine, how he quickly bounced back from unease or displeasure.

What a contrast, to be a Fire who easily angers but also a calm and composed Water. The witless side of me wondered how soon I would see the bravery of an Earth and the wildness of an Air within him. My rational side reminded me that all I would ever get from Bellamy were lies and betrayal, regardless of his mood.

I knew I never would move past the way he had deceived and manipulated me. How long was I carefully watched and assessed by him? Just as he was doing now. Eyeing me like I was an anomaly that he needed to study so he could find advantage within it. To him I was little more than a means to an end.

Each thought swirling through my head sparked my anger like a flint, lighting a fire in me. I desperately wanted to knock him to the ground.

"That is it Princess, let your wrath loose," he said teasingly. I balled my fists in an attempt to resist his taunts. He took a step forward, but I refused to back down from him. His smirk irritated me, but I was here to learn, not be made a fool of. "Come at me Asher," he encouraged.

I shook my head, prepared to protest. In the blink of an eye, he closed the space between us, and without much thought, I jabbed my fist out. I struck him in the nose, his head jerking back from the force.

Screeching at the pain shooting through my hand, I tried to hold back the tears, but still they relentlessly ran down my cheeks.

"I think you broke my hand you dimwit," I hissed, panting heavily through the pain. Blood was pouring from his nose, but still he laughed.

"You broke your own hand. I cannot believe you just hit me." The surprise in his voice brought a scowl to my face. As if he thought I would just sit back and let him attack me. Perhaps I should have hit him harder.

"Maybe if you would have—oh I do not know—told me we were starting rather than running at me like the lunatic you are, then I would not have hit you!" At this point I was shouting, but I could not help it as the pain and shock mixed with the rage within me. Would it be ludicrous to hit him again?

"I think you like that I am a lunatic, Asher," he said, somehow flirting with me through the pain he had to be feeling. His teeth were crimson from the blood that seeped into his mouth, matching the red of my split knuckles. "And anyways, I was hoping to gauge how much you know and what instincts you possess. Apparently, I underestimated you."

Another casual shrug of his shoulders sent my rage climbing once more. I would get nothing done training with him.

"I want to train with someone else," I blurted through clenched teeth. If the searing pain was not enough of a sign that this pairing ultimately would not work out, then the way we seemed to gravitate towards each other was. We stood there, nearly chest to chest again somehow, both staring at the other as if we could will submission.

Bellamy turned to spit out some of the blood in his mouth onto the dewy grass, then glared down at me.

"And who exactly would you like to learn from?" The bite of his tone did not go unnoticed, but I could not afford to spare his feelings when this information was fundamental to not only my escape, but my survival.

"What about the pumpkin demon? He seemed fit enough," I offered, waving my good hand towards the double doors behind us. When I did, I took in the sheer size of the estate that Bellamy called his home. It was a mirror of the interior, a towering dark presence. In the distance I could see the village and the market beyond, which were all so white they practically glowed in the fading moonlight. An interesting contrast.

A short stone path ended at the double doors that led inside, which were shaped like an arch. Four large cylinder towers reached towards the sky, four stories in height, connected by flat structures in between and on either end that sat three stories high. Most of the windows were shaped similar to the double doors in the front, arches of glass rather than wood. However, the fourth story of the far tower facing the sea had what appeared to be floor-to-ceiling windows, replacing the walls. This tower was thinner than the rest, the odd one out of an otherwise symmetrical design.

It was undeniably beautiful, Bellamy's home. That much I could admit.

"You want Henry," Bellamy growled, cutting off my mentation.

It sounded like more of an accusation than a question, but my hand hurt, and I simply wanted to see a Healer and move forward with training, so I swallowed the bitter anger. I turned back towards the demon prince, first taking in a breath of fresh air before the scent of him distracted me. Then I smiled up at him and spoke with as much sugar in my tone as I could conjure.

"I would love to train with him, as well as see a Healer." When he did not so much as flinch, I gritted out, "Please?" Why was it so difficult to be kind to this male? Was it normal to simultaneously want to smack and kiss someone?

I tried to think of some way to salvage the conversation that I had already so foolishly bludgeoned. Glancing up at his bloody nose, which would heal incorrectly if not realigned by a Healer immediately, I saw that the red liquid had already stopped flowing. "You should probably see a Healer too," I pointed out.

He chuckled then. A full, deep rasp that nearly brought a smile to my face. When he closed the small space between us, I felt the rumble of his chest and the warmth of his skin through his clothes. I pictured what it would be like to spend our days like this, laughing and training and touching. Then I quickly shut down the thought, because what would never be was not worth fantasizing over.

"Careful Asher, it almost sounds like you care."

"I do not, demon. Now please, can we get to a Healer before the pain makes me throw up all over your extravagant cloak?" Each word took more energy than I seemed to have. His dimpled smile did not falter as he strode back towards his home, brushing my shoulder as he passed. Pivoting, I followed him.

Just beyond the castle, I saw the sun rising over the sea, slowly casting the sky a vibrant orange. Around the large manor were bright red flowers that seemed to glow in the light of daybreak. "What are those flowers called?" I asked. Bellamy looked to his left and smiled, eyes quickly darting my way then back to the delicate flora.

"Those are called Salvia Splendens. Of all the places I have been, I have yet to see them anywhere but here." Bellamy leaned down and plucked a long red stem, turning around to fully face me.

Slowly, he reached up and tucked it behind my ear, running his finger gently across the flat top. His caress felt almost...loving. But I knew that with Bellamy, nothing was real. Everything was calculated and planned. So I shook off his fingers, tossed the flower to the ground, and walked up the black stone steps to the red double doors.

Before I could reach the handle, Bellamy was there. He grabbed my chin, lifting my face towards his.

"Beautiful creature, how I wish you knew the power you held." His whisper sent a wave of excitement through me, but his fingers reminded me of another night full of sorrow, forced affection, and so much pain—of Sterling.

I flinched at the memory, and just like that I was inwardly begging to be released. I held back the tone in my mental voice that made it an order, but barely.

Decades, that was how long it had taken me to control the way my power demanded obedience. Sometimes when I was flustered or overwhelmed, I slipped. This might have been one of those times, because Bellamy let go of my chin, ushering me back into the castle of night and blood with a wave of his hand. I could see the hurt and anger on his face, but he said nothing until we walked through the doors.

"I am afraid I need to take a page from your book, Asher," Bellamy said. My eyebrows knitted together at his declaration. Gazing over my shoulder I saw he was wearing the same devilish smirk he seemed to prefer. "So here are the conditions I have if you want to train with my subjects, roam free in my lands—"

"What I want is to go home," I corrected. My left hand laid limp in my right, healing in a way that made it appear crooked and deformed. Even through the pain, I still felt that spark of anger in me that the male seemed to enjoy lighting.

"Regardless, you will not attack any of my fae or demons with your powers. You will take no minds under your will to harm them in any way unless your life is threatened," Bellamy ordered. Though he did not have the power I did, he knew I had no choice but to listen. To follow his commands.

Guilt washed over me, because I did this to others. I took away their free will and forced their hand. It was cruel. It was evil.

It was me.

So I nodded, knowing I deserved the leash.

"I need to hear you say it, Asher," Bellamy ordered. The wording and the tone brought my mind back to the changing room in Pino's

147

booth, and I felt the blush on my cheeks before I could get myself in check.

"Fine, I will follow your rules and will not use my power to harm any of your fae or demons unless my life is threatened," I huffed, adding, "I will play the good captive as long as I am allowed to train daily."

Taking no time to consider my condition, Bellamy agreed. "Absolutely. Despite what you think, you are not a prisoner here."

I thought back to what Lian said about being saved from a prison disguised as a sanctuary. No matter how this male attempted to spin my situation, I was a hostage—a pawn. One thing I would not be, was weak.

CHAPTER TWENTY-ONE

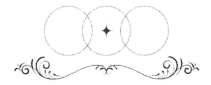

Navigating through the maze of a home was not as difficult in daylight. The arched windows allowed for the golden rays to shine into the manor, making the black and red seem significantly less ominous. The paintings were impossibly more captivating at this time of day as well. The rich and vibrant colors brought character to the black walls and life to the home itself. When we came upon hallways without a view of the outside world, what I assumed was demon light floated in the air.

Eventually we stopped in front of a red door that looked exactly like the rest to me. I was surprised anyone could find their way through the confusion.

"Do you live here alone?" I asked. Bellamy continued staring forward, not so much as glancing my way. "Is that really something I am not allowed to know? What would I even do with the information?"

His eyebrows lifted, amusement lighting his face. I knew though that he was afraid to tell me anything that was not necessary, which proved that he trusted me as little as I trusted him.

The door cracked open and a pair of jet-black eyes met mine before going wide and scanning over to Bellamy. He opened the door fully, showing his equally black waist length hair and scruffy facial hair that slightly came off his chin. The male was wearing all white clothing that covered nearly every inch of his dark skin, seeming to light up the hallways with his presence alone.

"My Prince," he said, bowing low. I caught his eyes flick over to me again before he straightened once more.

"Ranbir, there is no need to bow for company's sake." Bellamy chuckled, clapping the male on the shoulder with his clean hand. Ranbir looked at Bellamy's nose and clicked his tongue, shaking his head slowly. The sight of the demon prince covered in blood was clearly not surprising.

"What happened this time, Bell?" Definitely a regular occurrence then. Bellamy smiled, flashing his deep dimples and crinkling his freckled cheeks, looking every bit the part of a mischievous youngling rather than a grown male. It was so familiar to me for some reason.

"Ah, the beautiful Asher punched me square in the nose," Bellamy said.

Idiot.

"It was marvelous," he rasped, looking back at me in a way that made me feel bare.

I rolled my eyes, crossing my arms and bunching my good fist to keep the inappropriate feelings at bay. Ranbir looked over to me again with wide eyes.

"It was his fault. Besides, he could use a good punch to knock him back down to reality." I scoffed. "Plus, he broke my hand with his stupid face!" Shooting a glare at Bellamy, I reached out my crooked and bruised hand.

Ranbir gasped and stepped towards me. He cradled my hand, running soft touches over it. At first, I was confused, but then I felt the burn of healing. I hissed in pain when I felt his hand tighten and the power rebreak then heal my bones. When Ranbir released me, my hand was back to its former state.

"Thank you so much. My name is Asher, Asher Daniox. I appreciate your help," I said with a soft smile. At least someone in this horrid place was not a heathen. The Healer smiled back, warm and genuine.

"I am Ranbir Bhesaj, and it was my pleasure. You next?" Ranbir asked, facing Bellamy, who in turn nodded. I watched as Bellamy's nose was restored to its former glory, smeared blood the only remaining sign of my masterwork.

A shame truly, the shattered nose would have done wonders for his overinflated ego.

"Was there anything else you needed?" the Healer inquired with clasped hands and that same gentle smile. His accent was the sharp lilt of *home*, just as all the fae here still possessed. It made me wonder once again why they were here at all.

"No Ranbir, that is all. I hope you have a splendid day, and thank you for your assistance." Bellamy's words were soft, his tone almost familial. It was the same way he spoke to Lian and Pino, both fae as well. I might not have noticed, but I was trying to remain diligent, to glean any information I could later use to my advantage.

"Thank you," Ranbir said.

He looked between us once more, then settled his eyes on me, mouth open as if there was something on the tip of his tongue. Bellamy must have noticed the way that Ranbir hesitated, the eye contact we maintained, because he cleared his throat loudly.

"What is it, Ranbir? Please, speak freely." The demon prince's voice stayed kind, but I could tell by the tic of his jaw that there was tension. Whatever silent conversation the two had in that moment made me painfully aware that there was something I was missing, and it was important.

"I do not mean to insert myself where I do not belong, but I have long since prayed to the gods that you would come, Princess. Seeing you here is of great relief to me. I would like you to know that the fae of this realm fully support your—"

"Apologies Ranbir, but Asher needs to get ready for her requested training. I do appreciate your help this morning," Bellamy rushed, ending the conversation.

He placed his hand on the small of my back, pushing me towards the way we came. My head whipped back to watch Ranbir close his door, those black eyes never leaving mine. Chills ran down my spine as my mind raced through the possibilities of what the Healer might have meant.

I shoved off Bellamy's hand when we were out of Ranbir's earshot, whirling on the demon.

"What are you keeping from me, Elemental? Do I not even have the right to know the secrets that concern me?" I spat out, my finger tapping his chest in time with my words.

Had I always been this violent? No, I could not have been. It was this place, this house, this male.

"I owe you nothing, please do not forget that," he said matter-of-factly. I could tell he was on edge, but I could not care less.

"You stole me in the middle of my wedding after swearing to me you would never take me against my will again, then you murdered my betrothed. The least you owe me is honesty!" I shouted. My face heated up and my head pounded. I was uncontrollably angry, and barely containing my power that was trying to burst free from me.

"First of all, you can stop pretending that you were not begging for the wedding to end. I saved you from a man who would sooner murder you than respect you! I know you, and that life would have killed you if he did not," he said, arms flying in the air.

I refused to back down, to flinch. Instead, I squared off my shoulders, gritted my teeth, and steeled my heart.

"You claim to know so much about me, but have yet to ask me how your actions made me feel. I have been conscious for one night, and I already am being lied to and manipulated, as I have been by you since before we even met." Every piece of my rage accumulated into that seed of power within my chest, making my fingertips tingle, my ears ring, and my head spin. Everything was heavy.

"I realize I went about this wrong, Asher, but you needed to be removed from beneath their shoes to see what has always been in front of you. You have to realize that the life you were living had no purpose. That you were suppressed and secluded. There was nothing but death and sorrow awaiting you. Can you not understand why I would take you from there?" His hands went to my cheeks, but all I could focus on were the truth of his words.

The life you were living had no purpose.

Was that not the same thing I had been chanting to myself for so long? Still, it pained me to hear the words spoken aloud.

"I know you plan to ransom me, so please, just get on with it so I can go back to where I belong," I said, my voice sounding as defeated as I felt.

He winced, rearing back as if I had struck him. In fact, my words seemed to have hurt far worse than the punch that smashed his nose earlier.

"You know nothing, Princess," he rasped, voice full of raw hurt.

"I want to go home." I was begging, and I hated it, but my pride could take the hit if it meant I would be safely in my own bed tonight.

"I know, and you will." With that, he turned and continued his quick pace down the hall.

Like a trained pup, I followed. We wound through the three-story manor, and I thought he might be purposefully attempting to confuse me so I could not escape. The twists and turns were disorienting, and when we went down a set of stairs to later go up an oddly familiar set, I knew I had been right about his tactics.

At the end of a hall, we paused in front of yet another red door, exactly the same as Ranbir's in appearance. Bellamy rapped on the copper wood three times, the sound echoing down the empty walkway. There were a string of curses coming from the other side, then the shuffling of feet. The door swung open, revealing a barely conscious Henry. His orange hair stood up in every direction, mussed from his pillow. He wore wrinkled black trousers, but his toned torso and his feet were left bare.

At the sight of Bellamy his brow furrowed, but when his eyes met mine, shock crossed his face.

"What do you want?" he asked, gaze flicking back to his prince. Informality like that was rarely used between subjects and royalty, and it seemed as if this was the norm between the two. A weak point in his otherwise strong unit. I could sense it, their animosity. I would use it the first chance I got.

"Actually, it is not me who wants anything. Asher would like to ask you a question though," Bellamy said with a shrug of his shoulders.

Of course he would toss me to the wild beast with no remorse. His bitterness was a pain among other things. Henry once again eyed me, and I felt my body enter self-preservation mode, my feet bringing me a step further from him. Bellamy chuckled softly next to me when I swallowed loudly.

"Um yes, I do. First, I want to apologize for how I acted earlier. It was not right for me to use my power against you like that," I offered, hoping to bridge the gap between us before asking for a favor. His eyes formed slits, and I could sense his apprehension. The suspicion he seemed to feel was warranted, because I was about to request his help when I did not necessarily deserve it.

"Power, huh?" he asked.

"What?" I asked, confused by his question and annoyed at his condescending tone. Fae power was a blessing from Eternity. From our creation. It was utterly unique, even if the demons might not think so. Their magic derived from darkness, from the Underworld. We were not the same.

"You know very little for someone of your status. Anyways, get to your point before Bellamy lights me on fire for refusing to speak in innuendos." Again, the energy between the two grew thick, the anger tangible. I might get more from Henry than just training if I play the game correctly.

"I would like for you to train me in combat, if you have the time and are willing that is," I stated plainly. It seemed this male liked directness.

His eyebrows rose, and his attention went back to Bellamy. I glanced over to see that the prince's fists were squeezed at his side and every inch of his face had gone red. Fury radiated from him, pouring into the air. Henry smiled at that, then looked at me with mischief in his eyes.

"You do not have to ask me twice, darling."

CHAPTER TWENTY-TWO

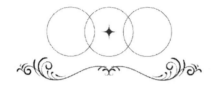

I let out a quick whoop at my small victory, causing Bellamy to cross his arms and pin Henry with a merciless glare.

"If you so much as look at Asher wrong, you will have me to answer to." The threat sounded serious, but pumpkin did not seem to be phased. His lack of fear must have set Bellamy off, because the ground shook slightly, rattling vases on tables and pictures on walls.

"Relax Bell, I will not hurt her. She seems fully capable of protecting herself anyways. Go paint another pretty picture and leave us," he scoffed, waving Bellamy away.

His words caught my attention, and I subconsciously scanned the nearby paintings. I had not realized before that, though they were a variety of styles and mediums, they all had the same feel to them. Passion and joy and sorrow and *life*.

"You painted these?" I asked with wonder in my voice. The gentle nod of his head and the shy smile told me that I still had so much to learn about this male. My captor. Or, as he would call himself, my savior.

"Yes, yes, he is very talented. Be talented somewhere else," Henry said, rolling his eyes and grabbing my arm gently. Bellamy's gaze went from soft to blazing in an instant, his hand reaching out for me. "Oh stop, she will be fine with me. Leave us be so we can begin."

The second my body was fully through the door, Henry slammed it shut on his prince's face.

I had never seen anyone disrespect a royal in that way, let alone one as powerful as Bellamy was. But the door did not smash open, there were no angry yells. Instead, I heard silence, then a moment later, furious steps retreating back down the hall.

"Interesting dynamic the two of you have," I noted, eyebrows raised.

Henry just flashed me an, admittedly dashing, smile and walked further into his chambers. His relaxed demeanor calmed my stormy mind, and I felt instantly comfortable in his presence despite our previous hostility. Perhaps that was why I followed him, plopping down on the edge of his bed while he sifted through his clothes.

"So, what will I learn first?"

"Have you ever had any lessons in combat before?" he asked, littering the ground with shirts as he dug through the wardrobe. I shook my head no when he looked back at me, slightly ashamed that I had never forced the matter with Xavier and Mia.

"Bellamy just attempted to give me a single lesson, and it ended with his bloody nose and my broken hand," I said. Henry snorted, but I was not amused. I left myself vulnerable in more ways than one.

Unwillingly, I thought back to a time when I talked back as a youngling. The way Mia narrowed her eyes, which told me I was too bold for my own good. How she called in Xavier to dole out the punishment in my room on the low level of the palace and watched. Or, just the other day, the way Xavier shook his head in disappointment before my beating.

I wondered silently if they never taught me because they knew how unpredictable I was, that I might fail them with fists rather than just words. A new fear came to life then, because Xavier and Mia knew best, that much I was aware. In every situation, their advice—whether I heeded it or not—turned out to be the wiser option. Was training a bad idea after all?

"Well Bellamy is the general of our armies. He sees things differently than the rest of us." Information I had not yet known. I liked this demon, if only for his big mouth. "Since you are completely new to it, we will start slow. Focus on getting you strong, then we can add in classic stances. From there I will teach you how to actually fight and eventually add in a weapon or two," Henry explained as he pulled on a plain black tunic.

Why had it taken him so long to find that? It looked like every black shirt sprawled on the ground.

"Are you not afraid that teaching me to fight will make me more dangerous?" I asked, curious if he had similar opinions to Lian.

He dismissed that notion with a wave of his hand, a gesture he seemed to use often. Were all demons so boisterous and bold? No one, not even Nicola, had an aura like his. Energy and charisma seemed to ooze out of him, seeping across the floor and latching onto me. Next to him, I felt admittedly less aggressive and stressed.

"You need to learn this stuff to protect yourself, relying on your magic as if it is infallible is ignorant and risky. Besides, you being dangerous does nothing to hurt us. Hopefully you will figure that out soon enough," he stated offhandedly. More nonsense, more half-truths. Seemed common among the beings of this realm, though Henry was decidedly more forthcoming when he wanted to be.

"For some reason, I feel you will not be elaborating further," I stated, eyebrows raised. Henry chuckled, but did not deny the statement.

Predictable. "Does that mean you forgive me for manipulating your mind earlier?" I asked, not making eye contact.

After a moment of silence, I peeked up through my lashes to find him looking over at me, his expression incredulous.

"You are a moron if you think that is true, but you are not so bad from what I can tell. You just need to let loose a little," he said. The way he phrased it sounded almost scandalous. "I would love to help you loosen up any time you would like, little brat." Yep, definitely inappropriate.

I shook my head at Henry, scoffing.

Looking around more intently, I noticed the interesting choice of furniture and decorations, which stood in great contrast from the rest of the home. The room around me was full of pastels. Blues, greens, yellows, reds, purples. So much color that it went past overwhelming. Despite the little rhyme or reason to it all, the décor managed to remain perfectly cohesive.

Not a single piece of furniture matched. The dark brown wood of his bed was the direct opposite of the light, raw color of the dresser. His desk was bleached white as if exposed to the sun too long, matching the driftwood on the beach outside. I saw another sort of table in the far-right corner, stained with smudges of color. He had a large open wooden case that held weapons of different sizes and types, which proved he was a good choice for a trainer. Above us, at least a dozen balls of demon light floated midair, the addition of the black ceiling seemed to mimic the night sky.

The rest of the room was just as chaotic.

One wall was completely covered by a tapestry that was the most gorgeous color of blue, as if the thread was dyed with ink pulled from the sky on a clear summer day. Running horizontally across the fabric were three black rings overlapping one another, joined. In the center of the middle ring was a white star that glowed like the floating demon light.

The colors among the other walls came from paintings. These were similar to those hung in the hallways, the sight challenging my previous assumptions regarding animosity between Bellamy and Henry. I stood, walking over to the wall that held the exit, where the story depicted seemed to start. Within clouds rose two hands, a ball of light and a ball of darkness hovering above them. In the next, rain fell from the cloud, both onyx and white droplets, as if the light and darkness were blessing the ground below. Mortals, it seemed, were dancing under the water, hands in the air and smiles on their faces.

I slowly rotated in the room, taking in the tale of sorrow without fully understanding. I was far too encompassed to notice Henry approach me from behind, but when I made the full circle there he was, watching.

"Would you like to hear the history aloud?" he asked, his voice hinting at the emotion under the bravado. I nodded, and he began.

"Everything that makes us special, came from Stella, the goddess of the Above. She loved the innocence many mortals possessed—the sort of genuine love and joy that had long since been missing from the gods. From her hands she rained her power down on us, giving the humans of this realm the ability to wield the raw magic from the light of the sun and the dark of the moon. From then on we were identified as either Suns or Moons. With this came the blessing of long life. Our sigil represents the ring of light on the left, the ring of darkness on the right, and the ring of demon kind in the center, with the Star of Stella at the heart of it." Henry's voice became haunting as he spoke, calling to me.

"At first, everything was blissful. Our kind thrived as we mastered the gifts Stella gave to us. But that all changed when a goddess fell in love with the demon king." At that, I gasped.

Henry's mouth tilted down, his eyes half closed. A sign of the turn the story would take.

The painting depicted a beautiful female with wild ebony locks and equally dark eyes. Her full lips were a bloody red, and she wore scraps of gold that barely covered her voluptuous curves. She was reaching down from the clouds towards what appeared to be a mortal, but must have been the demon king. His tall and muscled frame was covered in a white blouse of sorts, the sleeves tight fitting. It was open at the center, the ties hanging loosely down the front. His jaw seemed to be carved of marble, sharp and fierce. His ears poked out of his brown hair, the smooth arch surprising me.

I pulled my eyes off of the mural to zero in on Henry's ears, which were...round. Stella gifting the mortals magic did not change what they truly were, mortal. Strange that she would so cherish them, enough to sacrifice a portion of her magic. It seemed rather foolish, honestly. But if this were true, then their magic did not come from the Underworld—from evil—but from the blessing of a god.

"Asta was enamored with our king, Zohar. Their love story was rather tragic, as her mother, Stella, forbade her from ascending the prince to be with her in the Above. It was not that Stella did not see greatness in the king. She loved us all dearly, and he was the strongest Sun that walked the world. More than that, he was an incomparable monarch, bringing rest to our kind as we integrated with the other beings in the land. He was not a god though, and his power was miniscule in comparison, as it was merely a gift from Stella herself, a scrap of her magic distributed amongst us all."

I remained silent, taking in the tragedy of loving what you cannot have. Of fighting a world which wishes to tear you apart.

"Asta was set to be married to another god who was powerful in his own right. An incredible match, but not her love. So, one evening, as she peered down at her lover below, she made the decision to run. That very night, Asta wed Zohar under the veil of twilight, becoming queen of our realm. Our kind rejoiced, so very proud that a god would choose our honorable king as her husband." I smiled at Henry's words, but his own face remained forlorn. This was not the ending it seemed.

"Her mother was intent on letting her go, simply banishing her from returning, but the other gods wanted retribution for the way she slighted her godly betrothed. Many months passed, and Asta became pregnant. The day she gave birth, Stella appeared to her, celebrating the birth of her grandson. Joy seemed to be in abundance that day, but the very next, the gods took their vengeance." My eyes went wide, because I had a feeling I knew how this would end.

Henry grabbed my hand and tugged me to the last wall, and a small sob left my mouth.

The painting was of Zohar, his brown hair soaked in thick, red blood. It was pooled all around him as he lay lifeless on the floor, Asta pictured in a fit of rage and sorrow, screaming up at the Above with her hands on his open chest, now without a heart. Stella watched from the sky, a silver tear streaming down her golden cheek. It was gory and horrific. I reached up to my own chest, as if it too were being ripped open.

I realized after a moment that I was accidentally tapping into Henry's emotions as well when I felt sudden rage mixing with a deep sadness. I looked over at him to see a single tear running down his face, just like Stella's. I squeezed his hand, wanting to comfort him in some way, despite not knowing him.

"Their son possessed the magic of his father as well as his mother. His dual magic passed down the royal line, becoming a symbol of not only the strength of demon kind, but of love. Every heir born since has wielded both," he stated, grief pouring from him.

I wanted to ask for further details of Asta, Bellamy's ancestor, but it seemed rude to pry any more than I already was. Plus, I was rather certain Henry would not tell me. Or could not. I silently considered the possibility that Bellamy had not descended from fae, but had instead gained the power to harness the elements from Asta.

"Why did Bellamy paint this here?" I asked instead, as it was clear that these were done by his hand.

Henry, who was seemingly a full-blooded demon, was openly emotional about this history of theirs, but Bellamy had not mentioned it, had not cared to spark conversation in that way. Though, he also did not have the chance in hindsight.

"He began painting them one night in a spark of outrage. I believe he stayed in here for nearly a week to get them all done. He can be over emotional at times, but in this instance, it was warranted. He, more than any of us, feels the need to uphold the legacy of Zohar and Asta, to be worthy of them," Henry said, his voice soft and raspy, as if speaking the story had exhausted him. "But that week was dark, full of bleak terror. I believe he wanted to avoid this room at all costs when he was done. Actually, the chambers were vacant until I commandeered them."

I had so many questions, but I knew that if I asked too many he would stop answering all together. Why had he taken over this room? What happened to Asta? Had the gods felt satisfied with their revenge? A tornado of questions spun through my head and wreaked havoc on my brain. None of those questions would help me in any way, and it seemed that he was done speaking of Bellamy, so I opted for another form of information that might come across as innocent but was vital to my escape.

"You mentioned that there were *other* creatures the original demons had to acclimate with once gaining their power. Are they still around?" I asked. He rolled his eyes at me instead of answering, tugging my hand and pulling me out the door. I grunted in protest, but he maintained his speed, weaving us on a much straighter path than Bellamy had. "Fine, who makes those portals?"

"Makes portals?" he repeated, his eyebrows scrunched together in confusion. We stopped there in the hallway, as if I stunned him. "Do you mean how do we portal?"

I just stared, hoping not to give away my ignorance. I had a feeling I was about to discover another of Bellamy's lies.

"We use our raw magic to portal, it is fairly simple once you understand the concept of it and practice enough. Though, not many demons can do it. It takes an incredible amount of magic."

Thinking back, I realized I never saw the green ball in Bellamy's hand when he took me from the ballroom. In fact, I now remembered that I even noted how the smoke of darkness smelled like him. Stupid, I was so incredibly stupid. Henry seemed to notice that my thoughts had taken a turn for the worse, because he started pulling me forward again, changing the subject.

"Let's get you some food, then we can start training. I do not want to have to carry you back inside if you pass out from hunger," Henry reasoned.

Fair point. I realized then that I was ravenous. I guess I had ignored it before due to my stubbornness and fear. Hopefully demons did not eat children or something equally heinous.

CHAPTER TWENTY-THREE

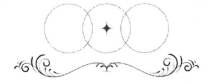

We came to a stop in front of a pair of double doors. Henry pushed them open, revealing a large dining area. This room sported the same red and black of the rest of the home, with a long, glossy, black table and chairs. The walls were decorated with Bellamy's paintings, still a hectic grouping of different styles and colors strewn about in a way that made the room feel cozy. Sat in the chairs were Lian, Pino, Ranbir, and two others.

Henry was the picture of comfort as he strolled down the table and claimed the seat next to Ranbir, who quietly listened to the others talk, still sporting his all-white clothing and looking noticeably more relaxed than he did when he healed me earlier.

Lian sat on the other side, chatting with a female who had golden brown hair that seemed to reach her midthigh, though it was hard to be sure as she sat. I was unable to see much of her at all from the back, but her sensual voice rang throughout the room, drawing in everyone at the table.

The last female had hair the color of moss, which was wrapped in intricate coils along her head. She sat on the other side of Ranbir, and I saw her irises matched her vibrant locks. She had generous curves and an overall roundness to her. A small black cloth covered only her breasts, held up by a delicate chain that wrapped behind her neck. She was beautiful in a way that I had never seen before.

Everyone at this table, apart from Pino, seemed to be young—perhaps even near my own age. Their lively and casual conversations signaled they were also quite close, as if mornings like this were a regular occurrence.

Pino turned to face me, his gray hair and wrinkled skin giving him a warmth that I did not see within the others. He stood from his seat beside Lian, drawing my eyes to his tunic. The chest was a deep violet, but the stitching and the wrist-length sleeves were a beautiful gold shade that shone in the demon light. Though I loathed how little color was in the fae palace, Pino's top reminded me of where I was, of my plans. I ached to go back, to find comfort within my home that I was now fairly convinced lay an entire sea away.

The Tomorrow walked towards me, his bright smile soothing my unease and anxiety. "I hope you find the clothing suitable," he said. I returned the smile, though it did not meet my cheeks, and nodded. Beaming, Pino took the silent compliment and bowed low.

"I love them, I do not believe I have ever had clothes that suited me as well as these. You are truly a born talent," I gushed, wanting him to understand just how much having clothing that both fit and flattered me meant, despite my morose look. At that his smile turned even brighter, lighting up the dark room.

"You, Asher, are a delight to have among us."

With the word "us," I suddenly felt five pairs of eyes land on me. I looked to the right of Pino, and sure enough, all of the table's occupants were staring our way. I felt uncomfortable under their scrutinizing gaze, though I knew Henry, Ranbir, and Lian were likely just tuning in rather than making a judgement. Theirs had already been formed.

Henry flashed me a distinctly feline smile, clearly aware of my unease and enjoying it. With the other female fully facing me, her hazel eyes alight with curiosity and perhaps a bit of mischief, I could sense the thrum of her power. It called to me, nipping at my own, as if it were begging to be not only deciphered, but understood.

"Hello, I am Noe Tristana." Instead of reaching her hand out, the female pulled me into her chest and squeezed me tightly. When she released me from her grip, I felt darkness lick up my spine.

"Stop taunting her, Noe, or she'll make you stab yourself in the eye," Lian said offhandedly, as if it was not a threat and an accusation in one. I raised my eyebrows, feigning shock.

"I think I recall telling you that I had no interest in harming you, Lian. If I wanted you dead you would be," I spoke with equal ease and comfort, adding in a swift shrug. Creeping towards the small, blue-haired Air, I flashed a ruthless smile. "Plus, it is not nearly as exciting to play with the dead as it is the living."

Lian shivered, but beside me I felt Noe's excitement peak.

"Henry is right, you are quite riveting. Perhaps we can all see you in action sometime," Noe spoke. Moving my eyes back to the brunette, I tilted my head, sizing her up.

The female with green hair cleared her throat, smiling at me warmly as she summoned a ray of light in her hand. She blasted it towards Noe, who in turn shot shadows at her, the two convulsing together like they were both at war and in love. I had never seen anything like it in my lifetime.

"It is so wonderful to finally meet you, Asher. I am Winona Nayab," the female with the green hair said right as the pair let their power go, the light and dark sucking back into their palms. "Ignore these animals, they rarely have company beyond those in this room."

I chuckled softly at that, shoulders loosening as the fear and discomfort left me. Distinguishing between fae and demon would be easier than looking at their ears it seemed, because Henry, Noe, and Winona all spoke in that same accent as Bellamy now did.

"My wife is right. Please, sit and suffer through breakfast with us," Ranbir spoke, gesturing to the seat beside the head of the table, which remained noticeably vacant. Almost painfully so.

My eyebrows shot up in surprise. Not only had a Healer married outside of his faction, but he wed a *demon*. The two of them smiled at one another, and I thought, not for the first time, that perhaps we were wrong to enforce that restriction on our kind.

With a gentle hand on my upper back, Pino encouraged me forward. I plopped down in the seat across from Henry, holding in my need to enter the minds of those around me—fighting off my curiosity. When I felt them all stare at me once more, I decided to speak.

"Is there something you all would like to ask, or am I simply so good looking you cannot divert your gaze?"

A snort sounded from Henry, and beside him Ranbir blushed faintly. Noe and Lian on the other hand, looked amused in a way that made me wonder if in another life I would fit in well with this group.

"Well, yes you are, but I am actually quite curious. The rumors of your power are so very exciting. Can you show us?" Noe asked, her tone not mocking, but inquisitive. Genuine.

I reached out, just to douse her curiosity. I knew when I had her, because the darkness enveloped my senses. Every ray of sunshine, every flame of fire, every bit of light was sucked out of the world. I saw nothing for what felt like a lifetime, but eventually came back up for air. Her intrigue was at the forefront of her mind, and when I attempted to creep further back it was as if there were no other thoughts, emotions, or memories. Just distinct interest.

I opened my eyes, which I had not realized I closed until then. Noe was staring, waiting.

Stand.

Noe stood.

Jump.

Noe jumped once.

"Tell me a secret, Noe," I said, dropping my voice to the commanding tenor of my mental one. A couple of the others gasped, each of their faces full of concern. I rolled my eyes. "Fine, a secret of little consequence."

Noe looked like she was intoxicated on my power, as if this experience was a rich wine she could not get enough of.

"When Bell and I were young, I sent a pyrien after him because he would not kiss me, but I never told him it was me."

My eyebrows furrowed. What was a *pyrien*? Before I could ask, the smell of cinnamon and smoke wafted in the air like a warm breeze. I turned to find Bellamy in the seat beside me, claiming his head spot.

"I always knew that you did that, you little heathen," Bellamy said.

He was still wearing the red tunic, though it was now hiding his chest. His dark hair was slightly tousled, as if he, or someone else, had been running a hand through it extensively. I also noted the bit of kohl under his eye, causing the blue to look terrifyingly—enchantingly—bright.

"Hello, Princess," he rasped, our eyes locking. Butterflies erupted low in my stomach, but I ignored them.

"Do not call me that, demon." I scoffed. Noe's lush laugh sounded behind me, followed by Henry's deeper, more earthy chuckle. Bellamy seemed unfazed by my tone. If anything, he smiled wider.

"I love it when you play hard to get," he purred. I rolled my eyes and did my best to act as though I was not fighting the urge to kiss him. He was the enemy, and I was not staying.

"On a more important note, has anyone ever told you that you sit funny?" Henry asked me, his green eyes alight with an emotion I could

Of Night and Blood

not place. My brows creased in confusion as I assessed my posture. I was sitting as any royal would. "Like you have a stick up your ass."

Noe giggled, Lian coughing to hide her own laughter. Winona and Ranbir looked as if they were trying very hard not to react at all. I merely glared at the demon, not wanting him to know just how badly that wounded me. With all the grace I could muster, I sat straighter.

Bellamy leaned over and smacked the back of Henry's head, causing it to fling forward and nearly land in his food. Then it was my turn to laugh.

"Anyways, Winona what was it you so desperately needed to make me aware of?" the prince said, looking my way with a dazzling smile on his face, as if he enjoyed the sound of my laughter.

The Sun opened her mouth to speak, but when her eyes quickly darted to me, she shut it once more.

"It might be a matter best discussed in private," she said. Everyone else at the table seemed to zero in on me as well, though I was unsure if they had ever stopped gawking. My own eyes narrowed, my fists scrunching in my lap in anger.

"Yes, you would not want to divulge too much to your captive, Prince," I added, eyeing her. Winona winced, as if prepared for me to harm her for what she said. I was both offended and thrilled by her fear, which was a new trait of mine that I was growing rather comfortable with.

"I do not mean to offend you," Winona responded, her voice soft and soothing.

All I could think of was how they might be attempting to take advantage of me. These were the same beings who were mass-murdering fae, who mercilessly attacked those who had done them no wrong. In fact, their kind had done more than offend me in the past.

"I feel the need to make something clear. I have no desire to harm any of you; I am no monster who finds pleasure in the pain of others. As someone who has been maimed by your kind, I think it more fair I question your intentions with me rather than the other way around." My accusation was plain as day.

It was them who could not be trusted. As pleasant as they seemed, they were also a viscous species who tortured fae for the fun of it. The very same creatures who cut my ears and murdered my family sat at this table, and it was a struggle to contain my pain in that moment.

"Actually, that is not—" Lian began, but Bellamy quickly silenced her with a raised hand.

I reached out to her mind as quickly as the snap of a whip, but the demon prince was somehow faster. The earth below my chair rumbled, sending me flying backwards, breaking my concentration. Wind, fierce and cool, hit my back, pushing me upright. I gasped at the jerking motions, feeling a tad nauseous.

"Now, Asher, I thought we agreed you would stay out of their minds," he said, a smirk on his stupid face.

I huffed and started scooping food onto my plate. No part of me believed he would tell me how he sensed my power, which rendered that question unnecessary and pointless. From the corner of my eye, I saw Lian glare down the table at Bellamy, as if she were angry at him for stopping me.

I ignored it, grabbing piles of eggs, pancakes, potatoes, and anything else my hands could reach. The assortment of spices wafted towards me, smelling far more exotic than anything I had ever eaten. From the corner of my eye, I saw Bellamy watching me, the heat of his stare threatening to undo me.

"Am I allowed to pick at your mind, oh glorious prince?" I asked. Without waiting for an answer, I looked away, shoving a few bites of food into my mouth and sending my power creeping towards him.

Whatever he did to block me was not in effect. In fact, his mind was unguarded, as if he was hoping I would invite myself in. The second I did, Bellamy startled me by speaking.

Would it be wrong of me to say I grow hard watching you devour your food like that?

I jumped, having never been spoken to through the mind. My power had only ever seemed to allow me to communicate to another, rather than the other way around.

"You are a pig," I said, making sure to bite into the greasy bacon as I did. Bellamy licked his lips, watching me finish off the piece.

"Asher, we have no reason to harm you. I think you have misunderstood your reason for being here, though I am sure that was easy with what little information Bell has provided," Pino said, his palms up, as if offering me invisible honesty.

Everyone at the table was watching me. I wanted to shout at them that I was not for their entertainment, their curiosity. I wanted to kill them all for their complacency in the murdering of my fae. So many horrible, intrusive thoughts beat down on me, and I knew that I had to be alone before I hurt someone.

As I stood to leave, I felt a prickle along my left arm and turned to see darkness creeping up my body. It seemed to be flowing from Noe, who was pouring tea into the cup beside my plate. The way it caressed my skin gave me the impression she was attempting to coax my own power out of me. Our eyes met, and a shadow slid under my chin. The table went silent, but I paid them no attention as I opened my mental gates, my power welcoming Noe's mind.

"Noe, come here," Father called. By the sound of his voice, he was angry. I held my breath, contemplating staying hidden. I knew though, that the longer I disobeyed, the worse it would be. So I pulled myself out of the small hole in the wall, crawling through my wardrobe and opening the doors. When I was out, I slid the wooden slab back into place, making the wardrobe appear whole once more, then pushed my clothes in front of it.

As I walked out of my chambers, an eerie darkness had encompassed the hall, devouring every inch of light. Before I could register the wrath that must have brought this on, I felt a fist slam into my back, throwing me to the ground. Searing pain shot through my wrist as I landed on it, my knees hitting with a loud thud. Crying out, I looked behind me to see father standing above, sneering.

"Let this be a valuable lesson, dear daughter," he snarled, his face scrunched in rage, so much like my own when I am angry. "I will always win."

This time, when his fist came down on me, my eyes shut and did not open.

When the memory faded into black, the heaviness of Noe's pain filled me. Then, as clear as Bellamy's earlier, her voice came echoing into my head.

We do not wish to hurt you, Asher. I do not. I know your pain, as you have seen. I feel it radiating from you as if it were my own. Let me say plainly what the others will not. If you go back to the place you call home, you will break, and no one will be able to put you back together.

Relinquishing my hold on Noe, I fell back into my seat and promptly heaved up the breakfast I had just finished eating.

ACT III

~ BARGAINING ~

CHAPTER TWENTY-FOUR

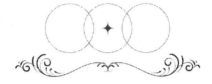

No one spoke as I uncontrollably vomited. Any other time I would have felt embarrassed, but in that moment I only felt weak. When my stomach settled, my mind cleared.

"Something is wrong," I whispered, face still downturned. Bellamy was on me in an instant, Ranbir not too far behind.

"How often has this happened, Asher?" the latter asked.

I thought back to the instances of pain that ended in me bent over this same way, with an awful taste in my mouth and a weakened body. But it was not only in times of great hurt. I remembered that every instance in which I expended too much power in the last few months I was left feeling drained, bilious.

"Lately it has happened often. I believe I have just been overexerting my power. A reminder to keep to my own thoughts I think," I hoarsely chuckled. Neither male was particularly interested in the joke though. When I tried to sit upright, I was met with a second wave of queasiness, this time also feeling off center.

"A well of power like yours is more likely to punish you for not using enough rather than using too much. I have not seen you exert the amount needed to even slightly quench the thirst that is probably building inside of you," the Healer stated, leaving no room for questions. Beside him, Bellamy's face was cold, calculating.

He looked over to Henry, and the two held a silent conversation that left me on edge. Sweat ran down my back, and black spots filled my vision. Noe whispered something to me that I could not quite make out, and Bellamy's cool hands grabbed onto my cheeks just as a thunderous pounding began in my ears, matching the erratic beat of my heart.

When Ranbir's fingers met my temples, some of the fog lifted, and suddenly sound came flooding back. Then the pain started, my veins feeling as though they might burst.

"It had to have been regularly administered to her if she is experiencing withdrawal like this," Bellamy said, his voice cold as ice. The Healer grunted with what sounded like effort as he continued to somehow pull the pain out of me.

"It tastes strong. By the way her body clings to it, I would say she has been taking it for decades, if not her entire life. This last dose must have been large, because it is still in her system. I can feel her heart straining against it," Ranbir said, his voice full of concern.

Their pity aggravated me, giving back some of the energy I felt deprived of. I shoved his hands away, grumbling to let go. He let out a small chuckle, but his fingertips went straight back to my temples. I refrained from arguing and opted to focus on staying upright.

"This would explain why it took her so long to wake up," Lian mentioned.

I tried to recall how long I had been asleep, or to think of how often I felt sick any time I used my powers throughout the years. I knew one thing for sure, I had gotten worse since Sterling arrived. Briefly, I considered yelling at them to stop discussing me as if I were not there, but my body and head felt heavy, my mind somewhat fuzzy.

"As well as why the mortal was capable of incapacitating her," Winona pointed out. "And based on what Luca and Cyprus told Noe, she received quite the beating the night before her wedding, which was followed by a Healer coming in and placing a blocker on her. She could have been injected with enough to make her complacent during the ceremony rather than to staunch her magic. Luca said she left the prince in tears with very little effort, I imagine the royals did not want to risk her lashing out."

The names of the two guards who pledged their loyalty to me days ago caught my attention. Were they spies for the demons? How had they been able to infiltrate the castle guards? I thought through the information they might have gleaned, trying to catalogue it all so that I could inform Xavier later. I would allow them the courtesy of getting free of course, but the Fae Realm would suffer if we did not protect our secrets.

Each second that Ranbir's power worked through my body left me more cognizant of the accusations these beings were throwing around. They continued back and forth, always coming to the conclusion that Xavier and Mia had been the ones to poison me, never including me in the conversation. Lian discussed wards and different defensive options. Henry addressed details his spies had come across recently. Apparently, they were no longer afraid to share information in my presence. Noe stayed silent, stroking my head and rubbing my back.

I realized quickly that they spoke of the times I was punished or beaten with no surprise. I loathed the idea of each of them being privy to my private life. It was Bellamy though that my eyes darted to as the last of the pain left my body, which now felt lighter than I ever remembered.

The demon prince was shaking with rage, his fists glowing an orange hue as the flames tried to fight their way free.

"We need to get Asher to the king as soon as possible. They will come for her," he spoke through clenched teeth. My fear rose at the reference to the demon king. If they were planning to move me, then I would need to escape sooner than I thought.

As their conversation ensued—arguments erupting here and there—and someone came to clean my mess, I detailed out everything I had learned so far. I knew we were near the sea, maybe the same beach Bellamy had taken me to just two weeks ago. The portals were a ruse, so I would not be able to steal one and run, though it was entirely possible that they left boats on the shore for quick leave. Going by water was the only way I could get back, but if I was in the Demon Realm then I would have to make it past The Mist.

No one who attempted to penetrate the thick fog had ever lived to tell the tale, but we knew that it was too thick to see through and seemed to behave as if it were sentient, reaching out towards boats in attempts to drag them in. Xavier himself was nearly snatched when the fog-like substance first appeared hundreds of years ago. He divulged that it felt as though it sucked all of the life out of one's body.

It was possible that my power might aid me. If it had even the smallest bit of conscious thought, then I could manipulate it. If not, well I would rather suffer The Mist than be at the mercy of the demon king. Especially now that Bellamy and his strange friends were assuming that Mia and Xavier had been the ones poisoning me.

I knew in my heart it had been Sterling, who had the most to gain from me being weak, but the others were inclined to believe the fae king and queen were guilty as well. If King Adbeel thought I was of little use to him, then he would sooner off me than return me to his sworn enemies. Or worse, attempt to force me to join his side.

I spent the rest of breakfast listening intently as the group made plans to prepare for the journey to where they called *Dunamis*, their form of a capital. Ever the observer, I also did not miss them address what I believed to be the Demon Realm as *Eoforhild,* which they suggested would take weeks to cross merely half of.

When the discussions ended, I told Noe I wanted to go to sleep. Bellamy seemed poised to argue that he take me, but Noe shot a wave of darkness at him that sent him toppling backward in his chair. If my mood had been better, I might have laughed along with the others or been surprised at how these beings treated royalty. Instead, I watched him fall, then turned and followed a smiling Noe through the maze of a home.

Noe took me up a set of grand stairs that looped in a spiral, appearing endless from the view below. This must have been the center tower, which had been slightly different than the others, thinner. We climbed them slowly, my eyes fixed on the sleek black marble below my feet. I nearly missed the break in steps and tripped, but Noe's strong grip held me upright.

I gave her a slight nod, an assurance that I was okay. Noe smiled widely at me as she opened the only set of doors ahead, which revealed what had to be the most beautiful room I had ever seen.

These chambers were vastly different from the majority of the home. Greenery hung from above and rested in large tan pots on the floor, which was a gorgeous raw wood. Windows made up the entirety of the walls, giving me a perfect view of the sea where the sun was beginning its slow descent, though it would be hours before it met the horizon. It almost reminded me of my chambers at the palace.

A large, round bed with sage green sheets and more pillows than I could count was pushed against the windows across from the entrance, the wooden headboard curving with the walls. Also in front of the windows was a piece of cream fabric hanging from the ceiling, making a sort of seat with a small pillow that matched the bedding.

As I turned to my left, I gasped. I had been wrong before, the room was not a perfect circle. A wall made up entirely of shelving sat there, holding enough books to be considered a small library. There was an assortment of colors and styles and sizes, each book a new tale. When I finally pulled my stare away, I noted the wardrobe and the vanity that sat against the windows as well.

I was amazed at the beauty of the space, which felt so unmistakably me, somehow. There was a distinctly earthy aura to the chambers, and it seemed to call to me. Noe walked up, a smile still on her face.

"Whose chambers are these?" I asked her, still awestruck.

"They are yours, Asher, for as long as you would like them to be." Noe's choice of words brought me out of the trance.

I pivoted to face her fully, wanting to gauge what innuendos were hidden in her words. Noe's red lips were set in a line, her eyes full of understanding. Every bit the kindness I wanted from others, but had come to not expect. In that moment I knew that this demon, regardless of feuds and bad blood, was kind.

"You think I plan to run," I stated rather than asked.

She offered a sad, knowing smile. A friend. Noe could have been a friend. In another life, under different circumstances. She had not shown me that memory to manipulate me or brainwash me into believing she was trustworthy. Everything I saw was to prove that she, more than anyone, understood what it was like to be hurt by the people who you love.

What Noe, Bellamy, and the others failed to see though, was that Mia and Xavier loved me too. Unorthodox as their methods were, it came from a good place. Above all else, the royals cared about my safety and my happiness. Before my wedding I questioned that, but now, looking back, I knew they had simply been pushing me towards my best option.

"I know from experience what you are thinking right now, Asher," Noe whispered, cutting off my thoughts. "You are hoping that they will be better when you find your way back to them. Or worse, you are convincing yourself they beat you because they love you. I went back to my father countless times over the years with the same thoughts and hopes, but the pain he inflicted never stopped, the wounds never healed."

Noe shivered at her own words, her face gaining a slightly green hue.

I thought of the wicked male, his beady black eyes so different than Noe's large hazel ones. Even his greasy black hair that hung limply from his shoulders was a contrast to her golden-brown locks. I had never consoled someone for loss or pain, so I struggled to find words that would suffice. Thinking of what I might want to hear, I spoke.

"I find that the strongest of us often have heinous histories. From the mere moments we have spent together, I can tell you are worthy of love and light and joy. I am sorry those who were supposed to give that to you did not," I offered.

Noe shook her head, "This is not about me, Asher. I have faced my evils and won. I want to encourage you to do the same. Think through your next steps wisely, because you might find you are sentencing yourself to a life of anguish for a duty that is not yours."

Her hand went to my arm, giving me a small squeeze before turning to leave. When she got to the doors, she looked over her shoulder and spoke once more.

"I know what he did to you, that mortal prince. If you were my daughter, no male would ever harm you and live to tell the tale."

CHAPTER TWENTY-FIVE

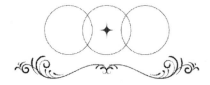

No matter what Noe said, there was no place for me here. Not unless I wanted to be tortured, brainwashed, and used.

That was the reality of the situation. These beings seemed nice, but that was because I had power they wanted. When I was a small fae barely able to walk, they attacked and mutilated me with no remorse. All because they had no use for me; I was not vital to their success. Prince Baron was not so lucky.

Which was why I was leaving.

Immediately after Noe closed the door to my chambers, I began frantically pacing, attempting to make a plan. It did not take long for me to form one, though the likelihood of success was low.

I would pack enough supplies for a fortnight, which was likely not enough, but truly all I could carry. From there I would manipulate whoever was standing watch to take me to whatever small boat they had that would be discreet but also functional.

No plans would get me through the journey past The Mist.

When I finished packing clothing in the conveniently placed satchels, I went in search for a bathing chamber. I figured the wall of books had to house it, because otherwise I would be stuck going down all of those stairs every time I had to relieve myself.

The center shelf had an indent in the wood, big enough to not be an accident but small enough not to be immediately noticed. I grabbed onto it, tugging slightly, and it gave way, swinging out towards me. Inside was the bathing chamber, which was much more Bellamy's style. Every inch of it was black marble, including the bath that was large enough to fit multiple bodies. I raised my brow, curious as to how the previous owner made use of it.

This room had curtains hiding the light from the windows, also black of course. But what struck me the most was the demon lights floating above. They were far smaller than the ones throughout the manor, looking even more so like stars than they had in Bellamy's chambers. Calling the sight captivating did it little justice.

After I finished ogling, I took another bath. My body had been through more than should be possible since my last one a few hours ago. Products of all kinds had been left in vials, the most common being vanilla scented.

Once I finished soaking, taking well over an hour to relax my growing nerves and tense muscles, I got dressed in another set of all black clothing. Then I waited until the sun set over the horizon and knocked on the door. To my dismay, Henry was on the other side.

"Hello, little brat. Pray tell what you might need?" he asked.

I rolled my eyes on instinct, but quickly flashed a smile to recover. I would need to do this without my powers, because there was no telling who might be on watch duty tonight. I could not risk taking control of more than one of them.

"Henry, I was hoping to take my dinner in my own chambers. I am in need of alone time to…process everything. Would you be able to tell me how to get to the kitchens?"

I knew he would not allow me to go on my own, but his chuckle still infuriated me. Despite Bellamy suggesting I was free to roam anywhere I pleased, his particular wording did not suggest I could do so *alone*. Stupid demon.

"Oh Asher, you wonderful, manipulative little creature. There is no world where we would set you loose on the unsuspecting residents of Haven, though I am sure you of all beings will do your best to try anyways." He smiled, leaning towards me slightly.

Was this Bellamy's new tactic? Revoke my ability to roam the grounds and send the pumpkin demon to seduce me too? I pushed past him, scoffing as I did.

"Well then please do lead the way, carrot top." My tone was not kind, but I did find myself not completely loathing Henry's company. He was entertaining to say the least. If I were to be seduced, Bellamy and Henry were not the worst males to do so. That was if I chose to forget the way the former deceived me and the way the latter attacked me.

Not that great of suiters actually.

Henry chuckled, placing his hand on my mid back. I flinched away, hating how his hand reminded me of Sterling's. The demon did not miss my reaction, but chose to say nothing while he removed his hand. More than likely, they all knew what had happened to me.

"So, since everyone seems to be privy to my life, tell me about yours," I said as Henry began walking down the many stairs.

"What could you possibly want to know?" Henry asked, his tone full of surprise.

"Everything." I shrugged, giving a shy smile. A short pause had me eying Henry, whose bewildered expression almost made me laugh.

Then, in an instant his eyes narrowed in suspicion. I just continued to smile expectantly. Finally, he caved.

"I am going on my two hundred and thirty-ninth year, I have no siblings, I enjoy riding horses, and I rather like when you pretend to hit on me in order to learn more information that you hope to exploit later on," Henry said, flashing a smirk. I clenched my teeth to prevent myself from saying something snarky in return.

Henry's orange hair was particularly vibrant under the strange demon light now that darkness had fallen. The sharp cut of his jaw cast a slight shadow on his neck, nearly hiding what looked to be a small scar. If it was enough to scar a demon, then whatever attacked had to have been gruesome.

"What cut you there?" I asked, not attempting to mask my blatant interest in the matter.

Henry stopped suddenly, then side-stepped so he was directly in front of me. I looked up into his eyes, the green irises suddenly alight with fear. I felt that if I looked into them long enough, I might be swallowed whole by the mere memory of the creature.

"There are some things that even your magic cannot manipulate, one of those is an *afriktor*. Our lands are mostly safe from creatures that feast on flesh and revel in fear, but even so, you would be smart to stay out of the Forest of Tragedies."

With that, Henry turned and continued walking, effectively ending the discussion. At least my plan tonight did not involve the forest, which was so poetically named. Though, I would take on whatever nightmare stood in the way of me and the Fae Realm.

I had to speed up to maintain Henry's quick gait, his long legs taking strides twice the size of my own. I let out a quick huff of annoyance, but he only sped up slightly, chuckling.

"So you like horses? I have never ridden before, but I hear it is exciting," I said, attempting to maintain some form of communication as we wove our way through the seemingly endless manor.

Henry ignored me, pressing on. We stopped in front of an open entryway that housed a grand kitchen, which was the same black and red that Bellamy seemed to favor. The wrap around red cabinets and glossy black countertops housed an assortment of tools and foods, with both demons and fae rushing around in what could only be described as organized chaos.

I spotted the head of the kitchen quickly, her booming voice demanding attention and obedience. Her cropped black hair and lavender eyes paired well with her high cheekbones and long eyelashes. She appeared almost ethereal, as if she were not a demon or a fae, but something entirely other. Her rounded ears made me assume demon.

"Hello, Calista," Henry cooed, causing the female to groan.

When she turned, her face was pinched in annoyance, which gave me the impression that Henry enjoyed irritating everyone rather than just me. Calista opened her mouth as if to retort, but then her eyes met mine. At the sight of me, she immediately paled, her throat bobbing as she swallowed back what I assumed was fear based on the way she stumbled.

"Um, hi, my name is Asher," I said, giving a slight wave.

My introduction snapped Calista out of her trance. She blinked repeatedly and shook her head, as if trying to clear it. Looking over at Henry did not help me. His face was perfectly neutral, bored even.

"Hello, Asher, it is so very nice to meet you," Calista said, her voice breaking midsentence.

Something was strange about the way these beings viewed me. I had always been feared, but the openness of which they showed that terror here surprised me. I knew I should take advantage of it, but I had always hated the way the fae cowered in my presence, had been raised not to capitalize on it unless in the pursuit of justice.

"You as well, the kitchen smells divine," I offered, smiling. "I was hoping to snag some food so I could have alone time, would it be okay if I took a plate as well as a bit extra?"

My attempt at flattery worked, because Calista nodded eagerly, running around to collect what looked like enough food to feed me five times over. Perfect. I hoped some of it was nonperishable, this trip would take a long time.

Calista came back with a basket full of food in her hands, a smile now on her face.

"Here you are. I added a few treats in there for you," she said with a conspiratorial tone. Then she turned towards Henry, a scowl forming. "You, go get Asher a cup of my famous cocoa. I already have an entire barrel in the dining area." Calista waved toward the door.

Henry betrayed his annoyance with the tilt of his head and the narrowing of his eyes. He stared at me for a moment, then allowed his gaze to bounce between Calista and I. She shooed him off with her hands, and finally he relented, leaving the kitchens. I let out a soft chuckle, reveling in Henry's sour mood.

Suddenly Calista cleared her throat. I turned to face her fully, the purple of her eyes bewitching me for a moment.

"I know the waters well. I implore you to rethink your plan," she whispered. I stepped back, my mouth agape. The surprise hit me so swiftly I was unable to speak. "Please, use your power on me; there is something I need to show you."

I was nervous to use my power again after my incident earlier, but her wide eyes seemed to beg me to do so even more than her words had. When I finally caved, entering her mind was easy. Like cutting through butter.

Flashes of a view underwater, so clear it was unnerving, ran through her mind. She showed me images of a squid the size of a house and fae-like beings with fishtails instead of legs. Then the image became darker, though still eerily clear. A thick, red haze could be seen in the distance, with flashes of white that seemed to charge the water. Shadows, large enough to swallow the giant squid whole, crept within the confines of the red haze.

I let go of her mind, gasping for air as if I had been holding my breath.

"The Mist," I rasped. "You showed me The Mist."

Calista nodded, her face grim.

"What are you?" I inquired, knowing that the depth she had to have been at and the clarity of her vision labeled her as other in the same way her beauty did. She sighed, grabbing for my hand and leading me towards a door. When she tugged my arm, pulling me into the room, fear crept in as well. Not mine, hers, I realized.

There was no light in the cramped space, but I could feel shelves and an assortment of items littering them.

"We can speak freely here, though how much time we will have I am unsure." Calista's voice sounded muffled despite being next to me, as if the lack of light was a ruse to hide some sort of barrier. "I am a siren."

She could not see me, but I still tilted my head in question. I had never heard of a siren before, though I was also unaware that there were other creatures besides demons and fae that existed within the realm of supernatural before today. "What is a *siren*?" I asked.

Her gasp told me that I was serving my ignorance on a silver platter.

"Those imbeciles will get you killed if they continue to keep you in the dark," she hissed. "Sirens are water folk. I have the ability to change my physical body at will, which allows me to have feet on land, but a large fin and gills in the sea. We are a deadly species, Asher. Our beauty, our aura, and our song will draw you in, then we will eat you alive."

I stepped back, my head smacking into a shelf. Sweat began to bead on my brow as I realized that I was in a dark room with a creature that had a taste for blood. I wanted to vomit, or run, or do something other than stand here next to her as she scented me. I heard Calista chuckle, a devious sound that did nothing to soothe me.

"Eating you is not my intention. I am merely hoping to shed some light on why your current escape plan is likely not the best," she said, her voice lowering to a whisper.

Relaxing a little, I thought over what she was saying. I would not admit that I was planning to flee, unsure if she used deductive reasoning based on my desire for extra food, my jumpiness, and my overall demeanor or if she also had the ability to know what I was thinking.

Calista stayed quiet as I attempted to formulate a response, but before I could, the door was ripped open, light filling what I realized then was a room for storing food. I blinked, trying to fight back the tears threatening to spill from the sudden light. Bellamy stood in the doorway, looking as if he might rip out our hearts. I forced myself not to cower, to remind myself how much stronger I was than all of them.

"Asher, let's go," he ordered.

I saw Henry glimpse into the room from behind him, his face betraying his discomfort. I chose to stay put. Bellamy let out a deep growl, causing Calista to flinch.

"Go. Now," he told her. Calista did a swift curtsy and hurried out of the small space.

I still did not move.

Bellamy scoffed, then he turned, pushed Henry back softly, and promptly slammed the door shut. As if having been in the storage area alone with a siren had not been enough, I had to be subjected to being stuck with The Elemental as well. Joy.

"You should really stop telling me what to do," I spit, hoping he heard the venom in my voice.

The air became charged, making the blackness seem alive. In fact, it felt as though small wisps of it tickled at my arms, my legs, my cheeks. My body stilled, waiting for Bellamy to speak. Move. Anything.

The silence stretched for what felt like minutes, hours, days.

Did he hope I would confess my plans? Could he be angry enough to attempt to kill me?

He could do it too, kill me. With his strange ability to block out my power and his superior combat skills, there was no competition. I would not go down without a fight though.

"If you try to kill me, I will shatter as many of your subjects' minds as I can before you take me down."

"Is that a threat, Princess?"

"It is a promise, Prince."

CHAPTER TWENTY-SIX

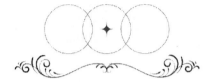

Bellamy went quiet again. I nearly offered another threat, but then he spoke.

"I would love to see you try, beautiful."

He grabbed onto my hand, interlacing our fingers as he led us out of the storage room. His free hand snatched the basket on the countertop, and I did not fail to miss the glare he shot towards a bickering Henry and Calista. The two silenced themselves as we passed by.

The moment we walked through the doors, black smoke wrapped around me. Bellamy portaled us, ripping our bodies through space until we landed in a grassy field facing a haunting forest. The chill outside was magnified by the sheer horror that dripped off the trees as their branches swung in the breeze.

"You want to act like a foolish youngling? You want to run through the forest and attempt to escape? Then please, be my guest," Bellamy said, his arms flinging up towards the tree line.

I wanted to be stubborn and march straight into the depths, but I knew I would never make it out of there alive. The demon seemed to be aware of my thoughts, flashing a triumphant smirk as he crossed his arms in front of his chest. I pictured smacking him.

"Obviously I would never go into the Forest of Tragedies, I am not an imbecile!" I yelled, not caring if I attracted the attention of a heinous beast if it meant getting Bellamy eaten.

On more than one occasion, he had acted as if I was incapable of rational thought. Yes, I was planning to sail through The Mist, but I was not doing it on a whim. I needed to go, the fae were counting on me. If I did not get home as swiftly as possible, then these demons, they would take over. They might even use me to do so.

I was still unsure of their plans for me, or for my realm, but whatever it was would not be good. My only obligation was to my subjects, and they needed me, now more than ever. I would give my life before I let them down. If Bellamy did not understand that, then he was not worthy of being called a prince.

"You would risk yourself to the creatures of this world in order to what? Run back to a mortal prince who wishes to enslave you? Torture you? Rape you?" he asked.

The words felt like an accusation more than a question. There was a tone of hurt in his voice that confused me, his face showing the betrayal that he would not admit to feeling. But his pain could not begin to match mine.

"What do you mean run back to the mortal prince?" I asked, my body beginning to violently shake. "Is he—is Sterling alive?"

Bellamy's eyes grew wide, as if just realizing his slip of words. But I knew before he spoke what the answer was.

"We received word this evening that Prince Sterling has made a full recovery," he said, his voice breaking.

I wanted to scream, to rage at him for not telling me. But now, with my engagement still intact, I was unsure what motivation I had. Did I want to go back? Could I survive a marriage to Sterling? A life of wearing a blocker and submitting to a mortal boy?

Bellamy seemed to sense what I was feeling. Or that was what I imagined the visible slouch of his shoulders and heavy release of breath meant. He was not the easiest to read when he blocked me so well.

"I am sorry, Asher, I did not mean that. But I see the way you flinch, I sense your terror when you are touched, and I know that you do not want that sadistic child as a husband. So why, Princess? Why do you insist on going back?"

"I do not want to be with him, but your kind, they kill fae. What am I supposed to do exactly? Sit back and play a good prisoner while you murder innocents? What kind of princess would that make me?" I whispered, the fight gone from me. All I could picture was the way that Sterling smiled at me as I walked towards him down the aisle. The gleam in his eye as he realized he had everything he wanted.

I closed my eyes, but the tears forced their way through, pouring down my cheeks at the same time raindrops began falling from the gray clouds above. I used to love the rain, how it made the air smell clean and crisp, how it seemed to wash away my worries. Then Xavier began having me carry out executions, and suddenly it felt like an omen. Similar to how the drops felt against my skin now.

Suddenly, I felt Bellamy's hand on my throat. I tensed under his grip, though it was rather soft, and grabbed onto his wrist. I wondered briefly why this act did not terrify me; why my skin did not crawl at the show of his dominance or the reminder of another prince's hand on my neck. His thumb slowly slid up my throat, my chest slightly grazing his stomach. The smell of cinnamon and smoke hit me, his breath caressing my ear.

"I am not the evil you should be concerned with, Princess. Your fae have nothing to fear from me. Not as you believe they do. Please, trust my words," he whispered. Then, even softer, "Please stay with me."

I shivered, opening my eyes to find his face now inches from mine. At this proximity, I noted his icy blue irises had a slightly darker hue around the rims. Each of his freckles stood out in contrast from his complexion, running across the apples of his cheeks and the bridge of his nose. His full pink lips parted slightly, and the rings on his fingers were cold against my skin as his hand slid down to my shoulder.

"How can I trust you?" I asked, my voice so incredibly weak.

Just as quickly as his fingers met my skin, they vanished, the searing heat leaving a chill in its absence. Pain flashed across his features before he turned to face the forest. He stood like that for a moment, as if contemplating his answer.

"Come with me to The Royal City, meet the king, and if you do not like what he has to say, then I will take you home," he said, his back still to me.

My mouth fell open, the surprise overcoming the suspicion. If he meant what he said, then I would not have to brave The Mist or the Forest of Tragedies or any other terrifying obstacle. He could portal me to my bedroom in the blink of an eye, but I would first have to travel with them to meet the most notoriously evil king to grace any realm. I thought it over, weighing out the pros and cons of this bargain.

Bellamy must have sensed my wavering resolve, because he turned towards me once more.

"Fine," I answered.

His eyes grew wide, and he stumbled back slightly. Then, he smiled, a deep dimple gracing each cheek. I could not bring myself to feel anything other than resignation and sorrow.

"But I want you to know, that if you do not let me leave like you have promised, I will kill you and everyone you love," I vowed. I had already lost my future—my joy—there was no use in maintaining a moral compass.

His smile faltered. I did not wait to see what he would do or say next, instead I turned around and started walking. I had seen the tree line before, and was fairly certain his home would be this direction. The thought of the dark and foreboding manor felt oddly comforting, familiar even.

Eventually, Bellamy caught up to me, and together we walked back to the manor, where he led me to my room. Before I could shut the door in his face, he handed me the basket of food. After setting the basket down on my desk, I walked to my bed and collapsed onto it, not bothering to change my clothes or even take off my boots.

I laid there, staring up at the cream ceiling until the darkness turned to light. Even then I did not move. A heaviness that made it hard to breathe settled over my chest, and I wondered if this was what being hopeless felt like.

Mia would be personally offended if she saw me like this, weak and full of self-pity. Normally I would get up and fight back simply because the idea of her being ashamed of me was enough to force me into action. I could not find that energy or willpower within me anymore.

When the sun began to descend, signaling the passing of midday, sleep finally overcame me.

***

Run!

The voice in my head was terrified.

I looked down at my bare feet. Where were my shoes? The damp grass was so cold my skin had begun to lose color. All I was wearing was a short gold slip, which was moving with the breeze. My hair was loose, providing some warmth to my back.

Why was I not moving?

A laugh that sounded like stones scraping together came from behind me. I turned to find Sterling wearing the same gold crown and outfit as he did on our wedding day, blood staining the fabric of his tunic where a hole exposed his chest. His smile showed off his white teeth, but the curve of it felt sinister, ominous.

"Sterling?" I asked, confused. "How did you get here?"

The mortal prince did not respond. Instead, he began slowly walking towards me. I tried to step back, that voice in my head screaming louder and louder to run, but my feet were stuck in place. Sterling was right in front of me.

"So beautiful, so unique, so devastating." His words were muffled, but they felt loud and all consuming, like I might hear them for the rest of my life. "You are evil, Asher, a plague on the realm. Your magic will be the death of us all if we do not contain you," he said.

It was then I saw the blocker in his hand, which he was clasping onto my wrist.

"Evil? What do you mean? I never hurt anyone with my power," I said, looking frantically around for somewhere to escape to. "I am going to save us all, that is why I am marrying you."

Even as I said it, my voice taking on a pleading tone, I did not believe it. Had I not always wondered if I were unworthy of this life? Perhaps I was the problem after all. I knew of one instance that would verify his claims, even if my magic had not been behind the tragedy.

"Oh lovely wife, how wrong you are." He let go of the blocker, rotating a gold band on my finger.

When had we gotten married? Before I could ask him, his other hand reached up and grabbed my neck. I remembered a time when he had done this before, then thought back to when Bellamy did too. The difference was stark.

Sterling squeezed, making my throat constrict. I was gasping, but I did not fight back, did not beg for mercy.

"You are a beast, a monster. But every piece of you belongs to me now, and together we will rule the world."

When his lips met mine, I screamed.

Instantly I was back in my chambers, my body shooting up as I continued to let out a piercing wail. Tears stained my cheeks and sweat left my clothes damp. Just as I registered that I had been asleep, my doors burst open, tendrils of black smoke wafting in.

Bellamy looked crazed, his eyes wide and body tensed for a fight. He saw I was in bed and darted to my side. I wanted to tell him that it was just a terror, that I was fine, but I could not seem to find my voice. His gaze raked over me, assessing every inch of my body. He scanned the room, and I wondered if he was searching for the threat. The way he poised his body was like a shield, prepared to take the blow of an unknown enemy if need be.

When our eyes locked, realization dawned on him.

I was not sure how I appeared, but I knew how I felt. Disheveled. Terrified. Broken.

So beautiful, so unique, so devastating.

A monster.

Light shone in from the windows behind me, the sun bright and high enough in the sky to tell me I could not have been asleep for more than an hour or two.

Neither Bellamy nor I spoke for a while. Instead, we sat in silence while my breathing steadied and my heart slowed. He was perched on the edge of my bed, mere inches from my arm. But he did not touch me, did not flinch from his position.

Regardless of where I went from here, I knew that I would likely be haunted for the rest of my life by those words. I was everything Sterling called me in the nightmare, there was no changing that. A part of me was fine with it. In fact, I reveled in the idea of living without a code which limited me.

Another side of me was disgusted by that. Smaller though it was, that voice was somehow louder. Damning. A life of joy and ease and comfort was not on the table, but Eternity did not seem done with me yet. I would be made a symbol no matter which of the two paths I took. My subconscious reminded me of that in my sleep.

Sterling would use me. Bellamy would use me.

Thus begged the question: which of these scenarios would I be able to survive?

Finally, Bellamy broke the silence, "Would you like to talk about it?"

I stared into his eyes, trying to see where the male I met on that balcony and the one who abducted me from my home met. Where the two converged and became one.

I wanted to believe him when he said he was not the one responsible for killing my kind, but it was as if all of my energy to feel and care and *try* had left my body. Bellamy lifted his hand toward my face, an act meant for comfort that instead left me cringing back. I saw it, the hurt on his face at my rejection.

"I will leave you to your thoughts," he rasped, his voice a broken symphony. "I have made sure no one is assigned to your door; you are free to roam if you would like."

With that he got up, walking back towards my doors. I had a feeling that he was attempting to give me space.

Just as his hand grasped the handle of the door, he turned once more to face me. His lips were pursed and eyes downcast, radiating nervousness.

"I have nightmares too," he spoke. "Maybe one day you and I will create a world where we can dream instead."

I blinked, dumbfounded by not only his confession, but his insinuation that there would be a future where we worked together. He had to know that the day would never dawn when we were a team, but still he attempted to speak that desire into existence.

Dreamers were foolish.

Disappointment fell across his face at my continued silence, but I could not bring myself to feel sympathy or regret. I could not feel anything. So I looked away, the only signal that I was alone once more being the soft click of my doors as they closed behind The Elemental.

CHAPTER TWENTY-SEVEN

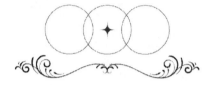

A knock came not ten minutes later. It took an embarrassing amount of energy and willpower to get up. I padded over to the doors, swinging them both open carelessly. Noe stood there, her long sleeve top and flowing skirt both a soft lavender that complimented her olive skin. Her hair was all pulled to the top of her head, messily held up by a large leather band.

Behind her, three buckets floated on a black mist, bobbing up and down slightly.

"I brought you water for a bath," she said, a smile lighting up her face. I attempted to return the smile, but by the way her face fell, I assumed I had not been quite so convincing. Nodding, I stepped out of the way, making room for her and the large buckets.

Noe waved her hand, a sideways flick that sent the black tendrils wafting towards the bathing chamber. Splashes sounded, echoing throughout the room. Neither of us moved, both prepared to submit to the discomfort—a hungry beast that would swallow us whole.

First to break was Noe, who let out a long-suffering sigh that would put any spoiled youngling to shame. The Moon crossed her arms, glaring at me.

"You are really going to ignore me now? After everything we have been through?" I openly gawked at her, the statement absurd among other things.

"I have known you for all of one day," I argued. "I have been better acquainted with local wildlife in the fae Capital."

Noe whooped, jumping up and throwing her fists into the air. My mouth hung open while I watched her celebrate as if she had somehow won.

"I knew that would get you to talk to me! Honestly, Ash, you are so predictable," she said with an eye roll. Before I could tell her not to call me that, she strutted over to my bed, plopping onto it so hard that the supports groaned in protest.

Not mine, Bellamy's. Let her break it for all I cared.

"I am not sure what you want from me, Noe," I said, standing awkwardly beside her laying form. She crossed her arms behind her head, snuggling her body deeper into the duvet. Her eyes fluttered closed, the picture of serenity and comfort.

The buckets slammed onto the floor of the bathing room as her concentration broke, the loud bang startling me. I glared down at her, wishing she would just speak her mind and leave like a normal female. Instead, she opened her eyes and stared right back, a smirk on her face.

"What do I want? For starters, I want you to start giving a damn about yourself." Noe shrugged.

I clenched my teeth to stop myself from spewing something genuinely hurtful, though many options came to mind. Tightening the hold on my mental gates, I offered no argument.

"And what else, dare I ask?" I responded, crossing my arms.

Her smirk widened into a toothy smile as she scooted her body towards the center of the bed, patting the spot she had previously filled. I hesitated, unsure of what she was planning. After a moment, I decided that playing along would get her out faster. I got into the bed, making myself comfortable, and waited for her to answer.

"Have you ever been in love?" she asked instead. I flipped my head toward hers, mouth agape and eyes wide—astonished at not only her audacity, but at her calm demeanor as well. "Oh come on. If you answer that question honestly, with at least some juicy details, then I will answer any question you ask."

An incredible offer. But answering her would mean drudging up a part of my past that I had long since hidden away in the depths of my subconscious. A painful memory that I was not confident I could survive.

She nudged my arm, eyebrows raised. What would I ask, if I could? Pertinent questions came to mind. Ones that would give me an upper hand on our journey to *Dunamis*.

Perhaps it was that fact, or maybe the way Noe looked at me as if she truly cared about what I had to say, that had me facing her and sharing a story I had never told another soul. Not even Nicola.

"There are not many rules placed upon me by the royals, but those lines that do get drawn are unmoving. One such edict is that I do not fraternize. In Academy, myself and three others would sneak away to hangout with each other, but none of us mingled romantically with those outside of our factions. I had kissed a male once as a youngling, but he left crying when I accidentally invaded his mind and spoke to him. Otherwise, I listened, confident that Mia and Xavier would find me a match someday." Noe listened intently to my story, not a hint of boredom in her eyes.

"It was not until our final year that I first made the decision to truly go against that rule," I shared, my heart racing. I felt as if my soul might split even thinking of him. "He was a Healer. Kind, gentle, intelligent. None of my friends were in that faction, so they were unaware he even existed. We had run into each other from time to time," a faint smile broke out on my face as I recalled the memory, "and once, he stopped me from splashing in a puddle when I was too distracted reading a new book."

Noe patiently listened, not moving a single muscle. I on the other hand, was a twitching mess. Fiddling my fingers, gnawing on my bottom lip, fidgeting. I could not stay still. But I pushed on, if only to get a single question answered.

"His name was Sipho. His hair was a fascinating shade of black, because it had a sort of blue hue in the light. He always fussed with it, leaving it constantly disheveled. And his eyes, they were a beautiful honey color." I gulped, the air difficult to take in. "I fell in love with him in the same way that water flows down the river—easily, naturally, as if it were my destiny."

Mental images of the male I once cherished more than anything flashed through my head. My eyes prickled, tears threatening to leak. I could do this. Share this part of myself in order to gain that precious answer.

"Sipho was brilliant and so very curious. No part of him held hatred for anyone. He did fear though, me above all else. To him, I was a terrifying and exciting anomaly. He began studying me during our...meetings, desperately seeking the results of his endless hypotheses. But not once did he treat me like a prize or a monster."

Sobs slipped through my lips as we neared the end of the tragedy. That was the problem with histories, they could not be changed no matter how horrific the ending. A wound that would not ever heal.

"Xavier found us one night. We had not met within the castle grounds before then, but Xavier and Mia were celebrating their anniversary on Isle Element, their home. I—I thought it was safe for him." Noe gasped, the first sound she made since I had started to speak. A sign she knew exactly what was to come.

"I do not know what set him off more, the fact that we were naked in my bed, or that Sipho was examining me. He was sending his power into my body, using it to form a better understanding of how I came to be. Where my powers came from when no one else in existence had them," I explained through my tears as they fell mercilessly down my face.

"In all my life I had never seen anyone as angry as Xavier was that night. He grabbed me by my hair and dragged me off the bed, completely nude, throwing me against the opposite wall. Then he—" my words cut off, a tremor running down my spine. It was nearly two centuries ago, but the wound was as raw as ever. I curled into a ball, needing to hold myself as I admitted out loud what I did to Sipho.

"Xavier burned him alive. In front of me. I screamed and cried as his howls echoed through my chambers, begging for help, for mercy. When no one came, I took hold of Xavier's mind for the first and last time, telling him to stop. But it was too late. All I could do was grant Sipho peace, manipulate the pain away and shatter his mind. I will never forget the feeling of his hand slipping from my own."

I did not speak again for a while, trying to calm my shaking body and swallow the sobs. Noe lay to my right, quietly crying as well. After some time, she began slowly stroking my hair.

"It took me decades to forgive Xavier, to understand what he meant when he said he had to do it, that it was my fault. And when I finally stepped back to look at what happened, I realized he was right. The only one I could blame was myself. I put Xavier in that position; I put Sipho in that danger; I put myself in that nightmare. So, yes, I have been in love. A brief and slow love that only served to make me realize just how dangerous I am," I concluded.

Noe went to speak, but I put up a hand to silence her. I did not need pity or justification. I did not need sorrys or condolences. What I wanted was answers, even if it was just a single one. Without thinking, I asked the first one that came to mind. The one that stuck with me even as I told that story of love and death and so much sorrow.

"What does Bellamy want with me?" I rasped, my voice sore from crying so profusely.

I hoped she would not tell a soul, but felt that she might run straight to the very demon I was inquiring about. A calculated risk, one I was willing to take. Let them think me a heinous beast, it was not as if I disagreed.

Noe shook her head, a sad expression still etched onto her beautiful face.

"I do not think anyone can answer that except for Bell. Not because I refuse, but simply because I do not know. We had all thought it was because you are powerful and could make a difference in the coming conflict. Yet, he does not seem to act as if you are a means to an end. He is more protective of you than he has ever been with anyone else. He watches you in the same way Winona watches Ranbir—as if you are a dream he never thought would come true and is terrified to wake up from," she said.

Valid as that seemed, I still did not believe she was being completely honest. How convenient that she would not know his true motives, that he would have shared them with no one at all. And her phrasing, *a dream*. Did Bellamy not just talk of dreams with me? Was this a planned speech, a diversion to avoid my questions?

I could steal the answer from her, convince her to tell me with a mere thought. I did not need permission, but what would I lose if I began taking so carelessly? I was unsure if that was a risk I would be willing to take or consequences I would be able to face.

Patiently waiting for my response, Noe hummed lightly.

"Perhaps I will save my question for another day. Would you retrieve Henry for me while I bathe?" I asked, feeling far too drained to fight for the answers I needed. Angry as well, that I had given that piece of myself to a stranger who did not possess the answers I needed.

Noe's eyes widened, "You want him to come in here with you? Alone?" She looked around the room, as if judging how appropriate it would be. Or how her prince would react to finding Henry in my chambers.

"First of all, I can tell without even using my power that you are horrified at what Bellamy will do if he finds out that I invited Henry into my bedchambers. So let me save you from the nightmares; I would like to *train* with the demon, not fuck him," I said, too much animosity lacing my words.

I fought to assuage the red-hot anger rising inside of me, taking deep breaths. Noe was kind and, for reasons I could not fathom, wanted to befriend me. She did not deserve my wrath.

Noe's shoulders sagged in relief, an amused smirk lifting the corner of her mouth. When she finally shimmied off the mattress, I had calmed down significantly. I fought to keep my anger at bay as she paused at the foot of the bed and said, "I do believe I have some bragging to do about being the first of us welcomed into your bed."

I took the pillow she had laid on and threw it with all of my strength at her. Normally, my strength was far superior to those around me, which was why I expected the pillow to smash into her. Instead, Noe swatted it away, only a soft grunt escaping her mouth. My brows pinched together as she chuckled, lightly tossing the pillow back and making a quick escape.

CHAPTER TWENTY-EIGHT

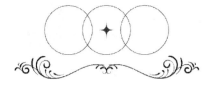

Hot water met my clammy skin like a lover's kiss, eliciting a groan from my lips. Slowly my muscles lost tension, and my body seemed to sigh in relief. My head on the other hand was a mess, refusing to allow me even a moment of peace.

Sipho came to the forefront of my mind, but thinking too heavily about him would do nothing other than breed resentment. Mostly for myself, but also that small portion of me that still blamed Xavier. Though I had forgiven him and accepted my blame, I could not help that voice in my head that pointed the finger at him.

Then I found myself thinking of Sterling and what kind of life I was running back to. Of course, those thoughts were even worse and made my temples throb. I did everything I could to push away all feelings, to make myself numb and calculating, the way Mia had always told me to be.

I thought of what training would be like, attempting to focus every bit of energy I had on what I would need to accomplish within such a short period of time. Realistically, this time with Henry would be my sole opportunity to learn combat skills, because Xavier and Mia would never allow it.

Maintaining that same train of thought until I was out of the bath was not easy, but I managed. When I was done, I padded over to the wardrobe. There were not many gowns. Apart from the red one Bellamy had purchased for me from Pino, I had only three others. One black, one lavender, and one a stunning blue that mirrored Bellamy's eyes.

Each of them was light weight with no corset, cinching just below the breasts—my preferred style. I grabbed the blue and inspected it. Everything about the dress was distinctly me. Just like the vanilla soaps in the bathing room, and the entirety of my bed chamber.

I felt the suspicion rise, but pushed it down. Shoving the dress back into the wardrobe, I grabbed a pair of soft black trousers as well as a red shirt that had buttons up the front and long sleeves. Bellamy's cloak lay on the desk, and I debated searching for another one. In the end, I decided to put on the stupid thing and leave my chambers.

He could deal with it.

I made my way down the stairs and out of the doors to find an empty hallway. Bellamy had told me as much, but it was strange not having a guard or someone waiting for me. Especially since I had asked Noe to send Henry, who I was hoping would lead the way. I was not too proud to admit that I would get lost in this maze.

Right on cue, I heard footsteps sound down the hall to my left. I leaned back on the wall next to the stairway doors, waiting for the carrot top to make his appearance. I was sure he would have a snarky comment or two, but if I could beat down my emotions about Sterling and Sipho, then I could ignore the moronic demon.

I turned my head towards the heavy breathing and pounding feet, but it was not Henry heading towards me. No, this male was far larger than Henry. Not in height, but in sheer muscle. His arms resembled small tree trunks, and veins protruded from his tanned skin, as if the muscles were forcing them to the surface. His jet-black hair and light brown eyes were nothing special, though there was a presence to him that, quite honestly, terrified me.

Looking away, I tried to seem uninteresting and bored, aiming to not draw attention. I should have known better; I had not done anything but draw attention since the day my powers manifested. The male stopped right in front of me, a scowl on his face and violence in his eyes.

Great.

"Are you that filthy fae princess?" he snarled, his voice so deep it rattled my bones. Filthy? I smelled far better than he did, nasty demon. I could have sworn I saw a flash of black smoke in the corner of my eye, but the growl from the demon's throat held my focus.

"I am filthy? Are you aware that soap should be used daily? Or do you demons believe being wretched is appealing?" I shot back in answer. So much for containing my emotions. My power thrummed in my bones, a warning to myself and a threat to the male in front of me.

"Your bastard of a king killed my father," he said, his face moving uncomfortably close to mine. I imagined that if Xavier killed his father, then it was well deserved. Likely even self-defense. I tried to convince myself not to respond, but then he spoke once more. "Your kind will get what is coming to you. Starting with you, stupid fae whore," he spit.

I smiled, devilish and every bit The Manipulator I was feared to be.

"Oh sweet, hideous beast. You sure did choose the wrong day," I said, smacking him lightly on the cheek before diving into his mind. I squeezed, softly at first, then harder. Hopefully Bellamy considered this a threat to my life, because I sure did, and I was too angry to stop now.

I wanted him to feel every second of this pain. The very hurt I had suffered time and time again. I wanted him to beg for me to stop. And then, I wanted to show him exactly what this *fae whore* could do.

His screams filled the hall, a beautiful piercing sound that made me laugh with glee. He crashed down onto one knee, ripping at his head, trying to claw my power out of him. I simply lowered myself, flashing my teeth and staring straight into his dull, brown eyes.

"You should be grateful that Xavier was the one who got to your father, because I promise that when I am through with you, burning alive will sound like a *mercy*," I seethed, running the back of my knuckles down his pinched face. Never before had I felt such exhilaration from harming a stranger, taking away their autonomy. Yet, I did not balk at this side of myself. In fact, I reveled in it.

Right as I was about to torment his mind, to pull out all of his worst nightmares and force him to live them once more just for the fun of it, my legs were swept out from under me, causing me to easily lose balance in my squatted position.

The breath whooshed out of me as my back connected with the shiny black marble, my head hitting with a crack. The demon was still on the ground, whimpering slightly as he recovered from the pain, but now another stood above me.

The black smoke from earlier, that must have been them.

Their figure was blurry, though so was everything else around me. But I could just make out their outline, smaller than the first male's, but not slight in the least. Before I could so much as take a deep breath, I was ripped up into the air by my shirt, the red fabric ripping at the shoulder.

"And when I am done with you, your throat will be raw from my cock." He chuckled. I felt his hot breath hit my face, and then heard his intake of air as he smelled me. "Then I will bathe in your blood and pray to Stella that I can do the same to your lovely queen," he added, licking up the column of my neck as if I were his next meal.

I would not cry, I would not cringe, I would not cower. If this were to be my end, then I would go out swinging. I grabbed onto his wrist and stared him directly in what I hoped was the eye, still unable to see beyond the general outline of him.

"Eat shit, demon," I rasped right as I brought my knee up and into his groin.

He let me go, hunching over in pain from my hit. My feet found the floor and by some mercy from Eternity, I stayed upright. I started sliding away, following the wall to the right where I knew my chambers were.

Reaching blindly for the handle, I nearly cried out in joy when my hand made contact with the cool metal. I turned it right as my hair was yanked from behind, pulling me backwards. The first demon had me now, his monstrous arm wrapping around my waist and his mouth coming to my ear.

"Die, fae filth."

I waited for the blow to come, begging that Eternity took me despite my sins. But just as I resigned myself to this unavoidable death, I felt a wave of power fill the hall.

I knew who it was when the demon released me, his gasp sounding from several feet back. Warm hands met my cheeks, a blot of orange flashing in my vision. Henry's arms encircled my shoulders, Ranbir's power diving into me, healing my wounds from the inside out. My eyesight cleared in time to see Bellamy stalking towards us, death incarnate.

The demons tried to flee, but Bellamy disappeared in a waft of black smoke. I turned to face the other direction, where Bellamy had reappeared right in the center of the hallway, blocking their escape. The slightly smaller one whimpered, his body shaking so forcefully that he was practically convulsing.

Bellamy sneered at the two, walking to them leisurely. His eyes said everything. He was soaking up their fear. Enjoying it. Basking in it. White light began leaking out of the larger one, who stood in a way that made me think he was poised to fight.

The demon prince simply laughed once more, eager for the challenge. And then the big oaf charged at his prince, yelling as if he were running into battle. Bellamy summoned his black fire, willing it to take the shape of a sword.

Henry left my side to grab onto the smaller demon, holding him to prevent his escape. Though based on the fear radiating from him, I did not think he would have tried. Ranbir remained at my side, his power stinging its way through me. The big demon threw out a punch, aiming for Bellamy's jaw, but the prince dodged it with ease, dancing back and then kicking out his leg.

When his foot made contact with the demon's neck, it sent him flying. The male smashed into the red wall, his arm and forehead gushing thick, red blood. I could not stop myself from grinning as Bellamy picked the creature up and head butted that same jagged cut.

The demon screamed once more, this time cut off by the black fire that sliced his head off, severing it in one clean stroke. Bellamy watched as the body flew to the ground, but my eyes followed the head, which bounced into the wall and rolled across the hallway. A shiver coursed through me.

"Ah Diazo," Bellamy whispered, walking over to the decapitated head and kicking it back towards the lifeless body. "How you and Conrad disappoint me. So many years of aiding me with the fae, and you let one measly vendetta get in the way of it all."

All-encompassing, that was what his voice was. Bellamy spoke with the type of authority and foreboding that could command armies and tear down empires.

"Did I not say that no one touches my princess?" he growled, losing his previous composure.

I realized then that Bellamy was speaking to the demon who was now audibly crying in Henry's arms. I averted my gaze from the dead body, and saw Bellamy press his hands to the sides of the demon's head, cradling it. Hiccups escaped the demon's lips, snot pouring out of his nose and mixing with the string of saliva that leaked from his mouth.

From my vantage point, I could not see exactly what Bellamy was doing, though when the demon called Diazo started screaming, I imagined it was nothing kind or affectionate like it appeared. But I was still angry, broken, and so, so tired. Which was why I reached out and shattered the mind of the male yelling in agony, whose face I now realized was being slowly burned from the inside out.

It was a simple act, just a quick thought that squeezed his mind like a boil, popping it and leaving nothing behind. The male slumped to the ground, blood leaking out of his nose, mouth, eyes, and ears. Bellamy's face whipped towards me in fury, but Henry smiled, a wicked kudos of sorts.

"As I said once before, Elemental, I am no one's but my own," I rasped, reaching my hand up to my head to verify the bleeding had stopped. Bellamy seemed poised to argue, or possibly even dote on me. However, I was in no mood to participate in this dance of his. I would thank him later. "Now if you will excuse us, I believe Henry and I have a training session to attend."

CHAPTER TWENTY-NINE

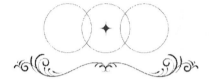

"You sure do love to piss him off," Henry said, amusement heavy in his voice.

I looked over to him and saw that he was, in fact, smiling ear to ear. I rolled my eyes, not responding as we marched forward, The Elemental practically steaming from his ears behind us, an incredibly stressed Ranbir beside him. I was still bloody, but the kind Healer had patched me up well. Enough so that I was itching to train. If this incident taught me anything, it was that I needed to learn to fight.

We continued in sweet silence for all of ten seconds before the demon spoke once more. "So do you want to talk about it?"

Yes. No. Both. I had no idea which was the correct answer, but staying quiet felt like a safe option.

Henry allowed me that space to sort through my head, a place I did not want to be, let alone subject another to. Truthfully, I was being generous by not discussing my feelings. I doubted Henry would enjoy the dark turn they had taken.

When we reached the double doors that led outside, I let out a sigh of relief. The grass was dewy under the morning light, a sign of the quickly approaching winter. A chill blasted through the air, and those holes in my top did little to combat the cold. Apparently, I lost Bellamy's cloak while I had my ass handed to me.

I ignored the discomfort, eager to learn all that I could from Henry.

At the center of the grassy lawn in front of Bellamy's manor, Henry stopped, pivoting to face me.

"Are you sure you can do this after, you know, all of that?" he asked.

There was a sincerity in his voice that made me miss the humor and snarky attitude he normally possessed. Rather than give that very attitude back to him and risk being left without a trainer, I simply nodded.

The demon eyed me for a while longer, judging for himself if I was fit to learn. Whatever he saw must have placated him, because he returned the nod and began going through what he called the "fundamentals of combat."

"Being smaller than your attacker does not mean you cannot beat them."

"Arm strength means nothing if you have no core strength."

"Your technique, such as stance and balance, will make or break you."

On and on he explained to me what it took to become a warrior.

"This is not something you will learn in one day, but it is something that you can hone as you practice. Dedication is imperative to the process, to keeping yourself alive in the face of danger." I nodded again, this time in understanding. I could do it.

Then we began.

Hours later I had decided I could not, in fact, do it.

Every part of my body ached from the exercises, slicing through me and shredding my already flimsy muscles. I had dry-heaved multiple times, each occurrence ending with Henry disappearing in a ray of light, just to return with water or food. I swallowed the liquid in a single gulp no matter how many times he brought me another, devouring the food just as quickly. After the third time I ate, I actually vomited.

By the time we got to fighting stances, I was already unsteady on my feet, my legs wobbling at the strain of keeping my body upright. How did they all do this daily? How did they survive it?

"This is lunacy," I said between the sharp pains in my side. Henry laughed, a full sound that made me think of a time when I was far more carefree. Something I would never be again.

Shaking my head to rid myself of that tragic thought, I flipped my hair over my shoulder. Henry tracked my movement, then left in a flash of white.

I waited impatiently for his return, going through the two stances he had taught me, trying to remember how to breathe properly.

"It seems my body is far superior to yours, it breathes on its own without my assistance," I had said when he told me I needed to think about my breathing. His laughs were the only response until he scolded me for not doing it correctly later.

I had angrily replied to his corrections by saying, "Perhaps you are doing it wrong, and my lungs are simply better."

With a heavy sigh, I switched to the first position, breathing deeply, channeling myself—whatever that meant.

The puff of white beside me was the only sign of Henry's return as he came up behind me on silent feet, and then the smell of cinnamon and smoke hit my nose.

Bellamy's ringed fingers grazed my neck, sending a shiver down my spine. I swatted his hand away, glaring over my shoulder at him. He flashed a smirk that did not quite bring out his dimples and held up a black band.

"Henry thought you could use some help with that unruly hair of yours," he said, his shoulders lifting and falling quickly, the epitome of casualness. A lie if I had ever heard one.

"Interesting ruse, but I am fine without your aid, thank you," I responded, once again pushing away his hand. He merely rotated his finger, signaling me to face forward. I huffed, but did as I was told. Honestly, my hair *was* becoming a hinderance.

Bellamy tugged his fingers through the locks, attempting to detangle the mess of caked blood and thick knots. After a painful few minutes of the demon prince combing through my hair, he finally finished.

Instead of putting my hair into the leather band and being done with it, Bellamy began softly massaging my head. Ecstasy rushed through me, that throbbing pain I had been ignoring finally easing up at his touch. When he felt satisfied with his work, the prince began braiding my hair back, his fingers skilled in more ways than I had previously fantasized.

"Are you okay?" he asked softly, his words as much of a caress as his fingers on my skin.

I loathed the way he affected me. How he made me want to share my thoughts and feelings, to trust in him. I forced myself not to speak, because even a crack in the dam was enough to bring the entire structure crashing down. I could not handle the flood of emotion right now.

Bellamy finished, my hair in a plait ending at my lower back. He brushed his fingers down the side of my neck before straightening the braid out. Quickly, I moved out of his reach, needing space between us to break myself from his spell.

"I am fine, just forget about it," I finally said.

"I cannot forget about it, Asher. In my mind I see their faces, two of my close companions, and I wish they were alive. Not because I regret what I did, but so I can slowly torture them. So I can make them feel my wrath," he seethed. I turned to face him, immediately locking onto his icy blue gaze. "Does that scare you, Princess?"

Subconsciously, I knew that his anger was likely due to the two demons risking his investment, his weapon. He had worked for who knew how long to obtain me, and in mere seconds, it all could have been for nothing. Yet, I could not help myself from wishing he had ulterior motives. Personal ones.

I was foolish.

"So, what next, pumpkin head?" I asked Henry, promptly ignoring the prince's question. We needed to get back to the purpose of being out in the freezing cold.

"We can continue to go over stances if you would like," the demon said with a laugh.

Dare I say he was getting fond of me? I smiled back, noticing Bellamy tense beside him, eyeing the two of us. Admittedly, it was rather juvenile of me to revel in his jealousy, but I did nonetheless.

I resumed with the two stances Henry had previously demonstrated for me, adding in a third once those were up to the demon's satisfaction. After Henry aided me with my legs when I struggled to get the new one just right, I saw Bellamy's jaw tick and his fists bunch.

Oh, he was not enjoying what he was seeing one bit.

When Henry seemed ready to end our session, an idea came to mind. Either incredibly brilliant or ridiculously stupid. Regardless, I wanted to test it out.

"Actually, can I watch you two spar for a moment?" I asked, trying to conjure a tone sweet enough that they would agree.

Not much was required in the end, because Bellamy did not hesitate to say yes, Henry's eager smile telling me he did not need to think twice either.

The two demons faced one another, Henry's height allowing him to smirk down at Bellamy—highlighting the two or three inches he had on The Elemental. Yet, Bellamy was not without his own advantages. The sheer build of him far surpassed Henry.

"Do not go crying on me when you lose," Henry said, shaking out his hands as he bounced on the balls of his feet.

Bellamy did not look remotely phased by the statement, an eerie smile splitting his lips and baring his teeth. He flicked his head to the left then the right, cracks echoing into the air. Then, as if he could sense me watching, his eyes met mine.

"There is only one thing I fear losing," he said to Henry, gaze still locked on me. Henry groaned, clearly uninterested in Bellamy's shameless flirting.

This win is for you, Princess of mine.

Then he was moving, ducking Henry's blow that should have knocked him to the ground, possibly even knocked him out.

I stood there, eyes wide, as the two of them fought. First with fists, trading and dodging blows. Then they added weapons, looking for all the world as though they were dancing, the clashing of their swords a beat like no other. The ballad of battle.

I focused, pushing my power towards them. Closing my eyes, I allowed myself to become one with their thoughts, bringing each of their strategies to me in real time. Never had I tried something such as this before, but to my surprise, it worked.

My mind flooded with their thoughts, techniques, and maneuvers. Relaxing my body, I attempted to *become* them, using it all as a blueprint for the warrior I might become if only given the chance. With little to no thought, my arms and legs started to move, a dance of my own. No part of me doubted that I was Bellamy. I was Henry. In this moment I was the two of them combined. A deadly weapon prepared to fight back, to end lives instead of always being the life at risk.

I heard the males stop their play fighting, felt their eyes land on me. And it was not until their final thought of fighting dissipated that I too snapped out of my sort of trance. I opened my eyes to find them both staring at me as if I had sprouted horns atop my head.

My hands flung to my hair, checking just in case. Thankfully, I was still hornless.

"What?" I asked, every part of my body aching and crying out. I would need to sit down soon.

"Did you just use your magic to do that?" Henry asked, astonished. I had thought it was a fairly ludicrous idea, but not impossible. Based on the way the two of them gawked at me, I figured it had not been a plausible option in their heads until now.

"My power, yes," I answered, my eyes darting back and forth between the two of them. I thought I heard Henry whisper "incredible" under his breath, but Bellamy clapped his hands together, a smile that reached his eyes and brought out his dimples plastered on his face.

Curiously, the two seemed to have very different reactions to me. Henry was in awe, his eyes wide and mouth hanging open. Surprise, that was what was written on his face, what I could sense now from him.

Bellamy though, he was not surprised, he was…proud, elated. What I felt from him was similar to a high, as if he had been the one to accomplish the task. He was not blocking me, in fact he was projecting. Over and over again he played the vision of me a moment ago.

I had my eyes closed and my mouth slightly open. My braid was whipping around with every turn, every slice. It was not a long sequence, but the furrow of my brow and the heaving of my chest had Bellamy enamored.

Some part of what I did fueled that already large ego of his, though I was unsure why. I meant to ask as much, but he spoke before I could.

"We leave in five days, Princess. Train up."

CHAPTER THIRTY

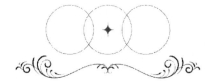

Moments turned into hours turned into days.

The night of our departure was upon us, and I was ready, dressed in a thick black tunic, matching trousers, heavy black boots, a sky-blue corset that was surprisingly comfortable despite its armor-like feel, and a cloak that shone the sparkling silver of moonlight. After slowly braiding back my hair, I left my chambers.

Henry had escorted me back from training earlier, my hot bath of the day waiting for me. So I was alone as I made my way through the corridors, but I knew my way around.

Being idle and solitary had done me no favors, which was why I found myself roaming as often as possible. Bellamy had always conjured a reason to be near me, though he never pushed for us to be alone. During meals I was regularly sat next to his spot at the head of the table. When I trained, he insisted that he could use the practice as well. He even joined

Noe and I on our walks along the beach. I never spoke more than necessary, much to Noe's dismay, opting to listen instead.

Only once did Bellamy stumble upon me when I was by myself. I had been exploring the manor three days ago, when I found a room that was entirely white. The quartz below my feet was perfectly polished, reflecting back my stunned expression at the black pianoforte that sat boldly in the center. A closer inspection showed small red designs gracing the smooth, black surface. A crystal chandelier sat above it, a single demon light floating in the center, casting rainbows across the white walls.

I walked over to the gorgeous instrument, running the tips of my fingers across the keys. It called to me, begging for my frustration to be let out in the best way I knew how.

Reading had done me no good. In fact, books only served to make me feel far more than I desired to. Which meant that was ruled out.

With everything taken away from me as of late, I thought that perhaps I deserved this moment.

I sat down on the black bench, which had an incredibly comfortable red pillow atop it. The moment my finger hit the first key, I was lost to the world.

No particular melody came to mind; instead I improvised, letting the anguish, heartache, and betrayal pour out of me. My fingers blurred as they sped, the notes climbing higher, matching how my loss had built into a mountain of pain.

Tears spilled down my cheeks, the only sign that I too could feel. My anger rose then, mixing with a sea of self-hatred so vast that I could only sob and rage like violent waves. I slammed my fingers down harder, hitting the keys with enough force to send the song into a tuneless crescendo.

A bead of sweat made its way down my back, my arms and fingers aching, but I would not—could not—stop. If I stopped, then where would I pour the glass of sorrow? Where would I set the plate of anger?

Where would I hide when the music was no longer there to shield me?

Then my sweaty hand slipped, ending the melody with a violent jolt of off-key exhaustion. Clapping sounded behind me, and I turned to find Bellamy leaning against the doorframe.

His dimpled grin and shining eyes trampled over my sadness and threatened to make me feel things that would only lead to pain.

He had said that his art studio was in the next room over, but I knew better. He had been following me.

I left the room and never returned.

Much of my time I spent burrowing down into my well of power, learning the new depths that seemed nearly never-ending. It was a strange feeling, that strength. Discovering the sheer force that I could be made it painfully obvious that I had the toxins in me for quite a long time. Though who had done it, I was still unsure.

My life had previously been spent fighting against The Manipulator. Perhaps the problem had not only been the poison in my system, but also the poison in my mind. Maybe I could be powerful and not care if it made me a monster.

After the five days of mostly eating, sleeping, and training, I had found myself numb once more. Panic attacks had shot through me, forcing emotions upon my mind that I could not take. Nightmares left me startling awake each night, an endless cycle of fatigue and stress and terror. Though Ranbir had offered tonics for sleep and nausea, I had refused the former, not wanting to incapacitate myself further. Instead, I shut down to block it all out, not allowing myself the opportunity to be sucked into the agony of my inner demons and thoughts. Now I was not quite sure how I would go back to feeling like a normal female when I found myself strong enough to fight it all.

Infinite time seemed to pass and yet none at all as I walked down the many stairs and through the hallways. No one came to collect me or guide me, though that might have been for the best. I was eager to have more time to myself before I was surrounded at all times by creatures who wished to see my kind slaughtered by the thousands. Honestly, they might prefer to see me dead rather than spend a moment with me. Maybe I would let them do it.

Before I could spiral too far into the pit of my despair, I made it to the entrance of Bellamy's manor, shaking off the horrid thought. I pushed open the two doors, welcoming the darkness that met me outside. Once my eyes adjusted, I was able to make out the group standing at the center of the grass field, a small ball of demon light glowing in the space between them.

Making my way to them, I opened the shield of sorts that I used to reign in my power, reaching for their minds. I could sense *everything* they were feeling, as if the emotions were my own. Their thoughts raced through my mind, like I had been thinking them as well. Every bit of my power told me to command, urged me to take control. I could not comprehend how small the effort was, how easy it had been since Ranbir had healed the poison from me. How very other it made me.

The Manipulator indeed.

Henry was eager to go home, his light sporadic. A mess of emotions he could not control, leaking into his magic. Then his mind veered, a mental image of me practicing today appearing.

Ranbir was calm, listing the supplies he had packed in his head. Healers always had a numb feel to them, as if my brain had been doused in morphine. Though it was much lighter tonight than it had ever been. Perhaps due to his wife who sometimes dragged him from those meticulous habits.

Lian was annoyed and slightly on edge. Her mind was ravaging through thoughts like a windstorm. Weapons, Bellamy, me, safe routes, and…royal fae guards.

Pino was a horrifying and exciting mess of the future, his mind racing quickly with images I could not comprehend. I had never seen a Tomorrow view what is to come in such a way, without touching another.

Were those memories of past prophecies? When he noticed me walking towards them in the distance, he critiqued my clothing, realizing he had not created travel worthy options for me.

My eyes swept across the group, realizing they all—apart from Calista and Pino—were dressed in leather of some sort, the matching head-to-toe outfits black with the sigil of the Demon realm in red across their chests. They also all wore red cloaks, which billowed in the wind.

Noe was eager, searching for me. I focused harder on her, trying to understand what it was about me that had her so deeply interested. But she saw me there, and her mind went blank, a flow of black clouding my internal vision.

Winona was incredibly similar in her hopeful and uplifting mental tone, though her magic was blinding where Noe's was deafeningly dark. She had a sense of awe as she watched me approach. She, along with the others, had been attending my practices and even lending aid.

Calista was practically shouting at me in her mind, that deeply rooted trepidation still ever present.

Ms. Asher, I implore you to keep your ears open during this trek. Listen to what you hear; pay attention. There is much to be deciphered from the vagueness of our crown prince and his Trusted, but the hints and the path are laid out for you, if you only open yourself to them.

Over and over the siren repeated herself, until I offered the slightest nod in acknowledgment. I wondered why she wanted me to know what the others did not. Where did her allegiance truly lie? If I could turn her against Bellamy, we could get away, I was sure of it. I would find time to make some sort of plan to win her to my side as we journeyed through the Demon Realm.

There was also another nagging thought—these beings knew how to speak to me through their mind. This was not something even I was aware had been possible, and yet more than one of them had done so already. What else did they know?

Bellamy's emotions interrupted me, coming into my awareness like a punch to the gut.

Worry. Fear. Excitement. Sorrow.

Every other feeling was instantly overpowered by tenderness and devotion. This feeling, it was similar to the way some worship gods, the way they sat at an alter and professed their unwavering support, their unending commitment. Never had I felt such deeply rooted passion. Not even when Nicola and Kafele's emotions accidentally found their way through one of my weak points, a crack in the gate. It was heavy and all consuming. This feeling was everywhere, blinding and immobilizing.

Love. Love. Love. Love. Love.

My head snapped in his direction, fueled by jealousy or curiosity or perhaps a combination of both. I wondered if it were Noe he was thinking of. But my eyes met Bellamy's, his gaze focused on me as if everyone else had disappeared, and I knew that he was either more manipulative and twisted than I thought, or the demon was in love with me.

Before I could dive deeper, a sea of black fire flooded his mind, pushing me out and back into my own awareness. I shuffled back, surprised he had suddenly realized that I was using my power on him.

"Such a nosey, beautiful thing you are," he said with a smirk on his face as I finally made it to them.

Of course, he was toying with me. He must have known I was going to try to break into his mind, so he was shooting false feelings at me.

"Prick," I said.

Bellamy's smile did not falter, but tension grew as the others looked back and forth between the two of us. Even the edge to their minds and the joy in Bellamy's could not get me to feel more than a spark of annoyance.

I had always been emotional. At least, Mia had said so. She believed I was ruled and guided by the kind of empathy that only my power could give someone. I had thought it a compliment, that I could feel so deeply and care for others to the extent I did. The queen disagreed, vehemently so. That was the first time I learned what it took to rule, the amount of indifference and coldness that came with the position of queen. From that day forward I found myself less and less interested in the throne, what it meant to be the one seated there.

Would I have to watch unperturbed as my subjects suffered? Mia seemed to think so. Standing here feeling the stress of those around me, hearing their concerned thoughts, and understanding that they saw me as a potential threat to their beloved future king, I knew she had been right.

To feel that deeply, to take into consideration the opinions and wants of those around you, it made you weak. My emotions surrounding Sterling were what led me here, trapped and surrounded by enemies. Now, those very same emotions might sway me into becoming comfortable around these dangerous beings. Or worse, wanting to please them, as I had so often with others. I could not afford to care about what they thought of me.

I was hollow.

"A dashing prick?" Bellamy asked, clearly enjoying himself.

I rolled my eyes and crossed my arms, probably looking juvenile doing so, but not caring enough to offer a retort. The prince laughed, husky and low. A quick look around the circle told me he was absolutely the only one who found humor in my foul mood.

Good.

I dared a glance at Calista, but she was talking to Pino, the two of them having a sort of hushed disagreement if their tense bodies and sharp hand gestures were any indication. Noe and Lian were also huddled together, watching Bellamy and I out of the corner of their eyes and attempting to maintain a separate conversation. The others more blatantly watched, stared even, as I went head-to-head with their prince.

"Regardless, this prick has some rules for you."

That got my attention. I snapped my head back in his direction, glaring up at his ridiculous dimples and freckles. Bellamy was like a carnivorous flower. Pretty and enticing, but deadly.

I thought back to my own reflection in the mirror of my bathing chamber. My long brown hair fell in loose, messy waves down my back. It was thick and prone to tangling, nothing like Noe's golden-brown hair which was straight and silky. My large eyes were the color of storm clouds and angry waters. I did not have a sharp jaw despite my high cheekbones. My full lips were often red and chapped due to my nervous habit of biting them. My body was soft, rounded where others were straight.

At no point did I ever consider myself ugly though. Even after Sterling came along and Mia insisted I eat less, I still knew that I was pretty. There was one male who told me I was beautiful rather often, though he usually followed the compliment with "despite the fact you are terrifying." I had had many casual romances that mostly involved the other enjoying the thrill of being with me, but each openly expressed their attraction to me as well.

That was the stark contrast between Bellamy and I. My beauty highlighted the danger inside of me. Behind the soft exterior there was a fear-inducing coldness. Farai had said it was in my eyes and mouth, my stance, my attitude. I was a walking nightmare to most.

Bellamy's beauty hid the danger he presented. One look at me told someone immediately that I was a threat. Looking at The Elemental was different. There was kindness in his smile, innocence in his dimples, and seduction in his eyes. The evil within him was deeply masked, concealed within his soul.

His heart.

"And what might they be, Your Highness?" I asked, my tone flat save for the bit of sarcasm I could muster.

Henry let out a cough that sounded suspiciously like a laugh, and from the corner of my eye, I saw Ranbir's hand fly over his mouth in surprise. I assumed I looked disrespectful, and likely rude, but that was because in their minds Bellamy *rescued* me. In truth, he abducted me from the only home I had ever known. He had done me no favors.

Bellamy's smile did not waver. As he spoke, I could sense his amusement, that feeling of warmth pouring out of him.

"You will not venture out on your own," he began, taking a step closer to me with each recitation of his so-called rules. "You will not harm any of us unless we are attempting to hurt you. And most importantly," his voice darkened, the eye contact he maintained giving off a sense of seriousness that was not there before. "If you are in danger, you *will* fight for your life."

We were toe to toe now, as we often seemed to end up. I wanted to claim he was ridiculous for even suggesting that I would not fight back, but I knew it was a lie. Days ago, I had fought for my life on instinct, but with time to rest and think I had come to a startling realization. Dying, especially when the outcome of survival would be Sterling, did not seem so horrible.

Running away to a far-off place and being free, that was the dream I had now. The only scenario that was not in play, the fate I was robbed of the second Sterling walked into my life. Death, it could take me there. Eternity might not accept me back, but that did not mean my afterlife would be horrible. Whatever existed beyond my final breath, whatever lay ahead of my end, perhaps it would be the bliss I was starved of during this lifetime.

Death, it would be a kindness.

Instead of admitting what he already knew, I just repeated him, my voice a bored monotone, "I will not venture out on my own. I will not harm any of you unless you attempt to hurt me. If I am in danger, I will fight for my life."

Before he could argue with my lack of enthusiasm, a shadowy figured appeared to my right. I jumped back, screaming at the barely corporeal form.

Henry laughed as the shadow took shape, forming legs, arms, a head.

"Cyprus you truly are the worst." Lian scoffed.

My jaw nearly hit my feet as the false guard materialized in front of me, a smile lighting his features. Cyprus' shaggy brown hair ran past his shoulders, shaking with him as he chuckled. Gray shadows still swirled around his russet cheeks, as if they were not ready to fade. When I backed up further, I hit a solid form. Turning, I saw nothing, causing me to yelp once again.

This time everyone in the group let out laughs as Luca, the other guard who pledged himself to me nearly a fortnight ago, seemed to become visible before my eyes. His blonde hair and blue irises brought his youthful charm into view, but his skin seemed nearly translucent rather than the cream color I remembered it as before.

"Hello again Your Highness, it is wonderful to see you once more," Luca said, bowing at the waist. He, too, had that drawl that the demons possessed.

As he straightened, the color of his skin returned. I was baffled, my mouth slightly open and eyes wide. What could I say? The two of them had appeared out of nowhere, as if flashing into existence. It seemed different than portaling. "Allow me to formally introduce myself, I am Luca Braviarte."

"What are you?" I asked, not knowing how to go about asking kindly. Luca did not seem upset, or even fazed. Instead, he smirked, eyes alight with a sort of mischief I had not seen within the palace.

"I am a *wraith*. I believe your fae call us ghosts." He shrugged. I was briefly stunned into silence once more.

Ghosts were terrifying. Every tale told in my realm about ghosts said they were evil creatures that haunted the living. That they were dead.

"So, you are not alive?" I asked, once again being quite insensitive.

I tried to remind myself to be more thoughtful in how I spoke to him, though I was unsure whether or not I would be able to at the rate this conversation was going.

"Last I checked I am very much alive," Luca chuckled.

My brows pinched together as I attempted to understand what the *wraith* was saying. He was a ghost but was somehow alive? He must have sensed my confusion, because he clarified.

"Wraiths are born with the ability to blend into our surroundings. We do not go invisible per say, though it is quite similar. Ghosts are a twisted version of a wraith, a lie created to isolate us from the masses I imagine."

"But," I said, turning towards Cyprus, "you do not seem as though you blend at all. It was as if you turned into a shadow."

Cyprus was equally amused at my line of questioning. He held up a hand, palm facing the night sky. Though the demon light did not allow for an easy view, I was able to make out a sort of black mist leaking from his skin. In a mere moment I could no longer see his hand at all.

Both mesmerized and horrified, I took a step closer. Cyprus did not seem to mind. He gently took my hand and placed it under his, allowing the mist to fall onto my skin. It was ice cold, but otherwise felt like air.

"I am not a wraith, I am a *whisp*. We are similar in many ways, seeing as we both function as fairly great spies." At that I raised my eyebrows, surprised he would so openly admit to being a spy. Then again, they all appeared to be relatively confident that I was not going anywhere, made all the more clear by his accent being revealed to match Luca's.

"I am able to turn my body into black mist, sort of like a shadow. It comes in handy at night more than in the day, but I can make myself unseen at any time," he explained.

Then, Cyprus lifted my hand through his, as if it were not there at all. I gasped, equal parts impressed and intimidated.

The whisp flicked his arm, causing the black mist to vanish and his hand to return once more. Both corners of my mouth turned up slightly, unable to hide the awe. Cyprus smiled back, wider than before, and leaned down to place a kiss on my hand he still grasped.

"Luca is right, it is amazing to see you again. I am Cyprus Papatonis, eternally at your service." I blushed at his flattering statement, which sounded far more inappropriate than it had when spoken by Luca.

"Okay that is enough introductions," Bellamy growled, grabbing onto my hand. Cyprus let go reluctantly, winking at me as Bellamy pulled me back to the other side of the circle. I rolled my eyes, but did not argue. If he wanted to act like a jealous idiot then that was his prerogative. No part of me had the energy to care, as my mind still raced through my impending doom subconsciously. "Now that we are all here, lets head out."

CHAPTER THIRTY-ONE

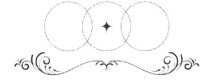

"Why not just portal us there?" I asked no one in particular, Bellamy's hand still wrapped in mine and guiding me forward.

I attempted to tug it back, but he only tightened his grip ever so slightly. The idea of traveling on foot halfway across the Demon Realm——Eoforhild——did not sound appealing in the least, especially in the cold.

Noe appeared at my side, her red cloak blowing back in the light wind. She was in good spirits as we made our way across the grass towards a large wooden structure in the distance. In fact, all of them moved with excitement and energy, a bright ball of light following each of us as we walked.

"We prefer to ride horseback. Ranbir and Winona are both research specialists. Ranbir studies the lands and Winona the creatures of the realm. They are likely the most well versed on their respective fields than anyone else in the world," Noe explained with a proud tone. "Bellamy actually introduced them to each other, hoping they would work together to catalogue information for him. The sex started fairly soon after," she said, throwing a wink at the pair.

"That is me, match maker extraordinaire," the demon prince teased.

Ranbir huffed, a blush creeping onto his dark skin. Henry whooped, smacking the Healer quite firmly on his shoulder, the loud whack echoing in the night. Luca and Cyprus burst into laughter as Winona shot a beam of light at Noe, nearly sending her to the ground. My arm shook slightly, and I saw from the corner of my eye that Bellamy was also laughing softly.

"Really, it is because you cannot portal into Dunamis, there are wards to prevent it," Henry added. "It is also dangerous for the horses, a risk I am not willing to take. That would leave us with no transportation or means of travel," he finished. I nodded, though I still felt as if traveling through this realm was a bad idea at best.

"Plus, the journey allows me to collect items that are wonderful for medicinal purposes," Ranbir said, sifting through his satchel. "Though I cannot say I am fond of the way horseback tosses around my vials."

Winona giggled, her eyes never leaving her husband's face.

I felt a pit grow in my stomach. I had never been on a horse before. A bead of sweat dripped down my back in spite of the cold as a faint neighing could be heard ahead.

When we were only a few steps away from the wooden structure, the ball of light moved, stopping just in front of Henry. The demon opened his hands, bringing them together over the iridescent sphere in a loud smack. At the impact, the light shattered, pieces floating to each of us. Bellamy urged me on, our respective beads following us to light our way.

I tried to swallow, but the lump in my throat refused to allow me that kindness. Sheer terror overcame me with the thought of being atop a creature so large. At that I recalled how Xavier had always told me that fear was inevitable, how pointless it was to run from it.

"Only fools deny and ignore something as inescapable as fear, Ash," he would state. **"What really matters is how you take that fear and *overcome* it."**

I would overcome this. If I could control the minds of all in attendance of my introductory ball while likely poisoned, I could ride a horse.

We rounded the corner then, and came upon the open entry of stables. Inside were at least a dozen horses, which was good because with each of us riding alone, we would need nearly all of them.

Bellamy's grip on my hand tightened while he pulled me past each of the stalls, the horses huffing at us when we passed as if displeased by the idea of not being picked. I chuckled lightly, enjoying the amount of personality the beasts had. At least I would die laughing. We stopped at the very last stall, where the sight of the horse made me gasp.

"She is beautiful, right?" Bellamy whispered, a small smile forming on his face. I nodded, my mouth agape. The mare was silver from head to toe, matching perfectly to my cloak. Her eyes were the same startling color, glowing in the night with the help of our demon light. "I had Pino make a cloak to match, I thought you might enjoy a break from all of the gold."

I tensed at the comment.

Gold. My least favorite color. Such a small gesture to anyone else, but to me, the idea of not wearing it was a dream. As soon as I got back to the Fae Realm, I would once again don the royal color. But, for now, Bellamy had ensured that I remained comfortable.

No, it was more than that. He had found a way to make me feel like *someone*. I was not a princess, The Manipulator, or a pawn. I was Asher, and that meant I could wear anything—*be* anything. Even if only for the length of this trip.

I tried to tell myself that he was tricking me. The horse, the perfectly decorated chambers, my clothing, all of it a bribe for my complacency and my forgiveness.

Yet, something inside of me hummed at his nearness, at his words. A part of me felt lighter, somehow. For the first time this week, I found myself smiling, truly smiling, and meaning it with my entire heart.

"Her name is Frost," Bellamy said. That got my attention. In the Fae Realm, we considered frost to be the antithesis of ash. The opposite of me.

Bellamy's gaze left my skin tingling. He was waiting. Hoping to gauge the way I reacted to the name choice, I imagined. Whether he was insinuating that I was darkness incarnate or perhaps making the analogy to convince me that he and I were the same, I was unsure. Either way, I had no interest in indulging him.

Instead, I slowly extended my arm, hand aiming for the head of the silver beast. She seemed docile, though I could sense a fire within her, those piercing eyes reading me.

Just like I read others.

I halted my movement just before I touched her, fingers and silver coat mere inches apart. I would let her meet me here—choose me rather than have me forced upon her.

Seconds ticked by, but I did not grow impatient. As always, I was aiming for acceptance, but this time it felt deeper. Frost was a different sort of hope. Jasper once told me that animals were astute judges of character. They could easily identify an enemy, but also a friend. Trust was something earned with animals.

The Single had said that while in his tigris form, he was able to *see* auras. Mine, apparently, was a pure white, like the midday sun on a bright summer day. If Frost rejected me now, I would have to smack Jasper for his lies.

Finally, Frost reached her muzzle towards my opened hand. She was soft, impossibly so. I pet her gently, a gruff exhale of breath, similar to a rough purr broke free of her mouth. I smiled, enjoying the way the horse nuzzled her nose further into my hand. In response, Frost came closer, licking my face.

Bellamy burst into laughter at my disgusted expression when I recoiled. The demon prince was bent over as the amusement shook his body, hands gripping his stomach while I wiped my cheek. Frost started lifting her front legs off the ground, huffing at the two of us.

"She either really likes you or the poor thing could use a little more salt in her diet," Bellamy said once his chuckles died down.

"Why salt?" I asked, ignoring the amusement still lighting his eyes.

I once again began petting the mare, giving her a warning look that hopefully conveyed my distaste with her choice of affection. I could gladly scratch her all day, but the licking just would not do. Her long tongue was not a particularly welcome feeling.

"She could be licking you to taste the salt on your skin." He shrugged. It was an interesting fact, and one I was surprised the prince would know. I was sure Henry would hold an extensive knowledge of the species since he mentioned they were an interest of his, but Bellamy had never mentioned them. Not that I had asked.

I knew so much about the Bellamy I met in The Capital, but I doubted anything he told me then had been true. Though his dishonesty and carefully constructed traits had been no fault of mine. While a part of me—the smarter portion—desired to maintain that distance we had forged, another wanted to know him.

And yet mere moments ago I had told myself that he did not deserve to know me.

Despite all that had transpired between us these last few weeks, did I deserve to know him? Was I any better than the demon at my side? A strange look passed over Bellamy, and I suddenly felt a sort of prodding at my power, like a tug. Then I realized it was Bellamy projecting his thoughts, practically screaming in his mind.

Pondering my next action for a moment, I decided it would not hurt to indulge my curiosity, especially when these beings repeatedly surprised me with their extensive knowledge of my powers. An understanding that went beyond even my own.

I would give anything to know what is going on in that beautiful head of yours.

Bellamy's thoughts rang through my ears as if he had spoken them aloud. Just as Calista's had. Just as Noe's had. I stared at him, assessing the playfulness in his mental tone and comparing it to the desperation etched on his face. He meant those words. Possibly had contemplated them for a while. I weighed my own response.

Answer one of my questions, and I will tell you.

I could lay myself bare if it meant gaining information, I had offered the same to Noe. Not that thinking of my past hurts would help me at the moment. While he considered my offer, I thought up a question that would aid me during this journey. I had conjured a fairly decent question when he tugged once more. This time, I did not hesitate to grab onto his mind.

What would you like to know, Princess?

Rolling my eyes at the nickname, or insult, I hurled my question into the black void, watching his face as he listened.

Why do you bring fae here?

I regretted my choice immediately, wishing I had opted for a more direct phrasing—specific, impossible to work around. I needed answers, not hints and riddles. Despite how little I knew about Bellamy, one thing I could be sure of was that he would only offer the bare minimum of information. He was secretive, hesitant to trust. The thoughts and truths he guarded and hid would not be found easily.

"Let's get you mounted, and when we are all moving, I will tell you," he spoke, opening Frost's stable door. The nerves came back in full force, making my breath hitch and my palms sweat. I could do this. I was smart, strong, powerful. I could ride a horse.

I watched as Bellamy hooked a black saddle onto Frost, the silver of her hair glittering in comparison to the dark leather. When he was finished with the complicated straps, tugging rather roughly to make sure it was secure, the demon prince waved his hand towards Frost. I slowly stepped towards the horse, patting her neck lightly to stall.

If he knew what I was doing, Bellamy did not let on. Instead, he nodded to me, moving across the stable walkway. His ball of light followed, highlighting a jet-black horse that was not only larger than Frost in height, but in sheer size. I wondered briefly how he would manage to get atop the horse, then decided that I should probably focus on how I was going to get onto Frost. I turned to face her once more, taking in a deep breath.

Then I did something I had never tried before—I reached out for Frost's mind. Mia told me many years ago that it was likely I would be able to manipulate any mind, even a common mouse. But she also told me it would be a waste of my energy, which before seemed so finite. Not like the well of power that thrummed in my chest now. Somewhere deep in my subconscious a nagging, gnawing thought tried to free itself. I ignored it, focusing instead on the horse in front of me.

When Frost felt me invade her senses, she became frantic, jumping and kicking. For a split second I let the panic sink in, thought perhaps I had harmed her in some way. But instinct took over, and soon I was ordering her much as I would any being.

Stay calm.

The horse settled, my words soothing her immediately. A sense of guilt came then, but I pushed it back. I would get nowhere with such an annoyingly persistent conscience. Breathing in and out slowly, pacing my own racing heart, I once again spoke in the mind of the mare.

Stay still. You trust me, and I trust you. We are a team, Frost. We will do this, together.

The horse let out a small huff, as if in agreement. I nodded to her, offering a small smile before hooking my foot onto what I assumed was some sort of footrest. I had seen palace guards do this time and time again, even Xavier had mounted a horse in front of me once or twice.

I allowed myself a brief glance back at Bellamy. He was still arranging the saddle, his back to me. This would be my only chance to avoid embarrassment. As a final precaution, I reminded Frost to stay still.

I pushed up with my left foot, grabbing onto the saddle with both hands. Using every ounce of my strength to get myself onto the horse, I hoisted my body up. Too much strength, I realized a moment later. My chest passed over the saddle, my stomach following suit. Then my hips hit the leather with a loud smack, torso slamming into Frost's side. She stood her ground, only letting out a short grunt of disapproval. I laid there, barely on the horse at all, while the blood rushed to my head.

How in the Underworld was I to get down? Or even right side up? I quickly became light-headed as I attempted to grab onto the rope hanging from the saddle. No amount of pulling was working, though.

Stuck. I was completely stuck. Like a bumbling fool.

Hands gripped my ankles, a chuckle sounding behind me. Oh please, no. I murmured a quick plea for him to just let me sit there and wilt, but it was no use. Bellamy was tugging my legs down, sliding my body slowly off of Frost.

His hands moved to my thighs, branding my skin through the thick trousers. Then he had me by the waist, his grip strong and unrelenting. One moment I was a dead fish on the horse, the next I was in his arms, a dimpled smile flashing down at me.

"I had a feeling you would not know how to ride, but I did not expect you to fail so miserably at mounting poor Frost," Bellamy teased.

I scowled up at him, picturing my fist connecting to that face again. A chuckle to our right caught my attention, my head whipping towards the noise. Anger filled me to the brim—the most emotion I had felt since I was attacked—when my eyes met a pair of amused green irises.

Henry stood at the opening of the stall. The second our gazes connected he began laughing so violently that tears streamed down his face.

Without thinking I called to Frost's mind.

Frost, I think Henry could use a bath.

I sent over an image to her, willing the horse to obey. Just like that, Frost leaned forward and rained spit down onto Henry's face. I burst into a fit of laughter of my own, howling at Henry's stunned expression.

"Good girl, Frost," I said between chuckles. Bellamy's own laugh rang through the wooden structure as he set me down. Henry attempted to wipe the spit onto his black and red leathers, but the fabric would not soak up the thick saliva.

I watched in glee as Henry stomped away to find something to clean himself off with. When he was out of sight, I stepped up to Frost and whispered into her ear, "That is my girl." Scratching behind her ear, I peeked over at Bellamy to find him watching me with that smug smile still gracing his face.

"Impressive, the way you manipulated Frost's mind. I knew that you two would get along," he said, dipping his head towards the mare. I froze, the shock of him knowing quickly fading to annoyance. Of course, he knew. The damn demon knew everything.

I rolled my eyes, once again stepping onto the footrest of sorts, hoping this time I would be successful. Bellamy closed the space between us, offering me his hand. Oddly enough, I took his help, shocking even myself. Together, we successfully got me onto the horse.

I beamed down at him, proud that I had at least done some of the work. He smiled right back, the picture of joy. In his eyes there was something more, an emotion I could not, and would not, allow myself to understand.

"Now, I know that power of yours can make the process of riding easier, but you do not have to use it. Henry worked tirelessly with Frost to make sure she was perfectly trained, and she will listen to your vocal commands. She is incredibly intuitive and intelligent, just hold those reins and tell her what you need of her," Bellamy explained, petting Frost as he did. He brought his nose close to hers, looking into her big, silver eyes. "Keep her safe Frost, she is important to me."

Below me, Frost stomped, moving her head up and down as she huffed at him. Those actions satisfied Bellamy enough to warrant a smile, and then he was off, heading towards the black horse across the way. Ignoring his comment to Frost, I watched as he effortlessly mounted the large beast, winking at me once he was up. I rolled my eyes again, then closed them.

I could do this.

Henry appeared once more, face clean and mood deliciously foul. I was pleased that I had successfully annoyed him at least. He walked up to Frost, grabbing onto the straps on her head, and led us out of the wooden stables. When we were back in the open air, I let out a sigh of relief, this was not so horrible.

Yet.

Bellamy and his horse came trotting from behind, stopping beside me. His horse was bigger than I first estimated, towering over Frost by well over a foot. The prince saw me assessing his stallion and tilted his head to the side.

"Lucifer might be bigger and stronger than Frost, but she is far more cunning and fast. You are safe and in wonderful hands. Or, well, hooves." He shrugged. I merely nodded, biting back my laugh, not wanting to feed his already inflated ego. As the others began emerging, tugging the straps of their own horses, I swallowed the rising fear.

CHAPTER THIRTY-TWO

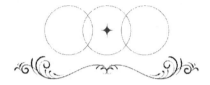

The group gathered once more outside of the wooden stables, eight of us atop horses. It did not escape me that Bellamy and I were the only two who rode steeds that were not brown. A message given and heard without having to be spoken aloud.

The demon prince circled our party, doing a final assessment before we departed.

I caught sight of swords securely strapped to each of them, everyone prepared for the worst. As Lian and her horse trotted towards me, I noted that she seemed to have more weapons than the others. I raised my brows, eyeing her stock. Lian laughed at my assessment.

"I am Bell's swordmaster. I maintain all weapons and I train every new recruit in his army with weapon work. You will rarely catch me unarmed," she said with a wicked smile.

Surprise left me without words. I had always seen her with some sort of weapon since meeting her, but she now was armed to the teeth with two swords, multiple daggers, a bow, and a quiver of arrows strapped to her horse.

"Here," she said, grabbing one of the daggers. Lian urged her horse up to Frost, and quickly grabbed onto my leg. I startled, trying to tug out of her hold, but she simply gripped me harder. I stilled when the realization of what she was doing hit.

Lian had strapped the dagger onto my thigh. The sheath was black with three red circles and a star in the center of the middle ring—the demon sigil. When she finished securing the straps, I removed the weapon, assessing it.

It was a gorgeous blade, the hilt the same silver as my mare. Red and black writing, jagged and sharp, covered it. Some sort of language that I had only ever seen once, older than even the demons perhaps. The same runes that graced the walls of my low level room, of my blocker. The sight of it sent chills up my spine.

"I cannot possibly take this, it is yours. Plus, your prince would not appreciate you arming me," I said, trying to offer the hilt of the blade to her.

The clothes were a necessity, but the dagger, though I wanted desperately to have one for my own safety, was not. No, this was something else. An unsettling coincidence that made my stomach turn.

Lian shook her head, directing her horse away from me. "It was made for you, Bell just had me hold onto it."

Made for me? That was enough to silence me. I held it in my hand, gripping so hard my fingers ached, and called onto my powers. No change.

So it was not the same magic.

As if the sound of his name was a pull, Bellamy appeared at my side, Lucifer nudging Frost's head in hello. I did not bother to ask about the blade when I knew he would not answer. If it did not stifle my powers, then I would take it, though I would not let my guard down while wielding it.

Calista and Pino approached Bellamy and I, the former holding my gaze. Neither of them were on a horse, neither held a satchel as the others did. They would not be joining us, I concluded. Behind them, Luca winked at me before disappearing into thin air. Clearly the wraith was not coming either.

Right on cue Bellamy spoke, confirming my suspicions.

"Be on guard and expect them to come. Your duty is to Haven, to keeping those who reside here safe. Do not fail," he ordered, his voice bleak and demanding. The Tomorrow and the siren nodded, faces unreadable. With Calista staying behind, I lost my chance at an ally among the group. What had she called them?

His *Trusted.*

Pino walked up to me, reaching a hand up to grip my own, giving a tight squeeze.

"When we meet again, I have quite a bit to tell you of your future," he whispered. To my left Bellamy let out a low growl—a warning. Pino merely tsked, waving a hand of dismissal at his prince. "You will return, Princess."

I raised my eyebrows, suspicion and curiosity battling inside of me. Calista nodded at Pino's side, the two of them offering no real help other than vague promises.

Bellamy huffed, muttering a quick encouragement to be safe, and then clicked his tongue. The eight horses all quickly obeyed, Lucifer and Frost vying for the lead. Henry must have been an excellent trainer, judging by the way that each of them followed commands.

We rode slowly, despite Bellamy's previous eagerness. For my own benefit, more than likely. Would that annoy the others? Make them resent me for the longer travels? None of them seemed to be uncomfortable with the pace, or in any sort of hurry, but I did not want to risk upsetting them. I would prefer sleeping peacefully rather than with one eye open.

"Have you ever heard the story of how the Fae Realm was split?" Bellamy asked, Lucifer and Frost nearly touching as we rode side by side. I did not bother to hide my confusion at his question, which had made no sense whatsoever. As per usual.

"It has always been that way," I responded, wondering where he might be going with this. Should he not be answering my question rather than speaking in riddles? I asked him as much mentally, letting my distaste sprinkle into my tone.

"I am answering your question," he countered aloud. I did not, for a moment, believe this odd line of questioning would tell me anything about why he chose to bring fae here. Why they willingly stayed.

Or were they somehow prisoners too? Abducted and brought across the sea, left on a coastal village that was utterly inescapable. It would not be the first time he had done it. Yet…I looked back at Lian and Ranbir, the two of them so comfortable in their places here. In Haven. With Bellamy.

"You did not think it strange that there were five islands, perfect for splitting factions and celebrating royals? Did you think gods did it?" Bellamy continued, inquiring as if he knew the correct answer. I hesitated then, trying to understand what he was insinuating.

"Of course not. The fae do not fall to their knees for gods or worship at the altar of an all seeing one. We follow the universe from which our powers came. We acknowledge the gods, respect them even, but Eternity, that is what we pray, swear, and submit to," I answered, ignoring the first half of his question.

Yes, it was strange that the islands were so perfectly made for us, but was that not divine creation? It was not so hard to believe that the ethers that were responsible for the existence of gods, fae, and the world were also capable of making our land suitable for our future needs.

Perhaps it would seem irrational if not for the power that coursed through my veins, through Bellamy's.

"It was none of those things that made the Fae Realm as it is. Your queen did it," Bellamy said, disdain and sarcasm heavy on his tongue.

I stilled, my eyes narrowing at the allegation. Here it was, the motivation behind his story. Turn me against Mia and he would have me, ripe for the taking. He knew that my family, the royals, were the thing that tugged me home the strongest. I wanted to protect my subjects and to make it back in time to watch Nicola be wed, but Mia and Xavier were the true reason I desired to go back. I owed them at least that much.

"And why, demon, would she want to do that?" I hissed, an accusation more than a question.

I wanted to scream, to tell him that he would never convince me that they were the evil he deemed them as. Poisoning me, lying to me, hurting me for their own sick pleasure. What would he say next? I sat up straighter as Frost moved at an unhurried pace, prepared to argue with him. But Bellamy, for all his faults, was not quick to anger. With me, at least.

"Long ago, the greatest Earth to ever be born was named heir to the lands of the fae, Betovere. A beautiful place, with an even more beautiful soon-to-be queen. She was magnificent, with hair the color of a flame and eyes like ice," Bellamy began.

A quick look behind us told me I was the only one skeptical of this tale. Lian and Ranbir were engrossed, eyes trained on Bellamy as he spoke. Noe, Winona, Henry, and Cyprus all listened casually, as if they had heard the story a hundred times.

"Her parents had found her a betrothed that was most likely to produce younglings that would far surpass even her power. The Fire, wild and untamed, was eager to prove himself worthy of being king when the princess's parents passed on unexpectedly. The queen knew this, so she used his desire for acceptance against him. She convinced him that splitting Betovere would strengthen the fae. If they could ensure that factions did not mix, then they could maintain the power within each." Without realizing, I had leaned towards Bellamy. His voice had lost its raspy tone, taking on a captivating timbre. I was unable to look away.

"After extensive planning, the two rose before the sun on one fateful day. The queen channeled all of her power, which was said to have sent waves of energy across the world. When she slammed her fist into the ground, Betovere split. Death wreaked havoc on the fae as giant cracks and flooding water awoke them. And when the ground stopped shaking, fae found themselves separated from their loved ones, ripped from their homes and the lives they had built."

Lian let out a soft sob, tears streaming down her face. Henry looked furious, as did the rest of the demons in the group. But it was Ranbir, his previously stoic face contorted in sorrow and pain, that caught my attention.

"Slowly, the newly crowned royals implemented designated areas, Isles as they would be called, for each faction. If fae had found love outside of their faction, then they would be outlawed from being together. Families were torn apart, never to be whole again. Fae without power disappeared throughout the years, and soon everyone seemed to forget the past, to settle into their new normal," Bellamy whispered, his eyes glassy as the story came to a close.

My mind was begging me to ignore him, to see the story for what it was, a lie. A fabrication meant to sway me. But as their emotions and thoughts crept up on me, seeping through the holes in that golden gate that held my power in check, I found a tear sliding down my own cheek. Mia and Xavier were kind. They ruled with love for the Fae Realm and its inhabitants. How much had they asked me to give up just to ensure the safety of the fae? Why would they do so much harm to those very same beings?

"You asked me why I bring the fae here, and I assume you also are curious to know why they desire to live in Haven. The answer is simple, laid out for you quite plainly in that piece of your history that is hidden from you all. The fae here seek joy and love," Bellamy said, his words laced with both anger and despair. "They wish to live."

I shook my head, trying to unhear the words, the story. I could not allow myself to believe the lies, to fall for the tricks. Because if I did, then I would understand his cause, I would agree with him. I would be a traitor.

But, had I not once wondered how it would be possible for me to find love with the way we were restricted? Did I not once think it ridiculous that they would limit us that way, all for the desire to have more power?

More than that, had I not always been aware of the hard choices that I would have to make as Queen one day because of watching Mia and Xavier do that very thing? A part of me knew that there had to be some truth to the story, because the fae in this realm and the perfect split of isles made no sense otherwise.

I felt seven sets of eyes on me and shuddered at the intensity thickening the air. I wanted nothing more than to forget this, to have asked a different question earlier. It seemed that I might be relieved of the expectation of responding as the vibrant green grass below our feet turned a darker shade, nearly black. The Forest of Tragedies sat in front of our group now, an ominous presence that requested our full attention.

Just when I thought myself free of the conversation, Bellamy added, "Remember when I told you that we often speak of the dark-haired beauty that will save our realm? I was not lying, Asher. I do believe you will save us all."

My head snapped towards him, taken aback by his proclamation. I wanted to ask him what he meant. To inquire about his intentions for me. I could not though, because we were now at the edge of the forest, and danger awaited.

"Remind me, Ash, what is it that the fae say when they stare death in the face?" Noe asked, a hint of trepidation in her voice.

"May I return to Eternity," I answered.

CHAPTER THIRTY-THREE

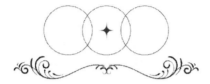

Every hair on my body stood on end as Frost took that first step into the Forest of Tragedies. The uneven terrain, overrun by twisting roots and invasive plants, made staying on top of the horse all the more difficult. My muscles would be screaming by the end of this, no doubt. I rubbed the side of the silver mare, speaking into her mind gently.

You are okay, girl.

Then, I grabbed onto the minds of the other seven horses, reassuring them as well. The ease with which I used my powers was still astonishing. I had never felt so unrestrained.

I fought back the urge to dwell on Bellamy's so-called history lesson. Surely Mia and Xavier would not keep such an important piece of truth from me. They respected me enough to be honest, even if they were not proud of their past. At least, I thought they did.

We sat in silence as we rode forward, the quiet a tangible, sinister thing. With every curve of the path, I felt the tension grow within each of

Bellamy's Trusted. Within the demon prince himself, who was usually so good at blocking me. I worked to maintain a connection to all eight horses and the seven riders, feeding strength into them, manipulating their thoughts of fear to those of confidence.

Trees swayed in a viciously cold wind, looking for all the world a pack of monstrous creatures ready to snatch me right off of Frost. I wished then that I would have been able to give myself relief from the stress and terror that sat heavy on my chest.

"Why are we traveling through this forest? And why at night?" I asked Bellamy, my voice a mere whisper. This close to the trees I could see that they were pine, their needles raining down on the ground, making the surface far more difficult to walk on.

Bellamy leaned closer to me, an attempt at staying as quiet as possible. "This land is bordered by the forest, which was the reason it had been previously unclaimed by a Lord before I created Haven. The only way out is through."

Sounded like the citizens of Haven were more trapped than I thought. Being held captive by The Mist on one side and the Forest of Tragedies on the other. How inviting.

"As for why now, there are wards on the forest. Ancient magic that prevents entry during the day. I believe it was used to warn off those who might let curiosity get the best of them. There are many intelligent creatures who do not wish to eat you, but instead wish to steal from you. Or simply steal *you*. They will try anything to convince prey to enter the confines of the forest," Bellamy said, his threatening words not quite matching the shrug of his shoulders.

Ice spread up my spine, a cool kiss of fear. Bellamy's foreboding tone made me believe that it was not coin or food that was being stolen. No, this was something far more precious. Irreplaceable.

"Like navaloms. They are greedy creatures who gorge themselves on that which you hold most dear, the very things that make you who you are—memories. They are not a particularly strong species, nor are they fighters, which is why they try to lure their prey into the forest with pretty songs. Then they eat away at your past like a sweet dessert, until you are driven mad, or die," Winona added from behind us.

As an expert on creatures, I imagined her word could, and should, be trusted. Secretly, I hoped that the group of them were simply trying to scare me. Unlikely as that was, it did help quench the fear somewhat.

"The wards were likely created around the same time as the one set on the creatures. They are unable to leave the forest. So they are quite eager for visitors, as you can imagine," Bellamy added. A shiver snaked down my back, a feeling of dread washing over me like a cool pool of water. Drowning me.

They were definitely serious.

I focused once more on creating a veil of peace for each of them. They had seen far more than I in my life, and it was clear not one of them was a stranger to horror of some sort. I might not have agreed with them, or even wanted to be here, but that did not mean they did not deserve comfort.

If only I could offer myself the same kindness.

"Listen, Asher," Bellamy said, his voice a quiet plea. "I know now is not a good time, but we do need to talk. You have been through a lot recently, too much, and I have been part of the reason. If you give me the chance, I can explain—"

The snap of a twig drew my attention to our right, everyone in the group immediately going on edge. My breath hitched as a daunting presence sucked the life out of the air. Whatever was out there, it was wrong. Evil.

And it was hungry.

My own mouth salivated when my power grabbed onto whatever it was, responding to the grumbling stomach of the creature hidden in the trees. I sent a placating thought to it, one of boredom and disinterest. Convincing it that there was nothing of importance here.

The creature froze, trying to decipher the new path its mind was taking it on. As if arguing with the thoughts I attempted to portray as its own. I tensed when I heard it make the decision to turn around, to leave us be.

Poised to go the opposite way, the beast halted. I knew it was aware of my prodding when I felt its glee as it faced us once more, heard its thoughts of violence and excitement. Then it spoke, not aloud, but within its mind. A voice of nightmares, like metal scraping glass.

Ah, The Manipulator. Tales of you span realms, worlds even. Feared by many, loved by none.

I shuddered, bile rising up my throat. The insult slamming into my heart. My soul. I frantically searched the tree line, catching Bellamy's attention.

The female who has a family that seeks to control her, use her. Did you know your queen puts hemlock in your food? Such a silly, pathetic being you are. So trusting. So naïve.

My breath hitched. Was it insinuating that Mia was poisoning my food? How would it know that? I shook my head, focusing on my body, my physical being. A metallic taste in my mouth startled me. I had bit through my lip, blood soaking my tongue.

Even worse, the prince at your side hides much from you. A liar, a murderer, a vengeful soul he is. Yet perhaps the only being in existence who does not fear you. Apart from the one who seeks you above all else, that is.

I tugged on the reins, urging Frost to stop with the ropes and my own power. I gasped for air, feeling how confident the creature was with its statements, an all-knowing presence that made me want to rip off my skin from the itch of its magic.

Bellamy noticed us halt, doing the same with Lucifer. His face did not betray his thoughts, though his eyes showed the concern he felt.

I latched on once more, urging my power to simply shatter the mind of the evil veiled by the trees. Laughter could be heard, echoing across the forest, baleful and unsettling. Whatever it was closed in on us, quickly. The others eyed me, as if they had suddenly realized what I was doing.

Ah yes, your tricks do not work quite the same on our minds. Oh, how that god will weep. Her Gift, the promised doom, dead before your destiny could be fulfilled. A tragedy. And I do so love tragedies.

That horror-inducing chuckle sounded again, no more than a hundred feet away now, but in a different direction. It was circling us, a predator taunting its prey, enjoying the game. Noe gasped as the creature spoke out loud, addressing us all this time.

"I will tear you all apart, limb by limb. I will suck the meat from your bones and savor the taste of your blood on my teeth. You, Manipulator, I will save for last—my grandest prize. I will make you watch as I eat them. I will make you watch as your future dies before you," it said, a promise and a threat. Joy, it felt so much joy at the idea of our demise.

"Afriktor," Henry rasped, his green eyes wide in fear.

Bellamy's entire body lit, black flames licking at the air around him as he steered Lucifer in front of me. I noted that this time, his clothes did not burn away, nor did they touch or frighten the horse.

Henry and Winona urged their horses forward from behind me, their bodies glowing as brightly as the moon and stars above us. The two of them were on either side of Frost and I, Noe—bathed in darkness—holding the rear.

Cyprus, Lian, and Ranbir spread out, a second line of defense in case the beast was not alone.

Protecting me. They were protecting me.

As if it had been awaiting my discovery, patiently allowing me to build up hope, the afriktor walked out of the trees.

Taller than any fae or demon, the afriktor towered above us, its smile showing yellow teeth as sharp as a blade. With the demon light coming off of Winona and Henry, I could see that its wrinkled skin was the dusty red of a lunar eclipse. An omen.

Talons the length of my forearm clicked together, the afriktor's leathery wings flapping in time with my breaths. Henry had been attacked by this? And lived?

I did not dare look back at him, though I was sure the demon was living in both the past and present as he stared into the all-white eyes of the creature before us.

"Stella save us," Cyprus whispered. Another laugh sounded from the afriktor.

"She learned her lesson the first time she aided the Blessed, named you such. You were a waste of her time, a stain on—" before the creature could finish, Bellamy attacked. Black flame shot into the chest of the afriktor, sending it flying back.

An ear-splitting screech rang through the forest.

Utter silence replaced all sound. I held my breath, afraid that even a soft exhale would unleash the darkness upon us. Bellamy waved a hand, a click coming from between his teeth. All eight horses shot forward, pushed on by a phantom wind that smelled of spring and flowers. Lian.

I nearly fell off Frost as she sprang through the woods, dodging trees and far outrunning the others. I held on with all of my strength, begging anyone or anything that would listen to keep me upright.

And then the thrashing came. Not from hooves, but *feet*. An avalanche of pounding steps and beating wings.

"Foolish prince. You think I would not share a prize such as this? We are all eager to taste the coveted one," it said, hidden from view once more, likely keeping time with us, maintaining our speed with glee at the chase.

Asher.

They chanted in their minds.

Asher.

They called.

Asher.

They hunted.

CHAPTER THIRTY-FOUR

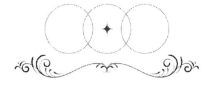

Frost seemed to sense the danger around us closing in, somehow speeding up, weaving through trees and over roots with incredible precision. But I was no rider. As she pushed on, faster by the second, I found myself slipping.

I urged her to slow down, but either she could not hear me or did not wish to obey. Frost wanted to live, and I did not blame her. When she leapt over a fallen tree, I knew I was doomed.

The moment her hooves touched the mossy ground once more, I flew off the saddle. The impact knocked the wind out of me, my back crying out in agony. Air did not return to my lungs again for what seemed to be ages, the cough that sputtered from my lips echoing across the forest.

In the distance, I heard Bellamy's shouted order to find me. His fierce yells of horror and determination as he fought one of the beasts, earning piercing shrieks from his latest victim.

I was not too proud to admit I was drawn towards Bellamy, whose fury was shaking the ground under my feet. Willing myself forward, I slowly moved to the left. To him.

A chuckle from behind stopped me dead in my tracks.

Decay, that was what it smelled like. An odor far more foul than any other. I spun myself around, and there it was. The afriktor smiled down at me, each yellow tooth visible. My eyes caught on the bloody wound the creature had suffered to the chest.

This was the same one Bellamy hit earlier.

"How did you know all of those things about my family?" I asked, a sad excuse at distraction, but also my curiosity making an appearance at the worst possible time. The beast stalled, its head tilting to the side much like Bellamy's often did.

"Interesting question," it said, that petrifying voice making my stomach roll. "One I will not deign to answer, because the others come, and I no longer wish to share."

Drool dripped from its mouth as it leapt towards me, those white eyes staring straight into my soul and far beyond. I dove to the right, barely getting out of the way in time. Then I was up and off, running as fast as I possibly could towards the sounds of Bellamy and his Trusted.

Fast was not quick enough. Beating wings could be heard from my back, and just as I jumped over a large root, the beast grabbed onto my shoulders, claws digging into my skin.

I screamed out in pain, which sent a rush of glee through the wretched beast. My left hand shot down to my thigh, unsheathing the dagger and plunging it into the arm of the afriktor. At the squishing of my blade cutting into its flesh and the scream that rang in my ears, I ripped down as hard as I could.

Suddenly, I was free-falling, my body barreling down towards the trees. A strong breeze slammed into me, slowing my descent. I was guided down between the branches, landing on the dead grass and moss with a thud. To my left sat the arm of the afriktor, which was twitching violently.

Scrambling to my feet, I moved away from the severed limb and searched desperately for whoever helped me. Lian ran through a dense pack of trees, blood splattered across her beautiful face and a sword in each hand. I still had the dagger gripped as well; my knuckles white from squeezing it so tightly.

"Are you okay?" she asked, appraising me. I nodded to her, my body shaking but overall, still intact. I knew blood was leaking from the wounds on my shoulders, but they were not so awful that I had to play the weak damsel. "Good, let's go."

The pair of us darted through trees and past a dead carcass of an afriktor that I assumed Lian had cut down. The sounds of the others grew nearer, and soon we could see the light coming off Henry and Winona shining through the trees.

Wings beat from somewhere above us, and I felt a constant probe on my mind, as if there was someone—or something—trying to project their thoughts my way. Relentless, that is what the push was. I shoved against it, attempting, and failing, to remain focused on the path ahead.

My heart thundered in my chest, pounding in my ears and reminding me that I was still alive. That I needed to push on. That there was a part of me that wanted to survive. And damn it all to the Underworld if that side would lose tonight.

A final jump over a mangled root and push through a patch of trees brought us back to the group. Five of them stood in a circle, fighting off the creatures left and right. Henry and Winona were lit up as bright as the sun, solid rays of light shooting from their hands and into the afriktors, burning through their bodies.

Noe was barely visible, a cloud of black encircling her like a vortex. She was slashing through the beasts with her shadows, cutting them as if they were butter. On her right was Cyprus, who was wielding blades and fighting the afriktors back with enough force to send severed body parts whisking through the air.

Ranbir was beside Winona, unmoving. His eyes were closed in what appeared to be concentration. I took a few staggered steps forward, but Lian grabbed my arm and pulled me back.

"He is sucking the life from them," she said, pointing to the afriktor that was writhing on the ground in front of Ranbir. I gasped, my hand flying to my mouth. I had never seen a Healer do such a thing.

With no other explanation or instruction, Lian leapt back into battle, fitting herself perfectly in between Henry and Winona. Watching her fight was startling. She was ruthless in her pursuit, killing at twice the rate of the others. Both of her swords seemed to sing through the air, as if she were using her powers to whip them faster.

Only one was missing from the group.

I searched the area, trying to find the demon prince, but he was nowhere to be seen. I could feel him though, somewhere out there. His aura pulsed, rage and adrenaline mixing into a dangerous combination. The ground shook, small cracks forming at my feet. Salt water kissed my cheeks, droplets of it washing through the air towards a dense patch of trees beyond the small clearing turned battle ground.

There he was. My feet moved of their own accord, taking me towards the roaring prince.

The area Lian had left me at was covered in shadow, not even the moon above or the Suns in front of me lit the patch of dead grass I stood on, or the path towards Bellamy. It should have been safe, but luck and I had quite the tumultuous relationship.

A solid force hit my back as I ran, and the smell of death burned my nose. I tumbled down, the slight hill giving me momentum and throwing me into a tree trunk.

Time seemed to slow then. The afriktor that I had mutilated came upon me, frothing at the mouth and dripping foul smelling blood on my chest. My dagger was gone, lost somewhere in the fall. No amount of training would have prepared me for this, definitely not a few days of lessons.

The wounds on my shoulders burned and my back felt as though it might break. And the afriktor knew that. It leaned down and licked at my right shoulder, laughing once more as its tongue ran over its bloody teeth.

Why would this thing not simply *die?*

Above, those white eyes stared at me with a hunger that sent shivers down my spine. I saw the sharp claws of the afriktor coming towards me and heard the shouts of Bellamy as he searched for me. Yet only one thing came to my mind.

The female who has a family that seeks to control her, use her.

The prince at your side hides much from you.

I was alone. Not only now, but in this world. A fae princess that had never known true love. Mia and Xavier used me, for what, I was unsure. They poisoned me, of this I was certain now, as I stared death in the face.

Bellamy was doing the same, though he disguised it as freedom. Really, I was his pawn, his tool. Maybe that was what I was to everyone. A sword and shield, rather than a sentient being.

But I did not want to die this way. No, I still had fight in me.

I would tear apart the world, destroy every one of them who wronged me, and I would start with this ugly, disgusting beast.

Inches before it gutted me, I reached out and caught the arm of the afriktor. It went wide-eyed, bewildered when it found my hold stayed tight. I had always been strong, but now I was also riding the high of my fury.

Pushing with every ounce of strength I had, I shoved the afriktor, sending it flying into a tree. A loud crack rang as it made contact with the bark, the large body then slamming into the ground.

Before, it had said my gift did not work quite the same on them, but had not suggested my powers did not work at all. I channeled everything I had, dove deep into that well of power that I had only recently discovered was so vast.

The beast moved, murderous thoughts attempting to jam through my mental gates. I stood as well, mirroring its need for blood.

Too often I had been used. Too often I had been belittled. Too often I had been exploited.

I lifted my hands, closing my eyes to focus on that thick and grimy feeling of the afriktors, wrapping myself around their minds.

Never again would I be abused. Never again would I be taken advantage of. Never again would I be weak.

They wanted me to be the villain? They wanted The Manipulator?

Fine. Then that was who I would be.

I threw my arms forward, releasing a piercing scream as I took my power and threw it into their minds.

CHAPTER THIRTY-FIVE

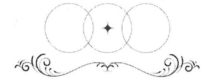

My power flowed through me and into the minds of nearly three dozen afriktors, all scattered throughout the forest. I did not manipulate or shatter them, but instead attacked them head on.

Every one of the creatures flew to the ground, wailing in agony and thrashing in the muddy grass. I screamed with them, the amount of power coursing through me a kind of pain in itself. I wanted to let go, but I knew that if I did those things would get right back up, and I would be the same helpless fae, ripe for the taking.

Tremors ran through my body, which begged me to stop, warned me that this was not safe. I simply reminded myself that safe had gotten me nowhere but alone and in danger, then I pushed harder.

The first mind to wink out was the afriktor in front of me, a personal victory of sorts. Then, one by one, every afriktor within the forest went still, death heavy in the air. Before I could give in to the exhaustion that threatened to pull me into oblivion, the bodies of the afriktors began to explode.

Bellamy appeared at my side in a burst of black smoke, shielding me from the raining gore that came from the beasts. His face was full of an anger that promised vengeance and haunted nightmares. This was The Elemental, the being that terrorized an entire realm and murdered without a second thought. Yet, I did not feel afraid, did not balk. Instead, there was comfort knowing he was now the scariest thing within the area.

My body slumped into his waiting arms, his warmth a welcoming feel. The scent of cinnamon and smoke was still there, though faint in comparison to the reek of the afriktors. Each rise and fall of his chest was soothing, the beat of his heart a melody.

Maybe it was because I was weak from the power drain, but I found myself snuggling into his chest, basking in the essence of him. When he wrapped his arms around me, squeezing with enough pressure to be more than simply holding me upright, I thought I might have felt a sigh of relief. Not from his mouth, but from his mind.

"For a moment there, I thought I lost you," he said into my hair as he stroked it. I sensed the others coming our way, but my eyes refused to open. Bellamy tensed when their footsteps sounded, his anger returning in full force.

I felt a kiss placed on my forehead, and my eyes finally snapped open. The six of them stood in front of us, bloody and torn. Cyprus had a slight limp, Winona was bleeding from the eyebrow, Henry had three slashes across his thigh that revealed a deep wound, Ranbir looked as if he might be sick, and Noe seemed to have been hit rather hard in the nose, as it was sideways and sort of…hanging.

Lian had made it mostly unscathed.

I stumbled away from Bellamy, pushing off of him to assess his injuries. His dark hair was matted with blood, his hands as red as wine. In fact, the majority of his body was covered in the filthy blood of the afriktors. Otherwise, he was unharmed.

The prince stepped forward, his glare sharper than the talons that tore through me mere minutes ago. He pointed his finger at each of his Trusted, not one of them resisting the urge to flinch under his gaze. Even Henry seemed to cower somewhat.

"I told you all to keep Asher *safe*," he accused, his voice deeper than I had ever heard it. I opened my mouth to argue, to say that I was not weak, to stand up for them. But a quick shake of the head from Henry told me that it was not my place. "Only one of you bothered to find her, and by then she was already *mangled!*" he said, screaming the last word.

As subtly as I could, I dared a glance at my shoulders. A mess, that was the only way of describing the pile of fat, tissue, tendons, and torn skin that I saw covered in blood under what remained of my top. My stomach flipped, but as the adrenaline was quickly replaced with exhaustion, I had little chance to dwell on the pain.

"I am deeply remorseful, My Prince. I vow to protect the Princess with my life," Henry said dropping to one knee. At once, the others followed suit, dropping to the ground and vowing their lives to my safety. As one the group unsheathed small daggers, bringing the blades to their palms and making quick slashes. They bowed their heads, lifting their hands towards Bellamy, who in turn stomped over to them. He removed his own dagger, slicing open the skin of his palm as well, allowing them each to drip their blood onto his open wound.

Unsanitary, horribly so. A blood pact of sorts perhaps?

Foolish beings.

"You are all idiots. I can keep myself safe," I said, my voice a raspy whisper. Not nearly as threatening or confident as I had hoped it would be. But I remained standing, my eyes roaming over each of them. "And honestly, get up out of the mud, our camp will smell incredibly foul tonight already."

My poor excuse for humor had each of them rising, though hesitantly. I scowled at Bellamy, wishing he would have simply kept his mouth shut. I would have commented on his absence when it came to rescuing me, but I had a sneaking suspicion that he had dealt with most of the afriktors by himself.

Noe walked over to me, offering support. All too glad to accept the help, I wove my bloody arm around hers, and together we made our way back to the clearing up the hill.

The black grass crunched under my shoes, the mud squelching beneath them and threatening to suck my boots right off my feet. The air was freezing, though my shoulders felt as if they had been lit aflame. Just to be sure, I glanced down at the injuries once more.

No fire.

Though I knew what that meant. Fever. If I did not have Ranbir heal me soon, I would be suffering far worse.

By the time we reached the crest of the hill, I was wheezing. Bellamy had been following directly behind Noe and I, and the moment I tilted too far into her, he snatched me out of her grip. With no energy left to fight him, I allowed myself to be scooped into his embrace, one of his arms tucked under my legs and the other around my back.

Unable to resist, I let my head fall against his warm chest. The muscles on his body were too firm to be as comfortable as a pillow, but suitable enough that I would not be lifting my head again anytime soon.

As our group made its way down the hill, Bellamy's steps providing a slight rocking motion, my eyes grew heavy. I tried to fight off the fatigue, but a headache bore down on my temples, sending a throbbing pain to rival the other injuries.

I knew we had made it to the bottom when Bellamy gently set me down on the forest floor, his fingers brushing my tangled hair out of my face. A second pair of hands worked their way across my body, and I suddenly felt the searing pain of fae healing powers.

"Please, leave the scars," I rasped, grabbing onto Ranbir's hand. He looked concerned at my request, as if he were considering whether or not my injuries had caused me to become delirious.

How could I explain to him that I needed these reminders? That without them, I struggled to differentiate between reality and nightmares?

"I want to remember," I said, hoping that it was enough to convince him. Above, Bellamy looked as if he might scream into the ethers, or perhaps burn the world to the ground.

Luckily, Ranbir asked no further questions, healing me until the tears on my shoulders were angry pink lines. I closed my eyes, basking in the thought of having that history remain on my body. Taking solace in it.

"She will not be able to travel for at least the night," Ranbir whispered from above as he finished.

I allowed my eyes to remain closed, both out of exhaustion and embarrassment. I wondered if I should speak up, convince them I was strong enough. If only to maintain my façade of vigor and assurance.

But Ranbir would not believe me, and Bellamy would not listen either. I would be at their whim until I was once more at full strength. So I would do what Calista suggested, keep my ears open and listen for what Bellamy and his Trusted hid between their words.

"Can she at least portal?" Bellamy asked, his voice breaking. The way he said it did not sound angry any longer, but rather fearful and grief stricken. Ranbir offered a hesitant nod, and that was all it took for the demon to haul me up once more. "You can all meet us one mile past the edge of the forest, we will be far enough out that setting up camp there should be safe. Just head to the Northwest sector of Sophistes."

And then we were gone, the feeling of time and space ripping my body apart, sending shockwaves of pain through me. When we landed outside of the Forest of Tragedies, I nearly heaved up the hefty dinner Calista had fed me earlier in the night.

Had that truly been this evening? It felt as if it were days ago. The events of late have weighed on me like decades rather than mere weeks. That small voice in my head reminded me that it would only get worse. It was right of course.

"Rest, Princess. You are safe," Bellamy whispered to me, his breath a caress against my hair. My enemy, the one I should despise, but still somehow found myself comforted by. Though I knew he had been truthful about the royals, I also was well aware that he had plenty of his own lies and half-truths.

If I had been born here, or he had been born in my realm, then I think Eternity would have brought us together. Instead, we were placed on opposing sides, bred to battle one another. And no matter what revelations I had, there was still a nagging thought, or perhaps a premonition, that only one of us would survive.

CHAPTER THIRTY-SIX

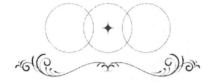

Bellamy scouted out the best area he could find about a mile from the forest edge. When he finally decided on a spot, I promptly sat in the grass, hugging my knees to my chest and trying to resist thinking. Or feeling. As much as I hated to admit it, Bellamy was a good companion. He let me be, content with giving me the space I needed. The demon asked nothing of me other than to drink water.

I sat there, staring at the star-filled sky while he made a fire, casting a dull light to break through the darkness. Then I watched as he somehow wove shadows into shelter and bedrolls. Words were inadequate to explain my utter shock at the magic. Bellamy must have noticed, because he let out a low chuckle and a quick explanation.

"Think of it like portaling, but rather than using the raw magic to transport myself, I am calling onto items I have laced with my essence." He smirked, the first smile I had seen from him since we entered the forest. It seemed he was over my near-death experience now that we put some distance between us and the battle grounds.

In fact, the demon looked almost energized. As if the fight had recharged his spirit. Or maybe, based on the way his eyes raked over me, it was the fact that we were alone. He was sorely mistaken if he thought anything would happen between us again. Ever.

"You better stop looking at me like that. If not for the fact that I have the distinct urge to murder you, then simply because I have somehow vomited more in the last couple of weeks than in my entire life, and I just might do so once more." Bellamy's stare suddenly felt heavier, full of concern. I could not stand seeing him look at me that way, with fake compassion. "Do not think I am unaware that you are the common factor, demon."

It seemed nothing could break his mood. Instead of responding, he simply pointed to the largest tent in the clearing. I looked over at it, raising a brow.

"Are you telling me to go to my room, Your Highness?" I asked with an eye roll.

"Merely suggesting. If not to rest, then to wash up. As much as I would love to clean every inch of you with my tongue, I imagine you would prefer the hot water."

His gaze raked over me once more, making my skin flush and my stomach knot. Then he was up, walking over to the tent right next to mine. I counted five in all, which meant I would likely be sharing with someone, but as long as it was not him, then I would be fine.

"There is warm water inside," he said over his shoulder.

I got up, my body cracking with each movement. The training had left me sore, but the fighting had done no favors. It seemed Ranbir's power did not extend to discomfort. I made my way to the tent, parting the fabric and stepping into a wonderfully warm enclosure.

There was a cot on either side, furs piled on top of both, and a small bath in the center. I struggled to see with the lack of light. I would need to either bathe in the dark or take a chance with allowing the flap to remain open. Unwelcome thoughts tended to find me without the light, so I opted for leaving them open.

I made quick work of the bath, which had warm water as Bellamy had said it would. My stare stayed trained on the opening of the tent, not trusting the demon to keep his eyes to himself. But he did, not once walking by the entrance.

When I was done, I dressed myself in the long-sleeved tunic and thick trousers that were folded in the corner, both all black. I could not find any undergarments apart from a small band that would support my breasts, which would have to do. I laced up my boots and latched my cloak before once more finding my way outside. Bellamy sat there, facing the fire with a small pile of dried meat next to him. I quickly swiped a piece as I passed, opting to sit across from him. Every part of my body cried out when I bent over to sit, a groan leaving my lips.

"The only moans that would escape that pretty mouth would be of pleasure if I had anything to say about it," he said, standing and moving towards me like a predator on the hunt. My eyes grew large, his insinuation sparking a fire in my core that I had been steadily snuffing out.

Stupid demon was being far more bold tonight than normal.

"In your wildest dreams you would still never have me beneath you," I hissed at him. Of course, that wicked smile appeared, as if he enjoyed the chase. Despite that, he still seemed to be assessing me, checking my wellbeing. Was he distracting me with banter?

"Well I can definitely confirm that you are wrong, but that is beside the point. You owe me your thoughts," he said, closing the distance between us and sitting beside me.

Black smoke curled around my shoulders, the smell of him stronger. For a moment I thought he was going to dump me somewhere, but then the smoke suddenly had weight to it. As it disappeared, a blanket emerged, covering my body.

I looked at him, noting the crinkles at his eyes and his soft smile. Who admits to having sexual fantasies about someone to their face, and then smiles like that? His confidence with me was jarring, as if he was just waiting patiently for me to submit.

Clearly, he thought that he was some irresistible prince that even his prisoner would fall for. He was sorely mistaken. Two could play at that game, and I did not plan on losing.

"You want to know what I am thinking?" I asked in a sultry voice. I allowed my eyes to float down to his lips, not having to fake the response of my body. I had tasted him before, and I knew that if I did it again, I would not be able to stop.

The demon gave a nearly imperceptible nod, his body otherwise stiff. Arousal radiated off of him when I leaned in, my own breath quickening. I maintained a slow pace, stopping just inches before our lips touched.

Heat filled the air between us, and I knew that I had him, though I also had myself unfortunately. A quick glance down told me that he was eager to see what I would do next, his leather pants straining against the size of him already.

"I am thinking of things that do not require talking," I whispered against his ear. A shudder ran through him, and his erection grew impossibly larger. I grabbed onto his chin, tilting his face down to my own. His eyes were burning, a blue flame of desire.

Once more I brought my face to his, this time our lips brushing together. Closing my eyes, I took in one last breath.

"Such as this," I rasped. And then I brought the meat I had snagged earlier between us, ripping a piece off with my teeth, before backing away with a smirk.

Bellamy's eyes bore into me, his stunned expression quickly morphing into one of need. He launched himself towards me, grabbing the nape of my neck and pressing his body into mine until my back was against the dewy grass. Gasping for air, I looked up at him with wide eyes.

Moments ago, I had told him I would never be beneath him, and yet, I did not think I would let him move off if he tried. His tongue darted out, wetting those tempting lips. I could feel the cool bite of the many rings on his fingers against my skin, and somehow it was a temptation rather than a discomfort.

Over and over again I reminded myself that he was the enemy. I told myself that he had kidnapped me, lied to me, betrayed me.

He was evil.

He was wretched.

He was The Elemental, the demon prince.

He was…so beautiful.

"Tell me to kiss you. Tell me you want this—that you want me. Give yourself to me, Princess," he demanded, fist tightening in the hair at the nape of my neck.

I swallowed, struggling to get the food down with the lump in my throat. Somehow the nausea had subsided, though a part of me wished it would return and act as an excuse. I would not, could not, give in to him.

He ground his hips into me, likely annoyed by my reluctance, that bulge creating a delicious friction against the wetness between my thighs.

Gods, if I did not stop this now, then I was doomed. I pressed my hands to his chest, my breath coming in strained pants. Bellamy stilled, waiting for me to push him off. Waiting for the rejection he expected from me.

I pictured the last time I was touched, kissed, held. None of them were joyous, in fact the memory brought pain. Sterling had been the last to taste my lips, and I had not wanted it. Perhaps he would always haunt my dreams, but I did not have to let him have that ownership of me. To be my last.

Acknowledging that allowed me to let go of the anger and betrayal I felt towards Bellamy, at least for the moment. Without those negative feelings, there was nothing stopping me. So I did something I had promised myself I would not do. I gave in.

My hands fisted the demon's cloak, pulling him down and crashing his lips onto my own. At first he did not return the kiss, though he also did not make a move to back away. Aggravated by his sudden hesitation, I wrapped my arms around his neck and bit down on his bottom lip, eliciting a husky growl from him.

Then he was everywhere. His tongue, his hips, his chest, every part of him touching every part of me to the point that I was no longer sure where he ended and I began. I struggled my way free of the boots that I had, thankfully, tied loosely. In response to my wiggling, his free hand moved to my own, bringing it above my head and securing it there. The one pressed against the nape of my neck followed suit, his thighs trapping my legs. I was left unable to move, and enjoying every second of it.

Bellamy broke the kiss, tracing his way down my throat, stopping at that sensitive spot above my collarbone. I moaned, a loud and untamed sound. I felt his fingers undo my cloak, tugging it from below me and tossing it to the side. No rational thoughts entered my mind, the need for him drowning me. All I could think was that his touch was electric, an intoxicating pleasure, and I never wanted him to stop.

"You are everything, Asher. The beginning and the end and every moment in between," he whispered against my skin. I had no idea what he meant, and the way that my head was spinning at the flick of his tongue stopped me from attempting to. His mouth began lowering ever so slowly, shivers following in his wake.

He made his way down my torso, stopping at the hem of my top. I peered down at him, catching the raise of a brow and nodding in silent confirmation. He flashed a devilish grin, and then ripped the fabric in half, exposing my bound chest. The cold air was a shock, and nearly enough to pull my wits back to the front of my mind. But this time, he did not ask for permission, opting to latch onto the garment with his teeth. The edges of them grazed my skin as he slowly tugged my breasts free.

His mouth was on me in an instant, sucking in a peaked nipple. I gasped at the heat of his tongue, which managed to make the chilly night a sensual caress. Every nerve in my body was alight with the very fire that ran through Bellamy's veins. The tips of his fingers tickled and warmed me, that same flame kissing me as well.

I wanted more. I *needed* more.

Grabbing his other hand, I brought it down my stomach and rested it on the button of my trousers—a demand. Bellamy's laugh vibrated against my nipple, sending waves of pleasure through my body. I leaned into him, far too tired to resist my natural response.

"I thought I was eager," he teased.

I opened my mouth to offer a sarcastic retort, but the damned male was faster. His hand shot into my trousers with a kind of efficiency that told me he was fairly practiced, fingers meeting flesh in a way that made the stars seem to shine brighter. My back arched up as he explored slowly around that throbbing bundle of nerves. I was horribly uncontrolled, a consistent low thrum of sighs leaving my lips.

"So wet," he purred as his fingers sped, then slipped lower to tease my entrance. Never had someone's voice threatened to bring me to the edge, but this cursed demon's did.

His lips met mine at the same time I reached between us, stroking the bulge in his trousers to tell him with actions rather than words that I wanted this—him. The moan that he offered my lips was erotic, a deep melody of longing and hunger.

He froze for a moment, then pulled back, separating our lips. There was something in the way his stare bore into me, as if he were peering at my soul and did not mind what he saw. I felt my heart skip a beat, a bit of panic finding its way into my chest. That look was more than simple lust.

"Choose me, Princess," Bellamy breathed. His hold on me tightened as he pulled me up, fingers slipping out of my pants and our bodies pressing together. The tone of his voice was more of a plea than a demand. A second passed before I registered what he had said, tensing at the request.

I had no words for him. My thoughts were utter chaos, my pulse a beating drum. Nothing and everything were being said at the same time with my silence. Still, Bellamy pressed on, as if the pain of rejection hurt far less than the agony of not trying.

"I can give you everything. I can make you happy. Stay with me, and I promise I will always be yours. Choose me, and I vow to never stop choosing you. Be mine, Asher," he rasped against my ear, his hot breath a tickle and his words a dangerous promise. My head was spinning with the need for him, my heart racing from the fear of what he was asking of me.

I could lie, placate him just to have this moment. But for some reason, I was unable to form the words.

That hesitation was all it took.

Bellamy kissed my shoulder softly.

"I think you should get some rest," he whispered.

He let me go, fixing the band for my breasts before leaning away from me to remove his top and place it over my head. The view of his exposed chest and arms was no help. He was all muscle, looking as if he were honed for a never-ending battle. Those strange tattoos stood out in contrast to the white of his skin, as if someone had taken kohl and drawn on him lazily.

After I pulled my arms through the sleeves, he reached down beside us, snatching up my cloak. He wrapped it around me, placing a soft kiss between my collar bones. Then he grabbed my boots, putting each one on my feet and lacing them before standing once more.

He made his way to his tent, his back flexed and emotions barely locked down. I waited for him to look back. To explain. To say anything else. But he did not.

CHAPTER THIRTY-SEVEN

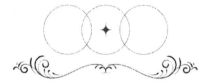

Hours passed and the others had still not arrived.

Most of that time I spent outside by the fire. I was shocked and embarrassed, but also furious. Bellamy had practically begged me to kiss him, and then he had the audacity to reject me while I was topless below him? My hand found my necklace, remarkably still intact, twirling it and resisting the urge to think of anything but the stupid demon.

Changing his mind was one thing, which I could respect, but this had been different. The demon wanted me to *choose him*. What did that even mean?

He was still plotting and playing games, not caring what it might do to my heart. And that pained me more than anything he had done to me before.

For a moment, I had thought I deserved it after pushing him away and rejecting him for so long. Yet, he had lied to me and betrayed me enough times that I was rather certain he had earned my poor attitude. So many times that a part of me despised him.

Ultimately it had been for the best. I would have regretted having sex with him later, no matter how great it felt in the moment. I was already angry that I had given him even the smallest part of myself after all he had done.

When I finally found my way back into the tent, my traitorous mind thought of him. What he might be doing. How he might have worshipped my body as if I were a blessing rather than the curse so many before had told me I was. I pictured what I would find if I searched for his thoughts, and then wondered if I should go to his tent and make some demands of my own.

While laying on my cot, an infinitely better idea sparked. I smirked, closing my eyes and getting comfortable. Using my powers this soon after burning out was stupid at best, but I was bitter, and pouting had done me no good. Plus, I could tell that my well of power was far deeper than I had previously believed. I could handle a small bit of revenge.

Reaching out, I tasted the air, seeing if his emotions had finally broken through that shield of his.

Eternity must have been feeling vengeful as well, because there he was, just as horribly disgruntled as I. But I did not risk attempting to read into his current thoughts, instead opting to feed him fresh ones. Better ones, if I dared say.

Images of me sneaking into his tent made their way to the front of his mind. I would be bare save the cloak he had leant me days ago, which would hang lazily from my shoulders. Then I altered the scene, flashing to me crawling on top of him, the cloak on the ground.

I could sense the arousal he was feeling, the excitement that set the hair on his body rising and brought bumps to his skin. A strong gust of wind hit my tent, and it took everything in me not to break the connection or show myself too soon as his powers got away from him. I gave him no mercy as I proceeded.

Then he was seeing me take off his trousers, my lips placing kisses up his thighs.

The demon was positively lost in the fantasy. Though I could not see what he was doing per se, I felt it, the unhinged chaos a relief from my own animosity.

I conjured up the sight of my mouth wrapping around his—

Black fire came at me, shoving my power out of his head and forming a solid wall of flame to keep me out. But the damage had already been done, and I was laughing as my power came back to me.

I gleefully hoped that feeling of unfulfillment would haunt him for a while.

Rustling from outside cut my joy short. I scrambled out of the furs, launching myself upright. Was he really going to storm in here?

But it was not Bellamy that popped his head through the opening of the tent. It was Henry, his orange hair a mess from traveling and his clothes still covered in blood. The shreds in his leathers remained, but the skin underneath was unmarred. Healed perfectly.

Surprise lit the demon's face. For a moment I was unsure why, but then he let his eyes fall onto my torso, a smirk forming. Glancing down, I realized too late that I was still in Bellamy's top. Horror filled me. I did not want Henry thinking I was sleeping with his prince. The two of us had formed a sort of friendship the last few days, and I hated to think he would pull away from training with me or spending time with me out of fear of Bellamy. I hastily wrapped my cloak tight around me.

To my astonishment, Henry closed the space between us and wrapped his arms around me in a bone-crunching hug. I stood there, arms slack at my sides, for a moment. But as the shock wore off, I found myself hugging him back. It was a warm embrace, and I was reminded how tall he was as the top of my head barely reached his chest.

"I am glad you are safe, Asher, I should have stuck closer to your side," he spoke, his breath hitting my hair. Not once had he offered this level of kindness to me. In fact, he was the only one I could count on to regularly offer me fearless taunts other than Bellamy.

"Honestly, if you keep saying nice things to me, I might gag, carrot top," I muttered into his chest. I felt the vibration of his full laugh rattle my head and smiled at the return of his former self.

Now that I had calmed down, I did not think I would attempt to kill Bellamy or any of his Trusted. I could count on them to protect me in the face of danger—they proved that tonight—but I knew they still lied through their teeth when they spoke to me.

Henry was slowly becoming the exception. Being around him was easy. He made me laugh, taught me without holding back, and often gave me truths that others would not dare offer. But that was seemingly due to the animosity between him and Bellamy. If they ever reconciled, I worried how that would change his treatment towards me.

"I sure do enjoy that annoying voice of yours, little brat." He laughed, lightly flicking my nose before walking out of the tent, tugging me along by the hand. Outside, the sky had turned a brilliant shade of pink, like the hyacinths that were scattered across the field of grass. The group was sitting in front of a newly lit fire, still in their battle-torn clothing.

Bellamy walked out of his tent, a long-sleeve purple tunic replacing the old one he had put on me. The demon prince looked my way, as if sensing my stare. His gaze was scalding, the slide of his tongue across his lips sending my heart fluttering.

Then my hand joined with Henry's caught his attention. In an instant his face was blank, controlled save for the tick of his jaw.

Noe followed his line of sight to me, a smile lighting her face. I offered a small one of my own in return, not wanting to offend her. Noe was the most eager out of Bellamy's Trusted to befriend me, and I had to admit she was slowly wearing down my defenses.

Henry sat us down in between Cyprus and Ranbir, Bellamy across the way. The six of them who had finished the trek through the vile forest looked positively exhausted, so their choice to stay awake surprised me. Rest seemed like the least they were owed.

"How did you all fair? Everything went smoothly?" Bellamy inquired, looking over each of their faces. I noted the obvious concern in his voice, different than what Xavier used during council meetings. This was more familial, a loving warmth.

The group all nodded in response, none of them eager to speak after the hours of what was likely a fear-inducing journey after the attack. I could see that Ranbir had patched up each of them up, but sleep would still be needed to get them back to full health. The mind needed rest just as much as the body.

I thought of my own experiences with Healers. Tish had been around for most of my life, though two had come before her in short spurts. All had been instructed to heal me to the point I would not scar. Even my latest two healing sessions with her left me in perfect condition, not a scar or bruise could be found. I thought it was so I would not be subject to the memories that scars would call upon, but now I wondered if it was to assuage the royals' guilt. Or perhaps to maintain the appearance of a loving family.

What it had really done was nearly drive me mad. The first few times it happened, I had thought I made the entire thing up. I spent days on end not sleeping or eating, thinking I might hallucinate once more. When I caught onto what was going on, I felt violated, as if I was missing a fundamental part of myself that had been stolen from me.

Looking down at my skin now, it was like I had never lived—like nothing and no one had existed within this body. Other than the scars from the afriktor attack. The ones I needed Ranbir to leave behind, if only so I could stay sane.

The fae king and queen's betrayal stung me far worse than it should have. Love was not something felt between the royals, but I had always believed that they held the emotion for me. After all, they told me they loved me, that I was cherished. Through each beating and scolding, even the many rules in place, I had been under the impression that love was at the root of it all.

Maybe I was foolish to so easily believe the afriktor, but something about the feeling in my stomach that came when the beast delivered the news made it feel true. Never had I considered the idea that the couple who raised me were plotting against me, but now I was fairly sure they had been all along.

I shook my head, trying to prevent the grief from swallowing me whole.

"Hey Ash, any chance you want to turn in for the night?" Noe asked.

I looked over to her, surprised. Her eyes held a knowing sorrow, as if she had been privy to my thoughts. Realization hit me then. Noe, for all her joy and exuberance, had lived through a similar pain.

I nodded, not wanting to speak for fear those walls I had crafted around my emotions might break if I tried. Noe walked around the fire, reaching a hand out to me. I grabbed on, standing to walk with her towards the tent. She bid everyone goodnight for the both of us, and then we made our way to the safety of our shelter.

Overwhelming sorrow left me sobbing by the time we closed the fabric behind us, my body shaking and head spinning with too many thoughts to comprehend. I sat on my cot, Noe moving to rest on her own; allowing me the silence that I needed to finally feel what had been building up for so long.

I was alone. Truly alone. No family, all of my friends a sea away, not even the comfort of my own bed below me.

After a few minutes of my tears, Noe spoke.

"I know you feel as if no one is on your side, but I am here if you need to talk. To let it out," she whispered. An offer of sorts. One I had not realized I needed until then.

Loneliness was terrifying in many ways, but it was also safer. I was taking a risk allowing Noe in, accepting the friendship she had so adamantly been attempting to form.

Yet, I knew I could not last much longer tucking away every memory and feeling that might hurt, especially now that I was aware it had been Mia who poisoned me. Not just in the last couple of months, but for *years*.

Somehow, I would seek the vengeance I was owed. Mia, Xavier, Sterling, even Bellamy, would get what they were due. I would be their karma.

But for now, all I could manage was to slump down on my cot and look into the hazel eyes across from me. They were warm and welcoming, eager to shoulder some of the burdens that weighed on my mind. Noe was kind and genuine, I could see that now. Whatever lies and secrets existed between us, they came from duty on her part.

"I think I have decided on my question I am owed," I said.

Noe's brow furrowed in confusion, taken aback by the seemingly random change of subject. However, she still nodded, willing to answer whatever question I wanted to ask.

"Would you perhaps consider being my friend, Noe?"

The Moon went unnaturally still. I waited, eager for her to answer. I had not expected rejection, but now I wondered if I should have. Noe was always moving, always speaking, always doing something. Seeing her simply stare was unnerving.

Then she smiled.

In an instant she went from her position perched on her cot, to up and bounding my way, barreling into me. The embrace was the kind that could stitch a shredded heart back together or heal a broken soul. It was a breathless, painful hug that brought the sobs back with twice the force.

"I would be honored to call you friend, Ash."

For the first time since Sterling attacked me, I felt peace.

CHAPTER THIRTY-EIGHT

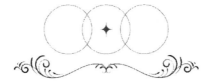

Noe and I had pushed the tub to one side of the tent, placing our cots beside one another. I was unsure whether my untamable sorrow came from the royals' betrayal, the afriktor attack, Bellamy's rejection, or finally having someone to lean on here in Eoforhild.

All of the above, most likely.

Noe did not balk, instead choosing to hold me as I cried and told her of what Mia had done, of what both royals had done. She stroked my hair as I spoke, and when I could no longer talk, she began sharing stories of her childhood.

Her mother had disappeared shortly after giving birth to Noe, running from her abusive husband. Noe had been left behind, suffering the wrath of her father who blamed her for the loss of his wife. She had met Bellamy not long after her magic manifested, when she was five years old and Bellamy was nine, still without powers.

She told me that around the age of maturity, about twenty-five years after their birth, a demon goes through something called The Almavet. In the year or so they remain in The Almavet, their magic doubles, and at the end their aging drastically slows. It was a difficult experience, as they often lost control and had to be secluded. Noe had been confined to her father's home without visitors.

It was interesting to learn of the difference between fae and demons, as our aging slowed far sooner, occurring when we mastered our power rather than at a certain age. About ten years after birth, a fae's power awakens. They are then sent to Academy, where training will begin to aid them in controlling the power they had been blessed with by Eternity. Once they were able to contain it, they would be scored on how much power they had. A series of battles and tests are recorded, determining where each fae ranks among their sub-faction.

Demons did not have rankings according to Noe. Instead, no matter their power, they were allowed the freedom to choose their own path. Apparently, even the strongest demons opt to run businesses or farm or sew or mine. Anything they wanted to become they could. Though it sounded beautiful, there was no denying the fact that such autonomy could weaken their entire realm.

Yet, I found myself thinking of what I might choose to be if given the chance.

Noe, unlike most of her kind, was not awarded the same privilege. She had been an assassin and spy long before Bellamy had created his Trusted. In fact, she often portaled to the Fae Realm—*Betovere,* if Bellamy was to be believed—and spied on the royals. Noe's father had rigorously trained her to take down his enemies, utilizing her exceptional magic ability as a weapon for his own selfish needs and desires.

She spoke of her isolation growing up, the longing for companionship she would feel as a result.

Noe gave such detailed descriptions of the places she had portaled, that I found myself lost in them, dreaming of visiting the far off cave where she uncovered a small group of rebels or the rain forest where she had found large cases of smuggled goods to blackmail a Lord with.

It was all so fascinating and inconceivable. She and Bellamy both had memories of grand adventures and the desire to be something more than what their parents wanted.

I had never wanted to be anything other than good enough.

It was pathetic really, that I had spent over two centuries pining for the love of a couple who had poisoned and beat me. Even more embarrassing that I still found myself dreaming of being loved by them, seeing their proud faces and knowing that my life had meaning. Somehow, I remained unable to hate them, that small part of myself insisting they were innocent, believing I deserved it all.

Would it be ridiculous to think that? To see my own faults and conclude that I had been the catalyst to the downfall of our bond? I did not believe so, but I knew Noe would. And so would Bellamy. Neither of them believed the royals held any good within their hearts, that they were capable of redemption.

But I knew without a shadow of a doubt that there was no good without evil. Life was not black and white; it was gray and gloomy, and we were all the villain of someone's story.

No matter what path I chose, I would be the worst of them all.

I scooted further into Noe as her words became softer and her breaths became even. When she fell asleep mid-sentence, I forced myself to not close my eyes. I fought it with every ounce of energy I had, but there was very little left.

My body begged me for relief and rest, but my mind reminded me of all I would see when I gave in to the fatigue. Slowly, trying not to wake Noe, I edged my way off the cots. Her soft snores stuttered at one point, but she did not wake, nor did she stir again after.

I snatched my cloak off of the floor, securing it swiftly, and made my way out of our shared tent. The morning sun burned, but the chill came with a satisfying jolt of awareness. Allowing my eyes to adjust, I stretched my arms and took in the empty field through squinted lids. Surprised to find no one keeping watch, I halted. What if someone—or *something*—attacked?

Bellamy was hardly an incompetent leader, and I doubted Henry would allow us to have no one keeping watch either. Someone had to be around here somewhere. I moved through our small camp, noting the dying flames of the fire and the snores coming from all five tents.

Figuring I should trust that they could manage their affairs, I wandered away from our site. There was a fresh taste to the wind as it blew my hair back, the sun overhead assuaging some of the frosty bite. Overgrown grass and hyacinths made for a fairytale-like scene.

Our horses remained nearby, untethered. I was once again amazed at Henry's impeccable training. Frost had found a comfortable patch of grass to sleep in, Lucifer not far away, his black eyes scanning the area.

Those two seemed quite cozy.

I did not rule out the possibility that the two were mated. Bellamy would give me his steed's mate only to later suggest it was fate. Stupid demon.

I walked around the sleeping animals, careful not to scare them. Lucifer watched me, tracking as I walked away. Promising myself I would not be reckless by straying too far, my feet pressed on for only a bit longer. When I felt satisfied with my distance from the camp, I collapsed onto the dewy grass near the edge of a cliff. The view was astonishing, but I resisted the urge to explore more, instead lying back all the way.

Basking in the light, I let my arms and legs spread wide. It felt like I was being cleansed—made new. I was far more comfortable than I had any reason to be. Exposed and exhausted, I risked my safety doing this. But I had fought so hard not to be still these last few weeks, and I craved that serenity.

So I laid there, breathing in the smell of flowers and autumn. I felt the cold seep through my clothes, welcomed it even. When my eyelids grew heavy, I allowed them to close. Perhaps I needed to see what would haunt me.

The thoughts that broke free terrorized me, and I let them.

Weak, they pushed. *True,* I conceded.

Worthless, they said. *Yes,* I agreed.

On and on images of every soul I shattered, every brain I manipulated, every light I snuffed out flashed before me. I relived every gentle hug from Mia, every proud smile from Xavier. Then the words of the afriktor echoed.

Such a silly, pathetic being you are. So trusting. So naïve.

I was all of those things and more.

End it. The voices of the fallen urged. Yes, the world would be far better that way.

I saw the cliff's edge again, and this time I walked over to the very cusp of it, ready to jump.

Sterling's charming face appeared next to me. He was living gold, the embodiment of fae royalty in a mortal body.

"Asher, beautiful Asher. Please do not leave me again. Who else will love you if not me?" he asked in a sultry voice. For some reason, I was tempted to take his outstretched hand. To submit to a lifetime of torture.

But I hesitated when a familiar voice sounded from the other side of me. It was a husky rasp, one that held love and fear and strength. Sterling scowled at the looming presence, trying to snatch my hand.

I pulled away, my back hitting Bellamy's chest. He wrapped his arms around me, holding on tightly.

Too tightly. He was crushing me against him, leaning down to kiss my disfigured ear. A voice came that was not his, but the afriktor's once more.

Even worse, the prince at your side hides much from you. A liar, a murderer, a vengeful soul he is.

Bellamy spun me around, his black flames burning my arms. I cried out in agony, but The Elemental merely laughed, as if he enjoyed my pain. The icy blue eyes I had come to know so well slowly became overrun by black shadows. He pushed, causing me to lose my balance.

I toppled over the edge, a scream ripping its way up my throat. My hands flew out, trying to gain purchase on something, anything.

Sweaty, desperate fingers met cold, calm ones. Bellamy was there, holding onto me, his grin wide. He tugged me up as if I were weightless, bringing me into his arms. I hugged him back, thankful that the one who had nearly killed me, saved me. Was that not how I had always been?

"You're a fool, Princess." The voice was different, the embodiment of death, ice cold and disorienting. "Though, it seems to run in the family."

Bellamy's words ended with a heated kiss, his tongue slipping into my mouth. Instincts failed me, because instead of pushing away, I pulled him closer. Relishing in the feel of him, I did not notice the pull between my breasts until it was too late.

He sunk his hand into my chest, ripping straight through skin and muscle, grabbing hold of my heart. His grip was excruciating, screams escaping my mouth in torment.

"Consider this a final warning, for I won't give another. You are doomed to a lifetime of loneliness. Any who you allow into your heart will surely betray you. The prince will sooner cut your head from your neck than love you. Guard this heart of yours before someone much hungrier feasts on it."

When Bellamy pulled away, it was no longer the demon prince at all, but rather a different fae of sorts. The creature had ears that came to a sharp point, though they slanted outwards instead of up. Its skin was so pale it seemed almost translucent, revealing a blue blush. Purple hair that was nearly black fell down its back, a shiny sleet of silk. Its eyes were white and narrowed, as if assessing me. High cheekbones and a chiseled jaw made the thing hauntingly beautiful, which only added to the horror of it. The black robes adorning its body blew in a phantom breeze, and its smile revealed teeth that were too white.

"Sleep well, Asher, we shall meet again."

***

I woke up with a jolt, eyes flying around the area for potential threats, but there were none. Only Lian sitting nearby, watching me. There was a furrow to her brows that told me I must have been a sight to see, asleep in the grass.

She stood, walking my way and plopping down on the grass beside me. I sat up, my body still shaking so violently that I could do nothing but hold my legs to my chest and breathe.

"I went back and retrieved this for you after Bellamy portaled you guys out of the forest," she said.

In her hand she held out the dagger she had given me, which was now clean, the blood washed away as if it had never been.

My hand shook as I gripped it, but I fought to bring the weapon to my chest. A single tear fell from my eye, hitting the demon sigil on the hilt. Nodding a thanks at Lian, I stood, making my way back to camp on silent feet.

"Perhaps I was wrong before," she whispered. I froze, the words she spoke next nearly breaking me. "Fear is not always healthy. For what it is worth, I am no longer afraid of you, Asher. I trust you."

Without a word or a backwards glance, I made my way to my tent.

I did not sleep again for three days.

I knew what awaited me when my eyes closed.

ACT IV
~ DEPRESSION ~

CHAPTER THIRTY-NINE

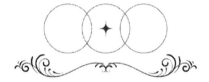

With the Forest of Tragedies at our backs, we were able to travel during the day.

Exhaustion weighed on me as we rode, Frost remaining steady below as if she could sense that my fatigue would throw me off her back if she so much as breathed too heavily. Henry, who I found out on our first day of travel after the afriktor attack was Bellamy's highest ranking captain—second only to the lieutenant general—trained me after dinner, not caring that I was exhausted.

We worked to keep a healthy balance of using my power to fight while also learning to survive without it. Lian offered to help, and together they had me past basics and onto more intermediate combinations after the second day. On the third, I was asked to wield my dagger.

The runes on it still gave me chills, still called to me as if they wanted me to know their meaning. I ignored them, but argued against using it.

My protests of fear that I would hurt them were met with laughs. Henry offered a snide remark, of course.

"As if you could hurt us when you tried, let alone by accident. Please, Ash, do be realistic."

Ash.

Noe and Henry both seemed to feel they were entitled to call me that. A nickname that was reserved for friends. For family. At first it upset me, the memory of those who had called me that before leaving behind an ache I could not free myself from.

But as the days went by, I found myself considering them friends too. Especially Noe, who had accepted my friendship and cared for me every day since.

When twilight came and went, the others slept. I offered to take watch the first evening when we once again made camp. I had not woken another to take over, opting to stay awake and practice most of the night away.

The second and third nights were far less convenient. Bellamy and Ranbir had timed our travel rather perfectly, landing us in small villages with even smaller inns just as darkness fell. It was then that I learned Eoforhild was home to more than mere demons.

On the eve we arrived at the first inn, we were greeted by the owner. She was a blue skinned female with five small, cream horns sticking out of her black hair. They looked almost crown-like, as if she were born to be a monarch. She was beautiful in only the way a faerie could be. Yet, the fae had been under the belief that faeries were completely extinct, wiped out by the demons in the Great War.

Bellamy used my curiosity as an opportunity, eagerly answering any questions I had, so long as he could ask his own. It turned out, many creatures had fled to Eoforhild during the Great War. He told me of the days when creatures were not separated by seas, but were mingled on land. I gasped at the idea of fae and demons and humans all living together, as if they were not so incredibly different after all. Apparently, that did not turn out well though, seeing as there was a war.

I did not sleep at the inns. At first I blamed it on the curiosity of the newness. After that wore off, I realized I was simply afraid of what resting would bring.

Instead, I wandered, rejoicing in the freedom and running from the monsters that loomed in my mind. As far as I was aware, Lian had not told Bellamy about my nightmares in the grass, but her discretion did not come without a price. She was never out of sight, always keeping an eye on me, even if from a distance.

Out of everyone, Ranbir's company was the most soothing. He was an early riser, hunting each area to find plants and berries and anything he could use for natural healing. I had never seen a Healer take so much interest in non-power methods, so I could not help but tag along those first three mornings.

He was not one for small talk, but he could not resist the opportunity to discuss his work. I learned about aloe, lavender, hyssop, tulsi, goji berries, and walnuts. So many natural ingredients that supported the body during recovery, even sped it up.

When I had asked why he would need to have anything of the sort when his patients were always quick healers, Ranbir's eyes went wide. I could sense his nerves and fear, feel his panic. Whatever reason he had was apparently one I could not know. Eventually he offered a vague response.

"They might not always be."

I did not ask again.

On the third day, Ranbir and I ran into a plant called prunella vulgaris. Ranbir nearly sobbed with joy at the sight of the plant that, according to the Healer, was not native to the region. He had left me after collecting what he needed to share the exciting news with Winona.

As he did each morning, Cyprus found me immediately after Ranbir and I parted. We were on our fourth day of travel following the Forest of Tragedies incident, and Cyprus had taken to getting to know me.

"Okay, today we talk about something you failed miserably at accomplishing," he said, a smirk gracing his face. Cyprus had pulled back his hair, wrapping it in a leather tie at the base of his neck. He was a similar build to Ranbir, the two of them both tall and thin.

Today he wore loose black trousers and a dusty rose colored long sleeve top. His cream boots matched perfectly, pulling the outfit into a beautiful statement. It had a certain Tomorrow's name written all over it. In fact, every one of Bellamy's Trusted wore clothes that screamed Pino.

My own outfit did as well. The seamster must have known I had an aversion to gold, because he managed to add every color but that to my wardrobe. Each night, Bellamy brought me a pile of fresh clothing for the next day that made my eyes bulge. Today I wore skin tight trousers that matched the sand at Haven. Around my thigh was a sheath that appeared black, but glittered an assortment of colors in the sunlight, my dagger tucked safely inside.

On my upper half was the true statement. The sage green long sleeve top wrapped me like bandages, twirling up my torso and around my arms. The chest was missing, covered instead with black lace and cloth designs that deigned to cover my breasts somewhat. Over top I was given a leather corset the color of spiced cider, which stopped just below the lace and tied at my back. Like every other piece of clothing I received from Pino, it fit like an incredibly comfortable glove rather than suffocating me.

To tie each outfit together I had taken to copying the group and adding kohl to my eyes, the same black as my ankle high boots. Instead of smudging it onto my lid or under my eye, I dragged it from the outer corners and up, creating wings that would never fly. But a fae could dream.

No matter the outfit, I always wore my silver cloak. It seemed the only article of clothing we repeated were the covers, as the others sported their matching red ones daily too.

Winona was the best dressed of us all. Every piece was spectacular. The day prior she wore a top that appeared to be made of diamonds held together by thin gold chains. Her tanned skin was visible below, only a small gold wrap covering her breasts. Black leather pants adorned her bottom half, and thigh high boots that reflected in the sun topped the look off. According to her, being cold was worth looking extraordinary.

She had been doing my hair every morning and telling me of fantastical creatures that existed nowhere else in the world but Eoforhild, which had been both exciting and terrifying at once.

I eyed Cyprus as I thought of something I failed at, other than being as mystical as Bellamy's Trusted of course.

"I once attempted to learn to sing, but my instructor was appalled that even after a fortnight I had not shown a hint of progress. The only thing I failed worse at was learning the language of The Old Ones. My tutor yelled at me for a year straight before finally giving up. I can pick up on a few words here and there, but it mostly goes in one ear and out the other."

At my admission, Cyprus let out a laugh that echoed across the small dining area of the inn. This had been the first one to not be enthralled by the idea of the crown prince residing in their establishment. Instead, these demons were hostile and ignorant. They had refused to allow Ranbir and Lian in at all, though they would have gladly thrown out Bellamy as well judging by the looks they had given him. There were no faeries here either.

It seemed a half-fae prince was not enough to eradicate the hatred for the inhabitants of Betovere. Perhaps the feud would never die, fae and demons alike always at war over prejudices that had been engraved into them since birth.

Bellamy had been prepared to concede, suggesting to us in a hushed voice that we would all make camp somewhere else, but something in me raged at the way they were ostracized. Based on the anger that poured off of the prince, I knew he was barely leashing his own frustration, fighting that reputation of ripping out hearts and burning beings alive.

Without hesitating, I latched onto their minds, burrowing my way in. I had taken to silently practicing on the others for fun lately, not saying anything until they managed to find me in their heads and nag at me to stop. But that had been entertainment. This was business.

"You will allow us to spend the evening here. You will show us kindness. You will kneel for your prince and treat him with the respect he deserves," I had ordered them, the tenor of my voice dropping to a low and seductive tone. I could sense the others tensing at my back, the way they all radiated fear despite knowing I would not harm them. Not now when I was just beginning to enjoy their company that is.

The two males had fallen to the ground, tears streaming and apologies spewing from their mouths. I had rolled my eyes, past the point of forgiveness. However, I had not missed the way they seemed to face me as they bowed. No one had scolded me, but the others did keep their space for the rest of the night.

The two demons had not bothered us again.

Even with my power, I knew it was not ideal to annoy the hosts, so I quickly jabbed Cyprus in the gut with my elbow, earning a satisfying grunt from the whisp. I moved my hand to my mouth to stifle my own laughs at his slightly bent form.

"What about you, oh great shadow? What is something you have failed at?" I inquired.

He pursed his lips, looking off to the side as he mulled over the question. Whatever answer he might have found was lost when his eyes went wide. My nerves skyrocketed as I turned, praying to Eternity that there was not a rabid beast at my back.

Eternity must have felt humorous today, because it was not a mere monster that stood behind me. No, it was Bellamy. He was only a few feet away, scowling at Cyprus over my shoulder. The nerve of that demon was absurd. But I could not bring myself to think of anything other than the fact I had not seen him today, and I was not prepared for his appearance.

We matched, which was now our new normal. I was unsure if Pino or Bellamy was responsible, but I had come to expect the demon prince to use our coordination as a way to initiate conversation, and then proceed to shamelessly flirt with me for the remainder of the day.

That was not what left me breathless though, not in the slightest. It was the utter indecency of his clothing. His sandy pants fit him as snugly as my own, better even. The sage top he wore had loose fitting sleeves that were rolled up to the elbow, showing his cream skin and the black tattoos atop it. The neckline of the shirt cut down in a low V shape, nearly reaching his navel. Black strings laced up the opening, though they remained untied, matching his black boots.

His dark hair was a mess, but it only added to his appeal, much to my disdain. Bellamy was aggravatingly handsome, even more so as his eyes moved from Cyprus to me. The blue was not nearly as startling as when he chose to wear cosmetics below them, but they still captivated me. An odd sense of déjà vu hit me while I stared into them, one I could not quite place.

"Well, I better go relax in a real bed while I have the chance; I know this will be our last inn for a few days. You will have to let me hear that incredible singing voice of yours later," Cyprus said, pressing a quick kiss to my cheek and then winking at Bellamy. With that, Cyprus was gone, fading to shadow. I rolled my eyes at his hasty exit.

Coward.

Bellamy stared at me for another moment, looking me up and down with that fire in his eyes I had come to know. I blushed, much to my annoyance and his smirk-filled amusement. Before I could brush off my reaction, he spoke.

"Cyprus seems to like you a little too much."

I had learned from Cyprus that Bellamy's Trusted were like a family. They did not act as if they had any particular power imbalance, nor did Bellamy demand their compliance. In fact, he had apparently urged them to speak their minds, to fight against his poor decisions.

That was, until I came. Now there was a tension in the air, one that seemed to follow me everywhere I went. I was the outsider. Either the problem to be fixed or the shiny new toy, and I hated that.

"What ever happened to beginning a conversation with 'hello' or 'good morning' or even 'thank you for not murdering us all in our sleep'? At least something more interesting than petty jealousy. It is truly beneath you, Your Highness," I said with a smirk of my own, hoping to antagonize him.

"Hello, Princess," he offered with a smile, bringing back that softness to his otherwise hard features. Bellamy took the handful of steps needed to close the distance between us, leaning down until we were breathing the same air.

With a raised hand, the demon pinched the lace of my top, toying with it. I swatted his hand away, coaxing a laugh from him. Those fingers came back up, lightly tracing my collar bone. I gasped despite myself when he leaned down to my ear and whispered, "You look positively ravishing today, Asher."

My eyebrows shot up, face feigning bewilderment. I did my best to seem offended as I brought my hand to my chest, mouth popping open. Anything to hide the heat that was trickling down my body to my core.

"Here I thought that I always looked stunning," I said.

He laughed, a short and crisp chuckle that I felt in my bones. It was a lovely sound, one that made someone want to laugh along, to enjoy themselves. I tried my best to fight his charm, which seemed to grow stronger with each passing day.

His dimples made an appearance on his cheeks, signaling a full and true smile. Despite myself, I did enjoy the sight of them paired with the crinkle of his eyes.

He was dazzling, annoyingly so.

I wanted to hate him, but was unable to. Dislike, yes. Hate? I did not know if I ever could.

"Are you implying I do not suggest so daily?" he asked, his own mock hurt shifting his face. I nearly rolled my eyes, but knew better than to give him the satisfaction of winning our little play fight.

He smirked, as if he knew how hard it was for me not to show my irritation.

"Of course not, I am merely saying you are not nearly as appreciative of my gloriousness as you could be." I made sure to lift my chin slightly, knowing it brought our lips closer. He took the opportunity to bring his chest to mine, our breaths matching pace.

With the movement of his body, our faces were now merely inches apart. If I wanted, I could lift onto my toes and taste him. Memories of his soft lips and wicked tongue fogged my brain. I knew I should protest the closeness, but I could not remember why.

"Let me make myself clear then. You, Asher, are the most gorgeous creation to grace our world. To see your face is to know true divine beauty," he whispered. Then, with a sly smile that lifted only one side of his mouth, he added, "The only thing better would be seeing the rest of you."

I reared back slightly, smacking his arm, laughing despite myself. He too joined in with a deep laugh, his arm looping around my back to pull me back into him.

Ever the obnoxious flirt.

Such a silly, pathetic being you are. So trusting. So naïve.

Ever the idiotic princess.

I placed a palm to his chest, pushing him back. He complied, stepping much farther than the strength of my shove had warranted. A kindness, but no more than I deserved. Because no matter what I thought or others attempted to make me believe, my body was mine and mine alone. A part of me knew that he agreed, but I could not shake the feeling of Sterling against me.

"You are lucky to have me, lucky to be mine when you are so unwanted by your own kind."

With the mortal prince's voice still ringing in my ears, I turned and walked to mine and Noe's room, not allowing myself the chance to do something I would regret.

I was broken and tired and lost. No one needed to hold my hand and watch me sink. Bellamy, who was willing to kidnap me to save his realm, least of all.

CHAPTER FORTY

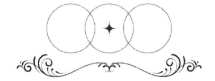

It had been forty-two days since the afriktor attack.

I had never been more sore in my life. Even the three breaks we had taken, staying at inns for an extra night, could not alleviate the pain that radiated throughout my entire body. I had recently taken to walking when the pace allowed for it, though it rarely did.

Last night we had made camp in Lady Odilia's territory, Kratos. Henry and Bellamy explained that Eoforhild was made up of seven territories: Dunamis, the lands of the five Lords and Ladies, and then the Forest of Tragedies. Very few knew of Haven, though it apparently was well known that Bellamy's Trusted had fae within.

Lady Odilia Nash was a Sun and Henry's mother. I had been fairly surprised upon finding out, but Henry had brushed it off. He went as far as to say his mother was an overpaid nanny, which earned a chuckle from me. And a story of my horrid nannies when I was a youngling, of course.

But inside I wondered what else I did not know about those within Bellamy's inner circle.

According to Ranbir, we were no more than a fortnight from Dunamis, from meeting the demon king of Eoforhild, Adbeel Ayad. I had shook at the thought of what otherworldly magic he might possess, courtesy of his ancestor Asta.

The sound of Noe's laugh brought the present back to focus, ripping me from my spiraling thoughts.

I often found myself wandering at times like these, when everyone was full of joy. The terrors of my mind left me waking in cold sweats and screaming into the night, so I did everything I could to resist sleep. To not show that weakness.

The first time it happened—the fourth night of travel—Noe had been so frightened she portaled to Bellamy and screamed that something was attacking me. When the prince appeared at my bedside in a cloud of smoke, his hands flying to my cheeks, I could do nothing but sob.

Bellamy had not left me for the remainder of the night. I had let him hold me while he whispered tales of dragons and gods and other worlds. I let him rub my back and caress my hair as he spoke of his own nightmares. I let him tell me that the fear of losing his friends, the emptiness of being alone, and the beings he had killed rained down on his mind in endless sequences of horror. I let him kiss my forehead and tell me I was stronger than I knew.

Beside me now, with the sunset casting a golden hue over his freckled face, I allowed myself a moment to imagine what life with Bellamy would be like. I knew he would hold me when I felt as if my heart might fall from my chest. He would be there when I was scared and reassure me that I was capable of anything—everything.

My eyes roamed over our group, the beings I would call my family if I chose Bellamy.

Noe would never allow me to give up, would fight anyone and everyone on my behalf.

Ranbir would always listen, would patiently teach me.

Winona would push me to be bold, would brush my hair and tell me stories.

Cyprus would make me laugh, would divulge secrets he knew were not meant for my ears.

Lian would make sure I was strong, would give me a weapon and a will to survive.

Henry would banter with me, would make fun of my height and embrace me in the same breath.

And Bellamy…he would treat me well. But he would also lie to me, would use me to whatever extent. There was no escaping the fact that I was a means to an end for him. The answer to the question he had been asking. The weapon in his war.

I could not allow myself to care for someone who would never see me as more than a tool.

When Bellamy turned towards me, those blue eyes finding my own, I looked away. Caring for him would be as foolish as loving the royals, and I had already made the latter mistake. No need to repeat it.

"I distinctly remember winning that bet, actually," Lian called out, her cool gaze directed at Henry, who smirked back at her. The two had been bickering all day, Cyprus and Noe offering opinions here and there to fuel the fire.

"Actually, that recruit still cannot shoot a target to save his life. One good shot at practice does not negate the rest. So I think you decidedly lost," the Sun shrugged. I could not stifle my laugh when I heard Lian curse and threaten to show Henry what one good shot could accomplish. Of course, that set the demon's eyes on me.

I heard his horse gallop to my right, Bellamy still on my left. Tilting my head towards Henry as he approached, I found him already looking at me with a wicked grin. I had not slept the last two nights, and I knew Henry was aware of just how cranky I could become, yet he did not hold back.

"And what is it you are laughing at, little Manipulator? Perhaps you can share with the group what you recently stole from our minds so we can be humored as well?" Henry prodded. I knew he was simply aiming to get a rise from me, a reaction, but I could not stop myself from taking that bait.

I squared my shoulders, glaring daggers at him. He wanted some secrets? Then I would give him some.

"Well, sweet potato, I am glad you asked. Last night in my boredom, I thought perhaps I would use you for entertainment. And imagine my glee when I found you horny as a rabbit and thinking of—"

"Woah, okay, never mind. Nope. Let's move on. Did anyone notice the way Bell nearly ripped Cy's head off when he whispered in Ash's ear at lunch? We should talk about that instead. The scandal of it all," Henry said, his words coming out in a rush of nerves and fear. His feelings projected my way, but I did not need powers to know he was quite frazzled.

Served him right for saying what he just did. I peeked back at Cyprus, whose smile had widened. Letting out a breath of annoyance, I slowly slid my eyes back to Bellamy. To my own surprise, the demon prince was smiling as well. Not a hint of anger or jealousy graced his perfect face, only amusement.

"Slander. As your prince and leader, I vote we discuss the fact that Ranbir's tunic was suddenly on backwards after said lunch. Does anyone else recall when Winona whisked him away to pick stinging nettle?" he asked, those haunting eyes never leaving mine, captivating me.

Laughs burst throughout the group, with Cyprus whooping and nudging Ranbir, who looked horrified. Winona on the other hand seemed pleased, flicking back her bottle green hair and winking at Bellamy.

"It helps with inflammation!" Ranbir insisted, defending himself. Of course, in his embarrassment he had not considered his words carefully enough, much to Noe's excitement.

"Interesting, I had never been aware sex could do such a thing," she said with raised brows. She flashed Ranbir a coy smile. The Healer's dark cheeks seemed to deepen in color, blushing at the teasing. Ranbir was too kind for this world.

Fortunately for him, I was not.

"Well Noe, perhaps you have only had terrible sex then. I for one find that a good orgasm can do wonders for inflammation, among other things," I cut in, flicking a speck of lint from my shoulder. Henry burst into laughter, Lian snorting. Noe's cheeks flamed, taking her turn to flush in mortification, though that smile still graced her face.

From the corner of my eye, I noted Bellamy coming closer, Lucifer and Frost touching slightly. Lust poured off of him, a hunger that throbbed and a thirst that ached.

Ranbir gave me a thankful smile, Winona blowing him a kiss from her horse. They were a beautiful couple, the fae and the demon. Unique in more ways than one, the most interesting being that they were natural born enemies.

Apparently, no good deed goes unpunished.

Cyprus pushed his horse into a trot, slowing when he was directly behind me. Over my shoulder he looked as if he were about to say something incredibly foolish, but before I could give him the benefit of the doubt, he proved my suspicion right.

"You know, I have been told I am rather skilled at loosening joints and stretching backs. Perhaps you could let me see if I am any good at *lowering inflammation*," Cyprus hinted, his voice dripping seduction. Bellamy, who was still visible in my peripheral, stiffened.

I did not fully know why I did it, shut down the male once and for all. My initial instinct was to deny that I cared about Bellamy's feelings or saw any future for us, but I could not pretend that deep down a part of me did. Which might have been the main reason behind my next words.

"Intriguing offer, but alas, I must decline. Sadly, as adventurous and curious as I am, I draw the line at sleeping with shadows, little whisp." My voice was light, but I knew that Cyprus had taken it for what it truly was, a rejection. To my left, satisfaction bled from Bellamy, his thoughts forcing their way into my head, each intentionally dirtier than the last.

I did not dare look at him, though everyone else instantly did. I would not fuel their suspicions.

I did of course push into his mind and offer a few derogatory remarks.

When the group had once again become silent, I thought back to what Bellamy said all those nights ago.

"Be mine, Asher."

I was no one's but my own.

CHAPTER FORTY-ONE

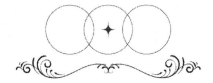

The next day, Bellamy found me awake before the sun, as I had been all night. I thought perhaps he had discovered my tendencies to fight sleep, despite not being told, but this was the first time he had approached me. We were camped in a low valley, the snow not yet sticking here but the air still frigid. I sat perched on a large rock, where I had laid out a thick quilt and bundled myself in my cloak as well as a large fur.

The demon came towards me on silent feet, his black hair messy, but still mostly swept to one side. The tip of his nose and apples of his cheeks were a vibrant red, nearly hiding the patches of freckles there. His full lips were slightly purple in color, as if he had been outside longer than the time it took to walk from his tent to my rock, but had not wanted to alert me of his presence by using his powers.

"May I?" he asked, gesturing to the space beside me, his head tilted in that infuriating way it so often did.

I eyed him for a moment, wondering what he was plotting. Begrudgingly, I nodded, scooting further to give him more space. He propped himself up on the flat surface, shivering at the cold that must have seeped into his body at the contact even through the quilt.

Sighing, I loosened the fur from around my shoulders and promptly wrapped some of it around him. Stunned, he looked at me with wide eyes and parted lips. I rolled my own eyes. I was not so horrid I would let the male freeze.

Suddenly, heat enveloped the space between us, radiating from him like a fire. Without much thought, I scooted closer to him, eagerly drinking in the warmth. Evidently, the demon did not need a fur to stay warm.

"Is this when you admit to me that we only traveled by horseback so you had time to convince me to join your cause?" I asked, eyebrows raised.

It was glaringly obvious that he had done this on purpose, though I was surprised that he found the wasted time was worth the effort. He could have made the same valiant attempt within the confines of The Royal City.

With a dashing smirk, the prince snapped his fingers. Appearing on my lap in a cloud of black smoke was a brown sack, lumpy and unimpressive. Inside I found my clothes for the day.

A deep red tunic, the fabric a soft cotton and appearing to be a tighter fit. Black, thick tights also lay within the sack. To top off the look of the day was a gorgeous chain mail vest. Instead of the bulky and tight stiches that normally made up the metal top, this one was thinner and looser, decorative almost with its twists and designs.

Pino was a genius.

I smiled, nodding a thanks. Looking him over, I realized he had already donned his matching outfit. Black trousers and the same loosely woven metal on top, though his traveled down the length of his arms and was red rather than silver. Below he wore a black tunic.

Bellamy had told me before that we each had a pack, which was filled with clothes daily. Pino had been in charge of mine, as well as Bellamy's. Paid servants had received the others', as they resided in the palace when not doing whatever work was required of them as a part of the prince's Trusted.

"So what did you need, oh glorious heir to the demon throne?" I inquired. The sooner he left the better. This time alone was the only chance I had to think and feel without caution. Despite how painful the long hours were, they were also a treasure.

"Am I not allowed to simply enjoy your presence?" he asked, the tone mocking and light.

"Not if you possess sanity," I answered.

Those crystal eyes met mine.

Blasphemy, he shouted into his mind, the sound reverberating into my own head. *I could never be insane, I am far too brilliant.*

Ah, but you do not deny my company is less than enjoyable? I shot back, appreciating the slight panic that lit his face. I chuckled, shoving his arm with my shoulder to break the tension.

"Your company is like the sweetest wine," he said, earning a scoff from me.

"I hate you," I said in response, not able to conjure a better insult.

"I think the only thing you hate is how much you like me, Princess." His voice was sultry, more than a simple tease. We needed to change the subject before I lost all my senses.

"Tell me what you came for, demon," I said. Whatever it was had to be important to come out here in the night. It was far from comfortable.

"Well in truth, there was something I wanted to ask." His statement was hesitant, as if he were nervous. Of what I was unsure. My reaction? My answer? Both?

I nodded, waving a hand to signal for him to continue. He did not smile, though to his credit, he also did not hesitate.

"What do you want in life?"

I reeled back, as if his question was a blow to my chest. How could he ask something like that when he had worked so hard to take my choices away from me? He certainly had not cared what I wanted when he inserted himself into my life in order to steal me away from the only home I had ever known. Nor had he cared about my wants when he hid secrets from me and refused to allow me the courtesy of knowing what my own near future would entail.

"Are you daft? Or do you simply enjoy being a prick?" I seethed, jumping down from the rock and stomping away from him, ripping the fur off as I went.

He caught up with annoying quickness, not faltering a step. His persistence only made me angrier. With every ounce of strength I possessed, I remained quiet, heading straight for my tent. Bellamy had other ideas, reaching out his hand and grabbing onto my wrist. Then I was spinning to face him, his other arm securing around my waist. I struggled in his grasp, but it held firm.

"I was not asking to annoy you or make you feel upset. Why can you not see that I care? That I want your joy more than I want air in my lungs? Ask anything of me, and I will do everything I can to give it to you. Talk to me, please."

That did it. I looked up at him, finger pointed to his chest and eyes blazing.

"Fine, you want honesty? You want to talk? Then know I am miserable. I have no home, no family, and my best friends are a sea away. I am surrounded by creatures who lie to me and follow a wicked prince that abducted me. Every night I think of that stupid little child's hands on me or Xavier beating me or Mia offering me tea that likely had poison in it. And here you stand, pretending to care, as if you are not keeping secrets and holding me against my will. As if you are not lying and plotting and using me just as everyone else has!" I said with a gasp of breath.

He stared, face unreadable save for the tick in his jaw that said he was at least mildly upset. Good, that made two of us. I would not let him recover. Would not give him the opportunity to hide ugly truths with pretty lies. Whipping back around, I made a dash for my tent. I was so close, a mere ten feet. Still, he caught me, grabbing around my waist and pulling my back flush to his chest.

"Ash, please," he whispered, leaning down to rest his chin atop my head.

I froze, not prepared to hear that nickname come from his lips. It sounded horribly perfect. As if he were always meant to know me well enough to use it.

"There are some secrets that are not mine to tell, many that involve you. But when we arrive in The Royal City, I promise you will be made privy to them all. I know this is unfair, and that I have upended your life. You were right before, about me stalling with this trip. Not because I wanted to change your allegiances. Rather, I wanted more time with you. Selfishly, I wanted you to have more time with me as well," he admitted.

My body seemed incapable of moving, as if I were rooted to the spot within Bellamy's hold. Nothing kept me together save for the feeling of those strong arms, tightly grasping my stomach as if he were afraid I might disappear.

Always, he found a way to pull me in. To assure me he was not the enemy. To convince me that he was my destiny. A part of me agreed, enjoying the way I felt at his side. In all my life I had never met someone so close to my equal, who rivaled my strength and power, who did not balk or fear me. We fit together like two halves of a puzzle, waiting for the other to finally be complete.

Here, in his warmth, that future felt right. That was what he hoped for. I knew it. Regardless of the scheming, he hoped that at the end of this, we would survive, side by side. Unrealistic as that was.

"What will she mean to you in the end?" Pino had said that fateful day at his clothing stall.

When I had eavesdropped then, I had been unsure what he meant. Now though, I realized Pino had been encouraging Bellamy to tell me the truth, to give me a choice that might salvage that future. And the demon had not done so.

Still, he believed he would have me. I could hear it in his voice and see it in his eyes and feel it in his touch. For whatever reason, The Elemental had set his sights on me.

Finally, I turned around in his arms, pressing my hands to his chest and looking up into those blue eyes that always made my stomach flip. He would not give up until I answered his silly question, though the answer was far too meaningful to be a joke.

I sighed, knowing I would lose this fight.

"I want to mean something," I said.

If my statement surprised him, he did not show it. His arms tightened, as if letting me go meant losing me forever. Then they loosened, his hands sliding from my back, to my shoulders, to my hands.

"Would it be okay if I took you somewhere, Princess?" he asked.

My eyes darted around our sleeping camp, trying to determine what might be nearby that would interest him. Nothing. The valley was low, grass crisp from the cold and leafless trees with branches that jutted out ominously.

Anger still pulsed through me, because he had done all those wretched things I said. He had stripped me bare—left me without family, friends, or a home. He had watched me lose everything with no remorse.

Still, I could not ignore that taking me also opened my eyes. I missed The Capital. I missed Nicola and Jasper and Farai. I even missed Mia and Xavier, though I would never say it out loud. But I would not deny the fact that Bellamy had rescued me in many ways.

I nodded, and he flashed me a dimpled smile before the smoke wrapped around us. The pain was still heavy, like being torn to pieces for that moment between time and space.

We materialized at the top of a canyon, overlooking a vast expanse of orange rock that was dusted with snow. The terrain was jagged and uneven, as if the years had eaten away at it piece by piece. Something I could relate to.

Straight ahead, the sun was rising over the land, bidding us good morning. Though I had not known true peace since that night Noe had held me, I felt it here once more. Next to Bellamy, who was as warm as the sun itself. Not just in power and magic, but in his soul.

A reminder of sorts that if we all had evil in us, maybe we all had good too.

With one hand still in mine, Bellamy leaned in and whispered, "You mean everything."

CHAPTER FORTY-TWO

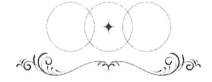

Eight more days of grueling travel passed.

In the night, I dreamt of Sterling finding me, his fingers turning to claws as they scraped down my torso. I screamed and screamed, but no one came. He spoke to me in a voice of velvet, promising to love me and take care of me, as long as I gave him everything he wanted. My crown, my immortality, my power.

When I begged him to stop, when I thrashed violently and refused him, the sultry voice disappeared, turning strained as he dragged those claws across my throat. He damned me to the Underworld, cursed my soul, and called me a monstrosity.

All the while I sobbed, wishing it would stop. Wishing I would die.

I awoke shrieking in terror.

Almost instantly, Bellamy appeared from a cloud of black, running to me.

I knew it was him, he was right in front of me, yet I fought to keep his hands from my body. I bared my teeth at him, opening my senses and shoving at that stupid mental shield of black fire. He lifted his arms immediately, backing away a step.

"Asher, it is me, Bellamy. You are safe. Please, I am here. You are safe, Princess. Please," he begged, his voice cracking with the plea. My eyes darted around the tent, desperately searching for some sort of sign that this was not a trick of my mind, that Bellamy would not attack me too.

Slowly, tentatively, he stepped towards me, noting how my eyes tracked his feet. How my body went rigid at his nearness. One step turned into three, five, and then he was there. Right beside my cot. Leaning down with caution, he reached a hand to me.

Tensing, I waited for him to strike. I deserved it after all.

A monstrosity, Sterling had called me. Yes. That was what I was.

Yet, Bellamy did not move to hit me, instead, he ever so gently placed his palm to my cheek, wiping a stray tear from under my eye. When his knees hit the floor, I finally snapped out of the crazed state.

He was real. I was safe. He was real. I was safe. He was real. I was safe.

I sighed, leaning into his touch. Relief washed over him as I did, causing his shoulders to slouch and his eyes to close. His other hand moved to my hair, massaging softly at my scalp and calming my pounding head, only stopping when my body lost the tension.

I would be okay. Bellamy was here, and he would keep me safe.

"Want to hear something funny?" he asked after a few moments of silence. I looked up, catching his blue eyes that appeared almost translucent in the demon light that Henry had crafted Noe and I last night. There was a devious look to them as he smirked to me.

"What?" I asked, eager to have anything else on my mind other than the nightmares. That hand remained gently clutching my cheek, thumb stroking my temple lazily. His smile grew, showing teeth.

"I once had a meltdown at a court function. Anger ruled me for a long time, and someone had made a snide comment about my ears. Many were unimpressed, if not outright disgusted, with the fae. A future ruler with pointed ears was enough to nearly start a civil war. I heard the carefully sculpted insult and everything turned red, a fire-filled haze blinded me with rage. My entire body erupted in flames. When the king finally calmed me down, I stood there, slightly hunched, and fully nude," he confided.

I burst into laughter, the thought of Bellamy standing without a speck of clothing on in front of a group of esteemed demons nearly leaving me heaving from hysterics. Though I could not help but feel a tinge of anger for his mistreatment.

He crouched beside me still, moving his other hand to his chest and popping his mouth open.

"I am wounded, Asher. You mock the single most embarrassing moment of my life," he said, feigning hurt. A devilish glint still lit his eyes, mischief heavy on his face. I flashed him a genuine smile, one filled with joy and humor, the nightmares far away.

His hand dropped, eyes blazing with that same fire. I froze, not understanding what had changed his mood so suddenly. Was it something I did?

"There it is," he muttered, that same dazed expression still lighting his face. I quirked an eyebrow, unsure of what he meant. "That smile. Your beautiful, wonderous smile which is so rare to see these days. But every time you flash it my way, I swear my heart skips a beat."

Now it was my turn to sit in stunned silence. I had no idea what to say to that, or how to react. Was there any option that would not hurt him? One that would not hurt me? His constant flirting and sly remarks, the way he managed to brush his fingers against my skin daily, every longing stare my way, they all pained me.

No matter what I did to push him out of my mind and heart, he always found a way to sneak back in, reminding me of the male I had met those many nights ago on a balcony. Back then I had thought of what life would be like with him by my side. Now, he was offering just that, and I refused him. Not simply for the lies or the plotting, but also because choosing him—as he so often begged me to—would be a risk. It would mean giving up on my family and my subjects back home. It would mean submitting to the unknown.

"Can I share something with you, Asher?" he asked, glazing over his comment as if it had never been said.

I quirked a brow, but curiosity left me nodding slightly without thinking. He smiled, a soft, reserved raise of his lips that did not quite signify joy.

"As a youngling, I never felt right here in Eoforhild. The others saw me as the enemy, as a pointy-eared traitor. I was an abomination that should have been dealt with swiftly, not given a title and space in the royal palace. Noe's father was one of the most adamant to speak against me. When I first met him, and Noe as well, I still had no powers. I recall him telling the king that I was a waste of space, better off executed than named prince."

Waste. That was one thing I had never been called. To belittle someone in such a way that reduces their life to nothing was foul and evil. Mia and Xavier would have never suggested I had no right to life, as awful as they had been in some ways. My eyes burned at the idea of a young Bellamy, blue eyed and freckled, hearing that spewed his way.

"Little by little, I lost myself throughout the years. I was secluded and ostracized. The king did everything he could to make my life easier, he loved me and taught me and stood by me. Still, the creatures of this realm found ways to make me feel less than. That is the thing about feuds and prejudices, they do not have room for exceptions."

His words sent chills down my spine, as I too had felt the weight of being different. I too had succumbed to the torment of being feared and hated by your own kind.

Perhaps that was similar to my own prejudice towards the demons. Bellamy's Trusted were kind and honest, funny and daring—nothing like the horrid beasts we had been taught they were. Bellamy himself, even with the scheming, was no monster. Not the one I thought him to be, at least.

"By the time I had my powers under control, I had long since lost my mind to the hatred. I was not good. I was ruthless and wicked. And I still am, deep down. I buried that darker side, hoping that I would never have to face it all, but it is still there, lying in wait for the day it can break free again."

That too felt too close to myself for comfort. For I also battled the evil within me. And like Bellamy, I sometimes lost.

"Noe and I became close after her own magic manifested, despite her father's agenda. When she limped up the steps of the palace decades later, bloody and bruised to a pulp, I lost it. I had called for help, then rode my horse to the edge of Dunamis and portaled to her father's doorstep."

He looked at me then, stare intense, as if gauging how I would react to the next part. Though, I knew what he would say. Whatever he saw in my gaze was enough for him to press on.

"I killed him. My hand shot into his chest and I ripped out his heart. But not before telling him that Noe was free. That he would never touch her again. That he would die a pathetic male with no love or success to his name. That he would die the way he deserved, alone. I killed him and I relished in the strength it seemed to give me. Desperation became my friend, retribution my lover. I was obsessed with violence and justice. With righting the wrongs that so many had committed," he said, his voice a husky growl that made me think he likely still had those urges.

"Not long after that, I developed a reputation. Demons and the creatures of Eoforhild feared me, they cowered in my presence. I was an outsider with more power than any one being should have, and no one was safe from my wrath. Once, when Noe, Henry, and I were out drinking mead and attempting to have a carefree evening, I let my rage get the best of me. A male had reached out and smacked Noe's behind as she passed him. When she reprimanded him, he threatened her body and life. In my mind, I was right to punish any that I deemed unworthy of existing. So I walked over to him, crafted a blade of black fire, cut his hand off with it, and then I split him from groin to head. It was a brutal death, one that sent others screaming from the tavern."

I shuddered at the image his story conjured. At the thought of such a deeply rooted love of violence. An addiction to feeling powerful through ending lives. I recalled how nonchalantly Bellamy had said he killed Sterling when I first awoke after my failed wedding. The fury in his face when he killed the two demons who had attacked me. The giddiness within him when we were entering the Forest of Tragedies. A part of the demon prince would always seek out danger, would always revel in death. And a part of me relished in that fact, as if I were pulled to him more for it.

"To this day I have to resist justifying murder for the sake of the greater good. Haven has helped, as did enlisting in our military forces. Adbeel had encouraged me to join. He had said that I was a slave to my anger, that I let it convince me I had the right to be judge, jury, and executioner. When I volunteered myself into our army, I found that I could show everyone who I was and what I was worth better than I could tell them. I quickly moved my way up, and now I am the general. I am the leader of a great force, and I am mostly respected and revered. A stark contrast to what I was," he said with a humorless chuckle.

Though he fought back that urge for violence, I could still see the shadow of his life haunting him. The guilt eating at him.

"I have nightmares that I will not be able to save those I love. That everything I have built will crash down. That I will once more worship pain as a god and lose myself all over again. That is why I tell you this. I want you to see that you are not alone, Asher," he said; his story coming to an end.

I pondered for a moment, considering how strangely alike we were. Two sides of the same coin, different, but the same. Still, I could not find words. So instead, I rubbed his back gently, a soothing gesture meant to reassure him.

He looked at me, those icy eyes landing on my own and seeming to seek an answer. Despite knowing he had lied to me and hurt me, I could not help but want to remind him of his worth. For reasons I might never understand, I thought he deserved to feel loved by me, if only for the night.

So I pulled him towards me, bringing his body to my own and allowing him to settle onto my too small cot. As we lay there, nose to nose and chest to chest, both of our bodies warming the other, I felt myself relax.

It was not the heat that brought me comfort, but rather Bellamy himself. His presence.

Perhaps it made me an idiot, maybe even a traitor to my kind, but in that moment, I allowed myself to imagine holding him like this forever. To picture loving him for not this one night, but for all nights.

He had given me a gift of sorts, the kind that could solely be offered by a being who had suffered the same self-hatred that could cause nightmares such as mine. Such as ours.

We were the worst kind of evil. The beautiful kind that inspired hope in others, then ripped it from them and brought only death. The kind of evil that had to fight itself every day.

I knew then the only words that I could offer. As the sun began to rise in the distance, as the light of a new day started to shine through the partially open tent flap, I put my arms around the demon prince of Eoforhild and spoke.

"I see you, Bellamy. All of you. And I am not afraid."

CHAPTER FORTY-THREE

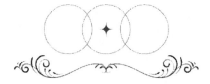

The following night we made camp on a snowy mountain side.

I had seen forests, deserts, mountains, seas, valleys, and so much more during this journey. Things I never had the chance to lay my eyes on before. With time, I found myself feeling more free as a captive than I had as a princess. Especially now that I was a somewhat decent rider. Frost and I maintained a far quicker pace, though I was still the least skilled of our group. I did not think I would ever be great at it, but the silver mare made up for my lacking with ease.

I had been training with Bellamy and each of his Trusted daily, quickly learning to balance the use of my power and my physical strength. The first time I disarmed Ranbir the entire group had screamed with joy. Then I bested Winona. Then Cyprus. Then Noe.

My victory over the Moon had been a shock. She was, after all, a trained assassin. Moreover, Bellamy had been instructing them all to block me. They each succeeded at various rates and capacities, but it did add to the already difficult task of fighting while trying to focus my mind and power. So I did not let the win go to my head, barely even allowing for celebration.

Harder and harder I trained, pushing myself every day with the image of Tish's face in my head, her horror at the sight of me bloodied and broken. Never again, I chanted in my mind.

Henry had been baffled when I finally took him down on day forty-three. Actually, the only one who was not surprised was Bellamy. The rest of us, including myself, sat still for a moment. We stared and stared and stared at my dagger against Henry's heart, his back against the snow.

But Bellamy started *clapping*.

When we finally snapped out of our daze, he ran to me, hoisting me in the air and spinning. I laughed, leaning my head back as he called a fresh wind to us, blowing my hair around my face. The others quickly joined in, Henry included, though he called it luck.

I had never felt so powerful, so unstoppable. Still, I reminded myself I had two more to take down.

Three days later, I beat Lian.

The swordmaster, who was also a Captain in Bellamy's forces, was the toughest behind the prince. She was strong and fast, incredibly dominant on the field. Unlike Cyprus and Ranbir, who held back and learned their lesson, she never once gave me anything less than her all. When I broke her shields and saw her next move, I jumped out of reach and smashed down on her sword hand with my elbow. The loud crack had been deafening.

I repeatedly told all of them that without my powers I would never beat them, that my ability to read their thoughts was an unfair advantage. But Lian disagreed, insisting that we all had abilities which helped us, even as Ranbir healed her shattered wrist. Henry's portaling had certainly made it hard. Lian's wind had knocked the breath out of me more times than I could count. Noe's raw magic had even taken out a chunk of my shoulder once.

When Bellamy and I fought, my protests rang true. He blocked my power, resisting my violent assaults on his mind and body. I was relentless in my attacks, but I never won. In fact, I lost quite easily. There was once when I thought I had worn down his mental shields enough to break through, but the second I had felt myself slip past, he kicked my feet from under me and I ate a mouthful of dirt.

Now we circled one another, both predators fighting for dominance. I had learned how to wield a sword, but often relied on the blade I kept sheathed to my thigh. That and my powers. Today was no different.

Bellamy struck the second he felt me within his head, which was guarded tightly by a wall of black flame. I could practically taste the smoke, feel the heat, sense the burn. But I welcomed it, parrying his swipe and kicking his back. He did not so much as stumble, spinning low to face me once more. Bouncing lightly from foot to foot, I scoured his shield for even the slightest weakness, the smallest hole.

The prince would not give me a chance to grab hold, charging me once more. Our blades sang to the mountain as they connected, steel meeting steel with a deadly kiss. Back and forth we swung until Bellamy drew first blood. My leg screamed in agony as he sliced through the area just above my knee. Blood oozed out of me, but I continued on, dodging his next attack.

Bellamy had told me in the beginning that those who I would need a sword against would not hear reason or hold back; they would kill me if I let them. Which meant no rules. I was to use every weapon in my arsenal, and he would do the same. Though he never did use his powers beyond a simple gust of wind or shake of earth. He had never so much as smacked me with snow or heated my sword. Still, I never came close to besting him.

Which was why I knew what I would need to do to beat Bellamy.

This time, when he came for my back, I turned, facing him head on. He ran into me, taking us both to the ground until he sat straddling me from above. I feigned exhaustion, allowing him to think me weak, because that would be my saving grace one day.

When he gave me a dimpled smile, his lips not far from mine, I reached up and cupped his face with both hands. His startled expression was all I needed to encourage my plan. I leaned in, letting my eyes flutter closed, and just when our lips met in a soft caress, I sprung.

My power flooded his mind, tearing through his shield. He was unsuspecting, confused, and unsteady. It was everything he could not afford to be in my presence, because it was all the opportunity I needed. Suddenly, I was him and he was me and everything I wanted was mine for the taking.

Hello, demon, I said in his head.

The prince flinched, rearing back at the realization that he was too late to stop me, though he tried to force my power from himself. He thrashed on the ground as I squeezed, adding more and more pressure in his temples. The others barely breathed, every one of them stunned into silence. Then, as easily as saying the words myself, I fed Bellamy a sentence I had been plotting for days.

He relaxed, straightening and moving to rest on one knee, bowing to me.

"I concede, for you are far stronger than I—a foolish demon—could ever be. All hail, Asher. A gorgeous and talented fae with skill beyond compare." With that, I too got down on my knees, placing my dagger against his throat.

"It seems you have been bested, Elemental," I spoke, exhilaration heavy on my face. I was bragging, being a sore winner of sorts, but I did not care. I had *beat him.*

The group burst into laughter, adding in cheers here and there. But Bellamy did not look away from me.

Our heaving chests met in steady intervals, the smell of cinnamon and smoke wafting to me and heating my body. In that moment, I forgot about the audience we had, ignored the warning bells in my own mind, and pushed away the hurt we had caused one another. Because the feel of him against me was intoxicating. The kind of addiction that tore you apart and left you shattered on a floor unable to think of, or want, anything else.

The prince seemed to understand, to follow my thought process and agree. His breaths came harder, loud in my ears and hot on my face.

"I do so love the sight of you holding that dagger to my neck, Princess. Perhaps we could do this every day," he said, his mouth forming into a smirk.

I knew what he wanted me to do, to say. My mind considered what it would mean to say I was his, to give myself to the demon who stole me two months ago. Who might still plan to use me. The strange fae's words from my dream all those nights ago still rang in my head, clear and foreboding.

"Any who you allow into your heart will surely betray you. The prince will sooner cut your head from your neck than love you."

Before I could say anything, or even think further, a slow clap sounded from behind me. The group went silent, all of us adjusting our bodies to seek the source of the sound. There, at the edge of our campsite, was a group of at least five dozen demons.

My body went cold at the sight of them, dressed all in black, with hooded cloaks and mighty swords that seemed to gleam in the fading sun. A rush of adrenaline, fear, and hatred washed into the air, stripping it of the joy that had been there before. Now, I was surrounded by the growing tension, digging into my head and making my body buzz with the need to fight.

The demon in front, a tall male with blush pink hair and dark brown eyes, lowered his hood. Bellamy and I both stood, his body moving to slightly cover mine. I wanted to argue, to shove my way to the front and prove that I could never again be harmed at the hands of a spineless male. Instead, I remained quiet, assessing.

The pink-haired demon was likely their leader, and I found my power urging me towards him, like an itch that needed to be scratched. I tested his mental barriers, finding them weak and flimsy. Inside his head was a mess of red, as if blood dripped from every surface. This male was vicious, killing for sport and regularly selling slaves on the black market. I internally shivered, not quite sure if I should attack now and ask questions later, or if that would be worse. Though I vowed no matter what, he would die for his crimes.

"What an interesting display. They told me you were powerful, but not once did they mention your ability to fight. Convenient detail to leave out," he said, his voice higher than I thought it would be, a sort of raspy whine. The second he said "they," images of Mia and Xavier flashed through his mind.

I watched as he struck a deal with them, vowing to bring me back alive and kill the rest. I listened as he promised to also deliver his own prince's head in a box to them.

Rage filled my vision with red, and I had to force myself to let go of his mind before I did something hasty. Bellamy reached back, his fingertips grazing my arm, as if he knew that I was close to losing my control. The one problem with having the hemlock out of my system was that now I had far more power than I ever possessed before. Maintaining a hold on it all was difficult, to say the least.

"Who are you?" Bellamy asked, his voice bored and uninterested. The pink-haired demon cocked his head to the side, eyes narrowing. Oh, he must have been quite notorious to have the audacity to show this type of vanity. Not only did he expect us to know him, he wanted us to. Needed, even.

"I am *the* O'Malley Harligold, renowned privateer, and I come for your lovely lady there. Maybe this need not be bloody. Hand her over to me, and you may all go about your evening in peace," he offered with a grand gesture around our campsite, his voice boisterous.

Bellamy's anger seemed to peak at the suggestion, tensing his shoulders. One fist lay clenched at his side, as if attempting to fight his urge to lift the sword in his other. His Trusted stood ready, each armed and eyeing the large group in front of us.

O'Malley Harligold straightened, and through his mind I felt his resolve mixing with excitement. He wanted the fight, the bloodshed. Gore was his entertainment. Unfortunately for him, I had recently discovered my own affinity towards violence.

"I highly suggest you reconsider, because I guarantee you that this will only end with your cock shoved down your throat and your eyes gouged from their sockets," Bellamy said, his voice a low timbre that sent chills up my spine. O'Malley scoffed, the group of demons behind him looking far more uneasy than their leader. "And when the Princess has had her fun with you, I will gladly remove your ugly head from your shoulders."

I laughed then, unable to contain it. The confidence Bellamy had in me was incredibly reassuring. I readied myself for the first test. A chance for me to measure what I had learned with no restraint.

The Manipulator eagerly awaited.

"Pity, it seems we will need to do this the hard way, Ayad. Let us hope your bloody death does not frighten the fae princess too much," O'Malley said, anger alight in his eyes. His pride was hurt, I could sense that without attempting to maintain footing in his mind.

I decided then that perhaps he would like an example of just how frightening this would become.

CHAPTER FORTY-FOUR

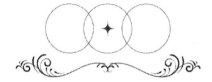

With little effort, I grabbed at O'Malley, whispering into his mind.

Did they warn you of my tricks, filthy pirate?

He froze mid step, eyes bulging and flying to me. His mind raged with memories. Mia telling him I would be skittish from mistreatment. That I was powerful, but they had likely been feeding me little and left the blocker on. Xavier had reassured him I was unskilled without my power, that I would be frightened and desperate to get home. They had prepared for a complacent and weak fae.

They had underestimated me.

Foolish of you, O'Malley, to trust royalty.

I stepped forward, a smile on my face as I took in his worried expression. He did not back down, readying himself. In his head he wondered if killing me would lead to his own death, and then I watched as he concluded it would be worth it to suffer the consequences of ending me if it meant saving his pride. He decided it would be an easy kill—after all, I was still a young and sheltered princess. Then he glanced over to Bellamy, and the way he gleefully pictured ripping his intestines from his stomach had me seething.

I shall show you who the weak one is.

Then I was upon him, drawing my sword from my back and striking swiftly. Lian had given me this weapon. It was a perfect match to the dagger, though far larger, the runes even more eye catching—even more unsettling. She said it was lighter than most, but it still had taken me awhile to learn to wield it. I was not perfect, but I was fast and strong. Not to mention I watched as he decided his moves, reacting before he could blink.

Without realizing it, I had held back with Bellamy and his Trusted, scared to hurt them while practicing. Now, I had no such qualms. I wanted to hurt this demon. He was the perfect image of everything and everyone who had beat me down. This would be my chance to show myself just how strong I could be. To remind myself that in the end, I needed no one.

That I was no one's but my own.

None of the others moved, opting to watch as we struck at one another, swords slashing through air and steel colliding. Each time he thought he had me, I adjusted just in time. He became sloppy with fury at my ability to hold him off, his pride becoming his downfall.

I simply laughed, enjoying the way my arms burned and my power hummed. Never before had I unleashed myself this way, controlled but free, like a waterfall. For the first time, I was flowing as I had always been meant to, and it was addictive.

Moods spiked at the sight of my growing advantage, and I felt the exact moment that O'Malley's group decided they might need to intervene. Which sadly meant my fun had ended.

I turned in a circle, whipping my foot around to catch the back of the demon's calf just as he had stepped back. He stumbled, crashing to the snow. As quickly as I could, I took my sword and stabbed it through his stomach, pushing until I felt it stick into the dirt below the snow. His scream was horrific, and also somewhat pleasing, sending birds flying from nearby trees. I threw my power out, grabbing hold of the minds of all sixty-three of O'Malley's group.

Stay, I told them. *Watch.*

None of them moved, though their eyes bore into me as I unsheathed my dagger from my thigh. I pressed the tip lightly against O'Malley's cheek, running it down his skin softly in time with a falling tear.

Did his victims cry as well? Did the slaves he bought, sold, and transported beg for a mercy he would not give?

His mind seemed to suggest he enjoyed their pain, relished in the way they grew weaker. He had taken many professional contracts, but when he transported goods and defended territories, he also committed atrocious crimes. His death would be a justice.

I leaned into his face, smelling heavy tobacco and nearly gagging. "Do remember my face as you burn, demon."

With speed I had not known I possessed, I took my dagger, cut a hole in his trousers, and sliced off his pitiful penis. He howled, vomiting from the pain and choking on it. But I was not done. I took the severed member and shoved it into his mouth until I heard him gag. The runes on my weapons seemed to glow, as if feeding on his terror.

Then I gripped my sword and yanked with all my strength, ripping it from his gut in one smooth motion. O'Malley sobbed in the snow, one hand freeing his mouth and the other holding his upper wound. Just to make sure I followed through with Bellamy's promise, I shoved both of my thumbs into his eyes, digging until a loud pop sounded.

He screamed until his voice became rough, cracking and breaking. I looked up, staring down his lackeys. As I released them, I pointed my bloody sword their way, eyes wild with wrath and eagerness.

"Think twice about your choice, now," I warned.

Some part of me deep inside begged them to lay down their weapons.

Of course, they did not. Instead, they charged me, screaming. I rolled my eyes, though I would not pretend like I was not eager for more. Behind me, Bellamy and his Trusted snapped out of their stunned daze. They too pushed forward, all eight of us rushing to meet the far larger group ahead. My well of power was nowhere near depleted, but it had lost a significant amount after holding them all still and forcing them to watch.

Still, I was ready when two males raised their swords to me. I swung, and then I was dancing, channeling everything I had learned these last two months. I cut through two, five, then six of them, blood soaking my white blouse. Each life I took made the runes on my sword glow brighter, until it was nearly as captivating as the demon light being wielded against me.

When someone landed a blow with shadows as sharp as steel, slicing a narrow cut to my side, I roared. I was not weak. I would never be weak again.

Sterling, Mia, Xavier, the two demons who had attacked me in Haven, even Bellamy flashed through my mind. Never. Again.

I ducked out of the way of a stream of light, rearing back and swinging to behead the demon. Her blood splashed across my face, momentarily blinding me. Wiping my eyes with the back of my sleeve, I steadied myself.

Behind, another demon came for me. This time, I allowed the fight to last, eagerly slicing him throughout our battle. When I heard Winona howl in pain, I shoved my sword through his face, kicking his body off with the heel of my boot.

Then, with little care for whatever morals I might still possess, I grabbed onto every enemy mind and slowly squeezed. One by one they fell to the ground, similar to the way the afriktors had. I watched with glee as they screamed, begging for help. Suffering was the least they deserved.

Inside, I felt that part of me, the one that had wanted to be better, tell me to stop. *End them quickly and be done with it,* the voice seemed to say. I wanted to argue, to resist and rain fire down upon the crying demons. I wanted them to feel every ounce of pain I had in my life, to know that, in the end, it was a foolish princess who bested them.

A hand on my shoulder brought my mind back into focus. I looked back to find Bellamy there, face unreadable and palm warm. I shuddered at the contact, at the way it grounded me.

"I see you, Asher. All of you. And I am not afraid," he whispered to me.

Just like that, I was reminded of who I was. Who I wished to be.

I shattered their minds.

All but O'Malley, who Bellamy then urged Ranbir to go to.

"Heal him only enough to speak," he ordered. Ranbir nodded, rushing over and bending to place his hands on the demon's stomach, eyes raking over his mutilated genitals and shivering.

I watched, thinking of all the horrible things I had ever been called, and knew they were all correct. The bodies that surrounded us were gruesome to view. Warm blood coated the snow, melting it in places and staining the world red. I wondered how many of them I had killed, and how many Bellamy and his Trusted had taken care of.

Noe walked over, eyes wide and hands raised in the air. Each of her steps were slow, calculated. She reminded me of someone approaching a caged beast. Looking down, I realized I still held my sword grasped firmly, knees slightly bent and eyes alight with havoc.

To our left, Bellamy called upon his fire, burning the bodies. I let my sword drop, taking in a deep breath and allowing a gore-soaked Noe to wrap me in her arms. When I felt her hands drag up and down my back, I exhaled the heavy breath and returned the hug.

"I know, Ash. The first time you take a life like that is never easy. I wish I could say that you will forget one day, but you will not.

Personally, I can still feel the blood of my first kill dripping down my cheek. We all know that pain, and we are all here to help you," she reassured.

Part of me thought I should tell her just how many lives I had snuffed out, like a strong breeze blowing over a table of candles. These demons were not the first to have been ended by The Manipulator, nor would they be the last.

Ranbir stood, walking over to Bellamy to speak softly, then heading to Winona and pulling her into a gentle kiss. When they parted, he assessed her, eyes roaming from foot to head. Then he kissed her once more, and I watched as her body quickly healed, how she relaxed into the touch and wrapped her arms around his neck.

Lian was once again unscathed, using a cloth to clean the blood from both of her long swords. Cyprus had barely been hurt, and I watched as his black mist slithered across the bodies before a flick of his hand snuffed it out. Noe released me, turning to face the whisp, who had on a face far more stern than his usual easy smile. Beside him, Henry let his narrow gaze roam over the carnage, blood that did not seem to be his coating his tunic.

Winona made her way to us, hair falling out of her braids. When she was close enough to smell her honey scent, the Sun pulled me into a tight embrace. Just like Noe had.

"You were so brave, love. You saved us all, do not let the weight of this burden overshadow that," she said against my ear.

I nearly burst into tears, unprepared for the onslaught of emotions that would surface within me. Regardless of what my actions cost my soul, I would have done it again. Anything to stop the image of Bellamy's head in Xavier's hands from playing in my mind.

When she too released me, I forced myself to watch the many bodies burn to ash. Forced myself to see what I was at my core. I had liked hurting them, killing them, and I could not bring myself to regret it. So the pain I felt at the sight of it all, it would be mine alone to shoulder.

Across the clouds of smoke, Bellamy stood, covered in more blood than any of us and still burning black fire around his arms. He had his eyes trained at his feet, where O'Malley Harligold lay clutching at his groin, as if he could will the appendage back onto his body.

"Nothing to say? Strange, you seemed to really enjoy the sound of your own voice before," he said, dripping rage. O'Malley moaned, body tensing at the sound of Bellamy's voice. When the prince reached down and grabbed at the pirate's jaw with a flaming hand, ripping it to the side so he could look into his bloody eyes, O'Malley began to sob.

Taking that as my cue, I made my way around the bodies, coming to a stop before the two of them. The pirate flinched when I dug into his mind, seeking out information about the royals and what they wanted. He knew very little, only having met with them once and then portaling back to Eoforhild and seeking out our group. It had taken him two months to find us, and he was running out of time.

I nodded to Bellamy, letting him know I had everything I needed from the demon at our feet. Then an eerily familiar smile formed on his lips, as if he had been holding back his blood lust and this signal was a relief.

"We are on a bit of a time crunch, so I am unable to take my time with this," Bellamy said. I could not force myself to look away as he lifted his blazing arm and seethed, "Perhaps we can settle this in the Underworld."

Then his arm swung down, fire ripping through the skin and bone, severing the demon's head.

CHAPTER FORTY-FIVE

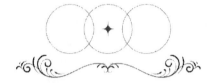

Bellamy allowed us one day to recuperate. When his fire had burned the bodies to ashes, we packed up and moved camp enough of a distance away for the smell of blood and burnt flesh to fade. Still, I thought the smell might never go away permanently, and it reminded me so much of Sipho that I sobbed all night, not daring to close my eyes.

The sight of the bodies, of the singed hair and my bloodied hands, had me reliving the night of his death over and over again. I could hear my own screams echoing in my head, see the blood from my bare body being thrown against the wall so hard my skull cracked, feel Sipho's pain and agony being projected into the air, taste the rage on my tongue, and smell the fire burning through the male I loved.

I recalled my shame and how it prevented me from telling anyone what happened, how the grief had left me in bed for weeks. Xavier had visited me, apologized for what he had done, but ultimately blamed it on my own stupidity and recklessness.

Forgiveness had not come swiftly, but I had never outright shown my anger to him. He and Mia were all I had, their love and generosity had gotten me to where I was. Without them, I would probably have been dead. How could I not forgive him after everything he had done for me?

With their love in mind, I never argued or fought, never brought up what happened. When they told me I would not be permitted to visit his grave on Isle Healer, I waited until I was once more in my chambers to cry. When I wrote a letter to his family, Mia had stopped me from sending it, and I had said nothing.

I had been weak.

The following night, and the next, I dreamt of Sipho. I pictured what our lives could have been, the way our younglings might have looked, what sort of home we would have built. And at the end of my dreams, I killed him. Every time. He would die in my arms, begging me to spare him, just as he had that night so long ago. I would shatter him, watch his soul leave this world, and then I would weep upon his body.

On the day we were supposed to begin our final stretch of the trip, Bellamy awoke me from a particularly bloody variation of the nightmare. He had looked into my eyes, his face full of an anguish that likely mirrored my own, and opened his mouth to speak. I quickly shook my head, not needing the reassurance that they had all been trying to give me. I knew what I was, and perhaps it was time I embraced it.

I was the death of all things good, it was what I had always been, what I was meant to be. I had no idea where I would go after I met King Adbeel, or what I would do. Going back home was unlikely, and even I knew that there was no real place for me in Eoforhild, unless I wanted to be used as a weapon and then discarded. So maybe I did not have to grasp at that conscience that I had so desperately clung to as a fae princess. There was no longer a need for it.

Bellamy handed me the satchel of my clothes, staring at me for another moment before exiting the tent. Noe was already awake, her eyes trained on me just as her prince's had been. She was worried, I could feel it tainting the air.

Noe had weak mental walls, and it was all too easy to see the images she remembered of me taking my dagger to O'Malley, of the way I murdered with ruthless efficiency. Her excitement, her sense of rightness at my actions, jarred me. She was not scared of me. No, she respected and agreed with my choices on that battlefield.

That was far worse.

After getting dressed and eating a hasty breakfast, we set off, pushing on until the sun began to set. The group spoke on and off, laughing and arguing as usual. I reinforced my mental shields, not wanting to hear any projected thoughts or feel any heavy emotions.

My own head was enough today.

The others asked for the information I gleaned from the mind of O'Malley Harligold, and I told them with as much strength as I could manage, detailing out his slave trade, the royals contacting him, and even their desire for Bellamy's head.

It jarred the Trusted, the idea that demons would turn on their own. Bellamy, on the other hand, had scoffed, deeming it "predictable."

"They hate me; they always have. I am an outsider. Seeing me dead and off the throne would please more than it would anger," he said.

The next few miles were spent strategizing for this new discovery, attempting to outplan and outsmart the royals. Surprisingly, no one suggested just sending me back.

When we stopped, I refused the training session with Henry. He had tried to joke, saying that slitting a few throats did not make me an expert. At my flinch, Bellamy smacked Henry upside the head. When Cyprus laughed, Bellamy smacked him too.

They all walked on eggshells around me from there on, too afraid that they would be the reason I tipped over the edge. Even Noe, with her loud personality, did not dare to say more than a few words to me. They gave me space, and I took it gladly.

When we finished eating, I wandered over to the edge of the mountain side, staring off into the snowy distance and wondering how I would feel when this was all said and done. When I refused whatever the offer would be from the demon king, maybe I could travel.

I had always wanted freedom to see the world. There were far more mortal lands than demon or fae, I could always go to one of those kingdoms. But then what would happen to my friends back home? To Bellamy and his Trusted? War would come, and no one would be safe. There had to be some way I could change the tide. For all my many faults, I knew I had the potential to prevent total destruction, it was the how that evaded me.

Bellamy walked up behind me, cutting off my planning. He said nothing, merely calling on his fire, creating a flame in his palm the same way he had the night we met. Just like he did then, Bellamy held the fire in front of me. I smiled in thanks but remained quiet.

It was not long before he broke the silence.

"A gold piece for your thoughts?" he asked.

I snorted, looking over to him with raised brows.

"That is a hefty price for a mere thought," I said.

"Yours are worth far more," he responded with a dimpled smile. His body slid closer to mine, the air around him warm and inviting.

I rolled my eyes but smiled back despite myself. Hating him would make this all easier. He waited for my answer, but it would not come. Any plans I made would need to stay private, because I doubted he would let me leave if his king—his father—ordered me to stay.

"Okay, how about I tell you what I am thinking? Free of charge." When I said nothing, he continued. "I am thinking that you are being too hard on yourself."

Huffing out a low breath, I relented.

347

"I know what I am. I have always known. There is no reason to deny or fight it anymore," I muttered, looking straight ahead at the snowy scene. Bellamy scoffed, extinguishing his fire. Peering at him from the corner of my eye, I saw him cross his arms. "What a noble and mature prince you are."

"Taking life is never easy, but sometimes it is necessary. Doing so does not make you evil," he whispered, as if it were something he still needed to convince himself of. I nodded absently.

There was no such thing as good and evil, nor had there ever been. But I knew who I was, I knew how little good existed in me. My powers had never been pure like that of other fae, and that tainted me, blackened my heart. It was far more than any one being should possess— the ability to manipulate the minds of others. Like playing a god or masquerading as Eternity.

The demon seemed to notice how little his words swayed me, because he heaved a sigh and grabbed onto my hand, dragging me back to the others. I allowed him to pull me, thinking of how his hot skin felt against mine, the sense of rightness that always came with his presence.

I watched him as they all talked amongst themselves, noting the way he seemed to lean towards me. It was the same way I always gravitated to him. Bellamy and I were both fighting to be something we never could be—resisting the urge to be what we always would be.

Out of thin air, a pencil appeared, wrapped with a piece of paper. I jumped, the sight catching me off guard and sending me sprawling to the snow. Bellamy chuckled, catching it and standing, his free hand reaching out to haul me upright.

"How?" I asked as he lifted me to my feet, intrigued by the sight. In the Fae Realm, we used messenger ravens. Never whatever that was.

"I laced the pencil with my essence. Our king has long since studied ways to intertwine our magic with objects. Similar to how I am able to call upon tents and cloaks and quilts, so too can I be made aware of someone touching those objects. I felt the pencil being used, and when it was let go, I called it to me. Quite an effective way of communication," he bragged.

Cocky demon.

Panic seized me though as I watched Bellamy's face contort from humor to fear. Whatever he was reading, nothing good would come of it.

The others seemed to agree, rushing at us with concern and apprehension. The demon prince did not notice, did not so much as move as he stared at the paper in his hands. I wanted to beg him to just tell us already, but Noe beat me to it, snatching the paper from his hands and reading once. Twice. A third time.

She looked up, her eyes roving over the group, then landing on me. She stared at me in horror as she spoke.

"Pino says he sees danger ahead. Something is coming."

CHAPTER FORTY-SIX

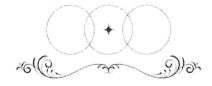

Gathered around the fire, seven of us remained silently sitting while Bellamy paced and murmured to himself. I had wanted to say something encouraging, to lead the way I had always been taught, but nothing came to mind.

Pino had not specified who or what was coming, but the urgency in his written words were clear: they needed to prepare, now.

Suddenly, a question came to me.

"Wait. How is it that Pino knows something, or someone, is coming?" My words sounded strange as they tore through the hollowness that had come from our lack of talking.

The group stirred, looking my way. Then, as if needing permission, each of their gazes found the, now still, prince, who merely eyed me. When no one responded, I continued voicing my thoughts and confusion aloud.

"I just mean that I have never come across a Tomorrow with the ability of foresight to that extent. Well, apart from my friend Nicola, who sometimes has dreams that manifest. That, though, was previously unheard of. I guess I am wondering what makes Pino believe that there is danger lurking? Did he touch someone and see their death?" I asked, ceasing my nervous rambling.

The others allowed their eyes to roam to Bellamy once more, not daring to speak an answer. Another secret, another lie. Was Eoforhild really in danger, or was something more convoluted occurring? I meant to ask when Bellamy finally found his voice.

"Every couple of millennia, a Reader is born with a power greater than their peers. What they see is not limited to yesterday or tomorrow and no touch is required, they simply see what the gods deem worthy. The past many have forgotten, the future many have feared, and the present many have avoided. A fae such as this is not called a Tomorrow or a Yesterday, for they are far beyond. They are called *Oracles*," Bellamy said, the word sounding foreign and strange.

Yet another term I was not privy to. Annoyance was beginning to form at the realization that I was far more ignorant to my own subjects than I thought. There was so much more to them than I ever knew, to the extent that I was starting to wonder if I would have been the queen I had always imagined myself as.

Ranbir spoke next, a voice of reason among the panic.

"What is our next move then? We cannot simply leave Haven without forces seeing as it is a border land, but someone must rally our armies. And we need Asher to meet King Adbeel so that—" Ranbir cut himself off midsentence, grimacing as he looked my way in apology.

I rolled my eyes, crossed my arms, and promptly pouted like the grown fae I was.

Noe and Henry both let out low chuckles, but quickly reverted back to seriousness as Bellamy once again paced. His face was scrunched together in concentration.

From a political standpoint, the best thing they could do would be to immediately meet with their king and allow for the monarch to weigh in, if not make the final decision. But I could see how their priorities might be the defense of a village they all deeply loved.

Without thinking it through, I allowed myself to weigh in.

"We should split up. If you think about it, this group is probably perfect for the divide we need. Bellamy can take Lian and Henry to your armies and ready them. While they are doing that, Noe, Ranbir, and Winona can all head back to Haven to prepare defenses. Little shadow should be more than enough to get me safely to the clutches of your demon king. I myself am eager to find out what ploy is in place that requires my abduction, so truthfully this scenario works perfectly," I said, sarcasm heavy on my tongue. I was still a bit bitter, obviously.

Yet, the wisdom and reasoning to my plan was solid. Noe nodded, Henry agreeing silently. Cyprus looked positively giddy, smiling from ear to ear at the prospect. The others also seemed to agree that this plan, which I so nicely provided, was probably the best course of action.

Bellamy's was the only face that grew angrier. The demon's cheeks went red as he stared my way. I waved a hand at his disapproval, standing up to square off with him. He did not back down, coming over to tower above me instead.

"Now is not the time for territorial jealousy, you prick. Not to mention that you have no right to dictate or disagree with who I allow around me. We need to split up whether you like it or not!" I hissed.

He merely stared at me, contemplating.

How was it that I—someone with no reason to help these creatures, who had thought them to be monsters only two months prior—was the one fighting to protect their realm?

"Fine. We split up then," Bellamy said. I nodded, thankful he was finally agreeing with me. About time. "With one small change. I will be accompanying you to Dunamis instead."

I groaned, rubbing my temples to give relief from the headache forming there. Jealous idiot. No one objected to the plan, but anyone could see that the best option would be for their general to lead the army. If it were foreign forces coming, then they would have to make it past The Mist to reach the realm, which in itself was horrifying as the capability to pass through it was beyond any knowledge. No one with enough power to do that should be overlooked, especially not for me.

"Once you are safely settled, I will head to the base," he added on, nodding to himself.

"I really think—"

"Enough Asher. We all depart in the morning," Bellamy said, promptly cutting me off. The demon sat, not willing to speak further. I gasped at his sheer audacity, poised to do something reckless. Henry reached his hand up to grab my elbow, shaking his head as he pulled me to him.

I huffed, but conceded. The fight would be pointless when they would all listen to Bellamy regardless of my protests. Still, I felt angered by his refusal to see reason.

"Where do you need me, Bell?" Cyprus asked, not sounding the least bit perturbed by having his spot taken from him. I admired that about the whisp, his ability to adapt and smile through challenges. He was incredibly optimistic and energetic, never faltering in his mood.

"Betovere. Something about this feels wrong. Bigger than us having Asher. We make no real moves until I get to the king. He will want to know what is happening," Bellamy said, his voice grim but strong. He was rising, as those in power must do during times of fear and danger.

Bigger than me? Did Bellamy think the fae were fighting back against the demons' attacks on Betovere? I grew angry at the idea, the simmering heat of fury boiling over and spilling out of me.

"Perhaps if you would simply stop attacking the fae, then your subjects—your entire realm—would not be in danger," I seethed. This argument had been a long time coming. I knew it. He knew it. We all did.

For every move I took towards them, I also took two back. My own ears were a product of their violence as a species. Any war that came would be born of a natural feud, but would be urged on by their bloody choices.

Ranbir gasped, his eyes wide. Winona grabbed his hand, squeezing it in comfort. Lian glared at me, as if I were wrong for standing up for our kind. Noe, Henry, and Cyprus remained silent, though I could see the judgement in their eyes.

Did they all truly justify their actions? How could they possibly sit there and know that innocent fae were being murdered at the hands of demons, and still support that? It was disgusting.

Bellamy stood once more, my words stoking the fire within him, feeding that anger that was such a fundamental part of the Fire sub faction, his preferred power.

"You know nothing, Asher. Nothing. We have not laid a single attack on Betovere since the Great Wars, even when warranted. That king and queen that you so deeply love are framing us for murders they have committed. They want you to think us the enemy, they want divide, because they want war. They want power!" he shouted, causing me to shrink back into Henry.

The tattoos on Bellamy's exposed forearms writhed, as if they were alive. Pulsing and stirring, they slithered like snakes, roaming his cream skin. The angrier he grew, the faster they moved.

"Why do you think that we have fae here in Eoforhild? Have you considered that there must be a reason for fae to *escape* your realm? Well there is. Eighty years ago, I was in Betovere and came across Lian screaming over a bloodied body while three guards in *gold* aimed at her with fucking swords." Lian cringed, eyes clamping shut against the onslaught of emotions that the story brought out of her, tears streaming down her face.

"She begged—*begged*, Asher—for them to stop. She had done nothing wrong, her lover had done nothing wrong. When they attempted to drag Lian from her bloody body, I killed them. All of them. From then on, I found a way to rescue those who had been so brutally treated. I found fae who were about to be executed for daring to love one outside of their faction. Fae who were two millennia and considered expendable. Younglings who showed little to no power. So many that your filthy royals have deemed unworthy of life."

The silence among us was painful as Bellamy neared me. His breathing grew heavier, eyes blazing with a rage that seeped from him, assaulting my senses. Fists clenched and jaw tight, Bellamy stopped his approach, as if he were too angry to keep walking.

Hot tears met my cheeks, but I did not allow myself to look away from the rage on his face. The pain.

"Do you think I do not want to wage war on them? Of course I do. Henry has been pushing me to do so for decades. How do you think I felt when I found out that they beat you to near death? What do you think I wanted to do when I heard how they treated you like a puppet? The moment I was made aware that they allowed that foul little mortal boy to *touch you* and live, I nearly stormed the castle. I would have done it, Asher. I would kill them all to save you, make no mistake. For you, I would be the villain."

His words were like a slap across the face. It felt as if my heart were shattering to pieces, hearing him speak and seeing the look on the two fae faces in front of me was gut-wrenching.

"But I will tell you right now, I have not attacked Betovere, and neither have my kind or any of my subjects. That is because I do not want death and carnage and the loss of innocents. So please, tell me again how I can stop this war that the royal fae are so set on beginning."

Seven pairs of eyes looked upon me. In the distance, a bird screeched. Otherwise, the silent air was thick with unspoken words and the truth that parted ways from Bellamy's lips. My hands grazed my ears, the tears still racing down my face. Had Xavier cut them? Mia? Were they the ones who murdered my parents? Had they been the ones to rip their own son's life from this world?

They lied to me, all of them. The royals, Bellamy, his Trusted. It was not my fault I lived in ignorance of the truth. Yet, I felt guilty. So immensely guilty that I had thought the beings around me had been mass murdering fae. Because they had proven themselves just and kind. Taking me was horrible, yes, but had Bellamy not saved me from Sterling? Had his Trusted not treated me as a comrade and cared for me like their own?

I considered how quickly Bellamy and Henry had come to my defense when those two demons attacked me. I remembered the circle the seven of them had formed around me when the afriktor threatened us. I thought of waking up in the grass to find Lian watching over me. I recalled how Noe held me when I cried. How they trained me and laughed with me and…loved me.

This group of beings, so different from one another, loved without hatred or judgement. They cared so deeply that they would lay down their lives for each other. For me.

And I accused them of attacking me and slaughtering my fae.

"I am—I just—" Words were failing me. No apology could make up for the lies that I had let sway my attitude and thoughts all this time.

At my back I felt a warm pressure. Henry had placed a hand there, comforting me as my mind reeled with the life-changing information. I offered the best smile I could muster in return, hoping that I did not look as pathetic as I felt.

Eighty years, that was how long I had been sitting idly by as fae were murdered by the couple I had considered my family. Nearly a century of strengthening our defenses, building prejudices, and honing powers for a war that could be avoided.

A war that would leave land decimated and lead to the death of thousands.

"I am sorry, Asher. I know you have been through a lot, and I would take away that pain in an instant if I could, but we are running out of time," Bellamy rasped, his voice a plea of sorts. The prince walked over to me, kneeling down at my feet and grabbing my hands in his own. "You have to pick a side, Princess. You have to make the choice that you have been avoiding. Because there is no room to sit in the middle when a war begins."

Bellamy reached up to cup my face with one of his hands, palm blazing on my ice-cold skin. He was asking for too much. How could I choose between the male in front of me and my friends back in Betovere? If I promised to aid the demons, would that threaten the innocent lives of those back home?

My breathing picked up, the tempo of my heart increasing to a dangerous speed. I needed more time. I needed Nicola's wisdom. I needed to find a better way.

I needed someone to bear the weight of the world that was upon my shoulders.

At my feet, Bellamy continued to stare into my eyes—my soul— searching for the answer he wanted. For the first time, I acknowledged that I did want to choose him. In a better world, we would be together. It would be as easy as breathing, loving him. Laughter and joy would fill our lives, perhaps even younglings one day. We could spend evenings with his Trusted and my own friends. A family of sorts.

That world was far different than this one, in which I was forced to witness my life crumble. Piece by piece it all crashed down around me.

Who was I? Certainly not a princess when I had been content to laugh and smile and breathe while my subjects were ruthlessly murdered by their king and queen.

I felt the moment when my mental shields fell. A cataclysmic shattering of that last mercy. When they toppled, every emotion and thought of the others bombarded me.

Suddenly I was feeling the rip in Lian's heart at the thought of her Yuza dying on the ground. Ranbir's thoughts of his own family being beheaded in front of him were horrific. Noe's anger towards Bellamy as she stood to her feet hit me violently. Cyprus was a whirl of stress for us, for Haven, for Luca, for his parents and sister. Winona was calculating, thinking of what war would mean for the inhabitants of Eoforhild, for her abnormally large family of parents and siblings that had no idea what was to come.

But it was Henry, who still rubbed circles on my back, that pushed me over the edge. He thought of watching me practice, the speed at which I learned. The demon conjured images of me on a battlefield, cutting down fae with eerie precision. He imagined what it would be like to watch bodies fall as I shattered minds. In his head, I was the monster that woke fae younglings from their sleep, terror ripping screams from their mouths.

The one thing their thoughts had in common was their belief that I could be a solution. To all of them I was a creature of the Underworld. Everything I had never wanted to be. Everything they needed to win the war.

I screamed, clawing at my head as if I could dig out their mental voices. My own voice, that deep tenor of The Manipulator, urged me to end them all. To shut them up swiftly. I fought against it, heaving and screeching for anyone to *please help me.*

Hitting the ground with a smack to the snow, I writhed, body convulsing as my power attempted to dig into the minds of those around me. I sunk into each of their heads, fighting my own urge to attack as I did.

Bellamy seized me, pulling my body into his arms. No pain from portaling could break through the torment occurring in my mind as time and space tried to rip us to shreds for daring to defy them, for my soul had long since been torn apart.

ACT V

~ ACCEPTANCE ~

CHAPTER FORTY-SEVEN

We appeared atop snow, a crystal-clear pool to our left which was fed by a waterfall pouring lazily from above.

The sky was infinitely more beautiful. Green and purple streaks lit it up, zigzagging over the stars and casting an ethereal glow onto the scene below.

Hands gripped me tighter, as if the prince thought I might flee or fall. I urged my heavy limbs to wrap around him in reassurance, causing him to loosen his hold.

The snow covered nearly every inch of the sunken waterfall. Walls of black, glittering rock rose on every side, the obsidian peeking out here and there. I had never been anywhere like it. We had seen a beautiful mountain a couple weeks ago, which shone in the light of day and rose past the clouds. Three weeks prior we came across a dazzling valley that held a quaint village. The warmth that radiated from it seemed to push away the winter chill.

Yet, neither could compare to this place.

My tears were beginning to freeze to my cheeks, mirroring the icicles that hung from a cave just behind the waterfall. I wiped at them, wetting the sleeves of my red tunic. The leather vest I wore atop it was cinched across my chest, holding in some of my body heat, but not nearly enough.

A shiver made its way through my tired bones. Silently, I wondered what the demon's plans were. We would be here in the middle of nowhere, far from the planning taking place at camp, and for what? To allow me the chance to breakdown in seclusion? It seemed rather pointless.

Unfazed by the chill, Bellamy walked us towards the opening of the cave, finding a path behind the falling stream with an ease that told me he had been here many times before. The sound of the water as it hit the pool below was melodic, soothing my sobs to a weak sniffle. I relaxed into him, but my mind remained a violent storm.

Bellamy maintained his own shields, the wall of black fire pushing back my reaching power that I had lost control of. So I was left to my own head. Mia's face came to me more often than anything else as the demon prince walked us farther into the darkness. One memory in particular, repeated.

Mia had been doing my hair, as she often did. The braids were exquisite, wrapping around my head and weaving together like an intricate basket. I remembered the way she covered my ears, pulling the hair down and over the mutilated tips.

"So you will never have to see yourself as anything less than wonderous," she claimed.

On that fateful day, my powers came to me in full force, lashing out and nearly killing the fae queen. I remembered the fear in her eyes, which would then turn into excitement.

Then the deaths began.

Quicker than I thought possible, Mia had a blocker made. I wore it every day, apart from practice hours, suffering in agony as my power was siphoned out of me.

I had thought it a mercy, to spare the world from me. A monster, Mia had said. I would become a vicious beast if not taught and restrained. Without fail, I thanked them for keeping me. For loving me despite what I was. Hatred filled me, for I was no better than a demon. I was horrid in every way, and I despised myself.

All while they murdered their own kind. All while they poisoned their ward, a female who had practically been their daughter. Perhaps after killing their own son.

A faint glow could be seen now, the color similar to the rays in the sky above. I squinted, trying to understand what could possibly make that light. As we neared, I gasped, seeing that small turquoise lights dotted a vaulted cave ceiling, reaching far higher than I would have expected. The lights wrapped around the walls, the cave bigger than a large home.

"Orfelia fultoni," Bellamy rasped to me. "Glowworms."

I looked again at the lights on the wall nearest us. I had seen drawings of worms that could be found on the isles, especially Isle Healer. But this did not appear to be any type of insect. They looked like demon light, glowing a different color, but still the same uncanny bright sphere.

Bellamy looked down at me, a soft smile on his lips, dimples hidden away. I wondered if he might have been making things up to distract me. While my curiosity was piqued, I would not be worth trying to please. Sorrow felt permanent at this point. As if it were a core piece of who I was now.

Right on cue, I felt my body begin to shake violently, the lack of sleep and the loss of control both fighting to break me.

I was spasming still as horrific thoughts of hemlock and Mia's smiling face bore down on me from memories and conjured nightmares. It became hard to distinguish reality from fantasy while the weight of the world crushed me beneath it.

Time passed both slowly and quickly, the cave becoming lit by nothing save for the glow of creatures around us. All the while, Bellamy held on, arms keeping me together while everything within me fell apart. I cried endlessly, begging to know why. Why did they betray me? Why had I not been smarter? Why was I always poisoning what I touched?

Bellamy brushed his hands through my hair, moving us to a sitting position and holding me in his lap. I felt every beating I had ever taken from Xavier. I remembered their warm embraces, the sound of their voices when they told me they loved me. I saw Mia's silencing looks and listened to her scathing remarks. I thought of each life I had been told to end. I recalled every ounce of joy that I had felt.

Honey eyes and blue-black hair materialized in my head then, finally pushing me over that edge I had been on for months. Xavier had burned him alive. He had tortured him as I sat naked against the wall, curled in a ball and begging him to stop. He had forced me to end the life of the male I loved, stole him from me, made me sleep in the room where he was murdered.

He blamed me, and in turn taught me to blame myself. And after, as I sobbed beside the charred remains of the male I had thought was my destiny, he beat me into unconsciousness.

And I had loved him like a father.

Everything I did was for them, always. They were my family.

Now I was alone.

I was alone. Alone. Alone. Alone. Alone. Alone.

And I deserved to be, because as much as I now knew that what Mia and Xavier had done to me—to Sipho—was wrong, I also knew that I would always hold blame. No matter what excuses I made for myself, there was still fault in me. So I chanted it over and over again, unsure if it was only sounding in my head or if I were uttering it through my lips.

Likely the latter, as Bellamy responded to my cries.

"You are not alone, Asher. I am here. I do not care what I said before. Any piece of yourself that you will give, I will take with honor. I will treasure you, hold you, and support you. My heart belongs to you, Princess. Never will you be alone again," he said, his voice a doting whisper.

Firm hands heated by the fire within grazed my cheeks, then guided my head towards a pair of icy blue eyes. All at once my shaking ceased, sobs slowing. Bellamy was staring at me like he never had before. Determination and devotion lit his gaze, sparkling in his eyes like the stars in the sky.

I shook my head, trying to free myself from the feeling that had been growing over the last couple of weeks, months really. The emotion I had rejected. Because I knew those who I loved, left. Always.

Pushing away was impossible while Bellamy held me like this, trying to force me to understand. I refused to see what he was attempting to convey, refused to believe he was being honest. Yet, the demon merely waited. Pinning me with that stare.

"Please, do not do this," I begged, weak from the months of torment and constant pain. I could not take another loss. Could not bear one more heartbreak. Surely I would not survive it.

His hands pulled my face closer, our breaths mingling in the small space between us. He smelled of smoky cinnamon and snow, and felt wonderfully warm. Everything I ever wanted, he had promised me before. It seemed now he was prepared to give that to me without any vows on my part.

"I love you, Asher Daniox. You are the breath in my lungs and the beat of my heart. And I am yours. I was yours yesterday, I am yours today, and I will be yours every day after. Even if you do not choose me, I will spend the rest of my life choosing you. I will love you until my final breath and long after. I would crawl from my grave to find you once more if it meant even a single moment with you."

My own breath hitched at his words.

They hurt just as badly as I thought they would. Another to love, another to lose. Every bit of happiness he brought me from here on out would simply make the inevitable pain that much stronger. Yet, admitting the scope of his feelings forced me to acknowledge my own. Which left me unable to do anything but let them swarm me.

Every crack and fissure that the days, the months, the years had created in my heart felt as if they were being cauterized. A painful burn and ache that came from being re-fused, remade. All with the fire that coursed through Bellamy's veins. That fire that he seemed to wield stronger than any of the other elements. The fire that I could feel radiating from him now, as he held me tighter in his arms. Skin of fire and eyes of ice burning me to my soul and freezing me in his grasp.

Before I could second guess my choice or over think, I closed the space between us. He reacted slowly, surprised at first, but then with eagerness to meet me with as much force as I was giving. And he did, tenfold.

The kiss was claiming, full of pent-up need and the high of his declaration. Without a moment of hesitation, I pushed his body down onto the cave floor, placing my knees on either side of his hips to straddle him. He moaned as I ground myself on top of him, desire driving me and leaving caution behind.

I gripped his shirt with one hand, pulling him further into me and lacing my fingers through his thick, dark hair.

"Asher, I do not think you are in any state to be—"

I kissed him harder, fiercer, wrapping my tongue around his and drinking him in. He moaned, but I could feel him slowing down, thinking far more than he should be.

"Princess," he whispered into my mouth, tugging his mouth away from mine to stare into my eyes. I knew what he was searching for in me, the reassurance he would need before he would allow us to go any further.

"I will not choose between the fae and the demons," I said. He stilled, looking up at me with half closed lids and rosy cheeks. His swollen lips were a temptation that I had to look away from to resist.

Closing my eyes, I pushed on.

"I will fight for freedom. No fae or demon or mortal is entirely innocent, but none deserve to suffer through a war. My allegiance lies with those who stand to lose the most, those who have been looked over, those I have wronged. I may not be worthy of their love or the title of queen, but none will suffer if I can help it. I fight for them, as I should have before," I proclaimed, not daring to open my eyes until I was finished.

When I did, Bellamy's mouth was parted slightly, his blue eyes glittering with something akin to pride. His fingers met my cheeks once more, sliding down slightly to grip my jaw and neck.

"I will stand beside you, a soul far more deserving of a crown than any before her. Your wish, your fight, your will, it is all my command. If you will have me, Princess, I am here." His heart sped up beneath my palm, as if perhaps he expected me to deny him. Somehow, I knew he would still love me after, no matter what choices I made. My own beat quicker, the sound drowning out my heavy breaths and invasive thoughts.

I recalled the strange fae's words in my dream and Sterling's insults. Considered the possibility that Bellamy might be tricking me. Each horrible moment that led us here flashed before my eyes. Every fear came at me, told me that I only stood to lose more.

Yet, staring at the demon prince, I had no doubts that he loved me, more than anyone ever had. More than anyone ever would. I felt it radiating from him as he slowly dropped his shields, allowing what little power I had regained to taste the adoration in his mind.

Yes, he loved me. And I loved him too.

I loved the sound of his laughter. I loved the way his cheeks and eyes crinkled when he truly smiled. I loved the way he held me when I was breaking without judgement. I loved the way he pushed me to be strong. I loved the way he conveyed his life and emotions through paint. I loved his heart and how deeply he cared for creatures of every kind. I loved his devious side, how he would purposefully brush his hand against my thigh and send deliciously inappropriate thoughts my way. I loved his remorse and strength and recklessness. I even loved his past and his anger.

Somehow, during the last two months, I had fallen for someone who I had once thought was my enemy. I had lost my family, my life, my home. But in that loss came something new. Yes, I lost more than I ever thought possible, but I found more than I could have ever asked for.

I found freedom. I found love. I found *myself*.

And though I knew I did not deserve love, I accepted it. Took it in and gave it right back.

"I choose you, Bell. Now and always. Wanting you is as natural as breathing. No matter what has happened, despite everything we have done to one another, I have never stopped wanting you. And now, if you will let me, I choose you. I choose you because I love you too."

A breathy moan left him at my words, and then our lips were meeting once more.

CHAPTER FORTY-EIGHT

Kissing Bellamy had always ignited a visceral spark within me. This kiss though, was something else entirely. It sent a wave of pleasure down my body, and made me feel as if my skin was on fire. Perhaps it was. I could hear the way the waterfall outside began to pour faster, timed with the beat of the prince's racing heart. The loose gravel beneath us shook slightly as well, with wind coming in bursts down the tunnel of the cave.

I would not be surprised if Bellamy's fire was being called upon, heat pouring from his skin and onto my own. And I could not deny that it felt wonderful in contrast to the cold of the cave floor that seemed to seep through my trousers.

Everything about this moment was blissful.

My hands roamed down Bellamy's neck, reaching his toned chest and dragging down his arms. I felt the cords of muscle beneath his tunic as they flexed under my fingers, and when I reached his hands, I guided them down my cheeks and neck. I continued to slide them until they met my breasts, and then I let go, giving the demon all the encouragement he would need.

His answering gasp was euphoric, the breath whooshing onto my mouth. Then his tongue was at my lips, sliding across the seam.

Playfully, I kept them sealed. Bellamy of course, had other plans. One of those hands reached down and squeezed my backside, earning a yelp from me. He took the opportunity to slide his tongue inside, wrapping it with my own and tasting me with a feverish hunger.

I moved my hands to work on the buttons of his cloak, unfastening it and letting the cloth fall to the floor. Then I began swiftly untying his tunic, my nails grazing his skin every so often, earning encouraging moans from him. I smiled into our kiss, enjoying this untamed version of the demon. Enjoying being in control.

Slipping the red tunic off his shoulders, I saw the rise and fall of his muscled shoulders, the black tattoos there writhing on his skin under the green hue. Or were they tattoos? I had never seen any sort of ink *move* like that. Before I could inquire about them, his lips began traveling at an achingly slow pace down my throat, settling for that spot where neck and shoulder met.

Humming softly with the contact, I brought my fingers to his hair, tugging lightly. His hands flashed to my chest, lips and tongue never leaving my neck, and removed my cloak. Then he uncinched the brown leather vest that had been layered over the red top below. When he finally tore me out of it, his quick fingers found the hem of my tunic and tugged up, leaving me topless and exposed to the frigid air.

For a moment, he simply stared at my upper half, drinking in tanned skin and peaked nipples and every soft curve. Normally, I might have been self-conscious, worried he would find me unappealing. But he had seen me this way before, and thoroughly enjoyed the image. And had he not told me how beautiful I was on countless occasions?

He had said he loved me, and that was enough to not flinch at his unyielding stare.

He placed tender kisses to my breasts, my stomach, my shoulders, as if he could hear my thoughts. Then his face was inches from mine, eyes such a clear blue that they reflected back the green light around us. When his lips brushed mine briefly, I thought I might die of bliss.

"Do you want me?" he asked into my ear, taking the lobe into his mouth briefly before offering a kiss to the jagged tip. I groaned, nodding my head in confirmation. "Tell me what you want, and I will give it to you. Allow me to make you feel like the queen you were always meant to be," he rasped.

His voice, as always, melted my core. It was erotic and deep, sending chills down my back that even the cold could not manage. More than anything, I wanted him to feel as out of control as I did.

"I want the demon prince, the untamed beast. I want you to wreck me, Bell," I whispered in a voice of velvet against his mouth.

A husky growl was the only response I received before he was ripping off my trousers, snapping the button on the way down before snagging my boots off with the ends. He shredded my undergarments, scraps of cotton meeting the ground on either side of my thighs.

Then he was clawing off his own tunic fully, pulling his trousers and boots off with an efficiency that made me question if they had ever been on. All he had left were his own undergarments, not remotely hiding the erection that threatened to burst free of the cotton confines.

I reached for them, pushing him back until he was lying down once more.

"Allow me, Your Highness." His eyes flashed with desire, irises a molten blue-green. I smirked, knowing that I had gained the upper hand. It had always felt like that with him. A battle of will and strength.

Slowly, teasingly, I slid the undergarments down his legs. Had his thighs always been so large? Or was I simply out of practice? I had no idea as I struggled to stretch the material down. When his member slid free, a slight bounce catching my eye, I gasped. He was…well, he was far bigger than I had anticipated.

He moved up onto his elbows, gaze trained on my movements. I held that stare as I finished removing that last barrier between our bodies. And when it was off, I peppered kisses up his legs, licking his salty skin as I went. He moaned at the touches, and when I reached his upper thighs, I bit down, his head lulling back momentarily.

I decided I liked him best this way, free and reckless.

When our eyes met once more, I knew he would tug me up onto him out of impatience and need if I did not move quicker. So I reached out and took him into my hand, stroking up from the bottom of his shaft to the soft pink head. He hissed in pleasure, encouraging me to continue.

I did, bringing my mouth to his tip, licking up the small bead of liquid that had gathered.

"Gods, Ash," he groaned, his hand moving to my hair, pulling slightly. "I have dreamed about this for so long. You have no idea how perfect you are. How much I want you. How much I *need* you."

My cheek flamed when his other hand grasped it, his thumb rubbing the corner of my mouth. I continued stroking him with my hand as I captured that thumb in my mouth. He gasped at the swirl of my tongue around it, then groaned loudly when I sucked on it, letting it leave my mouth with a pop.

Not wanting to allow him time to do anything that might give him back control, I eagerly brought his hardened member to my lips, diving my head down. An impressive string of curses came as shouted whispers from him while I continued to slide my hands up and down too, my lips tight around him.

I worked him, timing my hands and mouth to make sure I had every inch of him. His fist tightened in my hair, and I could not stop my own moan at the tug. The vibrations of my voice sent him into a frenzy, legs shaking.

He yanked me up, as if he could no longer wait to be inside of me. He sat me atop him, straddling his body. Leaning up, he offered me another kiss, this one sweeter than before, with far more love than lust.

Realization hit me like a solid force as we broke apart. I had been correct that night we departed Haven. Bellamy had loved me even then. I wondered silently how this male could have felt so deeply for me those many weeks ago. He had only known me personally a short time, though I supposed he had watched me from afar before we ever spoke.

Looking in his eyes now, the devotion he held was an extent of love I might not reach for quite some time. I kissed him again, meaning for it to be a light peck, but instead was turned starved when the devious prince deepened it.

Talented fingers met that sensitive spot between my legs, finding it wet. Another deep moan left his parted lips, and I could not help but grind against him at the sound. Twirling those fingers in a relaxed circle, he grabbed my hair once more, my head tilting back with the pull.

"I love you, Asher," he said into my ear. I hummed, enjoying the sound of those words coming from his mouth. To be fair, I quite enjoyed most of the words that came from his mouth. Most.

He slowly laid me down once more, repeating his declaration as he kissed his way down my body. I shivered when he nibbled on my hip, his fingers sliding up the opposite thigh. The bioluminescent glow was bathing his porcelain skin, giving him an ethereal look, as if he were a god.

"Good thing I saved room for dessert," he murmured against my skin.

I gasped at the insinuation, watching as his head dipped between my legs. His tongue made its first slow lick, and I arched into him, the pleasure great and wicked and all things unspeakable. He moaned onto me, as if the act was just as pleasing to him as it was to me.

Then he was feasting on me like I was the most delectable item the world had to offer.

I would be forever ruined. How could I not when Bellamy seemed to hear everything my body asked and provided it with deft answers?

My breath got stuck in my throat as he continued, adding a shake of his head here and there that made my stomach clench. His tongue slipped inside of me, thumb replacing it on that bundle of nerves, and I nearly screamed.

When a finger entered me, his tongue still inside, I finally sucked in air, trembling at the feel. Bellamy removed his tongue, adding another finger, then another, watching as all three worked me, that thumb still paying expert attention above.

I was a mess below him, trying and failing to maintain control. He stopped suddenly, both of his hands moving to the under side of my thighs. I whined in protest, but when I felt his chuckle ghost over my entrance, I quickly silenced myself.

He placed my bent legs over his shoulders, and then got to work once more. The new position made my stomach tighten, and soon the build up was so great that my body felt as if it might explode from the pleasure.

When I found that edge, I did not hesitate to dive off it. Nothing could compare to the weightlessness that came to me then, how my body seemed to be so full of pleasure that I wondered if I might never touch the ground again. The green on the ceiling of the cave blurred, and all I could think as I plummeted was that I loved this stupid demon. I loved him more than anything.

Riding out my high, Bellamy watched my body slump, pulling out his fingers when I stilled and sucking. I groaned, the image of his wet lips nearly sending me into a frenzy.

"Delicious," he whispered.

Then he sat me up, lifting me by the hips and bringing me down onto him, thrusting the entirety of his length inside of me. I screamed out, the sound echoing off the cave walls. His own cry of ecstasy mixed with mine, creating a symphony of pleasure.

He offered no reprieve, no time to adjust to the sheer size of him as he continued raising my hips and slamming me onto him. My nails dug into his shoulders, his lips sucking in one of my peaked nipples and pushing me that much closer to shattering once more.

It was then, as we both panted, that I felt somehow *whole*. When a Healer fixed ripped skin and broken bones, it was sort of like being sewn back together. While Bellamy held me, mumbling filthy words against my chest and worshipping my body like I was his own version of Eternity, I could not escape the feeling that my soul was being healed. That it was being stitched to his, like two halves coming together for the first time.

Just when I thought it could not get any more euphoric, Bellamy gripped me tighter and—with a deftness I did not know was possible—stood up. He remained inside of me as he walked us over to one of the cave walls, this one near the entrance and bare of the glowing creatures. He pushed me up against it, kissing me once more as one of his hands held my rear and the other found the back of my head. Those many rings adorning his fingers were ice cold, but his skin was nearly steaming, making me almost too warm.

"Hold on tight," he rasped with a sly smirk on his face. I did as I was told, digging my fingers into his back. "Just like that, Princess."

Then he was thrusting his hips once more, bringing him into me over and over again. I could feel the bruises forming on my skin from his tight grip, identical to the ones he was likely creating as he nipped at my neck. I relished in the thought of how he was marking me.

Lips numb and thighs spasming, I clawed my hands down Bellamy's back, a throaty moan slipping from my lips. I was coming unraveled, like a spool of yarn being unwound to create something beautiful. All the while, he watched me with those piercing blue eyes, staring at the way my face contorted in pleasure.

"You mean everything, Asher. Everything. You are the beginning and the end and every moment in between," he said, the tempo of his thrusts speeding. His voice of sugar and gravel sent tingles down my spine.

I was too enraptured by the feel of him inside me to speak. Close, so wonderfully close, to that edge again, I bit down on his shoulder to rein in my screams. He moaned my name, doing things to me no one ever had with just a sound.

As if he could read my mind, the demon prince moved one hand to rub that spot between my thighs once more.

"You are *mine*, Princess," he rasped into my ear.

It was all I needed to tip over, coming undone in his arms, the wall of rock behind me pinching my skin. I did not care as that incredible pleasure pulsed through me, dotting my vision with stars.

The demon continued on, sending wave after wave of ecstasy through me. Right as his body tensed, that crescendo approaching quickly, I grabbed his face, bringing his eyes to mine.

"My heart is yours, Bellamy. I see you, all of you, and I am not afraid. I love you," I said.

He roared, thrusting himself in to the hilt as he followed me right over that edge.

The well of power in my chest hummed, and I felt that sense of rightness and completion solidify.

His head fell to the crook of my neck, the two of us shaking as we both came down from the high. When he lifted to look at me, a tear rolled down his cheek. I quickly swiped it away with my finger, to comfort or erase, I was unsure. He smiled then, a soft upturn of his lips that did not show either dimple.

Bellamy carried me over to our discarded clothes, laying me down on top of them and pulling my back to his chest. He wrapped us in his red cloak, breaths still uneven. As he held me, I felt two more tears hit my neck, and I knew that there was far more the demon was hiding than I ever expected.

CHAPTER FORTY-NINE

As we lay there, I wondered what he was keeping from me. There was a reason he needed me to meet their king, his father, as soon as possible. Likely also more information about Mia and Xavier he did not wish me to know just yet. Some sort of timeline existed in his mind, one that determined when I would be afforded such secrets.

I turned around to face him, our bodies pressed together firmly. His eyes were pink, a slight puff to them. I wanted to believe that things between us had changed, that we would become a team. But that was not true, not while so many untold truths lingered between us.

"Is it safe to assume the sex was not so terrible it made you cry?" I asked, aiming for a laugh. His eyes grew wide, as if in panic. He grabbed my chin tilting my head up to his fully.

"I have been dreaming of doing that since the moment I laid my eyes on you, and it was far better than I could have ever imagined," he said, voice raspy and tone earnest.

"Then why?" My voice broke on the words, my pain surfacing. I had not fully forgiven him for what he had done, the way he had taken me, but I knew I would be able to if he only told me the truth now.

"Some things should not be known, and this is one of those things. Can you trust that I would tell you if I thought it could be of help?" he asked, bright eyes searching my own.

I wanted to tell him yes, but I did not believe him. There was so much I deserved to know that he would not tell me. The why did not matter when I was being actively denied information that I knew with every fiber of my being involved me. Even knowing that to be true, I nodded, changing the subject.

With my choice now made, we would have very little time together. I did not wish to spend it arguing.

Instead, I offered up my own truths, horribly ugly ones that I had never wanted him to know. Still, I gave and gave, hoping he too would give someday. I told him of each body I watched slump to the floor, shared with him the times I tortured fae into admitting their crimes, spoke of the many lies I told to hide my transgressions.

Finally, I told him about Sipho, through shuddering cries and hiccupping sobs. He held me the entire time, and when I finished, he kissed the amethyst on my neck.

"He will always be with you, Asher. Never will he leave you and never will he blame you. Think of him every day. Do not forget how beautiful that love was, how it shaped and remade you," he said.

I thought of the sound the chain had made as it snapped off Sipho's neck, my hand clutching the amethyst while I flew through the air.

We lay there awhile longer, and then he told me more stories of his days when he felt lost, when he killed simply to kill. He shared tales of fear and hatred, told me of how little he felt he deserved in life. I reassured him, kissing away his frown, begging him to understand how much he mattered to this broken world.

When neither of us felt like talking further, we made love. Not the frantic sex from earlier, but a slow and gentle joining. We savored each other.

"Why do your tattoos move?" I asked after we had caught our breath, tracing my fingers along the now still lines. He shook his head, sighing at my curiosity. I had a feeling that for as long as he knew me, I would be able to pull those glorious sighs from him, an annoyance until the very end. The thought made me smile despite his clear refusal to tell me.

"Next question," he answered. I huffed at him, pulling away my hand. Then a brilliant question came to mind.

"Fine, will you tell me what your super secret magic is?" I asked, smirking up at him. His brows furrowed for a moment, then at once his face went from confused to amused. He rolled his eyes, placing a soft kiss to my nose.

"Why is it that my initial instinct upon hearing that question is to throttle Henry?" he inquired.

I laughed at his tone, silky from the intimacy but also light from the humor. It was strange, feeling so content while simultaneously spiraling. A part of me drowned in guilt for enjoying myself when I knew so many others suffered. When I knew of the wrongs being committed by the fae royals. Another attempted to peel apart Bellamy's lies and evasions, to piece together what he was hiding. And then there was the part of me that seemed to hum at his touch, to settle into him like I had been made to lay there.

"Likely because he is the only one of your little Trusted that is willing to share any information other than, 'today we will be riding a horse, Asher' or 'did you know that the sky is blue, Asher?'" I remarked. He barked a laugh, the sound echoing back at us from the depths of the cave. "You are unnervingly joyous."

"I was not aware it was a crime to be happy, Princess," he teased. I eyed him with suspicion, not quite sure what to make of this sudden change in mood. Bellamy merely rolled his eyes again, flicking my nose before speaking. "Honey Tongue."

Furrowing my eyebrows, I regarded his smirk and light tone.

"Is that supposed to be pillow talk? If so, I prefer something more interesting when referencing my talented mouth. Such as goddess lips," I quipped. Another throaty laugh, and then he was kissing me. I reciprocated, questioning how I ever refused him, how I ever denied myself this pleasure.

When we parted, our breath was once again uneven, the air charged. But I wanted answers. I deserved them. He seemed to understand my thoughts, because with a rather dramatic sigh, he leaned back.

"Honey tongue is the magic that is passed down between demon royals. Asta, whom I imagine Henry must have told you about, had a rather impressive talent. She was able to sway beings with her words. When she spoke, everyone followed. Sometimes it would take convincing, other times it would fail, but more often than not it was as if her voice was hypnotizing those she spoke to. They usually relented, submitting to her will. Many even questioned whether or not she had seduced Zohar, though he adamantly fought the rumor. At least, that is what our history says. Truthfully, I do not believe she did. While the magic is not infallible, Honey Tongues are still considered quite dangerous," he explained.

Perhaps it was the realist in me, but I could not prevent myself from wondering if Bellamy had used that very magic on me. Was I being slowly seduced by his words? Could someone like me, with an ability to control minds, be overpowered in that way? He did always seem to have an affinity for captivating me.

Regardless of whether or not he had used that magic to sway my mind, I knew now why he was able to block me. Because he had grown up with a father, and likely a grandfather, who possessed the kind of magic that required mental blocking. Not to the extent in which my power called for, but still necessary.

"Before you ask, no, I have not swayed you in any way. I know I have said to use every power in your arsenal, but I do not believe in stripping someone of their right to choice without cause. I would never, ever do that to you," he swore, his tone far more serious than it had been before.

I nodded, feeling guilt rise at the way I had done that very thing. No words could take back the sins I had committed, but I could be better. I would be better.

After a moment, Bellamy kissed me. Though impossibly tired, we came together again. It was rough and hasty, our attempt to show each other just how deep our love went.

We got dressed after—me putting on his tunic with my cloak over top to avoid the buttonless trousers—and when we were finished, he portaled us back to the campsite. Right into his waiting tent.

Without so much as a second thought, he grabbed me by the waist and pulled me down onto his cot, settling the two of us together before covering our bodies with his quilts and fur.

"Rest, Princess. Tomorrow we travel to The Royal City. But tonight, I ask that you sleep here in my arms, where I promise to keep you safe for as long as I live," he said against my head, fingers dragging through my hair.

I nestled deeper into him, my head against his chest and my arms around him.

"Forever," I whispered, my eyes fluttering closed. "I will keep you *all* safe, forever."

I thought of Sipho, how he had once held me the same way, promised me the same things. The warmth of the demon prince and that feeling of rightness that still hummed in my chest allowed me to dream of joy for the first time in so long. Of beautiful memories rather than terrifying futures.

"Hello, Ash," Sipho said as he approached me, the hood of his cloak not able to hide the dazzling flash of white teeth and full lips.

My breath hitched, and suddenly the autumn night felt incredibly warm. He was stunning, as always. He walked with the confidence of someone who knew their worth and would accept no less.

Trying to remain calm and mysterious, perhaps even sexy, I simply gave a small nod of my head. "Sipho."

His smile turned devious, the moonlight glinting off the amethyst at his neck, a piece of jewelry I had marveled at more than once. It had been his mother's, but when a demon attack led to her death, his father had gifted it to him. Admiring it up close had become a regular activity of mine, though I was not always afforded the chance to see it, or Sipho, daily.

"My sweet Asher, you look wonderful this evening." Sipho sat down, pulling his hood back, our arms and thighs touching.

The lake in front of us was as black as the night, the grass below us cool. I wondered what he saw when he looked at the world around us. Did he too feel the unsettling calm of the dim light? The discomfort of the darkness?

His hand moved to my thigh, and I smirked at his infatuation. The male was not led by desire like the rest of the males in Academy. No, curiosity was his god. The slight sting of his power pulsed in my leg, and I could not help but peek in his mind as he worked.

Power radiated through him and into me, his thoughts racing through my healthy prognoses and searching for more. Where did my power come from? What limits existed? Why did I have it?

I laughed when nothing came up from his short assessment. He smiled back, not fazed by the failure, as usual. I feared he might be more upset if he did discover an answer to his questions. One less thing to obsess over.

"So disquisitive," I murmured with a giggle.

At that, the male leaned over, placing a soft kiss to my lips. Everything about Sipho was wonderful, from his soft skin to his honey eyes to the perfect mess of his curly hair. I loved him. More than I had ever loved anything. He was the force that held me to the ground, to reality.

He had told me many times before that he loved me as well, though I knew he also feared me. In fact, his thoughts and inner turmoil told me that his terror outweighed his adoration for me. I did not mind though. I imagined I would always be feared, but at least he would also cherish me.

"One day, I will discover more about your power, and I believe it will help you. We all have a destiny, Asher, you more than any of us. Perhaps I will stand by your side as you follow it," he whispered against my lips.

I smiled into the kiss, loving the way he inspired that hope which always seemed to find a way to evade me. Sipho believed I had a purpose even when I did not. No one else had ever made me feel worthy like he did. No amount of fear had kept him from me. Not the chance that our relationship could end in severe punishment, or even the possibility that I could hurt him with my strange and confusing power.

He was no Tomorrow, and neither was I. The future was not ours to see, especially since we could not tell Nicola or any Reader of our relationship. Still, we made promises of a lifetime together, and I knew he was being honest when he said it all. He truly believed we would be together until our last breath.

"You will always have a place at my side, Sipho. Now and forever."

He broke the kiss, leaning back to look into my eyes. I felt the devotion then, his mind unknowingly projecting the emotion towards me. It was strong, feverish. I stared back, baffled at the turn his thoughts had taken. Though, mine had done the same, to be fair.

"I might not be worthy of being king, or even standing next to you, but I would follow you to the end. No matter what, Ash. I love you."

We slowly stood, making our way to the wooded area on this side of the lake. There we made love, and through the night, Sipho held me, his fingers massaging my head and playing with my hair.

He whispered of theories and hopes and his love. We imagined a world in which we could be together openly. We talked of our future younglings, what they would look like and what power they would possess. We argued over names and both agreed that we would continue the conversation when the time came. We pictured a small cottage out on Isle Healer, one where Sipho could own a farm and I could read under the sun, leaving my title far behind.

He promised me forever, and in turn I promised it back.

Forever was so very short.

CHAPTER FIFTY

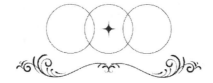

I awoke the next morning to red hair and a face of freckles.

"Do none of you heinous Trusted understand the concept of personal space?" I asked, hissing the words at him.

Henry lay next to me, Bellamy nowhere to be found. His smile was teasing, eager to make comments. I groaned, not ready to deal with him so early, but knowing I would be unable to fight him off for long.

"What first, pumpkin, the size of his cock or how long he lasted?" I asked.

Henry's eyes widened a fraction, green irises shining in the daylight that seeped through the tent opening. Then he burst into laughter, rolling onto his back and clutching his stomach.

I smiled, though the fatigue of the burnout, the sex, and the emotional wreckage of the days prior weighed heavily on me. One thing was true above all others—wit could get me past the worst of it. That and some food. My stomach grumbled loudly, as if my thoughts had reminded it of that hunger.

"How about we get you fed and you can tell me all the dirty details?" he asked as he hauled himself up, face full of eagerness. I rolled my eyes, but gladly took the hand he offered. When I was on my feet, he pulled me against his chest, a coy smile forming. "Or perhaps you can show me."

Scoffing at his pitiful excuse for humor, I batted the Sun away. He chuckled, maintaining his grip on my hand as he attempted to pull us through the tent opening. I reared back, tugging my hand from his hold. Surprise left him momentarily still, then he realized what I was doing.

"Must you get fully dressed first? There is no need for this shy modesty, not when you look like you do. Plus, I think breakfast might be far more enjoyable with you in only Bell's top. Watching him get worked up is like free entertainment," Henry said, shrugging.

I eyed him as I grabbed my trousers from last night, dirty and wrinkled and buttonless, but the best I could do other than listen to the carrot top and eat breakfast nearly nude. He watched me, all the while that stupid smirk still graced his freckled face. My head hurt, my stomach groaned, and my core tightened at the very thought of the demon prince.

Eternity save me from what I had awakened in myself.

There would be no going back now. Fae were territorial, to say the least. When we loved, we did so abundantly and without restraint. There was no limit to what we would do for love, no line we would not cross. I had no idea if Bellamy's demon side altered that, but I knew myself, and I had to be careful. I had a tendency to err on the side of dramatics.

Henry still stood there, eyes alight as I attempted to straighten Bellamy's tunic. It was disheveled, and even my weaker nose could smell the scent of sex on it. It would have to do though. I shook out my hair, hoping that smoothing out the tangles with my fingers would hide the mess of his hands running through them all night.

The thought of his hands on me, in me, brought a fresh wave of arousal, flooding my cheeks with heat. I would need to fight that once I saw the wicked demon, or else everyone would definitely know.

"My oh my, I cannot wait to see what Bell does when you walk out looking as you do. I would bet fifty silvers that your little lover snaps when he hears Cyprus hit on you. Though, I would not be able to blame him, you look quite incredible. The sex glow is truly working in your favor, little brat," Henry said, messing my hair once more and laughing as I slapped his hand away.

I gave a long-suffering sigh, having little confidence that he would find me boring and simply leave me to my stress.

Last night, as sleep overcame me, I had thought of what Bellamy was to me. Not a friend, not a husband, something strangely in between yet also far more. I had decided that he must tell me what it was he was hiding, that we would be nothing if he did not tell me everything. He promised that our arrival to the palace would lead to answers, and I would hold him to that.

Yet, I did wonder how he would act now that I had vowed to be his. It was not a simple thing to give, the heart. My body had been given before, but my love, that had only ever been awarded to Sipho. And it had ended in such tragedy that I feared what it would do to Bellamy and I. Especially when I told him of the choice I had made.

Henry seemed to think it would be entertaining to watch the prince squirm, though there was also some strange tension between the two that I had never understood. So perhaps he was hoping for a horrible ending, for Bellamy to fall. I had no idea, though I did not see Henry as the vindictive and hateful type.

"Why do you not like Bellamy?" I asked, my curiosity winning over my sensibility. It was not very respectful to outright ask, especially when Bellamy was not there to defend himself or tell his side. But I simply had to know.

He blanched, the confident stance he always held faltering. Oh, color me intrigued.

I pressed my power to the painfully bright barrier of his mind, caressing it with feather light touches. The demon relaxed, as if comforted by the way I sat at the edge of his consciousness. There was a tiny gap there, small enough to squeeze through. Then I was inside the vast expanse of his head.

I had always loved this, the way minds varied from being to being. How it felt to be inside of someone's soul in this way, to truly know them. Three months ago, I would have hated myself for the way I enjoyed this feeling, but no longer.

I rather liked being the villain, as it turned out.

Henry's mind had a tangy taste to it, the tip of my physical tongue could nearly sense it, though not quite. His mind was light not only from his Sun magic, but also because of who he was. Henry was an incredibly bright soul—a beautiful one.

Please, Henry, will you show me what I wish to know?

He complied, so quickly I nearly lost my footing in his mind. The memories raced, past our journey to Dunamis, past my arrival to Eoforhild, past Bellamy bringing me to the market of Haven.

I came to an abrupt halt in front of Bellamy, dressed in red finery, hair arranged perfectly, mischief in his eyes. This was the night of my introductory ball.

I saw Bellamy through Henry's eyes, as it always worked when looking through the lens of another being's memories. That also meant that I was privy to the thoughts that he had at the time of this discussion. As Bellamy looked into a large mirror, arranging his golden rings and straightening his jacket to perfection, Henry watched on.

I tugged the image, allowing myself to fall into it, embrace it. Suddenly it felt as if my conscious were falling, straight into that memory.

Bellamy was at it again. Lying, plotting. It was so very *him*. The only difference this time, was that he was not including me in those schemes. My best friend, my brother of sorts, leaving me out of something I could tell was monumental.

Never before had he dressed so impeccably for a trip to Betovere. What purpose was there to wear finery when rescuing the fae?

There was none, of course. No, he had other plans. And I wanted to know.

"Do share with the group why you are dazzling the needy fae with such an outfit," I drawled, smirking at him through the mirror as he meticulously arranged his clothing.

He seemed...nervous. Strange.

He eyed me through the mirror as well, his mouth in that perpetual frown he had worn for the last few months. Bastard loved to ruin a good time before it began. So serious. This though, was something new entirely. Whatever he was not saying must have been juicy.

"I am taking her. Tonight," he said, shoulders shrugging as if it were a trivial task.

I knew exactly who he meant, and it was no such thing. He planned to abduct the princess of Betovere looking like a twat? What would he do, charm the poor thing into submission?

I stared, mouth slightly agape. Idiot. Such a fucking idiot.

Finally, I snapped back into myself, shaking my head violently at the notion. He could not be serious.

Please, do not be serious.

"Ah yes, a mundane mission such as robbing the Fae Realm of their greatest weapon and sole heir should only require you and a bad haircut. Smart," I quipped, already growing angry with his vague explanation.

He turned, facing me head on. I could tell how little patience he had as well by the stern look he offered, though I could not imagine why. I was a joy to be around after all.

"I cannot tell you why, Henry. I promised Pino. You know how he is about risks when it comes to sharing—"

"Futures, as they are ever changing and evolving. Yes, yes, we know this. Now get to the part where you concede and tell me anyways," I said, cutting him off from the tangent he would have surely used to get out of the conversation.

A brilliant idiot is still an idiot, after all.

He huffed, rubbing his hand across his face. One more look at my resolved face and he sat, leaning his elbows on his knees and smacking his head into his waiting palms. What could possibly be this stressful?

"You will not understand," he said, voice wavering. I had him. I stared on, crossing my arms. Finally, he relented. "I love her, Henry. She is my future, *our* future. I need her. We all do."

I froze.

Never, not once, had I heard him utter such a sentence.

I love her.

Who could he possibly love? He had never even said those words to Noe or I, and he has known us for over two centuries. Nearly his entire life.

Love?

I shook my head once more, as if I could weed out the thoughts. Bellamy did not love. Bellamy could barely handle himself, let alone someone else. I had told him as much to his face.

What was happening?

"Whom, may I ask, is the unlucky, and likely unknowing, female that is cursed with your unheard of affection?" I asked, not able to drop the sarcasm from my tone.

If I did, I might explode. I might tell him he could not be more foolish. I might say that whatever infatuation Pino had planted in his head was a fever dream at best, and a disaster at worst. I might say she was not worth the pain.

"The princess. Asher, is her name. She is, well, she is everything. Brilliant, funny, talented, strong, caring. Luca says she is an incredible monarch in the making as well. And she is stunning. Her magic is unlike anything I have ever seen. Incredible really. She is my future, and I am hers. I need her, as soon as possible," he confided, letting loose a heavy exhale upon finishing.

I was swimming in the idea of Bellamy deciding to not only steal the princess to use as a weapon, but attempting to seduce her as well. It would not end well. It could not end even somewhat well. We would all die. This was the war I had fought for, because the fae rulers needed to be dealt with, but him stealing away their heir, that would be bloody.

"Let us say you are not being horribly foolish, and you do, in fact, love this Asher. What if she does not love you? What if your tricks only push her away from you? Will you tell her of the future Pino prophesized for the two of you? Or will you attempt to trick her and lie your way through a relationship you plan on fabricating? You must see how *wrong* this plan is. I understand taking her for her magi—wait. You said *magic,* not power. What do you mean by that? What are you leaving out, Bell?" I asked, panicking now at the thought of the unknown.

She was not demon, but we had also never heard of a fae with power like hers. He knew something, and he was keeping it to himself. I was livid, because never before had he done this.

Withheld information vital to the lives of our race, of all the creatures in Eoforhild. Not from me.

Bellamy though, did not seem to care as he watched the hurt from betrayal cross my face. Nor did he apologize. Instead, he quickly stood, offering me a final nod as he called to his shadows. To the moon.

The last thing I heard as I lunged for that smoke and mist were two words.

"Trust me."

That I would not do. Nor would I forgive him for putting our entire realm in danger for a dream as impossible as The Manipulator.

CHAPTER FIFTY-ONE

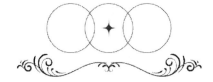

I was stunned, reeling from the information. Pino had, what? Shown Bellamy a future where we were together? Had he really made every decision since to find me and bring me to him?

Henry had been right, it was ludicrous. The future was uncertain, a series of events that depended solely on the behavior and decisions of those it involved. Bringing me here could have altered that future he seemed to desperately cling to in the memory.

My head pounded, angry at my reckless use of power when I was already exhausted. Or, was it magic? What had Bellamy meant by that? I attempted to further search Henry's memories, looking for anything that might indicate he discovered what it was Bellamy hid from everyone about my power.

The effort only bought me about three more seconds before I was swaying on my feet, power seeping out of Henry and back to me like a leak in a dam as the Sun forced me out with beams of light. I would see no more, though that did not mean I could not convince the lying demon to tell me anything.

"You were never meant to see that," he whispered, green eyes distant and full of sadness. I tilted my head, curious as to what he would need to feel emotional about. Was I truly the beginning of the end for them? The rock that shattered their friendship like glass?

"Do not feel guilty for having an opinion. They are like asses, we all have one," I said with a smile, walking over and hugging around his waist. A comfort for the both of us, I realized when he hugged me back with a raspy chuckle.

This made sense of the hatred Henry had seemed to feel when we first met. It seemed instant back then, as if he had merely been waiting for my arrival to dislike me. He had shoved me against a wall after all. Though, I had also invaded his mind, in his defense.

"I cannot tell you any more, Ash. You have to let Bellamy do it. I was mad too, in the beginning. He had been right though, and I should have listened. I do not blame him for the way he feels. There was far more disrespect on my end than you saw, and my apology perhaps was not enough," he said, placing a warm kiss to the top of my head.

Strange as it was that I somehow had grown to love these beings I knew for only a couple of months, it would be impossible to ever deny. They were meant to be mine, all of them. I leaned back, smiling up at the orange-haired demon who had been such a wonderful constant in this hectic adventure.

Before I could respond, Henry was thrown back, body crashing onto the ground with a loud thump that made me wince. I turned, readying to fight whoever—or whatever—had just attacked. But it was no enemy stalking into the tent.

Nothing could have prepared me for the red-hot rage that radiated off of Bellamy in heavy waves as he walked up to me.

What a ridiculous display. I thought I was dramatic.

"Okay alpha-male, back it up a few feet," I said, pressing my hand against Bellamy's chest. He merely looked past me, glaring daggers at Henry, who was standing with a groan. I gestured between them as I said, "This little feud is over. You will stop acting like younglings and apologize, the both of you."

Bellamy finally looked at me, mouth agape. I placed my hands on my hips, glaring right back, daring him to argue. The demon prince snapped his mouth shut, crossing his arms with a pointed *hmph* and looking at the ground. A quick look back at Henry showed a nearly identical expression and stance. Males were so fatuous.

My hands moved up, cupping either side of Bellamy's face. I saw it there, though he had closed off his emotions from me—the hurt. He was scared and confused, possibly even jealous. Not unreasonable feelings. Actions were the problem.

"Forever is far too long to feel this way, Bell. I am sure a part of your anger comes from what you just heard, and that we can talk about later." I looked back at Henry, offering him a hand and pulling him towards us. He let out an impressive sigh, as if *he* was the one forced in the middle of a pissing match. "Now if you two do not make up and kiss, then I will likely beat the daylights out of you both."

Soon we would part ways, and there was no guarantee that this supposed danger would not claim any of our lives. He would need to find peace with Henry, whether he thought it necessary or not. I waved a hand at them, annoyed by their standoffish expressions and stances.

Stepping out into the light was jarring, the sun so bright it reflected off of the snow and burned my eyes. After blinking a few times, they adjusted, and I was able to see Winona, Ranbir, Cyprus, Noe, and Lian sitting around a fire, each of them nursing a cup as they talked and laughed.

I smiled to myself, feeling far lighter than I had in a long time.

Perhaps it was the relief of finally accepting my feelings for Bellamy, or maybe I needed to fully fall apart and hit rock bottom so I could begin clawing my way back up. Either way, my soul felt similar to the morning sun, brighter than it had been before.

Now, I had purpose. A reason to push on.

I would fight this war, hopefully winning it before it could start. I would stop Mia and Xavier, and I would rule Betovere. No one but I knew it, but I would make great change. Sipho had dreamed of a Fae Realm where we could be together, and though he would never see it, I would make that happen. For him, for me, for all the fae who suffered because of it.

Sitting between Cyprus and Lian, I listened in as the group bantered. As they always seemed to do. From across the way, Winona cut off the conversation.

"Asher, what have you done to your hair? It looks like a bird nest!" she exclaimed, the hurt in her voice likely not faked.

She got up and rushed over to me, her green hair looking stunning as it sat in two coils atop her head. She had on a purple top with long, billowing sleeves that cut low and showed her ample cleavage. It ended at her waist in the front, but pooled down to her calves in the back, like a cape of sorts. Around her midsection was a stunning black corset made of lace, which matched her black leather pants and boots.

Seeing her reminded me that I was still in Bellamy's top, and I realized it could not be more obvious what happened with my hair. She did not mention it, but Noe and Lian snickered as if they knew exactly what led to my hair becoming such a mess.

Winona combed through my 'bird nest' with a feather light touch. When she finished she began styling it for me, twisting my waves into gorgeous coils and braids.

During our journey I discovered that she regularly did the others' hair, including trims. Bellamy and Henry both enjoyed a clean shave, and the Sun was more than happy to oblige. Her love for doing my own hair brought a smile to my face, and I quickly reached up to tap her in thanks.

"Well, as I was saying before Ash so rudely interrupted us with her post-fuck walk," Noe said, smirking at me from beside a wide-eyed Ranbir. I scoffed, but did not argue. She was right after all. "I think that we need to vote now before Bellamy and Henry come back."

I quirked a brow, looking between the group. Lian nodded casually, as if either way was okay with her. Cyprus seemed to be thinking over Noe's suggestion rather seriously. Ranbir rolled his eyes, standing and swiping another cup off the ground. He headed to me, giving me the cup of his famous chai. My mouth watered at the heat and spices.

"Thank you, Ranbir. You are too kind, as always," I said, smiling up at him.

He returned the gesture, leaning towards me and placing a hand on my cheek. The sting of his power hit me, but soon the aches in my body were easing. The tension that had built seeped from me.

"Drink up. It will help with energy and aid in lowering your blood pressure," he said. I took a sip, ignoring the burn as the flavor enveloped my senses. Ranbir always made such incredible tea. "I would also say that it is an anti-inflammatory, but you once claimed a good orgasm was too, and by the look of you, I imagine you have that covered."

I nearly spit out the liquid at his words. Winona burst into laughter, a melodic sound that brought a smile to Ranbir's face. The kind of smile only your soulmate could bring out of you.

"Ranbir, did you just make a dirty joke?" I asked, full of pleasant surprise.

The Healer tapped my nose, leaning into Winona to offer a swift kiss and then headed back to his seat beside Noe, who was arguing with Lian. I attempted to tune into their conversation, though I could not help but look into Winona's mind, enjoying the way her amusement mingled with her adoration. The couple's love was practically inebriating, and I enjoyed getting doses when I could.

"I think that I am easily his second. You guys are foolish to believe my skills do not make that so," Noe insisted, pointedly looking between Lian and Cyprus. The former shook her head, blowing a breeze at an unknowing Noe, who fell backwards onto the ground. I could not prevent the giggles from slipping past my lips when she popped back up, her hair full of snow and her cheeks red from the cold. "Bitch."

"Seeing as I am a captain in his army, the swordmaster, and an incredibly skilled Air, I argue that I am far more qualified," Lian said with a smirk.

Noe curled tendrils of shadow between her fingers, almost looking as if she were holding a snake. As if she heard me, she opened her hand, the shadow taking the form of a serpent and crawling from the skin of her palm. It was unnerving—creepy.

The snake slithered towards Lian, who yelped when it wrapped around her ankle and attempted to *drag her* towards Noe. Cyprus, who had been mostly silent, disappeared in his own wisps of darkness, body losing shape and melting into that cold darkness I had felt those many weeks ago. The shadows struggled to blend with the unusually bright day, but soon he was gone completely, reappearing next to Noe and shoving her back in the snow once more.

"Idiots, the lot of them," Winona muttered above my head.

I laughed, enjoying the scene as the three of them got into one of the most hilarious fights, each using their abilities to trip or push or knock over the other. That continued on as Winona finished my hair, and even proceeded as I ate.

When Henry and Bellamy emerged from the latter's tent, the trio froze, soaked in snow. Bellamy laughed at the sight, clapping Henry on the shoulder, who smiled over to him. Apparently they had made up.

Seeing the two of them together reminded me that I needed to speak with Bellamy about Pino's vision, about all of his many lies and evasions. But doing so would also mean needing to admit that soon I would leave him and go back to Betovere, where I would conquer and rule. Where I would prevent another Great War.

"It seems we missed all the fun," Bellamy said. He came over to me as Henry disappeared in a cloud of white light, only to reappear next to Cyprus and tackle him to the ground. Bellamy had changed, now sporting the same leathers he had worn on the first night of our journey.

I relished in the way his muscles flexed through the leather. How the fabric clung to his thighs. My cheeks warmed as I pictured the way he had felt against me, his skin scorching and his voice rough as he told me over and over again that he *loved me*.

Silently, I begged myself to get it together. I had not acted like this in nearly two centuries, there was no reason I should be doing so right now. He was still the same insufferable demon from before. The only difference was that now I had seen him naked. And really that made no difference.

Why did it matter that the very tongue that darted out to wet his lips was the same one that was on me mere hours ago? That the fingertips currently grazing my thigh had been inside of me not long before the sun rose?

I squirmed, working myself up like a love-sick youngling who had just lost their virginity.

Bellamy smirked, eyes of ice looking me up and down, moving slower over his rumpled red tunic I had confiscated. Then they moved to my lips, halting there for a few moments before meeting my own. His fingers continued to tease as I felt something—or someone—projecting. I pushed back, knowing it was him and not daring to let his words catch me off guard.

A mistake on my part.

"Good morning, Princess," he said, inching closer to me. He leaned in, smelling the air between us. My breath hitched, his exhale wafting across my collar bones. "Is that a new perfume? You smell absolutely…delicious."

I felt the blood spread from my cheeks to my entire face, reddening even my ears and neck as the mortification rained down on me.

Someone coughed, and I shook my head to bring it back into focus. Henry and Noe were snickering from across the way, Lian holding her hand out to Cyprus who begrudgingly offered her a handful of coppers. Ranbir and Winona remained silent, though they both had smiles upon their faces.

"Is it time to go?" I asked, trying to swiftly change the subject. The others lost their smiles quickly, tension growing.

"Way to kill the mood Ash," Henry said, scooping up a ball of snow and throwing it. I was too slow, too baffled, to dodge it before it smacked me in the face. My head flung back, and I accidentally inhaled some when I gasped from the sting.

Wiping it away, I glared at the demon. Bellamy seemed to be equally annoyed, conjuring a ball nearly as large as Henry and throwing it at him with his Water power. Henry was unable to move before it struck him. We all burst into laughter as it sent him flying backwards, his body hitting the snowy ground with a loud thud.

"Yes, we are," Bellamy responded, smiling down at me as he wiped stray flakes from my cheek. "We already rode the horses to a nearby village, and I sent word for someone from the palace to retrieve them. Time to say goodbye, for now."

I nodded, feeling my sadness mix with the others' in the air around us. Saying goodbye to them felt nearly as hard as missing my friends back home. Though they did not know it, this was likely the last time they would see me.

The more you love, the more you lose.

Mia had taught me that, and she had been right.

CHAPTER FIFTY-TWO

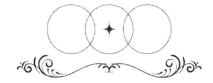

Bellamy had provided me with my very own set of the Trusted's leathers, which turned out to be surprisingly comfortable. The gesture felt like an offering of sorts—a chance to become one of them.

I said nothing as I dressed myself, choosing silence over the hard truths I needed to share.

Our farewells had been short, not wanting to waste any more time. We would need to get everyone in place as soon as possible to avoid whatever danger Pino had seen. The Oracle still had not responded to Bellamy's inquiries, which only further stressed the prince.

They all promised to see me again, each of them placing kisses to my cheeks. I did not return the vow. Cyprus had offered to punch Sterling in the face, which had earned a chuckle from me and a long-suffering sigh from Bellamy.

Henry had offered the longest goodbye, to my surprise.

"I am eager to hear all about the impression you leave on our great king," he had said.

"Oh, carrot top, we both know he will be utterly delighted by my greatness," I had responded.

He had laughed, bringing me in for a tight embrace and kissing the top of my head.

"Until we meet again, little brat. Try not to miss me too much," he spoke into my hair.

"Impossible. No one else is nearly as entertaining to make fun of."

And then we were all separating into small groups, each portaling at the same time.

Bellamy and I had landed just outside of Dunamis, the wards on the territory preventing us from entering with magic. We were met by a demon wearing faded brown riding leathers. She held the reins of two white steeds, and Bellamy thanked her before lifting me atop one and hastily mounting the other. The sun had just risen, but we would still barely make it there before it set.

"So, when are you going to ask me about Pino's vision?" Bellamy asked not long after we had begun riding.

In truth, I had been planning to ask, but I was angrier than I wished to be, and I feared what he might say when I told him the truth I hid.

"I do not believe you will tell me, truthfully," I responded, voice curt.

He did not look at me, though I saw a muscle in his jaw tick. I continued, relentless in my honesty.

"You have no right to be angry, not when you acted upon an uncertain future and ripped me away from my life. You thought of only yourself, and you decided what was best for me. But you do not know that, only I do," I said, my tone cold and biting.

He went quiet, not even glancing my way. I tried to calm down, to remind myself how tantalizing those visions could be.

Seeing the future through the eyes of a Tomorrow was incredible, so vivid that it could be confused for current reality. Some who saw the future became obsessed with obtaining it, though Tomorrows always warned of its uncertainty. It was worse with Yesterdays, who showed the past one could never have again.

"I never meant to hurt you, Asher. The vision, it was everything I could have ever hoped for and more than I ever thought I would have. You were the center of it all, and waiting was agony. I kept telling myself that you would find your way to me, that you would run away and seek me like so many other fae had. But you never did. And it was not long before I found myself hidden in a wooded area of The Capital, watching as you read a book in the grass," he confessed, his knuckles turning white as he gripped the reins.

"You were even more beautiful than the visions had suggested, even in the gaudy gold. I had Cyprus and Luca take shifts at the palace, keeping an eye on you to make sure you remained safe. And then you became engaged, and I nearly lost it. I painted the walls of my chambers for hours on end. I refused to speak to anyone. I did not even eat.

"After about a week of sulking, I began plotting ways to take you. You were mine, or that was what I told myself. And as I watched you grow less and less fond of the mortal prince, I thought perhaps you might choose me on your own," his voice broke.

"The night we met, I had been so nervous. You had looked as beautiful as ever, and the stupid prince rarely left you alone. I had to be bold, to convince you that you could love me the way I had already loved you. To prove to you that your future could be different than they had written it. When we kissed I nearly took you away then and there, but you ran, and I had to find another way to you. So, I portaled into your chambers a few days later, and I waited for you to return. I decided I would beg you to let me whisk you away. When you agreed to come with me, I thought that would be it. You would never leave my side. But you did, and I made a foolish choice in my despair. I went back for you," he admitted.

"Instead of finding you roaming the grounds, I saw you unconscious on a bed, sleeping in the way only someone who had been newly healed and forced into unconsciousness could. My rage took over when I found out what happened, and I nearly killed the prince then and there. I thought about how I would do it. Pictured the glorious feeling of his blood on my hands as I whisked you away, but I still wanted you to choose me. I could not just steal you away while you slept. I had to be smart. When the wedding was moved up, I knew it would be my only chance. So I took it, because I saw our future and knew you were all I have ever wanted, Princess."

I stared at him, his face contorted in both pain and determination. To him, the ends justified the means. But to me, who had not seen that future Pino prophesized, it was a gross manipulation of fate, carefully crafted to fit the future he wanted for himself. He had never forced me to love him, but he had upended my life in the hopes I would.

"I deserved to choose. I have not ever been able to make my own decisions. My life has been a series of choices made by everyone but myself. Never did I get a say in it, never did my opinions matter if they got in the way of those plans set forth. You took another choice from me, just as the royals always have. Every plot and scheme, every lie and half-truth, they all suited your wants and needs. What about me, Bell? What about my joy? My autonomy? My life? Does it mean so little that you feel it can be molded to fit your own?" I asked, watching as he winced at each blow.

I could not bring myself to regret the words, because he needed to hear them. He needed to feel the pain, to understand that his dreams had contributed to my nightmares. Perhaps a part of me needed the scolding as well—the reminder that I was no better.

"I am sorry, Princess. I should have put you first. Perhaps even left you alone. I would understand if you do not want me any longer. My offer to take you back to Betovere still stands, if that is what you wish. I want you to be happy, even if that is not with me," he stated, his voice falling off into a broken whisper.

Heart racing, I looked at him. He stared forward, body tense and hands shaking. I could tell him, end this now before either of us were hurt further. It would be better, cleaner. But I could not force my mouth to form the words, my voice to speak the end. I did not want to, I realized.

Selfishness won out, and I sat up straight as I finally spoke.

"Bellamy, look at me," I said. He turned, his eyes slightly pink, as if he were near tears. "I forgive you."

His mouth dropped open, arms tugging back the reins and forcing his horse to a stop. My own trotted past a bit, before I too urged him to a stop. Bellamy looked baffled, unable to do anything else other than stare at me with his lips spread apart in an O shape.

When he was able to speak, it was slightly incoherent.

"You…me…sorry…okay?" he said, stumbling over the words. I rolled my eyes, smirking over at him.

"Yes, I forgive you, silly demon. I hate what you did, despise that you felt it okay to make those choices for me, but I am also thankful. You saved me, you held me, you gave me freedom for the first time in my life. I will not pretend to agree with your tactics, but I know why you did it. I love you, you love me, and—together—we can move on from this. That is, as long as when we arrive at The Royal City you share every detail of each secret you have been hiding. There will be no more lies between us, okay?" I questioned, my tone more of an order than a request.

He nodded fervently, a stunned expression still on his face. I reached out, and he urged his horse forward, stopping beside me to take my hand. He leaned in, kissing both of my cheeks, then my forehead, my chin, my nose, and finally my lips. A simple gesture, but one that sent my heart fluttering.

He was an idiot, but apparently, he was my idiot.

For now.

I decided I would wait to ask about my powers. It needed to be the right time, and I had to make sure he was incapable of lying about it. He had promised answers, and I would not let him leave any out.

We pushed on, not stopping again other than to water the horses and relieve ourselves. Despite our quick pace, we maintained light conversation, neither of us caring to bring up the previous argument. It seemed we were both eager to move forward.

Just as the sun began to descend, we stopped atop a tall hill. Below, the sight of The Royal City took my breath away.

Rows upon rows of beautiful white and brown cottages covered in vibrant green vines lined cobblestone paths. Lilies of the valley could be seen decorating the city, blooming despite the snow. In the distance, upon a hill right along the coastline, sat a towering castle.

It was white with gray pointed rooftops, large windows lining the walls. There seemed to be no method to the madness of the design, random peaks and towers meeting rectangular structures, forming the largest palace I had ever seen.

Beyond, the water splashed at the hillside, violent green-blue waves nearly reaching the white stone. Despite the hour, many residents still conversed and roamed throughout the city, the sound of chatter and laughter reaching us in the distance.

"What do you think?" Bellamy asked, his dimples coming out in full force. I could feel his excitement at being here. The way he seemed to glow in the fading light of day, his relaxed posture, even the sound of his voice radiated the peace that comes from returning home.

"It is like nothing I have ever seen before," I said, words failing me. Bellamy seemed to understand, because he nodded, his smile growing impossibly larger.

"Haven is where I live most of the time, because the fae there need me, though I travel to our military base regularly. But The Royal City, it will always have my heart. Dunamis will always be my true home," he whispered, as if wanting to preserve the serenity of the scene. I nodded, though I did not understand.

An ache started in my chest. As I looked upon the home of the crown prince of Eoforhild, I was forced to accept that I would have to say goodbye to him. I did not belong here. Going back to Betovere, to the one home I had ever known, was the only option. The only way to save the innocent lives that would be used as shields and pawns in the war.

If I was going to prevent the coming conflict, then I had to kill Mia and Xavier. I had to take my throne.

I tried to force back the thoughts, the impending loneliness and heartbreak. For now, I had him—we had each other. Enjoying this would not make what was to come easier, but it would be worth that extra pain.

So I smiled at him, and together we made our way to the demon king.

CHAPTER FIFTY-THREE

BELLAMY

ONE YEAR AGO...

Lian and Noe were nagging, as they always did, Henry laughing beside them at my suffering.

Haven needs supplies. The army needs improved drills. An upcoming mission to Betovere needs to be planned. When will you date? Have you dated recently? When was the last time you even had sex? Wow, that long?

On and on and on.

As if we were not facing a possible war. As if those things *and* the war had not been invading my mind at every possible moment of each day.

Well, except for the sex. That mostly haunted me at night.

"Do you guys ever shut up?" I hissed, rubbing my temples.

The three of them laughed, like it had been some kind of joke. To them, everything was a joke. With all my heart, I did love them. They were family, more so than the one I had been born into. But they were all so exhausting, so infuriating, lately. I felt the elements stir inside of me, reacting to my anger and mixing with the magic that invaded my body.

The magic that *my mother* had ordered be put inside of me.

I felt the wards around my heart fight against it, like a wall blocking out poison. Looking down, I saw the black writhing inside of me like moving ink, itching to break free. I took deep breaths, attempting to calm myself enough to fight it off. If that did not work, then I guess I would need to go exert it somewhere.

I stood, not waiting for them to respond. I needed to get to Isle Reader anyways, or else I would miss the meet.

Throwing up my middle finger behind me, I quickly called upon that very poison, using it to portal. Below my feet the black marble turned into green grass, and as the darkness disappeared, I saw Reader River.

Easily one of the most beautiful parts of Betovere, the river split Isle Reader in half, a large zigzagging line of crystal-clear water that the Readers used to project their visions.

An interesting mix of power and magic, though the fae did not know about the use of the latter. I could not help but sigh at the many things they did not question, the lies that they allowed the fae king and queen to spoon feed them.

Then again, I myself was a lie. How many had been given the false story of my parentage? Been made to believe I was actually part demon? I thought they hated me now, I could not imagine the fury they would feel upon discovering I was fully fae.

Even worse, a fae that had been infused with their magic at birth. Who had stolen their gift from Stella.

Not that I had chosen it.

Not that I did not suffer from it.

Trying to maintain focus, I looked around, hoping to find the fae Noe had scheduled me to meet. Strangely enough, no one was there. The river seemed almost deserted, as if everyone had disappeared.

I made my way East, walking aimlessly. We had agreed upon the West end of the river, but being forgetful or late was not a crime. The alone time was far from unwanted, anyways.

"Hello, Your Highness," a voice said from within the tree line. Of course, that was when the male would choose to show up.

"Hello. Pino, is it?" I asked, turning to face him.

The male was visibly aged, gray hair and wrinkles forming on his face. I was surprised, not many fae cared to live that long. I knew I would not let myself.

He wore fine violet-colored clothes, his name stitched in gold on the right of his chest. There was a peculiar artistry to them, one I could appreciate. If he was the one who made those, Winona and Lian would go haywire. To be fair, I also enjoyed a quality wardrobe.

"Yes, Bellamy, it is," he said, his voice that intimidating tenor of a Reader.

Creepy creatures.

I nodded, offering my hand to take him to his new home. Pino stepped back, shaking his head.

"I must show you something first."

Watching as he walked to the edge of the water, I tried to assess the situation. Was this an ambush? A trick? A way to gain my confidence or my debt? I was not sure; it had never happened before. After a moment of deliberation, I made my way to his side, deciding the risk was worth it to assuage my curiosity.

Pino got down on his knees, gesturing for me to follow. I begrudgingly did, my trousers instantly soaking up the mud. I scowled. As if this day could not get any worse.

Pino placed his hand into the water, which began to stir around him, a small whirlpool forming at his fingers. I gasped, having never seen the water in action. It was remarkable, watching the images form in the previously clear liquid.

I appeared, my fighting leathers on, standing with my Trusted. It was a normal scene, unremarkable except for one interesting addition. A female was beside me. She was beautiful, with big gray eyes and full pink lips. Her brown hair cascaded down her back, thick and wavy. She too wore the fighting attire of my Trusted, the leathers fitting to her body as if they were made for her.

"Who is that?" I asked, gesturing to her.

Pino smiled, a soft upturn of his lips that felt slightly condescending.

"She is everything," he said.

The images changed, flashing scenes of me with the female. In one we danced, her golden dress wrapping around my ankles as we spun. In another she seemed to be yelling at me, though I could see my face held a smirk. Then the next showed the two of us…holy shit.

"Woah woah woah," I said, trying to splash away the vision of me holding the female, bouncing her naked body up and down on top of me.

I felt my cock twitch in my pants, the image likely egging on the teasing from dumb and dumber earlier. Taking a breath, I again focused on the water as Pino laughed and the image changed.

Now it showed me, looking like a nervous lunatic, down on one knee. The brunette smiled, a dazzling show of white teeth and rosy cheeks.

Just as I was beginning to enjoy this, to revel in a future that I had previously thought unobtainable, it changed. I gasped, rearing back at the sight of the new image.

"Explain," I ordered, my voice shaking.

"I am no mere Reader, prince of two realms."

"Do not call me that," I growled.

He shrugged, unphased by my sudden anger. The way he interacted with me set my hair on edge. It was as if he knew me. Not as a prince or as The Elemental. No, he acted as if we were friends, family even.

"I am an Oracle, cursed to see far more than a quick image upon touching another. What you just saw, it is a future I needed you to be aware of, for this will set in motion the beginning of the end," he said, his voice still that eerie tenor.

"Who is she? What will she be to me? What occurs for that to happen?" I asked, questions whipping through my brain and out of my mouth like a fierce wind.

I felt the panic growing, the magic inside of me stirring with it. I needed to calm down, but how could I?

"She is Asher Daniox, the fae princess, The Manipulator. You will love her, and she will be the end of us all," he said, the clouded look in his eyes slowly fading. I imagined that whatever trance his power put him in had released him.

Good, he was really freaking me out.

"Do go on, oh mighty Oracle," I drawled, feigning boredom to mask the sheer terror that had enveloped me. He nodded, starting from the beginning.

As he told me of a history forgotten, a princess stolen, and a bloodline corrupted, I felt it all sink into place. I watched image after image in the water, seeing more than any one being should. Pino shared with me truths long since hidden, lies long since buried, and promises long since broken.

In the end I looked down, watching once again as the female I now loved more than anything sobbed over my body. My dead body.

EPILOGUE

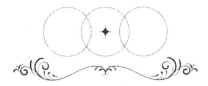

On a rocky shore, black smoke materialized from thin air. The wisps of darkness snuffed out every ray of light they came near before fading into nothing, the day once again bright. In its place stood a fae queen and a traitorous demon, both sets of lips upturned in delight.

They were beautiful smiles. Terrifying smiles.

The queen, made of harsh lines and porcelain skin, flicked back her amber hair. She narrowed her eyes—so blue they mirrored ice—distaste palpable on her tongue.

"I never thought I would see these shores again," the demon mused. His own eyes of pure black sparkled with excitement at the thought. His mahogany locks blew in the breeze of his homeland. The land he betrayed.

"No time to reminisce, Malcolm," the queen snapped, bored of his company already. The beach remained quiet, serene despite the evil that now lurked on its shore.

Though, a certain princess might argue that evil resides in all. Perhaps the beach knew that too, felt safe in the comfort of a familiar wickedness.

The demon turned towards the queen he had chosen over his realm. His family. His crown.

There was love in his eyes. One that was crafted from ambition, lust, and a darkness even the magic under his skin recoiled from. The kind of love that could convince a brother to slit the throat of a sister. The kind of love that began and ended in death.

The queen felt no such emotion. Not for the demon, nor her husband, whose dimples and dark hair had left many swooning before her. Not even for the child that was taken from her. The one she looked in the eyes mere months ago, his irises a mirror of her own.

No. She loved nothing but her throne, as she was raised to. Sooner would she perish than see the day her rule ceased.

For this reason, the queen walked from the rocks onto the soft sand, determination turning the grains into stone beneath her slippers.

"Ah yes, we must make haste lest someone else take over the world," the demon said as he trailed behind her. A joke that straddled the line between humorous and insolence.

No matter, the wicked queen had little desire to argue. Her interests lay ahead, where a black castle loomed in the distance. With a wide smile that bared perfectly white teeth between pink lips, the queen responded.

"Precisely. Not to mention it seems my son has stolen something of mine, and I plan to take her back."

LOVELY READER,

YOU ARE NO ONE'S BUT YOUR OWN.

ACKNOWLEDGMENTS

There are so many people who made this book possible. I wish I could thank every reader, every listener, every person who took the time out of their day to escape into my little world. You all mean everything to me, and I cannot wait to continue sharing Asher's journey with you.

To my mother who read the first book I ever wrote, I thank you always. At nine-years-old I was not making masterpieces by any means, but you read every single one and encouraged me to follow my passion. You sparked a fire in me with your continuous support and love. You bought me book after book when I refused to put anything else on my Christmas wish list, and you never once told me I could not one day be like the authors I adored. This is for you, mama.

To my husband who listened to me rant at three in the morning about afriktors and mountain sides and smutty scenes, thank you. I love you more than words can ever express. Your endless patience and support do not go unnoticed. And you, of course, inspired Bellamy. A win is a win.

To Savanna, the very first reader of ONAB, the one who has suffered through endless edits and ideas and corrections and confusion. You are an angel. Without you, this novel might not exist. You have brought so much joy and creativity to my life, and I am thankful beyond measure to have you in my corner.

To my sons, who can neither read nor understand what I mean when I say I wrote a book, thank you both for happy dancing with me when I hit a new milestone. By the way, I forgive you for every time you deleted chunks of writing by slapping my computer and for the many instances of interruptions. Honestly, it was kind of funny after I stopped crying. Also, please never read these books. I love you both. Again, please do not read these books. Thanks.

To my editor, Laura, you are a gem my little Scottish friend. Thank you for every time you corrected my misspelling of 'peek', and for your lovely and dirty commentary on Henry. It was always so wonderful getting your notes and reading through them. You are so so great at what you do, and ONAB would not be the same without your help.

To Annalee, thank you for working with me to perfect this book, to uplift it and me. Each kind word and encouragement pushed me to move forward and round out my vision. You are so wonderful at what you do, and I hope you know that it was your edits that made this book officially reader ready.

Finally, to my beta readers, your support throughout the final stages of this book was so deeply appreciated. You all have truly changed this novel and made it what it is. There will never be words to express how much you all mean to me. I am forever thankful.

ABOUT THE AUTHOR

Brea has been obsessively reading for as long as she can remember, consuming any and all books she could get her hands on. Thus sparked the dream of creating something similar—a book that would make readers cry and laugh and smile and feel all those big emotions that she did. At nine-years-old, she wrote her first book. Over the years she would write many more, but it was not until Of Night and Blood that she finally felt the book she dreamed of writing had come to life.

She spends her time working with the blind and low vision community, advocating for human rights, drinking too much coffee, chasing around her toddlers, and ordering new books for her endless TBR. She lives with her spouse, their two children, and their dog.

AUTHOR'S NOTE

Asher's story contains many heavy topics. I hold her dear to my heart as she has lived through much of what I have. Most of my life I have struggled with the concept of worth and how it is measured. Like Asher, I needed to learn that I was no one's but my own, and that my worth was mine and mine alone to determine. With all of my heart I desire each and every one of you to know the same thing.

That being said, I know these themes can be hard to read, especially for those of us who have had similar life experiences to Asher. However, I truly hope that as you follow her journey, you find solace in her resilience. Just like Noe, I hope you face your evils and win.

For those who are surviving similar struggles and need aid, I encourage you to reach out to your local or national crisis hotline. If you are in the United States, visit www.988lifeline.org/chat to immediately get into contact with a crisis support specialist. You can also text or call 988.

You are not alone, and you are worthy of life. All my love.